The God Curse

Levi K. Castle

◆♦◆ THREE SKILLET

THE GOD CURSE, Castle, Levi K.

1st ed.

 THREE SKILLET

www.ThreeSkilletPublishing.com

ISBN: 978-1-943189-24-3

"What kind of god art thou, that suffer'st more of mortal griefs than do thy worshippers?"

— Shakespeare, "King Henry the Fifth" —

—1—

IT'S NOT THAT I ENJOY PLAYING GOD. I just don't have any other choice. It's also the reason that my place has holes punched in all the walls. That's me, the part of me that I can't let anyone see. All those holes? Vanity. Vanity entwined in a desperate bid for survival.

I thought about having my knuckles tattooed once. You've seen them, the words love and hate in black on a fighter's hands. He grins at you with sweat running down his face, and he holds up his fist, and just before he knocks you out, he says, Love makes the world go round. Then he punches, and it's lights out for you.

The problem I ran into was my vanity. You see, I only have five knuckles, four if I want it to really work. The thumb hardly counts, but I was willing to play loose and free if I could use my vanity to punch a few holes in my life. It's like everything else about me. Round pegs in square holes, only my life is more like forcing the moon to fit into Lake Huron. First, you can't get the giant sucker out of the sky, and second, no matter how hard you pound it, it simply won't fit into the stupid lake.

You see, vanity has six letters. I never tried disgust. I can count, after all. I might rail, and my walls might suffer, but I did finish college. Not willingly, but I did finish. Tooth and nail, fighting every scholarship my ole alma mater stuffed down my throat every fall. I left my dorm room with a few holes, too. I just tried to hide them in places they couldn't be easily found.

You see, I really am a god.

You laugh. I can hear you even through the pages of this book. That's my god-thing, what makes me what I am, and even now, it's twisting me inside, clawing at the back of my eyeballs, making me want to change my words to describe myself the way you want me to be.

I can do that, you know, put a golden halo around my head, say pretty things to all the kids who live on my block, and knock your sniffles back to the other side of Monday just like Jesus did in the Bible. When you call me, crying, and you tell me it's been raining for four days, and you'll wet your pants if you see another raindrop hit your window, and then the sun breaks through the clouds, I don't expect you to make the connection, but yeah, that's me. I'm your god connection, your hot line to the Big Man.

Except in this case, I *am* the big man. Man, that sucks. And I'm not even out of bed this morning. What am I saying? I never made it to bed last night. I'm sprawled on the sofa, still in my jeans, with my shirt for a pillow. I think I left the TV on, too, because CNN is telling me all kinds of interesting things I don't want to know at six in the morning.

Oh, my head hurts! What in the world did I do last night? Sometimes it's best not to even care.

—2—

I FORGOT TO TELL YOU MY NAME. That's because I suck so badly at being a god. Well, I suck at everything else, too. Just ask my mom. I don't call, I moved half a continent away, and I have no real, burning desire to return home. Shouldn't I be a little more like Jesus, like when things were at the worst for him, his only thought was for his mother? If I were hanging on that cross, I'd be screaming out to anyone I knew to get me down, because those nails in my hands stupid well hurt like fire.

But then that's why I suck so badly at being a god. The god-things don't come naturally to me. Or, if I want to be honest with myself, and with you out there in the real world, I fight the god-things; I tear at them with eyes closed, punching and kicking, just trying to get through the day being a normal person, one who scratches his crotch when he gets out of bed in the morning, spits on the sidewalk when he thinks no one is looking, and sometimes forgets to brush his teeth and doesn't really care.

I have to fight, you see. There's nothing fun about being a god. Nothing fun at all. Forget those movies where God comes down and says, "Hey, you, Dude! I plan to take a vacation and let you play God for a few hours. Have fun, Dude!" That guy? He plays with the moon so his girlfriend will jump his bones, but it doesn't work like that. The god-thing doesn't do anything for the person who has all the power. I can't, like, get rich and drive fancy cars just by snapping my fingers. In that movie, the god-guy gets stuck in traffic, and he snaps his fingers, and all the traffic just scoots out of the way, and he has a clear shot to work. Can I tell you all the times I've been stuck in traffic or picked the slow line at the drive-thru? Nah, I can't, because I lost count about ten years ago.

What have I found out in all this? Lots of stuff, but the biggie is that being a god is not what you think it is. That's why I'm writing all this down. I want someone to understand just what it's like. And I'm not asking for sympathy. I understand how the world works. If you've got any measure of success—and I do hold a job with a regular paycheck—no one wants to hear about your problems. People want you to feel sorry for *them.* It's the game we play, the way we get through the days, weeks, and years until the Grim Reaper finally lets us free from this mess we call life. I get it, but I just want the chance to say, The Game Sucks. See my capitals? I wrote it that way intentionally. I want you to know, The Game Sucks, and if you're on the outside, you can't tell. You think I'm all halo, little kids, and sunshine. And you know, I am, because I can't do anything else, and that sucks so badly I want to punch a hole through my morning and make it back into night again.

Right. I already did that, and more than once. All I have to do is look around my house. It's also the reason I don't invite people inside for burgers. We stay on the patio, and I never, never let them use the inside toilet.

But, since I'm a god and all, and I have to do the halo thing, I had a toilet installed in the garage, with a door directly onto the back garden. It's even air conditioned and heated, with a tub-shower combination, and double sinks. The women tell me it's really nice, and they wish their boyfriends would do something that considerate for them to keep party guests from dirtying their houses while traipsing in and out to the bathroom.

I didn't do it for that, but whatever. I mean, and here I'm getting frustrated, because even to me what they say sounds reasonable. I'm not stupid, not if I believe five years of full scholarships at NYU, but as angry as I get at the world, I listen to my friends, and I actually agree with them. It is nice to have an outside bath opening straight to the party, where guests can go in and out at will, where no one has to ask where the john is. I even put a sign on the wall that people can flip over. One side says vacant, and the other, occupied. How cool is that? So, yeah, I can look at what I've done, and I can see the god-thing working.

That's not why I did it, though. The bath is there because of all the holes in my walls. I didn't exactly look forward to jackhammering lines through concrete, paying a plumber to put in the toilet not once, but twice, because I screwed up the drain lines and had to jackhammer the floor out *again*, and then have the electric box rewired for the baseboard heaters. I groused the entire time, and since I'm being honest here, I said a few bad words, too, when I was installing sheetrock, and I slammed my thumb with a hammer. Man, that hurt, and like holy fire.

My next goal? I need an outdoor kitchen. I'm tired of ferrying stuff in and out. When I put in the kitchen, it'll make my life easier, because I can let someone else run the show. I can invite people over, give them the keys to the gate, and watch the party begin.

I'm glad no one's asked for a pool. Ouch, that's expensive, and I don't make all that much money. And to dig that hole myself? I'm not sure even I could do that.

Okay, now I really do have to get out of bed. That heater in my garage bathroom costs a lot to run. I think I left it on after the party last night, and I've got an electric bill to pay.

Man, being a god sucks.

—3—

MY NAME. YEAH, SORRY. I'M LIKE THAT, sometimes, off on a tangent. I am out of bed, now. How's that for a tangent? I'm not a morning person, as you can clearly tell, but then, everyone who knows me knows that. Don't mess with me until I've had my first cup of coffee, or I might just as well bite your head off.

How's that for god talk? Words. It's all just words. Take offense, if you want, but words don't matter. It's what someone perceives that matters, and that's what the god-thing does to me. My "god-i-ness" makes it important to me what others perceive about what I do.

There I go! I was determined *not* to try and describe what this is all about, because you can't. You simply cannot put in black and white what all this god stuff is about. If the Jews couldn't do it in the Old Testament, how can I expect to get it down correctly in this little volume? I mean, after all, those guys knew what they were talking about, and I'm stumbling through the dark, blind every day, just hoping to miss the broken glass that litters the floor.

What I'm *supposed* to be doing is showing you how this god-thing has screwed up my life. Showing, not telling. Life examples, real things I've lived through, that type of non-sense. Things you wouldn't believe, and still, I'm here, and people love me, and all I want to do is get on with it, and by that I mean, being normal, scratching, spitting, and all that stuff. Instead, I get the god stuff, and that means I can't live my life on the beach with the person of my dreams at my side, just chilling myself into old age. If you've ever heard that song by Jimmy Buffett, you know what I want my life to be like. Sponge cake, sun, and tourists covered with oil, my days buried in a margarita haze. I'd like that, to let my life slide on by without any responsibilities to anyone else.

Well, maybe one other person, but that'll never happen. Count on it.

Oh, my name. I may go off on tangents, but I do manage to pull myself back to the main question now and again. Chip. As in Chipper, Chipster, Chippy, or any variation you can imagine. One junior high buddy used to call me Jodhpur. I never got it for a long time, not until he passed me a note in sex ed with my name on it. For two years I thought he had a lisp. Turned out he was calling me a skinny good-for-nothing, although I guess he had the right, because I've always known I have no hips. Still, it's not fun to have someone make fun of your skinny butt, even if it really is skinny.

I'm still friends with Chalky Hollingberry, by the way. I gave him that name after I learned of mine, because of the color of his eyes. They're a washed-out gray, and I intended it to make fun, but I found I can't even do that. Chalky said it was his first nickname ever. He was thrilled, and he's been my friend ever since.

How's that for being a god? I make fun of someone, and they become a worshipful fan. I'm careful what I say to Chalky now. Next thing, and he'll be looking for a cross so that he can deify me. Ouch. I don't need to be elevated to that level of godhood.

You can probably guess Chip's not my real name. I got that because my mom said I'm like my dad. I don't see how. He wasn't a god, not by a long stretch, not unless he tried to drown his "god" powers in Kentucky bourbon. Although, now that I think about it, there have been a few times when I've thought about that very thing. If alcohol didn't taste so bitter to me, I might be more like my dad. Well, except he's dead, and I'm not sure I want to be that much like him, not for a few more years, anyway.

I'm officially Pieter Christopher Engelbrecht III. That's a mouthful, huh? I started my life as Chris, and that devolved into Chip. Well, I should be grateful. Chris is very close to Christ, and wouldn't that be a crock? Another Christ, here in the 21st century, and it's me. I don't think so.

How'd I get that wonderful mouthful of a name? My grandfather, lucky guy. He got it first when he was born in South Africa back in the twenties. He fled to the Big Apple, the family never got out of Queens, and here I am, NYU scholarships and all. Lucky me. I ran away from it all. Now I call Houston home. Texas is half a continent away from the Big Apple, and I can think here.

And you know what takes the cake? Chalky followed me all the way from New York. I guess I could call him my first convert. Now, understand that I'm laughing when I say this, but he could be my first disciple. A really good god has to have disciples, doesn't he?

Even if he doesn't want to be a god at all.

Okay, I'm brushing my teeth, now. I can't do that and talk, so I'll have to wrap this up for a bit. Oh, and in case you want to know? Colgate Tarter Control with Extra Whitening, and my toothbrush has a handle in the shape of a dinosaur. I've always had this thing for dinosaurs. My mom used to buy me T. rex sheets, and when I moved here, it took me a long time to find a place that could custom order them for me. I said they were for my nephew, but I don't have a nephew, so you know where they are. The dinos on my boxers? Well, we won't even go there. Just understand that I have a thing for the suckers, and they make really good quality boxers with anything you want printed on them. I like dinosaurs, and nobody sees my boxers except me, so I can do what I want.

Except with the god-thing. Then I do what the god-thing wants. The god curse. That's what it is, you know. It controls me, and not the other way around.

Well, I'm standing here with my dino toothbrush in hand, and I really have to brush. I have to be at work in 45 minutes, and I'm not getting there with my dinosaurs on display. So, for what it's worth, catch you on the rebound, dude.

—*4*—

IF YOU KNOW WHAT I DO FOR A LIVING, it might help you understand me. I forget how important that is for some people. Me? What I get to do is the god-thing. No, that's not really it. What I'm *forced* to do is the god-thing. I have no choice, just like when you go to a restaurant, and you walk by the dessert table, and there's no way you're getting out without at least one slice of chocolate cake. Oh, sure, you can walk on past, but you'll dream about that cake until next week, and maybe even longer than that, so you might as well indulge today.

The god-thing is like that. I can walk on by. Yeah, sure, I can do that. See a kid with a scratched knee, and I can look the other way like I never saw anything at all, and the kid'll never know, other than that some cheesy man ignored him in his darkest time of pain and peril. But me? I'll know, and I'll think about it, and I'll have regrets, and I'll return to that corner day after day, just hoping to see the kid again so I can reach out to him, to ease his pain somehow, even if the scrape is already well.

So, yeah, I can walk on by, but it's better to just do it, whatever I'm required to do, and that, I guess, wipes some spiritual slate clean, and I can move on with my life. You can see how my god-thing controls me, how it's what I *do*. However, it's not how I pay the bills. I may be a god, but I still have to eat and cover the electric bill, and keep a roof over my head. All that and buy Colgate toothpaste and dinosaur sheets. Yeah, those are important, too, for my mental health, if not for the comfort of my god-like tush.

So, what do I do? Duh, what all good godlings do. I teach school, but not just anything. I teach junior high, that funky age when kids don't know if they're undergrown or over-grown, but where they'll back you down in a heartbeat if you even suggest they're still little kids, which of course they are. Anyway, kids that age need a lot of healing-type stuff going on in their lives. Especially the emotional stuff, and guess who's good at that? A god, duh! And that has to be me, so there I am, teaching my science classes every day, trying to figure out how to work on kids without seeming to work on kids. That's tough, because I don't want to be arrested and sent to jail because I've got my arm around some crying fourteen girl whose stepbrother just jumped her for the fourth night in a row. Not even a god wants to do time in the slammer for trying to help out a kid.

But, hey, what am I supposed to do? Let her continue to get jumped night after night? I won't even consider that, so like the fool that I am, I leap (after I look), and I get involved. First, I let her know I suspect she's dealing with something big, and I let her know I want to help. Then, I start the process. Sometimes it's a call to the local police, but more often I get the school counselor involved. I have to be careful, though. I have questions I have to answer, like, How, Mr. Engelbrecht, are you aware of this instance of sexual abuse in Mary Jane's home? Has she spoken with you about this?

Mary Jane will deny it, of course, because she hasn't said anything to me, so it helps if I can get her to talk about it with me. That can get sticky, because Mary Jane's not saying anything if anyone else is around, and to spend time alone with Mary Jane can create a pretty dicey situation for me. Imagine this: Ah, Mr. Engelbrecht, just what were you doing with Mary Jane alone and in your classroom for twenty minutes last Thursday?

See my point? Yet, the god-thing won't let me look past the girl as if nothing's happening, so I have to figure out how to get her to talk without getting her alone behind closed doors. It's stupid, but it's tough walking through life with your arm twisted behind your back, forced to deal with everyone else's problems, even when you don't want to.

Well, with Mary Jane, I walked with her in the hall one day, with kids everywhere, and believe it or not, that's a good time, because there's so much going on that no one pays attention to a teacher talking to one of his students. This is junior high, remember. Kids at that age see a teacher in the hall, and they automatically envision a void right where that teacher's standing, sort of a no man's land black hole where nothing good or interesting could possibly be going on, because, after all, what interesting thing could there possibly be in the life of an adult? Anyway, I punched her lightly on the shoulder and said, "You're a good kid, Mary Jane. You need to talk, I'm your man." I winked at her and went on as if it didn't mean anything. The next day I was talking with another teacher, and someone bumped into me. It didn't register, and then I felt something pressed into my hand. I turned to catch Mary Jane walking down the hall, focused on something I couldn't see. Then she called to a friend, laughed, and they broke into a fit of giggles. Girl stuff, things shared in a strange language I wouldn't understand in a million years. My hand? I held a note, from Mary Jane, I suspected.

That was how it worked with Mary Jane. In that note, she made the connection I needed to broach the subject with the counselor, and we got her the help she needed. How was my god-thing involved in this? That was how I knew this bright, friendly, and beautiful child was suffering under the assault of a nineteen-year-old who couldn't keep his pants zipped around his step-sister. It was also what drove me to distraction until I helped resolve her issues.

Oh, and there's one more thing I can do, not that I enjoy it. I can see things others can't. Now, before you cringe, it's not like dead people or anything like that. As far as I know, dead people are really dead, and I hope they go to Heaven, but I'm not aware that any of them hang around here to haunt the rest of us. I can see things bad people don't want me to see, like stashes of pictures on memory cards hidden inside rolled socks in the top of closets. Of course, Mary Jane's step-brother denied molesting her, but with the pictures he'd taken, he was dead in the water. You can't have a picture of your own, um, personal member attached to another person's, um, equally personal member and deny that it was you doing the deed. Yeah, he got locked away, and Mary Jane was better. You see, that's the good part of the god-thing. I do all the rest because I have to. What I *get* to do is the healing part. When I was with Mary Jane in that courtroom, and the sentencing was over, she came up to me, crying, and she gave me a hug. It was in full public view, and with the situation, I was safe in letting her do so, but I could feel the terror still inside the girl. That was when I let the god power flow, and I healed her inside. I can do that. How? You're asking the wrong person the answer to that, but I know it works, because I can feel when I do it. The pain is like a piece of broken glass inside a person, and I can feel the sharp edges poking, jabbing, and slicing their emotions. The tears are the blood that leaks out when the glass cuts too deeply. Well, I just reach in, and with a brush of my hand, I smooth all the rough edges, and the glass doesn't cut anymore. I can't remove it, so I can't help them forget. Dear God, I wish I could do that. But I can't. So, I make it not hurt anymore. What I think happens is that I seal all the memories in a bubble, and the person can see inside, but they can't touch them anymore, and that makes it okay. Sometimes okay is the best we can hope for, and that's what I do, give them okay.

Well, Mary Jane cried for a minute, and then she stopped. And when she pulled away, she said, "You're special, Mr. Engelbrecht. Hugging you, I don't hurt anymore. I'll be okay after this. Thank you." I didn't see any real change in Mary Jane's behavior in school after that, and she didn't treat me as if I'd done anything special for her, but then, she hadn't seemed messed up before. She just giggled at silly jokes, sometimes turned in her papers late, and was a regular kid. Then, that was the point. Mary Jane needed the chance to be a regular kid, and with that step-brother of hers, that would never happen. I hope she grows up happy, but now, at least she has that chance.

So, the god-thing isn't all bad, not like I make it out, but if I could move to Hawaii and surf all day, that'd be stupid fine. Now, I've got a red light that doesn't want to change, and if I don't get a move on, I'm not getting signed in before the vice-principal closes up the book, and I'll get a demerit on my record. If only I could change the lights to green when I needed it, I'd be happy to put up with all the other god stuff I have to do. But I can't even get that, just one green light to make my life easier.

Like I've said, more times than I can count, being a god sucks if I can't use any of my powers for myself. That sucks like a lemon on steroids.

I don't even like lemons.

—*5*—

SO, OF COURSE, THE BOOK WAS GONE when I got to the office to sign in, but it had nothing to do with that sluggish red light. No, it had to do with the dumpster on West Dallas. I knew what it was when I drove by, and I couldn't keep my eyes off that rusted hulk of metal. I mean, it was a regular old dumpster, sitting askew in its dumpster bay, with one of its plastic lids up and the other closed. There was even a black trash bag sitting on the pavement beside it, as if someone couldn't be bothered to actually toss it inside.

How much more normal could you get? It was a *dumpster*, for heaven's sake!

After I drove by, it was stuck in my mind, though. Like, what goes in dumpsters? Last week's garbage, empty toilet rolls, and tons of dirty diapers. Oh, and old televisions, although those are supposed to be recycled, even if we know not everyone does that. Serial killers sometimes put in extra arms and legs, double wrapped in heavy duty bags, I suppose, so they don't smell before they make it to the dump. The news hadn't said anything about a rash of odd killings, so I shrugged that off. It didn't feel like that's what drew me to that rusty dumpster.

No, I thought, as I stopped at the next light, with the dumpster just visible in my rear view mirror, it was something sinister, but what, I wasn't sure. It felt like old greasy pizza boxes that have baked in the sun too long, and they've begun to turn rank. That type of feeling, something maybe not bad, not at first, but that's been allowed to go bad, like it could have been cleaned up earlier without too much problem, but now the stink has spoiled everything touching it.

I made it to school, but as I was getting out of my car, I was focused on that dumpster; and not thinking, I left my nametag and my room key in my console. I was at the front door before I remembered, and I had to go back and get them. My one redeeming action? I said good morning to the veep before heading back to my car. For that, she let me step into her office and sign without a demerit, although she gave me the "eye" and told me to plan better next time.

I've never had to use my god-thing powers with Mrs. Lamar, so she has no reason to be grateful, and that means I'm like a piece of sand in her shoe, forgotten when I get out of the way, but very irritating when she notices me. It's not fun to be sand in someone else's shoe. Then, Mrs. Lamar is very much in control of every part of her life, so I can't imagine anything she touches ever falling apart, no matter how hard life tries to beat her down. Still, if she ever needs my attention, I'll be there for her, because that's what I do, help people, whether they want me to or not.

Once I got to my classroom, I forgot the dumpster for a while. There on my door was a giant card signed by all the students in my last period class. The Friday before, I had to leave early to help with the school assembly. Our basketball team is going to regionals, and the student council planned an impromptu pep rally. Planned and impromptu used together in the same sentence make an oxymoron, I know, but then this is junior high. Even when seventh and eighth graders plan some-thing, trust me, it's still impromptu. So, I volunteered to help, and that's why I left my class early, to help set up the gym for orderly attendance. In the 20 minutes or so they were left alone, the kids had made me a giant card wishing me a good weekend. Now I wish I'd come back by the classroom to col-lect it. I would've enjoyed showing it off all weekend.

I put it on my desk, opening it to look at some of the inscriptions. There was Mary Jane's. *You're the best, Mr. Engelbrecht.* Nah, M.J., I thought. Just doing my job, because I don't have any other choice. Still, what she said made me feel good, like being a god was sometimes all right, even if most of the time it wasn't.

Then the teacher next door, Miss Mulford, rapped on the door, and when I looked up, she smiled and waved. Stefanie is single, like me, and she confides in me. Like, who her latest boyfriend is, and whether she thinks he's marriage material. I listen, mostly. Stefanie could use some god-like instruction, but until she really hits a brick wall, and I mean really hits a brick wall, my god powers aren't likely to kick in. At least they never have until now, and we've been in next-door rooms for over five years. With her romantic disasters aplenty, you'd think it would have kicked in, already, if it were going to. Then, that's not the sort of disaster I help people with, other than listening and refusing to offer advice. I just smile and say, "He sounds like a nice guy. Could you live with three Dobermans in your apartment?" That's usually all it takes, and within a week or two, Stefanie has it figured out on her own. Stefanie's a smart woman, and I don't think anyone has to worry about what goes on in her life. She can handle herself pretty well.

This morning she wanted to make sure I got the card. That's Stefanie, social queen, always checking up on people to make sure they get their due, that they get noticed when they do something right. I understood what she was saying. Your kids love you, Chip. Just look at that card, if you don't believe it. And me, I'm so lucky to teach with you, even if you never do ask me out on a date.

That last part? I made that up. In all actuality, I don't think Stefanie would go out with me if I asked. She has enough boyfriends without me getting in the way. But then, I don't have any Dobermans. That's one mark in my favor.

I am subscribed to a couple news channels that send in the latest on my email. The school doesn't mind that as long as we don't use our school email account to do personal stuff or send mass memos to everyone in the district. It was second period when I noticed my email icon at the bottom of the screen blinking, and I double-clicked it, wondering what was so important that it had a little red exclamation mark out to the side. That was when my morning dumpster sighting came back to me in full force.

There had been an explosion in one of the city's dumpsters. Guess which one. Yeah, it doesn't take much to figure this one out. West Dallas Street. Hm. Want to bet it's a rusty dumpster with a black plastic trash bag sitting beside it? Now I wanted to kick myself. I should have pulled over and checked out what was inside.

Of course, then I might have lost an arm or a leg. Being a god doesn't keep all your body parts together in an explosion, and it doesn't help you regrow any missing pieces when it's all said and done, either. Even a god has to be smart enough to know when to step back and leave well enough alone. That's how you keep on being a god, rather than a martyr that used to be a god.

You think I grouse about being a god? You don't want to hear how I'll grouse if I ever become a martyr. I said people don't hang around once they're dead, but don't bet the bank on us gods. Now, I've never seen a dead god, because I don't see dead people, but I bet that I could stupid well hang around to torment a few people if I were ever killed, and I'd do it just for the kick of it, all because I thought I could.

Yeah, that'd be fun, a little payback to whoever took me out. I wouldn't mind that at all. That dumpster? I was getting the strongest feeling that I wasn't through with that rusty hulk anytime soon.

Man, I dreaded that thought. Dumpsters stink to gosh-awful heaven, but how else am I supposed to find out if it means anything? I've got to climb inside and see if I get any "vibes" from the residue that's left. Once I've finished that, I get to drive back to my house, throw my clothes away, and shower five times. If I'm lucky, then the stink will be gone, and that's only if I'm lucky.

Like I said, being a god sucks, and there's no two ways around that.

— 6 —

I PUNCHED MY FIST AGAINST THE WALL in my supply closet. Dadgum, it hurt! It's concrete block, so I can't punch through it, thank goodness. After all, I don't have a magic hammer like Thor, able to break through solid rock with a crushing crunch, or super strength like Superman, with the ability to compress ordinary coal into diamond. No, I break knuckles and get bruises under my skin, more like a human.

Anyway, I keep an extra winter jacket hanging in the closet, and it pads the wall when I've reached my frustration point. Now, you think I'm talking about my kids, somebody backtalking me, setting me off just to get under my skin, but I'm not. No, they're a pain in the backside, sometimes, but I'm never angry at them, not enough to punch the wall. I save that for my god-thing, when it frustrates me so much that I simply can't get through another minute without doing *something*.

Mary Jane didn't show up in my last period class. I know, kids don't show up all the time, and we're supposed to count them absent and prepare a makeup packet for them to pick up when they return. No big deal. However, and there's always a however. Usually, anyway. There was this time. The however? Mary Jane doesn't miss. Ever. Even when she was going through all that bull with her crappy step-brother, she never missed a day. Smiled every morning, just like it was the best day of her life. We fixed that, but the fact was, she was the same ole same ole, and I depended on her to be in her chair like clockwork.

That empty chair was a handful of long fingernails scraping a chalkboard and digging into my psyche like bloody chicken legs in a pan of chicken and rice. Yech!

"Anyone seen Mary Jane?" I called it into the room, thinking maybe she had stopped by the nurse or something. Things like that happen, and if she showed up with a pass, I wouldn't have to count her as tardy. The boy sitting in the seat behind hers, Alfonzo Maldonado, raised his hand in an, "I'm cool, and I can't believe you don't know this," way, and he rolled his eyes as I nodded at him. "Alfonzo?"

"Hey, you know that brother love she dealt with last year, well, he got out on a technicality.

The latest dope on the line is he wanted to see his chick last night, and he got a little rough in the sack." Alfonzo shrugged and gave a little snort. It was more of a high school response than eighth grade, but Alfonzo was held back several times over the years, so he'd be a junior next year if he'd kept his grades up.

"How do you know this, homie brother?" I teased him with that sometimes, and I think he liked the corniness of it. It got a smile out of him, and he looked around the classroom at the other students, seeing them watching him, and warming up. Me? I was sick to my stomach. Not Mary Jane.

"Yeah, my sis, she got knocked up, and she thought she was gonna punch one out last night." He grinned, as if it were the latest episode in a soap opera. "We had to make a run to the doc, and while we were waiting, some ambulance stiffs brought a chick in, all messed up like, and I saw M.J.'s mother come in all teary eyed. That's what happened, Mr. E."

"And you were there." I tried to keep control. Alfonzo's clumsy English? That was his gang persona, because he used his verbs correctly. He was all about how others saw him. Still, he wasn't a liar, never around me. I trusted what he said.

"Yeah, man, and that's why I don't got my homework." He leaned back, working his shoulders, with his head all cocky-like.

"You don't got your homework?"

"Kay, Mr. E. I get it." He laughed and gave

me a half wink. "Don't have." He dismissed the conversation, turning away, and dug in his backpack, pulling out a spiral and a pen, and he started putting his heading on a fresh sheet like he was really ready to learn today. As if.

I saved the punching thing until I went in to get some supplies—test tubes or slides, I don't remember—and I think I punched the wall to get my mind off Mary Jane. A technicality? What sort of technicality? And the thing is, I hadn't known it was coming. When I've helped someone, then something about them hangs on for a while, and I sorta track them. It's not stalking, nothing like that. I don't drive by their houses and look in their windows. It's more like I'm aware of them and whether they're having a good day or not. Sometimes I can sense if they're struggling, or if something has come up that's setting them back. You know, like jailed, incestuous step-brothers getting-out-of-prison-on-a-technicality stuff. I can sense those things.

I don't know why I didn't think of that dumpster. To me, they were two entirely separate events, a blown-up dumpster and a girl thrown back with a jackal of a brother who didn't deserve to walk the streets of the same city with her. I guess it was teaching in the Houston school district. Here, half the kids in my classes have serious issues they deal with every day. Like Alfonzo, no father, a pregnant sister, and a mother who thinks her kids' problems are a punishment from God. Yeah, I've sat through a few teacher-parent conferences over Alfonzo. That woman is the punishment inflicted on her family. If I had real god powers, I'd give her a makeover or two. It doesn't work that way, though. I seem to find the out-of-the-ordinary stuff that makes your skin crawl. At least it does mine. I assume it does that to everyone. If not, what's wrong with you? Are you a pervert, like Mary Jane's brother? Man, I hope not.

After class was over, I asked around in the office to see if anyone knew anything about Mary Jane. I said Alfonzo had mentioned seeing her mother at the emergency room, and that brought a laugh from everyone. They all know Alfonzo, and him being at the emergency room? That was more normal than not. His mother, you see. She's a bit hysterical, and if she can pump up someone else to support her histrionics, she's game, anytime, anywhere.

Anyway, Mrs. Chen, that's our nurse, motioned me into her office with a finger to her lips. She's like that, all private and mysterious. I didn't see the deal, since we're all staff, but she likes to make a scene, and hey, it's no skin off my knees. So, I followed her into her office.

"You know Mary Jane had some issues last year." She looked at me over the top of her glasses. Yeah, I was at the trial, but I kept an interested look on my face. "Did you hear that her brother went to prison for his involve-ment?" She waited expectantly, as if she wanted me to answer.

"Sure. I remember that." Let her think she was giving me fresh news, and she'd bleed everything out. I could hear the ladies at the front desk getting ready to shut the office down, keys out and stuff like that. Mrs. Chen wouldn't mind, though. She might even open up if it was just the two of us.

"It seems there was no actual warrant to search his things, and in an appeal, all the pictures used as evidence got thrown out. Shame, because it was obvious he did it." She shook her head and pursed her lips. "Too bad, you know, with poor Mary Jane just fourteen. But I don't blame her."

"What do you mean?" My heart caught. Blame Mary Jane? What had she done wrong?

"You use Dallas to get to work sometimes, right?"

"Sometimes." Almost every day, unless there was a wreck or I had errands to run. I talked about it all the time, so it wasn't like she didn't know. She was putting off telling me something, and that meant it was bad.

"You've seen the car wash at Taft?" She peered at me, waiting. "White building?"

"Yes." I was making the connection, and I didn't like it. That dumpster from this morning was at Taft, cattycorner from the car wash, just across from the Gregory-Lincoln Education Center. My good friend Charisse Winston teaches second there. I could have called her to find out what was going on.

"Well," and she looked away, hesitating,

which is not like Mrs. Chen at all, "a dumpster across the street caught on fire this morning, and it seems Mary Jane's brother was inside when it happened."

Thank goodness, I thought. He didn't kill her. Then it hit me what I was hearing; and with the wham of an epiphany going off like a gong in my head, I put all the facts together. Brother, out of prison. Sister, in the emergency room. Dumpster, brother inside. Finally, there'd been a big boom. Something really bad had gone down, to say it Alfonzo's way. Some really bad stuff had hit the fan. I hoped the resulting effluent didn't get all over Mary Jane.

"And Mary Jane? She's in my last class of the day, you know." She probably did, but me saying it gave me good reason for asking. You know, keeping the air clean, all that teacher and student confidentiality mumbo-jumbo. "Alfonzo said he saw her in the emergency room." Not exactly, but it was what he had insinuated.

"Sent home; told not to pee; and to come back when the crowd thinned." What she didn't say was clear. It was standard operating procedure at an overcrowded free clinic. Typical free and typical useless clinic. Mary Jane had gone in, needing help, and they'd turned her away.

"Her step-brother again?"

Mrs. Chen nodded in reply, looking at me over her glasses.

"She was attacked, and they sent her home?"

I felt anger boiling up inside. After all I'd done to help the girl out last time, and her bravery in confiding in me. How could an atrocity like this be allowed to happen?

"I know, Mr. Engelbrecht, but there was a gang thing last night, and Mary Jane could walk. Well, I haven't spoken with her mother today, but someone needs to go over there. Do you think you, possibly?"

She didn't flesh out the question, and it was just as well. I got the picture, and I wanted to get involved. This was the perfect opportunity for me to jump in without appearing to jump in. Thank you, Mrs. Chen. You are the sweetest woman, and I love you very much, even if you do have a husband and seven grandchildren. I can still love you, because you did exactly what I wouldn't have thought of. You sent me straight to the source rather than to that dumpster. Now I won't have to throw my clothes away. Thank you, ma'am, and you are, indeed, my very favorite school nurse, ever.

I did go back and check my classroom door to make sure no one had left me a note. Nah, it was clean, but it was also locked. I saw Stefanie's light on, and I leaned in, calling to her to have a good evening. Even when part of the world is collapsing for some people, we should still be polite to the others, because if politeness falls into the gutter, what else do we have? Nothing much at all.

I'd have to work at being polite to Mary Jane's brother, if he was still alive. What I wanted to do was cut some stuff off, the stuff between his legs, not to be too specific. Yeah, I'd do that, and I wouldn't even think twice about it. Mary Jane deserves a better life, and besides, I'm angry with myself that I wasn't able to prevent this. If being a god doesn't let me help other people, what point is there? None, and I'll be more than willing to toss this god-thing in a dumpster, one that will hopefully explode just after I chuck it inside.

It doesn't work that day, but I can imagine. Better, I'll see what Mary Jane needs, and once again I'll try to make her life right.

I still refuse to admit, at least in this, that sometimes there's nothing I can do. The reality is that you can't always make things right, no matter how hard you try. Especially, and I mean this, if you're a stupid, useless god like me.

—7—

I REALLY WISH I COULD FORGET some of the things this curse has forced me to do. Really. Just to be able to walk away, see people as they really are, and not as the troubles that haunt them. Yeah, that would be nice.

Like when I was fifteen, and I was still back in Queens. Now, parts of Queens are like suburbia, but not all of it. Some of it's a little rough, and you want to stay away at night. If you have to go in after dark, carry a really big flashlight, and maybe a gun or two. Like a rocket launcher. Rocket launchers blow things up from a distance, and they give you plenty of time to run away before the bad guys can get to you.

Well, I was still in high school, probably tenth grade, and I knew something always smelled—in the god sense—a little strong out behind the auto mechanics building. I wasn't involved in it, so what the heck? I never paid any attention.

Then kids started getting beat up. Not always the rough kids from the wrong side of the tracks, either, but good kids. Little kids, big kids, even some of the honor kids. Some even got legs broken. Of course, along the way, a few roughies got their share, but mostly it was kids you wouldn't expect. That was what got my god sense involved, I think.

Anyway, I wasn't real good at all this then. All I knew was this *compulsion* to get back there, to find out what was going on behind the shop. I mean, it *stank,* and there was no way people couldn't tell.

I tossed and turned in my bed for several weeks, being preoccupied with my own troubles, and staying away from anything that reminded me of my dad. Now, in case you think of me as a goody-goody high schooler, that wasn't it. I'd just watched my dad drown himself in Kentucky gold, and his funeral was still pretty clear in my mind. Well, not the actual *funeral,* as I was feeling sorry for myself during the entire mess, so that was pretty much a blur, but before and after, my mom, she was a wreck, cursing Pops one minute and kissing his picture the next. Half the time she'd speak in the same butchered Afrikaans she'd yelled at my father from time to time, mostly cuss words, I suspected, as I'd never bothered to learn more than a few phrases, and I didn't always recognize what she screamed at my dad. The rest of the time she'd carry his picture around, stroking the image, and wiping her tears from the glass, crazy like a street queen tripping on LSD.

I'd suspected for a long time that my dad was crazy, and I was convinced by then that craziness rubbed off. I didn't want his crazy to rub off on me. I'd seen my father talking to shadows on the walls and once digging into his skin with a sharpened spoon. I wanted to blame it on Kentucky, but I'd heard stories of my grandfather, and like I said, I thought craziness was a communicable disease, and if you lived in the same house with it, you caught it.

My mother was pretty good evidence of that.

Now she's okay. Mostly. Pops is dead and buried, I burned all his pictures when I was seventeen, and we moved on. Then, after college, I really moved on, leaving all the craziness behind. Well, to be perfectly honest, I left it all behind, except the parts I brought with me. I've just learned that it's not craziness. It's my life, and I have to deal with that.

At fifteen, I didn't know how.

So, there I was, compelled, and I lay in my bed night after night with pictures of beat-up people I knew I'd never seen before running through my head. Nightmares, I thought. Truth, I eventually learned. Well, one day during lunch, with sweat running down my back, I dropped all my books behind the water fountain, and I opened the side door to the cafeteria, the one that led to the auto mechanics shop if it was raining and you left your slicker at home. It went the long way around, and that was fine with me. I was about to take a dump in my pants, and I wanted to take the long way around.

Now, before I tell you the whole story, let me give you a bit of my opinion. Teachers have to go to college, get a degree and all. I know, because I have one. That's supposed to make us smart. The shop teacher—Mr. Lowry, if anyone's interested—was running drugs out of the back of a school building. He was, get this, cooking right there on school property. Where did his brains get to? Sheesh!

Did I do anything that anyone else couldn't have done? Nah. The problem was, they didn't. How did I help? I began talking to the kids who were hurt, and eventually I convinced a few of them to speak up for themselves. They found the strength to band together and confront the evil right in front of their eyes. Now, you might be thinking, Chip, there's the good in what you do, but no, that wasn't it. They did that completely on their own. What I did was help them forgive themselves and forget. Mostly forget, forget the pain part, anyway. You remember the thing I did with Mary Jane, smoothed the glass so that it didn't hurt anymore. Only thing was, afterwards, I still remembered, and when I saw them, I knew what every one of them had done. I knew, and I couldn't forget. That changes your view of people, I can tell you that.

Now, if someone could smooth my glass, that'd be a fine help, because all the memories still haunt me, and that's not fun. Not at all.

I wonder what I'll find when I stop by to see Mary Jane? Swollen eyes and a cast on one arm? Will she even want to see me? After all, I did let her down. I rescued her, but then her nightmare came back to see her. Then, I deal with that every day. Some mornings I try to pretend for a few moments that I'm normal, just a regular-Joe science teacher, and that feels pretty good. Then the god-thing kicks in again, and there we go all over.

If I have to do this, why can't I at least fly? Why does Superman get to have all the fun?

—8—

I'M AN IDIOT. WHY AM I writing this down? Do you care? Do you actually give a rippin' torrent? Not a chance in Hades. Do I care? Only when I'm not smothered in the sweltering schizophrenia of godhood run amok.

That's where I'm at, too. Those holes punched in my walls? I'm about to punch one through my car window. I went by Mary Jane's house. Blast it, I went by Mary Jane's house, and I can't say I wish I hadn't, but for Pete's sake, I want to punch something out, because I'm stupid tired of this god-thing.

That said, let's move on a while, and if I get under control, I'll come back to what happened at M.J.'s house. I told you once I'd like to have someone at my side. Yeah, right, like that sucks to even want that, you know? 'Cause it ain't ever gonna happen. You know? I meet someone, I get attached, and oh, man, do I get attached, and then it gets all shattered, and, well, that hurts. It hurts like razors, and I want to slash and burn and do mean things to people who don't deserve mean things. I want that so bad that I have to curl up and cry until it all goes away.

Well, that's a crock, because while I've tried the crying thing—which never works, by the way—all the rest? The yelling and the striking out and the making others hurt as much as I do? That only makes holes in my walls. This god-thing has me twisted up tighter than a baby's diaper in a wringer washer. I dole out goodness to everyone around me, and they smile, and everyone's happy. Everyone except me, and I smile, and I take the pats on the back, and we're all warm and fuzzy. Except I want to die, to curl up and let life melt away, and just not be here anymore. And I can't, because I keep thinking of the people I do care about, and how they'd not understand, and then I get all soft inside, and I don't want to hurt them.

How does a god die, anyway? Can a god die? Is it, just maybe, possible for a jerkwater god who can't get even one break in life, to up and Sam Hill die just to get it all over with?

I'm sorry. I'm getting slobbery here, with all my guts out for everyone to see, and that makes me feel like a heel, because when you think about it, I've got it pretty good. Better than a lot of people, anyway. I've got a job. The pay's not great, but it's not minimum wage, either. My car starts and runs every time I turn the key. My house may have holes in the walls, but the roof doesn't leak. I do have a really nice bathroom in the garage, and I do have friends that come over from time to time, friends who let me restrict them to the back yard even in Houston's humid summers, and they don't complain. Sometimes I wish they would tell me, "Hey, Chip, it's hot out here, and you suck, man. You have air conditioning just inside that door." Yeah, and I have holes in my walls, too, big ones, and I don't want you to know. Be happy with your bathroom in the garage. Your girlfriends are. So, there.

No, they throw arms around my shoulders, mock punch me in the stomach, and tell me with alcohol-laden breath that I'm the best guy they've ever known, and when they have kids, they plan to name them after me. Like ever. If that were the case, there'd be fifty little Chippers and Chippettes starting up kindergarten just any day, and I'm not aware of any of those. Then, I'm a Christopher, so maybe if I looked for Christophers I might find out those drunken promises were more sincere than I took them for.

You gotta love friends, especially the drunken ones. But be careful around their women, because that's a line no one crosses, even off-duty gods.

Okay, okay, I think I can relax my fist. I've

had my moment, and while I know it's out there just waiting in the wings, I think I have it on hold for now. Scratch too deeply, and red hot fury comes bursting out. Sometimes it's better to keep it contained. Then, when I'm past it, I can pretend it was never there, and I can go on with my life, one step today and another tomorrow. I read something on a website once that said to wake up in the morning is human. To get out of bed is courageous. To try to live through the same nonsense you lived through yesterday takes a god. I guess that's why I get the pigsty life, because I can take it.

Not fair, is it? Not in my book. Then, who am I to complain? I just left M.J.'s house, and look at what's left of her. And me? I've got that dumpster. It's waiting on me, even if I thought I could get away without going there.

It's what M.J. said to me. "I didn't want him to die, Mr. Engelbrecht. I just wanted him to stop. And he wouldn't, and I knew he wouldn't no matter what anyone did. If you couldn't keep him away, I knew no one could, and it was up to me. I'm sorry about the dumpster, though. Do you think they'll make me pay for it?"

Cripes, was she admitting guilt, or accepting the responsibility for something she didn't do? Maybe it was that way in her family, there's one responsible person in the whole lot, so that person gets to handle all the crud. Today, it was M.J. owning up to something she didn't do. I hoped she didn't, anyway. But to pay for the dumpster? An ordinary dumpster, destroyed in revenge, after she endured the torture that man put her through? And at nineteen, he was a man, and he knew how to make the right decisions. Apparently he knew how to make the wrong ones, too. Like sticking his wick where it didn't belong, just because it felt good to him. You got to think of the other person, man, not just what you got going on between your legs. The other person counts, too.

Oh, man, I'm listening to myself, there, because I'm talking to myself, too. It's why my relationships shatter. I do think of the other person, and that's why my relationships never go anywhere. I want girlfriends around, but I don't want to hurt them. More accurately, I don't want what I can do to hurt them, and that's why I let them go.

You know, part of my problem right now is probably food, or the lack of it, to be precise. And I see a Burger King to the right. Sometimes all it takes is a soda and a pack of fries to make the world right again. Besides, I've stopped here before, and since I teach, and some of my ex-students work here, sometimes I get the supersize for the regular price. I pulled in, happy to be the only one in the drive-thru line.

"Hey, yeah, I'd like a fry and a coke." That's what I usually order. I like their burgers, but I'm not much of a meat eater. Grease packs my veins better. Keeps my blood from getting lazy. And, if I'm lucky, it might even kill me before I get old and senile.

That's called seeing the bright side of things.

"Hey, that you, Mr. E.?"

It's a boy's voice. I try to place it and can't, so I improvise.

"Yeah. Is that you, Emilio?" I have no idea, but since I can't see him, he'll laugh it off. I've done this before, and since I know Emilio works here, I always use his name.

"Nah. You said that last time. Connor. Remember? Eighth grade science? I'm a junior, now. I'll make it a large, and we'll call it even. Drive on up, Mr. E."

The boy laughed, and apparently he didn't key the mike off quickly enough, because I could hear him call out in the background, "Emilio, Mr. E. thought I was you again. He was my favorite teacher, ever."

I pictured Emilio Abasolo the way he'd been his first day in eighth grade. Thin as a rail, like kids who shoot up a foot over the summer. Dark hair, parted, and combed with a swoop in front. Working his shoulders as he walked into class. He was new to Houston ISD, and he was making a statement. I figured I'd have to back him down at some point, because in my class, I'm the king. I rule, and the kids can only get away with stuff up to whatever line I've drawn. To that point, I'm pretty lenient, but cross it, and I become spitfire and lightning all rolled into one, although I do it with kindness and whispers. Emilio crossed that line on the third day when he wouldn't stop a conversation with another boy after I started the lesson. I called him on it, and he cocked that shoulder and said, "You get your stuff together and teach, Teach, and I'll listen when I get ready. Maybe tomorrow. Sabe?"

Sabe? *Sabe?* That was when I got real quiet, and I asked the rest of the class to wait outside. Most of them had me in seventh, and without a word, they stood and filed out. I didn't hear a sound from them, either. They knew better. I put up with a lot in my class, but disrespect, intentional disrespect, wouldn't pass the muster, not then, and not ever.

"So, Emilio," I started, my voice barely above a whisper, and I checked my class walkie-talkie attached to my belt, just to be sure the volume was down. When I hit the switch, I knew it would sound like I was turning it off. Scary, huh? "You and me, we're going to butt heads, and I'm going to win. You know why? Because I'm a god, and you're not." I never cracked a smile, either. Kids, the thirteen kind that come to me at the start of eighth grade, they get the god-thing, even if they think it's just posturing. Some of it is, I admit, because I've yet to gain control of lightning, but anything's possible for a god. Maybe I haven't reached my prime, and that's something I'll get someday. Maybe.

He looked hard at me for a minute, and then he glanced at the empty seats. I think that got him to consider-ing how the other kids had walked out without a question, and he licked his lips, like he was thinking. Then he said, soft-like, "I won't cry." His jaw was hard, but his eyes were red, and he blinked several times fast.

"I don't expect you to." I was pretty sure I'd hit some nerve. What, I didn't know, but he'd already changed his tune. That's what I needed.

"I don't want no bruises anyone can see." He closed his eyes, and it dawned on me. He expected me to hit him. The other kids out of the room, and no witnesses? I wondered who had done that to him before. Dad? Step-dad? A previous teacher? I shivered for him to take it so casually.

"I don't give bruises." As soon as I said that, I realized it could be taken as a threat. I was right, too, because his face melted, and his body wilted. I knew I needed to get this fixed, and quickly, or I would lose him. I rapped the desk with my knuckles, and he jumped, falling right out of his seat and onto the floor, taking down the desk next to him. It clattered loudly. Oh, cripes, I thought.

"Emilio," I said, hard, to get his attention.

"I'm sorry, Mr. Engelbrecht." His lip quivered.

I held out my hand, slowly so he wouldn't think I was about to strike him, and I held it until he offered me his in turn. "Off the floor, Emilio. Who's hit you, and what for?" Then I pulled him back into his seat.

He looked around, his eyes stopping on the door, and he wiped his face with the backs of his hands, leaving damp streaks down his cheeks. He shook his head real fast and took several deep breaths.

"Can I get you to look at me, Emilio?" I watched him track the floor and my shoes and finally find my eyes. His were dark brown and glistening. "I don't hit my students. I don't tolerate disrespect, but I don't hit, either. Who hits you?" When I saw he didn't intend to tell me, I knelt beside him and said, "You deserve respect. Sometimes you have to earn it, but you deserve it when you do. Can we work together this year?" He nodded. "Good. Now you have your stuff together, and I'll work on mine. How about that? Deal?"

He actually smiled at that. "Yeah. Deal. You're cool, Mr. E. Can I call you that?"

"Everyone does. I like you, Emilio. We're going to have a good year together." I popped him lightly on the back of the head. He said, "Ouch," but he was still smiling.

I brought the rest of the class back in, and I never had another moment's trouble with Emilio. By Christmas, he had muscled out to become quite a good-looking young man. Now he had all the girls stopping by Burger King on the way home from whatever they did after school and on weekends to get him to wait on them at the register.

But think of this the way I see it. Emilio. Thirteen going on seventeen. I flay his emotions to the bone, exposing the very core of his insecurity, i.e., getting beat up by whoever beats him for no good reason, and I'm immediately a god in his eyes. Okay, okay, I can see you roll your eyes. I am a god, but not that kind. It's the same thing over again. I do stuff, and it's not always nice stuff, and it always turns out to be the right stuff. If I killed someone at random, they'd probably turn out to be a cannibalistic serial child rapist with detailed plans in their shirt pocket with the time and place of their next murder. And I'd be celebrated as a local hero. Nothing I do saves me from this.

So, there I was in my car with Mary Jane weighing me down, and I drove up to the window. There was Connor with his blond hair and blue eyes, and he looked back into the restaurant before leaning through the window. "Emilio's an idiot. Ignore what he says."

Then, there was Emilio, pushing Connor out of the way, and he leaned toward me, calling, "Connor's the idiot, Mr. E. You're the best." He grinned and shot me a hand sign, with some of his fingers curled and the others out. I just shook my head. They were both idiots, even if I really liked the two of them.

"Here," I said, and I put a five through the window. With my change and food, I pulled away, smiling when I heard the boys yelling out the window after me, "We love you, Mr. E."

And they're seventeen? Maybe physically. Mentally? I'd peg 'em at twelve, maybe twelve and a half, and certainly not a day over thirteen.

I did feel better, though. See? I told you I'd get over what ailed me. Now if I can just help

Mary Jane get over what ails her, we might be in pretty good shape.

Except for one thing. I've still got that dumpster to visit.

Well, it was about to be a good day. Guess I can't have everything.

—9—

SORRY FOR THE TANGENT. Sometimes I go off on those, what with all the god rocks that try to stone me all the time. Growing up I never understood that in the Bible, you know, stoning people. Like, just cut their heads off or shoot them or something. Make it fast and easy. Then it finally came to me just what it was all about. It was about making the guilty party suffer one impact at a time. It wasn't about killing them at all, although I'm pretty sure that was intentional as well. The real purpose was watching the victim cringe while crying out for mercy, and knowing you weren't giving them an inch. Then they taunted them, threw another rock, and gloated when the blood stared to flow.

Me? I'm the victim, even if most people wouldn't understand that. If I were an orphaned Rio kid forced to prostitute myself just to have food to eat, I'd think my American life was pretty sweet, and I've got to look at it that way. If I don't, I'll go down screaming in frustration, hoping to take as many losers with me as possible.

That dumpster was roped off with yellow "stay away" tape. I laughed. There were no police to monitor, and the traffic was light for a Monday. Besides, the dumpster was actually on Taft, and anyone on Dallas wouldn't particularly notice it as anything special, not unless they happened to look just as they passed, and most people don't. If the police were no longer here, I didn't expect anyone would care. And there were no houses, just the Education Center across the street, and it was down a bit, with an open recreation area just across from where the explosion had occurred.

The dumpster was nasty. When I pulled up my car and turned it off, I was several car lengths down the street, but when I opened my door, there was no mistaking the smell. You'd think a good fire could eradicate any smell-bad particles, just wipe 'em clean, leaving nothing but scoured, fresh metal. And, open to the air, with the plastic lids melted away, the sun would bake the smell of the fire away.

Nope, nothing that easy. I did notice the compulsion from that morning was gone. The step-brother was probably in the dumpster when I drove by, and I didn't know. If I'd stopped, would I have felt better? I don't know. Thinking of Mary Jane, well, that slanted my opinions a bit. Calf fries, anyone? That kind of thinking can feel mighty good when a pretty eighth grader has a broken arm and one eye swollen shut. No telling the damage he'd done to her that I couldn't see. Am I glad I didn't stop? Hard to say, but I don't think I would have felt better if I had, and I'd rescued him, and the guy had killed my M.J. That's what would have happened. Maybe not today, but eventually he'd have gone too far, and she would have been the one. Was it better this way? I'll let you make your own call, but I know which way I'm leaning, and it isn't on the side of compassion.

There was paint missing all over the sides of the dumpster, and it was freshly scoured away. How could I tell? There was no rust. Oh, and the blue residue on the ground around the perimeter of the dumpster. Fire-retardant foam couldn't make all that disappear. This fire had been hot, so what was inside should have been mostly incinerated. I wondered what the accelerant was. Gasoline didn't usually do this much damage. It was great for starting fires, but without air and combustible materials, gasoline fires usually left quite a bit of unburned residue. I was beginning to see this as a science thing, where someone might have mixed up something to get the job done right and without anything left for incrimination. Bones, maybe, but that would be for forensic identification of a person's remains, not indictment of the perpetrator.

I lifted the tape and stepped under it, even as I knew what I was doing was illegal. So? Arrest me. I was at work when all this happened, and I have a very stern and no-nonsense veep to verify it. They might cause me some grief, but they couldn't pin anything on me. And next to what M.J. had gone through, my problems would be nothing. This was one good thing I hoped I could do, maybe, if there was enough left to get a reading.

I grabbed the lip of the dumpster, wishing I had gloves. I did, but at home, and I hadn't been home yet. I gagged when I got my head close. It was a rotten egg smell, bringing to mind carbon disulfide. If so, someone was smart. Carbon disulfide is explosive, more so than gasoline, so it would have spread throughout the dumpster very quickly, in a flashpoint blowout. It was heavier than water, and it would continue to burn from the bottom, even if they filled the dumpster with fluids. Some- one wanted all the evidence gone, someone smart enough to know their chemicals and to have access to them.

I wondered if I should check the supply closet at the school. I'd used carbon disulfide in a demonstration earlier in the year, but I didn't think I had purchased enough to do this sort of damage. At least I hoped what I had left over was still in the lab. If not, that brooked a whole series of questions I didn't want anyone to have to answer.

M.J., M.J., I thought, as I stood there looking inside. What was your part in this? Notice, I never questioned why. Sometimes you don't have to ask why, because all that's there staring you in the face, bam, like a brick wall. You just know. And if you don't, ask the black eye and the broken arm. Then you'll know. Now I had to get inside.

I've tried this from the outside. Lots of times, but it never works. To get the real picture, I have to be immersed. That's why I'm not inundated with visions and other stuff from every Joe Crack on the street. Oh, sure, little things like scraped knees on little kids, but that's the obvious stuff. The deeper darkness? I'm not immersed in their lives, and so all I get is an occasional whiff. I lived with M.J. over the course of a year. Yeah, I only saw her at school, but I often get more quality time with my students than their parents do. They become a sort of family for a year, and for me, teaching both seventh and eighth grade science, I get two years with most of them. How many families get busted up in less time, and then they try to hold things together long distance? I had it pretty good, I thought.

So, I immersed myself. I pulled up and swung one leg inside, cringing when the crotch of my pants scraped the dumpster opening. And these were one of my best pairs. Out of public view, and I'd risk stripping to my shorts, but not this close to Dallas, and certainly not across from the Education Center. All it took was for one report to make it to the Admin office, and my contract was toast. I needed an income, and I guessed I could wear my second best pair for the rest of the year.

Everything inside was blackened. Some residue still clung to the metal, like around the joints and in the corners. Anything big? Either burned or scraped for forensics. I bet there had been bones, but there was no sign of them now. It's hard to incinerate bones, especially in an open fire like a dumpster. Even so, I was getting something, one of those other-worldly experiences that starts at the back of your skull and moves forward. Think headache, except it's not pain. It's more like it engulfs me, distracting me from real life. I'm aware of what's going on around me. I just don't want to pay attention to it any longer. Then when it completely overtakes me, I can't pay attention to what's around me. People talk to me, and I can't respond, not sensibly, anyway.

The dumpster began to take on a translucent quality, as if it glowed from the inside, and the sounds of traffic hustling down Dallas grew muted, like when you're in a plane, and the elevation makes the pressure differential affect your ears. You don't know you can't hear until your ears readjust, and then everything sounds stupid loud, like it's all yelling at you. It's really your brain, because we tune out most everything, except what we want to hear, and when the pressure is affecting our hearing, our brain quits tuning out and tries to pick up everything. At least that's how I had it described to me, and it sounds pretty good.

To get on with it, I was dimly aware of the sounds of traffic in the distance, and I knew the dumpster didn't smell very good, but those things were happening to another person. My skin tingled, and I felt the forensics experts crawling around, collecting, occasionally joking with each other, and one jerking back at something surprising that she found. That wasn't what interested me, though. I pressed harder, and that scene faded away, and flames were all around me. It was total, too. No eighth grader with a broken arm would be able to get together the supplies and set a conflagration in motion like this. I don't know if that pleased me or worried me. I still didn't have my answer, so I pushed harder against the fabric of the past. The deeper I go, the more difficult it is. I knew I had to aim for nine or ten hours, a timeframe I tried to avoid when I could. Doing this takes a toll on the psyche, and I was going to have a ripping headache when I finished. I tried to remember M.J., but anything outside of the dumpster felt really far away. I doubled my efforts, and that was when I became aware of the screaming. I saw him, off in the corner, jerking, his skin scorched, and his hair on fire. Harder, and then he was clothed, and the fire filled the floor of the dumpster, but he wasn't screaming, yet. He jerked, and in that pivotal moment, I knew his name.

Stupid me. How had I not thought of that? Had I tuned him out during the trial? I tried to think, but with the time differential pressing in on all sides, trying to spit me back to the present, it was really hard. I didn't know where his name had gone, but when he woke, there it was. Ryan Gallagher Simpson. I even knew his birthday and the type of coffee he drank that morning. His last morning alive. He'd taken more pictures of M.J., this time intending they would be his last of her, and he wanted to keep the memories of those explosive moments with her fresh in his mind until the moment he died. He'd taken a lot of pictures during the night.

Then I saw something else. Blood soaked the front of his pants. Lots of blood. The fire might have woken him up, but I didn't think that's the reason he was screaming. He was missing some body parts. I didn't think M.J. had done that to him, no matter what he had done to her. I hoped not.

I pressed harder. With this much stuff going on, I'd about reached my limit. If nothing much is happening, sometimes I can get back two or three days, but when the air gets thick with action, it starts to feel like I'm swimming in honey, and nothing I do takes me much deeper. I become stranded, and then the present starts to pull me back faster than I can stay where I am. When I'm moving backwards in time like this, it's move it or lose it. I was about to lose it, and I still needed to find out who had done this.

Then something glittered out of the corner of my eye, and I turned my head. Remember, every-thing was filled with honey at that point. In my mind, I just whipped it around. However, the honey made the motion oh, so slow, and by the time my head got turned, all I got was a glimpse of a sleeve and a black watch on a thin wrist. The time said 7:40. That stood out to me, 7:40, like it was important. 7:40. The honey in my brain had me thinking so slowly, and like a sleepwalker, I pictured the clock on the kitchen stove when I leave for work. It always shows 7:35 as I'm walking out the door. 7:35. Before I could think anything else, the honey started to get slippery, and the past started to unravel, faster and faster, and I was pulled through the events that had taken place in that dumpster. With a loud snap, I was back in the stink and the heat of a Houston evening, and I could hear a horn blaring off in the distance. It stopped with a crunching sound, and it sounded like breaking glass. I cringed. When I do this time thing, stuff like that happens. I think it pulls so much energy that when other people are too close, it slows down their thoughts, too, just enough that bad stuff happens. Cut fingers, bumping into doors, car crashes, that sort of thing. Man, I felt guilty about that, but there was nothing I could do. I would drive the back way home, though, so I didn't have to see it. That way I didn't have to feel involved.

Just as my mind began to clear, the fog of the past evaporating from between my eyes, a sharp *tat!* *tat!* *tat!* erupted around me, the metal of the dumpster ringing in my ears. I automatically ducked and cringed at the intrusive noise.

"Chip? Are you in there?" *Tat! tat! tat!*

Dear God, save me from friends who worship me from not so very far away. That voice could only belong to Chalky. What was he doing here? I called out, "Yeah!" Then I tried to shake the ringing out of my ears.

"Saw your car." His voice was headed to the opening in the dumpster. "Then I saw the dumpster, and I knew you wouldn't be able to resist." He looked in, and his voice began to echo. "Yech, it stinks in here. What do you find so fascinating about places like this? Come on. Get out before the stink becomes permanent."

He didn't offer a hand, though. I think he remembers the last time I did this, and he knows better now. I do, too, and I didn't intend to get in my car like this. I had that worked out, or worked out as best I could in a situation where I didn't have a change of clothes, and I lived too far away to walk there to change and make it back to get my car.

"You remember Mary Jane?" I didn't bother trying to climb out. Chalky was in the way, and I was a little irritated at him. That rapping had hurt my ears. A lot.

"Mary Jane." He frowned in concentration. "Blonde or brunette? A bra size might help. Is it important?"

"From that trial last year. I told you about it."

"Oh, oh!" He laughed, turning red. "That girl in your class. Didn't her brother go to prison?"

"And got out on a technicality. He beat her up last night."

"And this?" He turned pale, and he took in the crime scene tape. Finally, he leaned into the dumpster. "He killed her and dumped her here, huh?"

"Not exactly. If you'd watch the news once in a while, you might learn something. He was found burned alive in this dumpster today. Castrated."

"No!" He shifted, and one hand pulled at his crotch, adjusting. Probably checking to make sure his was still in one piece, if you ask me. "They said that on the news?"

"No, but he was." I motioned for him to move back. "Out of the way. I'm coming through." When I was about out, Chalky reached a hand to steady me. I was grateful, because the time thing takes a lot out of me. My legs were wobbly. I should have gotten the burger. Really. The grease pumps the energy for a quick burst, then it's all gone as soon as the food gets past my stomach.

"Mary Jane told you? She's a brave girl."

"She's fourteen. She did not tell me he was castrated. Give her some credit. After what he did to her, she was probably unconscious. I'm here looking for clues."

"But, how do *you* know he was castrated?" We were headed to the cars, and Chalky had this look on his face that told me he was working this out in his mind, and I knew, because Chalky working things out mostly has to do with screwing his face up and blinking his eyes over and over.

"The front of his pants was covered with blood. Nothing else would cause that much bleeding."

"And you saw him like this when?" Chalky had his keys out, and he rattled them once and caught them tightly in his fist.

"Just before the killer with the black watch set the fire."

"Oh, that explains everything. Thank you, Chip. I'm stopping for pizza. Follow me there?"

That blew my plans for not stinking up my car. I had intended stripping to my shorts and tossing my clothes out somewhere. Not if we're heading for pizza. But the change in topic was very apropos for Chalky. He had gotten into doing that to signal me that I'd lost him, and he was through trying to figure me out.

"Oh, here." Chalky reached inside and pulled out a bag, throwing it my way. "My gym clothes. They're clean. You might want to put them on, because you stink. See you there." He dropped into his car, started it up, black smoke billowing from the tailpipe, and pulled away with a wave.

I picked up the bag and walked to the back side of my car. The building had an offset in the façade just where I'd parked, and I looked to make sure no one was watching before I pulled off my shirt and dropped my pants. My dinosaurs? They hadn't touched anything except me. They were staying on. No sense in taking things that far.

And pizza sounded pretty good to me, because I was starving. Thanks, Chalky. Sometimes a good friend is a very nice thing to have around.

—10—

THE PIZZA WAS JUST WHAT I NEEDED, and as importantly, it was stuffed crust with extra hamburger, just the way I
like it. With God as my witness, everyone should make such
good pizza, but then, if they did, that'd set the bar pretty high,
and how could anyone else measure up? It'd just be average,
and I'd expect something even better. Like Chalky. I complain
about him, but I only complain because I have a very high
caliber of friends. As a teacher, most of the people I interact
with on a daily basis are highly motivated individuals that care
more for how they can help society than how society can help
them. Sure, we grouse about the pay, but we stick with it. That
says something in itself. As for me? You know why I'm there.
It's for the kids. Still, most of my fellow teachers feel the

same. And since I teach with them, I'm friends with most of them. That sets a pretty high bar for Chalky to measure up to.

Tonight? With the pizza? Chalky outdid himself. Shot for the stars. Hit a double and came in on a home run. Yeah, as I finished off my third slice, I was thinking I was pretty lucky to have Chalky for my friend.

Then he dropped the bombshell.

"I've got a favor to ask of you, Chip." Chalky licked two of his fingers and sat back, one arm over the back of the bench seat. He reached to the pizza pan and pressed a damp finger into a pile of shredded mozzarella, and then he sucked it off with a wet sound.

Humph! He didn't fool me. I've known this guy too long. This wasn't a favor. He wanted something big, like when I got this job with Houston ISD, and the next week he met me at the gym with those same eight words. When he dropped that bombshell, it was, "Can I have some space in your moving truck for my bed? I've already taken an apartment in Houston a couple blocks away from your new school."

"No." I laid it out plainly, because sometimes Chalky doesn't get it when I try to be subtle. It just goes right past him. When he looked at me, surprised, I said, "Whatever it is, the answer is no, because you always take advantage of me. So, no, and I mean it."

"But you don't know what I'm asking, yet."

He actually looked hurt that I hadn't listened. I

put that aside, and I repeated my refusal very strongly.

"You're asking, and that's enough. Thanks for the pizza, and I'm glad you're my friend, but no. I won't do it."

"No, wait. I've got this all worked out. And it's not permanent, not if you don't want it to be. The air is out in my apartment, you remember, and now they think it might be another week." He grinned, as if this were the best thing that had ever happened to him. "They're letting me out of my lease."

"And you want me to help you move?" There had to be more to it than this. Chalky's surprises were never simple and easy, and so far, this seemed too simple.

"Yeah. Sort of." His eyes started doing his blinky thing, and he looked at the pizza pan, dabbing his damp finger into more mozzarella.

"Describe sort of."

"Well, you've got the good job, and I really need a new car. Really, and you know that for a fact. If I moved, I could save for a down payment for a few months and go car shopping." He smiled hopefully.

"You could. Do you have a new place lined up?"

"Chip!" He leaned forward and tapped the table right in front of me. "What are we talking about here? You and me, we're best friends, right? That's why I know you'll let me do this, to help out a good buddy, right?" Those washed-out eyes crinkled, and he winked at me, grinning.

I hated to ask, but I climbed out on that limb, anyway. "Help, how?"

"Chipper, do I have to spell it out? You've got three bedrooms, at least. I know. I helped you move in, remember? Surely you can squeeze me into one of them for a couple months. Please?"

He was right. I had three bedrooms. And I wondered, how had I not seen this coming? Had M.J. thrown me that far off track? While I was running all that through my head, I guess Chalky decided my dumbfounded look meant acquiescence, because he grabbed my hand, telling me thank you over and over, and then he started in on new Mustangs and which ones had the best sound and what he could probably get with what down payment and for how much per month. Once he started on that, how could I say no?

My big hesitation was my walls. Those holes. How would I explain that? Giant sheetrock-eating rats? Knowing Chalky, he would believe me, but I could hardly lie to him. Not about that. I had some old pictures stored in the garage, but not enough to cover all the holes, and anyway, who hangs pictures at waist level?

Then it hit me. What the heck? This man was my friend. He had followed me halfway across the continent, and anyway, what would my life be without Chalky? Better? Well, easier, perhaps. Less jumbled. More orderly. More in control, as if my life is ever in control, at least by me. So, I relaxed in the moment, and I smiled at my friend.

That just set him off again, reminding me that while I was in college, he'd worked as a residential construction helper for a year. Need anything fixed around the house? He was my man, and while he hinted he was by no means an expert in any field, he had helped in just about all of them. He could rewire a plug, fix a broken drain, and even sheetrock a wall.

Sheetrock? That got my attention. Maybe he would see my holes as pre-demolition. I could tell him I'd had a premonition this would happen, and I've been preparing for it. For five years. Would he believe it? Somehow I thought he would. After all, he believes I'm a god, a real lightning-flinging, bring-you-back-to-life god.

Maybe I am. People used to believe the sun was a god that gave them life, riding in a chariot across the sky each day. If Chalky's life revolves around me, I guess it would seem that way. So, maybe I can take some pride in how I look in Chalky's eyes. I am Ra, the Egyptian god of the sun, and those who are in my presence are blessed with life and happiness and the bounty of all creation.

That made me laugh, and as I was getting a drink of soda at that exact moment, I spit it out on what was left of the pizza. That hit Chalky just right, and he started laughing, too.

See how this god-thing works? I flat out tell

my best friend I don't want him living with me, dashing all his hopes for improved circumstances, and he winds up thinking I'm so excited to have him move in that he's beside himself. I might as well marry the guy and call it a life.

But then, that would be no life at all, and besides, Chalky has always been about searching for the next-larger bra size, and I don't wear one. Thank God for that.

Sorry, Chalky. Find yourself someone else to marry. I can't help you there. That brought another round of laughter, and Chalky didn't even seem to mind that his workout clothes now had soda all over them.

I guess he wouldn't. Not only was I the one wearing them, but he would be washing them in my machine.

When we got ready to leave, Chalky picked up the tab. I threw out a couple dollars for a tip, and as we stepped out into the heat of the evening, I was telling Chalky what color Mustang he needed to buy. After all, if he'll be living with me, I'm driving it, too. That's part of the price he has to pay. Oh, and refinishing all my walls. Maybe this wouldn't be too bad after all.

Like I've said before, sometimes a friend is a very nice thing to have around.

THE LIGHT WAS BLINKING on my hardline when I got home. I rolled my eyes. I could not deal with a phone call right then, not after Chalky's revelation. If he was to be my houseguest, I had a bedroom to attack. I might be single, and yes, I do live alone, but that doesn't mean I have two extra rooms sitting empty, just on the off chance a good friend will want to move in with me so that he can buy himself a new car. However, knowing Chalky, somewhere along the line I should have figured out something like this would happen.

Just before we drove off from the restaurant, I asked him if this weekend would be good enough. If it were me, I'd have things to pack. No way would I box up stuff without knowing I was headed someplace. I've been to Chalky's, numerous times, too. His apartment came furnished, so I knew all the stuff wasn't his, but after several years, I guess I'd started to picture him along with the faux leather sofa and the orange upholstered dining chairs, and I somehow expected him to have collected at least some personal stuff in the years he'd been here with me.

"All I have to do is break down my bed," he told me happily. Turns out his furnished apartment came with bathroom towels and everything, and he'd had the rented bed put in the building's basement storage. He had clothes and a gaming system, that and his mattress. Oh, and four concrete blocks for a bed stand. I offered my extra bed frame in the garage from when I'd gone from full to queen, and he threw his arms around me and slapped me on the back, telling me, "Love you, man. You're better than a brother to me."

I hope so, although that's not saying much in Chalky's case. He doesn't have a brother.

Anyway, that's where we were, and I had to make room. I flipped on the light in the hall, cringing when I thought of how my walls would look to someone for the first time. I was rather used to them, but under my newly critical assessment, I realized that not all of them were actual holes. Not see-from-one-room-into-another holes. A few were only imprints of my fist, from those times I'd been frustrated at my life, but not angry enough to punch all the way through. One just beside my bedroom door gave a view of my bed from the hallway, and I remembered why. That was one of those moments when you feel life has decided to treat you decently, holding out a romantic attachment that is so real and so close that you can see into each other's soul, and then I had to cut it off. That had ripped my gut out.

For weeks, every time those memories rose up in me, it had been like a giant fist grabbing my heart and twisting, trying to rip it free. That night I'd stood there, wrapped in memories that were only a week old, hoping we'd see each other again, but knowing all the pitfalls along the way, and all I could think was, "We were just together, and I laughed with you, and now we're not together at all." The pain choked me, and I couldn't breathe, my body jerking with the intensity of it all. I yelled out, and I had to do something to offset my lack of control in the situation, and I slammed my fist into the wall. I think I might have bruised a knuckle, because my hand ached for weeks after that, and I could barely write or type my attendance reports at the school.

What had really hurt at the time was knowing it was me that had walked away. For years I watched my mom suffer around my dad as he wasted himself with liquid medication. She loved him, and even when she knew he was killing himself, she couldn't bear to leave him. What if I go down that road? Sometimes drowning myself in alcohol looks pretty appealing, and can I saddle a woman with me, knowing what I might become?

Psychological problems run in families. Science has proven that, so the chances of me living out a normal, undamaged existence are pretty dim. Add the god package to the pot, and I think I just got the golden ticket. I can be charming in short bursts, but to have someone living with me for the rest of my life? I can't be charming for years on end. Can't be done. What if I punch her because I'm so frustrated with my life? I guess I'd rather jam my fist through a wall, rail at the injustice of my life, and step out each morning into the normalcy of teaching at the local junior high school in very ordinary, very unremarkable Houston ISD. Then, for just a few hours, life can be normal and easy, and I can learn to breathe again before my reality comes crashing back in.

I chose the bedroom farthest from mine. That way Chalky and I would have at least a little separation. Besides, it had the least stuff in it. Most of it was in plastic tubs that I brought from home and never bothered with. You know the stuff everyone has, old mementos, yearbooks, and stuff like that. When I was getting ready to move this way, my mother spent weeks packing up my stuff. After a few days of phone calls, asking, "This valentine from your girlfriend in fifth grade, do you want me to send that?" I just told her to pack everything. I had no idea how much stuff there was until I opened the garage door to find it stacked to the ceiling. Then I still had my bedroom and the old den furniture she was sending with me. I didn't want to take it, but she said she'd always wanted a yoga studio, and she planned to start a class, since no one else was interested in sharing her life. I got her jibe, but what could I do? I already had the job in Houston, and besides, I remembered Pop's drunken rages. I recognized I was running away, but I'd repaired a few holes for Mom over the years, and I swore I'd never be that way. Ha, ha, there.

I was done with stacking about half the tubs along one wall, covering the two biggest holes, when the doorbell rang. You remember I hadn't been interested in my phone message when I got in. That's because I was emotionally drained. I might be a guy, but I still get that way. Guys do, you know. We just don't go around crying about it on everyone's shoulder. No, we punch holes in walls, drive too fast, and shoot at poor animals in the woods. That's how we deal with it.

I groaned at the doorbell, but my arms were about tired by then, and I decided I could use a rest. I stopped by the kitchen first, pulling a water from the fridge, and I unscrewed the top, taking my time. I think I hoped they would go away, but the bell sounded again, and this time someone pounded on the door.

"No," I muttered. "Leave me alone." Of course, I kept that under my breath. For crying out loud, I'd never be rude, even though I wanted to most of the time.

"Lights are on, Chip. Come to the door." It was Chalky's voice, loud and clear. Yelling, if I was any judge.

"What happened to Friday," I yelled back. "I'm not a hotel." I bit my tongue before saying anything else. He'd warned me in his own Chalky-like way, and his enthusiasm should have been the key for me to predict what he intended to do. I wondered if he'd accept that dumpster tonight as an excuse and go away. I'm not kidding. My energy was gone. Doing the time dilation thing does more than drain me physically. My brain and all that honey I swim in, well, it takes a while for the effects to fade. I don't feel slow, but I miss things I would otherwise catch, and that makes me feel brainless. It also scares the bejeesus out of me, because I usually catch things no one else can. The real problem for me is that if I'm missing these little things like Chalky showing up at my door, what big things am I missing, like Mary Jane's story and one arm wearing a very big black watch? There was a good chance that figuring out that would be very good for Mary Jane's defense in court, if she needed one.

After all, who else would want to kill the sex-crazed sucker? Well, me, but I'd missed out on that, and besides, I don't know that I have the mental makeup for an extended prison stay. I'm glad I didn't get to him first.

The door banged again, and I yelled, "Meet me at the garage." I stepped inside and hit the switch by the door. The big metal monstrosity struggled for a moment, and then it began moving smoothly up and out of the way. I laughed. I couldn't help myself. There was Chalky's old car, and strapped to the top were his mattress and box springs.

"You ready for me?" He had his hands in his pockets, and he was hunched over as if he wasn't sure how I would take him showing up this way.

I had to laugh. I mean, what else was there for it, his old beater of a car, a bed tied on top, and that hangdog look? He was like a little rat terrier come in out of the rain with an old, dead squirrel in its mouth. How much more pitiful can a person get before the world simply has to break loose and show a little sympathy?

"Come here, you mutt." I held out one arm. Now, Chalky's my age, pushing thirty about as hard as a man can push without going over the edge. Still, he reminds me of fifteen when he does this, and I'm reminded of why I let him hang around back then. He has always looked like he needs someone else's bootstrap, 'cause he doesn't have one of his own. When he made it to me, I threw one arm across his shoulders, and I clapped his neck really tight before pushing him away and heading out to see how he'd managed to keep the bed on the car. I called back, "Buddy, I've been ready since we were fifteen. You and me? Hey, we've always been a team, haven't we?" I took two fingers, touched my chest, and then pointed them to him, giving him a nod.

That changed everything about him. He lit up, yanking his hands out of his pockets, and he danced sideways out of the garage. "See here? I used that knot we learned in Scouts back in seventh grade. Watch me untie it." He worked his fingers under the knot, and with a tug, it came completely loose. Then, as if to spite his good intentions, the bed started sliding off the top of the car on the opposite side. "No!" he cried, leaping on the hood and scrambling across to catch it.

"Got it under control?" I called out, shaking my head.

"Um, I think so." He was underneath the front end of the bed holding it up. The back end was still tied with the rope feeding underneath the deck lid. "Here's my keys. Pop the trunk, and let's get this into the house."

A tangle of metal came flying through the air at me, and I caught it just before the set of keys hit me in the face. One thing Chalky is good at is throwing. What he aims for, he usually hits. I had no desire for it to be me, however. I stuck them in the lock and released the catch. As soon as I did, the bed shifted again, and Chalky yelled for me to grab my end of the mattress. Together we stood both pieces up and walked them into the garage.

"You have a stand, you said? I left the concrete blocks at the apartment." He brushed at the fabric on the end with his sleeve, probably to get bugs off. Drive in Houston in the spring, summer, or fall, and you get bugs, lots of them.

"Are you bringing them when you go back for the rest of your things?" I'd told him I had a frame, and I did, but I didn't see it at the moment. He could use the blocks until we located it.

"The rest?" He looked at me like I was crazy. He stood by the bed, grinning and patting the mattress. "This is the whole showboat. Everything I own."

"You're kidding." I looked inside the car to see a pile of clothes. Inside the trunk was a television and gaming setup. "Where's your toothbrush?" I was teasing on that one.

"Here." He dropped in the car and popped open the glove box. He pulled out a bare toothbrush and a half empty tube of paste.

My word, what had I done? His toothbrush in his glove box? I took the toothbrush and toothpaste from him, calling out, "Okay, let me show you your room. I've already marked the places I want you to start my remodel."

"You have? Cool! So I can earn my rent. Have you already bought supplies?" His eyes glistened with excitement.

I guess I'd have to, now. Hadn't he told me I had the good job? And it was my house, so I guess that was fair. If I had to have someone living in my spare bedroom, who better than Chalky? It seemed that maybe this was in the stars after all. I refused to give any credit to the god-thing. No way. Even a god needs a friend that is just that, a friend, with no ulterior motive other than just hanging around because he likes my company. If all our friends are there because some exterior force twists fate and brings us together, it sorta takes something out of the mix, makes it hollow. A Potemkin village, where it's all window dressing, and there's no substance. Have you ever seen the movie *Truman*? His best friend since childhood was just an actor and nothing else. Truman believes in his friendship with Marlon, but it's all a construct for the show, and Marlon parrots what the director wants him to say, with no heartfelt substance behind it. I'd be very disappointed to find that all Chalky's adoration for the past decade and a half was nothing more than words and actions spouted because it was destined to be that way.

I suppose he'd feel the same about me. I hope so, anyway.

You know, I'm about to do something very unusual. I'm about to decide I wouldn't trade Chalky for any other friend out there, and I've got some pretty good friends. Most of them, if they took off to Timbuktu, I'd miss them and go on. If Chalky were gone, I'm not sure what I'd do, but I'd miss the stupid little turd. That much I know. And, as I'm not into missing stupid little turds, I think it's best he hang around a while, or at least long enough to remodel my house. That'd be nice for a change.

Boo-ya, Chalky Hollingberry, I thought, giving him a punch to the shoulder. Move on in, good friend, and you, my man, are welcome to stay awhile. I will expect some Mustang time, though. I've always liked Mustangs. I didn't say any of that, but he looked at me and grinned, and I think he understood what I meant.

Yeah, yeah. I'll be honest. It's not all about the Mustang. I've always liked Chalky. Now that I've vomited that up, I've got a bedframe to find, and then, I've got a bed to move.

Chalky. Chalky, Chalky, Chalky. What can I say? He is what he is, and that's all he'll ever be.

My friend.

—12—

WE HAD CHALKY SET UP BEFORE we got to the blinking light. I would have been content to continue to ignore it, but Chalky has this linear focus, and when something's happening, he's all there, in your face, one hundred percent. That blinking light was happening, and he was all there. He couldn't get past it, either.

"Chip, your phone there. It has a message."

"Yeah? So?" I was putting one of my fresh pillow cases on one of Chalky's pillows, and I tossed it on the sofa. The television was going, and I thought we might watch for a while. It'd be nice to do something brainless for a bit, like watch someone on TV screw up his or her life, knowing it has nothing to do with me, and no matter how bad it is, it won't trigger any sudden urges in me to get involved.

"Are you planning to listen to it?"

I wasn't, but I guessed I would now. I walked over and punched the button for it to replay the message. It keyed up with the usual introduction of, "You have one new message."

"Sure," I growled, looking at the machine. "That's what the light is for. So, tell me something new."

It did, and with no apologies.

"This call is for Mr. Engelbrecht. We have admitted a María Juana Noguerra to our trauma unit, and your name is on a slip of paper in her pocket. Please call us back at your earliest convenience. Houston Memorial at . . ." It went on to give two phone numbers and other additional information that I ignored.

It helps at this point if you know that Mary Jane isn't M.J.'s real name. In my attendance records, it reads María Juana. I asked her about it at the start of seventh, and she said it sounds too similar to marijuana, so she anglicized her name. I don't blame her, and she was always Mary Jane around me. Well, M.J. some of the time, but mostly Mary Jane.

"Mary Jane, you poor girl," I murmured.

Chalky looked at me, puzzled. "Mary Jane, like in dumpster Mary Jane?"

I glared at him. This was the part of Chalky that ground on my nerves, the insensitive part. I barked at him, "Don't call her that. Why's she in

Memorial?" I dropped to a chair, hitting my head with my palm. This was something else I'd missed.

"No problem. I can find out that." Chalky grabbed the phone and began punching in numbers. I looked at him, still mired in the evening's honey, angry at myself that I wasn't seeing things as they were, and now irritated that Chalky had jumped to do what I should already be doing. Gods have to stay on top of things. Let problems slide, and people could die. In fact, they usually did, especially when it was me not paying attention. I heard Chalky speaking into the phone, and then he handed it to me, shrugging. "They won't talk to me."

"Mr. Engelbrecht." I spoke the words into the phone as I looked at Chalky settling onto the sofa; and totally oblivious, he raised his shirt to pick lint out of his navel. Not finding any, he brushed his stomach and put his shirt back down, looking over at me and putting his hand to his mouth like he was getting a drink. Then he disappeared into the kitchen.

To sum up my conversation with Houston Memorial without boring you with the interruptions and the "ums" and so on, I'll give you the concise version. Emergency Medical Transport brought in Mary Jane accompanied by her mother. M.J. was unconscious with internal bleeding, and her mother was hysterical, speaking in staccato and undecipherable Spanish.

My name is all they could get out of her, and so, here I am. The contact person of note. Now all M.J. needs is for the police to show up to arrest her, and as far as I know, Mary Jane doesn't even wear a black watch. There was no way she had done this, although I might have cheered her on if she'd tried. Some people deserve to get their juice rockets cut off. Burning the man in a dumpster while he was still alive was perhaps a bit excessive, but then I didn't live through the attacks. Survive that, and I might well change my mind. My cry might be, "String 'em up, Sam!" That'd get someone's attention, that's for sure.

Yet, all that was not at the forefront of my mind. Remember my trip down memory lane, pulling me into that stinky dumpster? Something else happens when I bounce back the other direction. I don't always stop at the present. It's like walking down a corridor lined with doors. All of them are open, and I can see in each one. I can't walk through any of the doors. They're just there, with different storylines behind each one, all the events depicted in full, living color.

The only thing is, none of those events have happened, and most of them won't. The longer I stand there, the stranger it gets. One at a time, the doors start to slam in my face. I can open them back up, but if I do, there's usually nothing on the other side. Finally, there's only one door remaining, and that's the one I can walk through.

For a long time I couldn't figure out what all those doors meant. Now I've got a pretty good idea. They're possibilities. Each door is one way a person's life can go, but none of them are real yet, and that's why I can't walk through. I mean, look at it this way. You can't walk into a fairy tale, no matter how well you know the story. Maybe you can envision just what's happening as Snow White is about to eat the apple, but you can't leap in there and warn her. She has to eat the apple, and there's nothing you or anyone can do about that. Those doors are the same. I can see stuff happening inside, and all I can do is watch. Each one that closes means one of the possible outcomes in that person's life is no longer an option. For those of you who read, and not romances or historical fiction, but real stories, like science fiction, well, in science fiction terms, each door opens to an alternate reality, one possible series of events down which that person's life might go. Each change makes doors close to that particular opportunity. However, to actually step through one, the others all have to snap shut, those options gone forever. Most people don't know this is how it works, but being a god, I get to see it all.

Only once have I seen a door reopen and have anything behind it that later came true. That was right before my father died the last time. Humph! The last time. Like, what does that mean? Well, I'll tell you, my father died to me when I was ten years old. The bourbon didn't take his life until three years later. I saw the doors during that three years, even though I didn't understand them. The last time he was hospitalized, he went to rehab, and for three weeks he was sober. All the death doors slammed shut, and there was only one left open, one in which I saw myself graduating from high school, and my dad was there to see it.

You know that didn't happen, because I've already told you as much, but at the time it seemed it might. Like I'd been given hope. Then, the staff at the rehab clinic said my dad started screaming about having visions, and one night, in my dream, the graduation door slammed shut. There were no open doors. I ran down the hallway, desperate and afraid, and when I found one that would open, we were burying my dad, and I was standing red-eyed but stone-faced as they shoveled dirt in the hole. The next morning we learned he'd cut his wrists with the broken lens from his glasses.

Back then I dreamed the doors. Now I see them in the light of day, and sitting there in my living room, Mary Jane's doors swam before me. I knew everything that could possibly happen to her over the course of her life. Prison was one of them. Then I looked harder and saw suicide, a life of prostitution, and even one that showed her as a high school dropout with a kid and a habit that kept her stoned every day.

Forget those doors. I wasn't having any of it.

The one I grabbed at was the one that showed a smiling Mary Jane graduating from college, with her life held high, the spirited expression on her face telling of all the things she intended to do with the years she had to live.

That's the door I wanted for her, and the way I saw it, it was up to me to make sure all the other doors slammed shut on the way.

Oh, this sucks. The happiness of a fourteen-year-old girl is riding on my shoulders, and I haven't a clue what to do. So, what do I do? I grab my keys.

"Come on, Chalky. We're going to the hospital."

"Now?" He had a sandwich in his hand and a look of dismay on his face.

"Now. We've got some doors to slam shut."

"I have no idea what you mean, but sure. I'm game." He stuffed the rest of his sandwich in his mouth and grabbed his wallet from the table. He tucked that wallet in his pocket, and then, as if just remembering something vitally important, he snatched a water bottle from the fridge.

So, now it seems I've got a partner. Does that make us a crime-fighting duo? Good heavens, how comic book can you get! Now all I need are a couple of Transformers, a few super-powers, and maybe X-ray vision.

Now that I think about it, that would be so cool! A comic book hero. Not too bad a life, if I do say so myself.

—*13*—

I KNOW I HAVEN'T TALKED about it much, but I do own
a cell phone. Knowing that, you need to understand that I'm
not really a technology sort of guy, one of those nerdy geeks
that steps into a phone store and begins to ooh and ahh over all
the latest things each of the little black boxes will do. Don't
get me wrong, I'm not knocking geeks. They make the world
go round, and definitely, very definitely make my life easier.
When was the last time I had to get out of my chair to change
the channel on my television? I can't remember. See? Geeks
have a place in this world.

Smartphones? Well, not so much of a place in my life.

I did own one at one point, one of those glossy slabs with
no controls except one power button I could never find. I kept

it for two weeks, never was able to figure out how to answer a call, and when I did need to call someone, I always borrowed someone else's phone or waited until I got to a hardline. There's nothing I do that puts me in that big of a hurry. Besides, all the real messages I get, I don't need a phone to receive. They come through my interior "spiritual" nerve endings, and I can't turn the ringer off for those even if I want.

So, I went in the phone center, handed them my glossy slab, and said, "I want something that's just a phone and nothing else." Now I have a miniature flip phone that's about two inches by three inches, and it's perfect for fitting in that little pocket that men get on all their jeans. Why is that so important to me? Hey, how many times have you put your phone down and forgotten where it was? Me? Never. It's always in my pocket, right where I expect it to be.

On the way to the hospital, it started ringing. I worked it out, and I offered it to Chalky.

"What?" He looked at it like it was a snake. Chalky is worse than me. He can barely pay rent, and he's never had a cell phone. When I need him, I leave messages for him at work, and he returns my call on the pay phone at his apartment. Maybe that was why he wanted to move in. It alleviates that intermediate step in the communication process. Now the messages leap from my mouth to his ear and back again, and he saves a buck in the process.

"Answer it." I tossed it in his lap.

"Hello?" He held it to his ear like he'd never used a mobile phone before, and I laughed. It was funny, too, because he'd picked it up like it was a firecracker, and it might bite him. Then he'd tried to open the opposite end. Finally, he'd managed it, and he looked at the blinking screen for three rings before he found the talk button. How hard is that? It's big and green and says, "Talk."

Like I said, I laughed, but not in a mean way. I'm the same when it comes to smartphones, so I understand. Still, watching Chalky like that, it was funny.

It's better to laugh, I sometimes admit, than to give up on life. It's probably why I've let Chalky hang around all these years. When the god-thing grinds me into the ground, he keeps me rooted in a real life, ordinary sort of way, and I'm able to get up in the mornings and face the blinding sunshine of truth: I'm a freak that shouldn't exist. Not on planet Earth, anyway.

"It's for you." He handed the phone to me, rolling his eyes. "Latvian, I think. Only you would get a phone call in Latvian."

It wasn't Latvian. It was Mary Jane's mother speaking in a broken, pidgin Spanglish. The real issue was her speed. With M.J.'s mother, there's no slow setting, and she didn't pause between any of her syllables. It was a constant stream of vowels and consonants. I was used to hearing a similar patois from my students' parents, and I was able to catch some of it. My best guess was that she was so sorry she gave my name to the hospital, her husband had run away when her daughter was a baby, and there was no money in her Guatemalan bank account. Why she kept a Guatemalan bank account I had no idea, but then she might have meant her grandmother's account or even her Guarantee Bank account. The woman was a set of vocal cords on steroid overdrive, and I barely caught anything at all.

The last thing she said? "Take care of my baby Mary Jane." Of course, it sounded more like, "Cuidar de mi bebé María Juana," which taxed my limited Spanish. Bebé I knew, and I guessed cuidar meant protect or look after. The Mary Jane part was pretty obvious.

So, I said the one Spanish word I was sure of. "Si. I will."

"Gracious, Señor. Gracious." And she was gone. I closed the phone and slipped it back into my pocket.

The strange thing wasn't the conversation. It was what the conversation did to me. It was like a series of bright lights slammed into my skull, bam, bam, bam! Not that I saw them. That would be crazy. It was like my brain felt them, even though there was nothing there. Revelations, you might say. Insights. Electric power lines attached to my eyeballs that fed an overwhelming amount of brightly burning information directly into my head.

M.J.'s mother was running away, abandoning her daughter, and expecting me to take charge. Of a teenage girl! I don't even know the phone number of child services. By the hairs of Rasputin's hoary head, I don't even know my own cell number without checking my cell phone's settings menu.

Anyway, in my mind, I just saw one of Mary Jane's doors slam shut. That was the one with her mother at her wedding, hugging her as the photographer snapped a picture. How could her mother do that to her, and how was I ever shutting all the other doors that could not be allowed to become Mary Jane's future?

I was sick to my stomach, and I had no idea what to do. So, I did what all guys do. I hit the gas harder, and I ran all the red lights I had to, and I looked at everyone I passed by, and I thought, "Forget you, buggers, because you are screwed-up idiots who don't know what it's like to have a screwed-up life. You've got it good, and you don't even know, so don't give me any grief today."

It was in the hospital parking lot as I slammed my car into park that Chalky finally dared speak to me.

"Bad phone call, huh?" He looked at me warily. I couldn't blame him. I think I'd done a couple corners on two wheels.

"For Mary Jane. She doesn't deserve this." I hit the steering wheel twice, then I reached and turned off the key.

"None of them do."

I glanced over, and Chalky was blinking back tears. Hm. I'd never seen that side of him. I guess there's more to the guy than I'd imagined. Well, good.

Then it hit me. None of them do? None of whom? By then, though, he was out of the car, and when I climbed out and locked the doors, he was already twenty feet ahead of me.

"Hold up, Chalky," I called, and he just jerked his head for me to walk faster. His hands were stuffed in his pockets, and he was hunched over, so I knew something was going on in that head. I just had no idea what.

I wondered if I ever would. The way our friendship was headed right then, I guessed I'd have as good a chance as any. Chalky was mine, full blown, sleeping in my house, which was as good as God's truth.

I sighed. How did my life ever come to this?

—14—

I SAT IN THAT CHAIR in the waiting room, and all I could picture was that arm wearing that big, black watch.

For all that, it did me no good. I racked my brain for anyone I knew wearing a watch like that. Nope. I knew the real problem. I don't wear a watch, so I never notice them on other people. My phone has the time, as well as my car. I know how long it takes me to get to work, so what good would a watch do me? I make a point to check the time before I walk out the door, and then I know if I'll be on time or late. Who needs a watch?

I scrutinized the people coming in and out, several families, me looking for watches, when one big trucker-type dude entered. He walked in as if unsure, and then he found a seat and eased himself into it, like he'd been sitting too long already. He had a pink envelope, the kind you give cards in, and a bouquet of flowers. They were in one of those green plastic sleeves that are rubber banded around the stems to keep them moist. He sat and held them a moment, looking mystified, before he carefully laid them on the table in front of him. His daughter, I figured. Why else would a tough-guy type like that bring flowers to a hospital? It was actually sweet that he cared enough about someone to do that.

I caught sight of his arm when he reached to the table, and he had a watch on. It was black, but not like the one in my vision. His had gold hands and a gold band around the crystal. The face was white. The one I'd seen? All black. Face, hands, case. All black with a diamond at the twelve and at the six, and the hands were little more than hints of something against the face.

I blinked hard several times, for the moment wrapped up in that vision. I had seen 7:40 so clearly on that watch face, and how, I wasn't sure, but I knew it had two diamonds framed with those two hints of hands. That's all there had been on that face. How had I been able to make out the time so clearly?

I guess it was the moment, because normally I wouldn't stress over something so small. Just like I'd known Ryan's name in that inrush of infor-mation, I often "got" stuff in my visions that no normal person would catch in real life. It was like the world dropped out of focus, and for that one moment, I had tunnel vision, taking in one important fact that might otherwise have been unnoticeable.

What had I missed while I was seeing that watch? Still, my visions rarely led me off course, even though I sometimes had to figure them out. Like now. I was figuring, but nothing was coming to me.

That was when the room began to move in front of me. Remember the dumpster thing? Well, it was happening again, and I hadn't started it. That was what caught me off guard.

The really weird thing? What I saw wasn't even happening at the hospital. And it had nothing to do with M.J.

It was my father. God help me, my father was right there in that hospital waiting room with me, only it wasn't a hospital waiting room that he was in. See? I told you it was weird. What makes it even weirder is that my father died when I was thirteen, and by that time, I was glad to see him go. So, anytime I see my father, it's not a friendly family reunion. Far from it. I'd cleaned up enough of his putrid alcohol-fueled vomit to last me a lifetime, and I still carried a few scars from the times I hadn't been able to get out of the way fast enough.

This vision? It was funky weird, all fuzzy around the edges, and moving in jerks and starts. You've seen it in movies where parts of the scene are done in slow motion where everything seems almost frozen, and then in a blast of action, everything surges forward. That's the way this was. And you know? Even as freaked out as I was, it was very impactful. It came across like reality personified, like jumping off the Empire State Building and the force of gravity ripping the air from your lungs.

Did I pay attention? Holy humdingers, yeah, you bet I did!

You see, what I really remember about my dad is the bourbon. Kentucky, to be exact. Nothing much else, mostly just the bourbon. There were empty bottles sitting around all over the place, and the ones that weren't empty, he was trying to get them there as quickly as possible. Of course, there was the stink, although a lot of that could have been the showers that he never managed to get up and take. And shaving? Only when the whiskers got in the way of the bourbon. Yeah, I had a great childhood. If I'd understood what was behind it all, I might have been more forgiving, but I hated him for doing that to me. I hated him a lot.

In that hospital waiting room? What I saw there was an eye opener, I tell you. The father I knew was always sprawled in his easy chair, but not this one. He was running from something, a dark figure, robed and beaded. A witch doctor, maybe. Like me, my dad boasted tight hair and dusky skin. With a name like Engelbrecht, you'd expect us to be blond and pale, with blue eyes. Not a chance, except for the eyes. I got Gramps' gray-blue. The rest is from my mother's side of the family. In my vision? Pop's face was washed-out white. He was scared of that shaman. Scared out of his socks.

I knew how that felt. I'd been in that dumpster. That step-brother? That had been pretty bad, I'll tell you what.

Well, the look on my dad's face said more than anything he did, and he did a lot, like screaming, then falling down and trying to get away. And the pain. It looked as though the whole ordeal hurt like liquid fire poured into an open wound. It hit home with me that there was a reason he'd been crazy. This was why he drank himself to death.

Before I go any further, it might help you understand if I tell you I couldn't hear any of this. It was a vision, all in silence, but I could tell a lot of it by looking. When someone screams, you can see it on their face pretty well. You don't have to hear them scream to know they're doing it. It was as well. If I'd heard it, I might have been screaming, too, right there in that waiting room. That'd go off like a finely tuned fairy bomb, all pink feathers and happy "how-do-you-dos."

Then, just like that, the room cleared, and an emergency alarm sounded somewhere in the hospital. I could see the nurse behind the counter speaking to an older man with his arm around someone who was probably his granddaughter, as several white-robed orderlies ran by on the right. I sank into my seat. I knew what had set off those alarms.

Me. Me and my walk-on-the-under-side. Off to the right, a small boy was rolling a car across the floor. He looked up as the men ran by, then the alarm silenced, and he went back to his car. Directly opposite me an elderly woman with skin the color of tree bark and her hair wrapped in a bright scarf was trying hard not to show that she'd been crying, holding a tissue beside her face, and dabbing at one eye, while she was bravely smiling.

Then, something about that woman caught my eye, and I saw understanding there. I blinked, and I looked away. When I looked back at her, she nodded at me, waved, and then she stood and walked rapidly out of the room as if she'd been there for no other reason than to nod at me.

Weird.

I thought of my dad. When he died, I shut him away like a seersucker sport coat left to you by your grandfather, one that's too awful to admit you own but that's part of you, and you can't toss it away without making everything that's ever touched it even worse. Now I began to wonder. You see, I trust my visions. They don't lead me wrong. If I saw that with my dad, then it really happened at some point. I just had to understand it. I cringed at the thought, but I supposed my mom would be the first person I'd have to ask. Ouch. That was a lot of burnt crust to stir up from the bottom of the pot.

And that woman! What was that? Did I need to reforge my connections with my dad, maybe try harder to understand what his life had been about? Forget that, I thought. I wanted nothing to do with it.

I guess Chalky had started to notice something up with me, because he leaned in and punched me on the top of my leg.

"Chip? Everything okay?"

Luckily, I didn't have to answer, because just at that time, a nurse came out and said, "Anyone with María Juana Noguerra?"

M.J., I thought. Her name's Mary Jane, but I raised my hand, and she motioned us forward. She was in recovery, and she couldn't have visitors, but it seemed she would be all right. Eventually. That was a relief. When I told her my name, the nurse seemed reassured. M.J.'s mother had put me as next-of-kin, and I guess that meant they thought they had somewhere to send the bill.

If so, they had something else coming. That's what Medicaid was for. My insurance? It would barely cover me, and that was only if I forked out several thousand dollars first. I liked M.J., but I couldn't pay her medical bills, no matter how much she needed help.

Even a god has to draw the line somewhere.

—*15*—

I DIDN'T HAVE A GOOD NIGHT that night. My closet caught the worst of it. I figured out it's at the back of the house, as far from Chalky's new room as possible, and I didn't think I would wake him up.

It was the wretched nightmares. Man, they came and stayed, like I needed another guest to keep me company. They became the creepsters I couldn't get out of my head. When they got too bad, I stumbled into the closet and punched the walls. A couple times I got all the way through. I try to avoid pipes and wiring, although I know I'll get something live one of these times, and it'll bite me back. What can I say? I can't go out and punch people, can I? Wires are a chance I've got to take.

It was that woman looking at me, and my dad's face, as if there was something I should read in that, and M.J., knowing what she'd gone through, and that stupid black watch! How the heck was I supposed to figure that out?

They had to be connected, every one of them. I mean, I was at the hospital because of that watch, as much as anything else, and that's where M.J. was, and I'd never seen my dad anywhere else, and that woman. You think I'd see her looking at me like that at the local A&P? Not in a million years, likely. They were tangled up like spider webs on a broom, you can bet your sweet backside.

And I got to unwind it all. Holy frijoles! I mean, think about it. Have you ever seen how manufacturers make silk? I mean the natural kind, not the stuff from oil and plastic. They take cocoons and soak them into a tangled mess, and then they pull the threads without breaking a one until they have it all untangled. That was what I had to do, unwind that bowl of threads to see if I could weave it all into a silk shirt.

By the time four o'clock came knocking, my back was soaked, and I'd tossed most of the covers onto the floor. I finally sat up and ran my fingers through my hair, squeezing my eyes shut until I could see stars behind my lids. That was when I realized I might have hurt my hand during the night. Mostly I don't, anymore. Bare-knuckle fighters hit unpadded objects constantly to cause hairline fractures that heal and strengthen their bones. I think mine have done the same. They are stronger with all the hits they've taken, and I can get away with stuff that would drop an ordinary person screaming to the floor.

My left hand hurt, and when I rubbed it against my mouth, I tasted blood. Oops! Someone might notice that. Still, what was done was done. I stood and wandered to the kitchen, and when I flipped on the light over the sink, I found I wasn't alone.

"Bad night?"

I turned to see Chalky sitting at the kitchen table in the dark. At least he *had* been in the dark. Now he was in the light. I just turned on the water and began scrubbing my hand. When I finished, I tore off a paper towel and held it to my knuckles to keep any more blood from leaking out. Then I turned around to look at my new roomie. I laughed a snort sort of laugh, one of those chuckles that comes through your nose. "What's your clue, Sherlock?"

He grinned at that. "A little blood there, and maybe a little remodeling preparations during the night. About twelve-fifteen and one-thirty, to be exact. I did bring a clock, you know."

Hm. Chalky wasn't as dense I made him out. How about that? How long do you have to know a guy to know anything about him? I guess I'm the one who's dense that way. Thickheaded. A mother-of-pearl moron who's distanced himself too often from too many people to realize they actually care about him.

I guess you noticed what else I noticed. I was tacky with him to the point of rudeness, and it didn't faze him at all. See? Even in my own house, I can't get away from the god-thing. I don't try to be rude just for the fun of it. No, it comes out naturally, like some people are morning people, and others are not. Well, I smart off mean things, and no one takes them the way I intend them. Get a grip, people. Pay attention, here. I'm trying *not* to be a god.

Even that doesn't work.

"At the hospital, I saw something." I pulled out a chair and sat down across from him.

"So did I." He picked up a coaster left from a beer I'd had a week or two before, and he turned it over and inspected the bottom. It was one of those cardboard ones you get at a restaurant, and it was rumpled with repeated use. "What's her name?"

I looked at him hard. He wasn't looking back. That meant his question was a blind stab in the dark. He'd seen something, but he wasn't sure what it was. Just that it had happened, and perhaps it shouldn't have. Or, maybe, more to the point, it was out of place in his natural order of things.

Good ole linear Chalky. Things that didn't line up to him didn't make sense. Was that a good thing or a bad thing, for me, I mean?

Well, it was out of order in my natural order

of things, also. Dead people coming back to life in the middle of a hospital waiting room, and women who acted like they could see it all. Yeah, that was pretty much not in anyone's natural order of things.

I wondered how much Chalky was ready to know. About my god-thing, you understand. To tell meant it was known forever, and what I told, I could never take back.

It'd be nice to have someone else understand what tormented me in my head where no one else could see. But would it be fair? There are some things too weird to dump even on a friend.

I guess it was my nightmares and how tired I was. The stress of M.J. and my dad had broken me down, and it lowered my defenses. I got up and pulled a pan from the cabinet, tossing it on the stove, determined to let the god-moment at the hospital and all the weird nonsense with it die for the night.

"Eggs? I do a mean omelet." I looked at Chalky. "Cheese or ham? I have both."

Before he could answer, I was at the fridge pulling out eggs, cheese, and meat. Much as I wanted to, the old biddy from the hospital wasn't letting me alone. She was inside my head, scratching at my eyeballs, and wanting out. I looked at the two packages. I knew one thing. I'd prepare both, because I wanted to talk, and I couldn't do it sitting still with my new roomie looking at me.

"You eat breakfast at four in the morning?"

Chalky laughed.

"I am this morning." I cracked the eggs into the pan and dropped in a square of butter. "Pepper?"

"Sure, I eat pepper. If you're cooking, I eat most anything. Thanks for asking."

"Anytime." It was a polite response, not one that really meant I would do this for him anytime. I hoped he understood that. I was too tired for lengthy explanations. Rather than elaborating, I added spices and pulled out a wire whip, beating the eggs until the color was even. Then I turned the burner to eight, hot enough to get the pan warmed but not so hot as to scorch the eggs. My pan was nonstick, but if you work hard enough at it, you can stick eggs even to a nonstick surface.

I like my omelets. I didn't intend for anything to stick.

When the mixture started to firm around the edges, I turned it to four and called out, "Cheese or ham? You never said."

"Cheesy ham."

I looked over, and he was grinning. I shrugged and dumped a little of both over the eggs before folding it. It was actually making me hungry. I realized I hadn't eaten the evening before. Maybe that was part of my problem during the night. Hunger pangs. Lesser things had kept me awake before, and these were a crock. Flipping the eggs to brown the omelet evenly, I pulled out a plate and slid the finished product out. Sprinkling it with cheese, I set it on the table for Chalky.

"Silverware?" He pulled the plate to him, and I tossed him a fork and knife from the drawer, letting them slide across the table. "You want me to wait on you?"

"Nah. Eat while it's hot. I want to talk to you while you do." Having his mouth full would keep his responses to a minimum, and that would make it easier.

"Sure." He already had his first bite in his mouth. "About last night?"

"Yeah." I cracked two more eggs, but with the pan already hot, I didn't add more butter. I whipped them fast to keep them from sticking. "Tell me what made you ask about the woman."

"Yeah. Her." I could hear his utensils on the plate, and when he started up again, I could tell he had taken another bite. "She had this freaky fascination with you the entire time we were sitting there. And there you were off in one of your trances. I put two and two together, and there you have it."

"Freaky, how?" Not that I really wanted to know, but I had to ask. I hadn't really noticed her until after that dad-vision jarred my psyche. It might be important.

"It was that teary thing, and she was by herself. Like she was a ghost, waiting around, as if she needed to see the people who were in the waiting room."

"Ghost?" I looked at Chalky to read his face, only he was licking his fingers, and I didn't think him frowning at his fingers would tell me much. "You think she was a ghost?"

"Didn't say that. Like she was a ghost. You know, in that movie with Demi Moore where the dead people hang around until they get all their personal issues resolved. Like that. She was there, maybe, to see where her husband had been when he received the news she'd died. Or something like that."

"Did you ever see the movie *Odd Thomas*?" I was at the table by then with my omelet in hand. Just ham. I didn't think I could do cheese at four, no matter how hungry I was. I cut into my egg, and it smelled good. I thought about the cheese and wondered about sprinkling some over the top.

"Like the book by Koontz?" He laughed. "I didn't know that was made into a movie."

"Watch it sometime. So, the lady was a ghost, there to check out who was sitting in her husband's chair. Why hadn't she gone home?"

"Not a ghost. Only someone with psychic powers can see ghosts. Anyway, there are no real ghosts. Everyone knows that. She saw something, though, and it was just where you sat. Then, when you finally came to, she nodded at you and waved." He grinned. "See, I do pay attention to some things."

"I saw my dad tonight." I threw that out, bold as unbuttered toast, and about as dry. I wanted off the old woman, especially as Chalky was making no sense. I forked a large chunk of my omelet into my mouth just to fill it up, trying to distract myself, and I felt my eyes burn. That told me all the old memories weren't buried as deeply as I had hoped. Crumola. That couldn't be good, not with my dad just popping into my head, like a bad zit on the end of your nose on date night.

"Your dad, huh? Isn't he, like, long gone and buried?" Chalky sprinkled some salt in his hand, licked part of it out, and tossed the rest over his shoulder.

"Hey!" That irritated me. I may have holes punched in my walls, but I'm not a pig. Remember that bathroom in the garage? It's pretty nice. I keep it clean, too. My house? Now, I don't scrub my baseboards or anything, but things are put away, and I do sweep the floor every week. I like to walk in my socks, and dirty floors destroy clean socks. No telling what salt would do.

"What?" He still had his hand out, inspecting it, and he licked some salt that hadn't come off. Then he looked up at me. "Oh, the salt thing. I'm sorry. It's that good luck, over-your-shoulder thing. With you seeing dead people, I thought . . ." He grimaced. "Your floor. Right. I didn't think that through. I'll sweep it up."

He made to stand, but I patted the top of the table. "Later. I want to talk about my dad."

"Okay." He settled back in, only turning once to look at the floor. "What about your dad?"

"Back to the beginning. I saw him tonight." I

had my egg half finished by then, and I decided I was through. I pushed it back, glad I hadn't gone for the cheese. The ham was already a rock on my stomach. That was probably my dad, but then I didn't usually eat at four in the morning, so who knew?

"You saw a dead guy." It was a statement, not a question, and that said a lot. This wasn't all that much of a surprise to Chalky.

"Yeah." I let the word out without any inflection at all. I needed to see Chalky's response to the facts, not his response to the emotional wrenching it had given me.

"And?" He worked his fingers as if he wanted to drum the table, but he kept them in the air. That said he knew this was important to me.

"Yeah, and there he was, my dad. Pops." I worked my mouth, pressing my lips together, and glanced to the other side of the room. My house is all one big space, and the sofa was still mussed from our TV time earlier. No one had straightened it. I wondered if I was becoming a slob. I hoped not. I didn't know why that came to me, except maybe I was looking for a distraction.

"Doing?" Chalky fought a smile. He put his thumb to his mouth and made a motion like tipping back a cold one. "That's what you saw?"

"No." I stood, not irritated, but the reminder cut, anyway. Chalky had known my dad before, catching him yelling at me a couple times while walking down the street on the way to school. Well, he knew *of* my dad, anyway. In the years before he killed himself, no one really *knew* my dad, not the real dad that I might have had if Kentucky hadn't become involved.

Yea for Kentucky bourbon, may you all rest in peace, you rich, money-grubbin' whiskey mongers.

I turned away from Chalky and leaned my head against the fridge. The metal was cold pressed to my forehead, and the feel of it somehow reminded me of how horribly wrong every single day of my life had gone; and before I could stop myself, I began to pound the refrigerator door with the opened palm of my hand. I hit it over and over, not even thinking of Chalky just behind me. I didn't stop—I couldn't have—until I felt someone grab my arm and hold it firmly in both of his hands.

By that time the tears were flooding down my face, and when I couldn't pound anymore, I began to sob. Yeah, that sucks, and in front of another man, too. That really sucks. That's why I have holes in my walls. I'm not into the crying thing.

"I didn't know it was that bad." That was Chalky, and he released my arm. "Wanna talk about it?"

"Thanks, no." I had the weepy eyes under control by then, although I still faced the fridge. "And yeah, we're going to, if you still want to."

"If I still want to?" Chalky clapped his hand

on my shoulder, and he pushed it before turning loose. "Why do you think I'm here?"

"I don't know." I turned to him, snorting out a laugh, and wiping my face with the backs of my hands. "Free room and board?"

He made a sound with his mouth, one of those air sounds that says, "Fool!" before shaking his head.

"What does that mean?" I was okay by then, and I stepped to the sink and rinsed my hands.

"I know it looks like I'm here because you've got a house with lots of bedrooms, and I have nothing, but you can't think that's the real purpose. You can't think that's the only reason I hang around, can you, Chip?"

He sounded hurt, and the way he said my name, all broken, caught at me. I've always thought of Chalky as an accessory that didn't quite go with anything else in my life, and I've put up with him, even enjoyed him some of the time, but it's always been on my terms. He was just there, showing up, never getting his feelings hurt, and now, for the first time, I was seeing that there was something else in there that I must have been missing all along. Like he had real feelings, and they could be stomped on if I tried hard enough. And the thing was, I hadn't even tried this time. I was making a joke, a real joke, one I expected him to laugh at.

That made me feel low. I'm not even good with jokes. I insult people, and they love me. I joke with them, and I grind them into dust. How skanky is that?

Well, for the first time in my life, I decided I had to make an effort to fix something I wanted fixed, just because I wanted it fixed. Not because some god compulsion drove me to it, but because I wanted to be a good guy to someone who seemed to look up to me.

I wanted to be nice to Chalky.

"Hey!" I motioned with my hand, and I stepped to him, putting my arm over his shoulder. I looked at his face, and I could see his eyes glistening. Chalky's not a crier, either. Those tears were coming from somewhere he'd never shown me. I smiled, and I rapped him on the chest with my knuckles. "Now, I seem to remember a crazy nickname you gave me in junior high. What did it mean? Skinny—" I paused, giving him a chance to pull up the old memory.

"—good-for-nothing." He finished it for me, a silly grin bursting across his face. "Sorry."

"No, don't be. I'm not. That's why I named you Chalky. I was getting back." I rapped his forehead this time.

"Oh. I thought it was because you liked me." He took a deep breath and looked like he was trying to put the ramifications of my new revelation together.

"Who else has put up with me for all these years? Huh? Who else threw everything away and came to live in the great city of Houston, just because I ripped up my roots and moved halfway across the continent?" I rapped his forehead again.

"Me?" He looked better, like I was getting through.

"Who else can I trust to find me when I'm lost in a dumpster tripping out on dead bodies?"

"Me." He laughed at that, although it was quiet and he fought it. It came out more as an embarrassed grin.

"Stupid right. If I didn't have you, who else would I have?" That might have been forcing the truth, but then, it was true, too. I'd tried, and I'd run away from everyone I'd ever started to get close to. I'd have run from Chalky, too—heck, I did run from him—but the little doofus couldn't be beat off with a stick. So, in that sense, it made my question very, very true.

"Thanks, Chip." He threw his arms around me, pulling me tight, and completely taking me by surprise. That wasn't what I'd intended. He said, "That's all I ever wanted to be, your friend, from the first time we met. I'll always be your friend, as long as you want me around." He pushed away, and he sniffled, wiping his eyes, but he was smiling ear to ear.

Shoot me in the foot. I'd done it again. I lied through my teeth, and now I might as well exchange bodily fluids with him. Want to get a sex-change operation, Chalky? That's the only way I'm tying the knot with you. Sorry, guy.

The thing I tried not to admit was that I hadn't really lied. Shaded, yes, even hedged a bit, but what I said was all true. I trusted Chalky, and he was my only real friend, you know, the kind who can show up with a bed on the top of his car, and I actually invite him into my house to live. Shut the front door, if that's not real friendship, what the heck is?

And we hadn't even gotten to my dad, yet. At least it was only four-thirty. That gave us three hours before I had to get ready to go to work. Maybe, just maybe, we could get it all talked out.

With all that was going on, I guess I was distracted. I never gave that salt Chalky had thrown on the floor a second thought. Salt in a solution—any solution—is a perfect conductor. If you have to ask of what, you haven't been paying attention.

Dang. I knew I should'a stayed in bed. Will I never learn?

—*16*—

I DIDN'T MAKE IT TO WORK the next day. Not for lack of intent, be assured, even after Chalky and I tackled my dad. In the middle of a sentence, the man's face lit up, and he disappeared, only to return with one of the small storage crates I'd stacked along the wall in his bedroom. What the heck, I wanted to say, but he was grinning as he dropped it on the floor.

"This fell over. I found something inside." He had the lid off, and he was digging around. It was old pictures and stuff. I stood beside him and watched as he pulled out one and held it to me. "Is this of your dad?"

"Oh, man." I thought I'd burned them all. As I took it, my stomach churned. You know, the feeling that starts as a pinpoint in the bottom of your stomach. I thought that's all it was, but then it twisted into an icepick.

"It is him, isn't it?" Chalky looked so pleased with himself. "See, I do remember him."

"Yeah, so do I." With every word I spoke, the icepick got worse. Tingles ran down my fingers, and my heart began to pound. Then, without warning, I began to spit up blood.

Man, I hate the taste of blood.

I looked at Chalky, and I touched a hand to my face, pulling it away, and feeling this odd sense of disconnect, like this wasn't really happening to me. I'm a horse. I don't get sick, and yet, there was blood on the palm of my hand.

I didn't know what was in Chalky's head. I've known him over a decade, and I've never figured that out. But I do know what was on his face, and it was pretty close to what I was feeling. He had gone pale, and I thought he might pass out before I finished bleeding out, and then who would there be to call 9-1-1?

"Chalky?" I tried the word, whispering it to see if it jabbed my stomach with another icepick. Nothing happened, well, nothing except for the blood slurring the word. It also caused more blood to leak out of my mouth.

"Are you sick?" Chalky looked pale.

"I should have burned this picture, too." I held it out for him to take. Then, without warning, icepick, icepick, and dank underworld caverns, it hurt like the real thing. I doubled over, dropping to my knees, and I spat up more blood.

"Don't die, Chip." Chalky stripped off his shirt, and he used it to wipe blood from one side of my face.

I didn't know what good that was supposed to do. It wasn't my face that felt bad. It made me chuckle, and that made me cough on the blood already in my mouth.

"I'll try not to," I managed to get out.

"You think—" He paused, glancing to the picture and biting his lip before going on. "You think this might be caused by that picture of your dad?"

That icepick slammed me again, and I rolled up into a ball, screaming out this time. It was then that I felt it, the salt, and I knew. I *knew*. Dang. Why do I always figure out things too late? I tried to crawl away, but before I could move, it hit me again, the same criking icepick, coming right through that salt, but worse each time. Harder. Deeper. It was like something was sending me a message. Hey, I thought, as I coughed, wiping the blood away with my arm. I'm the god, here. Get off my case.

I was finding it didn't work that way. If I was a god, I was at the bottom of the totem pole, and someone else was determined to show me they could do to me anything they wanted. Like on a totem pole, they were all sitting on top of me, and my head was up their backsides. They were bouncing up and down on me, and doing a stupid good job at it, too.

Then I felt Chalky's hands on my face, and he was yelling at me. The only thing was, I couldn't hear him. I looked up, and he was pale and glowing with a white light, like an old tube television that's going out, and the picture gets smaller and smaller, and there's a grayish-white border surrounding everything, and you can only see what's in the middle of the picture. Then, one day, even that's gone.

I saw Chalky there yelling something at me, and I just smiled as he got smaller and smaller, and then he was gone.

That was when the nightmare started.

Nightmare? Hell on Earth was more like it. Any nightmares I'd had in the past were walks in the park compared to this. Yeah, one of those kind.

First, I was in this stone pit. It was hot and dusty, and stuff was swirling in the air all around me. The whole mess was brilliantly lighted and glaring enough that it hurt my eyes. I was still balled up, and I untangled my arms and legs carefully, not speaking, just in case the icepicks returned, only to find I was naked. Sufferin' succotash, totally, buck-jumpin' naked!

Big deal, you say. Everyone occasionally gets naked in their dreams. That's what tips them over into nightmares.

Okay, I'll go with that. The naked part was wrapped up in the nightmare, and I'll admit, it did little more than cause me to blink a few times. Even in the dream, I accepted it. You know, like you'll accept being a scuba diver even when you've never thought about doing that for a hobby, ever. It's like a *dream*, and you don't make any connection with real life, not at that point. So, I noticed I was naked, but my stomach didn't hurt any longer, and when I put my hand to my mouth, there was no blood. So, at that point, it was an improvement over real life.

I stood and began to check out my surroundings, what I could see of them. The pit was white stone, and the dust stirred like talcum powder. I moved, and great billows of it puffed up, like fake smoke made from dry ice. The stuff floating in the air was different, like it had a real texture. It felt alive, although I couldn't have said why. It was almost as if it was trying to probe me, maybe read my thoughts. Get into my head. I was a little creeped, but it was a dream, and I knew that. Or I do now, but at the time, it was that dream thing that feels right, no matter how goofy things are getting. It was more like the mist was *supposed* to be getting in my head. I brushed the feeling away, and it stopped trying to get at me. I laughed, pleased at my success, and getting a little cocky, I suppose. Buck-naked me, standing in a dusty pit, with live mist swirling all around me. I told it what to do, and it did it. I was the god here. I was the one in control.

I didn't realize that the mind thing was only the beginning.

I yelled out, "Hey!" I guess I wanted to see

what would happen. Maybe get a response. Then, part of it might have been that I was feeling so much better than I had in my house. My stomach was pain-free, and I was engaged in some sort of temporary euphoria. "Hey!" I called again, turning in a circle, all of it looking very much the same.

And just that fast, everything around me changed. And I mean everything.

The stone under my feet shifted, violently, and a section about four feet across began to unscrew, lifting me, and turning as it did so. I looked down, and the talcum powder dust kept the mechanism obscured, but the effect wasn't. It jerked and jumped forward in its twisting journey, unscrewing stone from stone. There was nothing smooth about the ride, either. Then lightning crackled overhead, and I looked up. The brilliant white mist was infilling with black, like those detergent commercials that drop dye into a clear tub of agitating laundry. The sudsy water is white, then the dye billows through it, leaving the water half white and half dark, with the dark quickly eating up the white. That's what the entire world was doing all around me.

And it didn't feel as kind and willing to back off as before. Instead, pressure began to build in my head, and I thought my skull would explode. Fingers of electricity crawled around me, filling the sky. I wanted to jump off the dais before it lifted me too high, but even with the swirling dust, I could see I was too late for that. I was on my knees holding to the sides just to keep from being jarred off.

I began to wish for the icepicks. Don't ever think it's better to trade your problems for something you don't know. I had wanted the icepicks gone. Now look where I was. Standing naked, on a pedestal, and being blasted by a building storm. This was about as bad as it could get.

So I thought.

That was when the wind picked up. The lightning had been frightening. I kept imagining that group of hikers in Colorado a couple summers ago. The husband woke up to find someone giving his wife resuscitation, only to find they'd both been hit by lightning. He lived. She didn't.

I wanted to be her at this point.

The wind tried to argue me out of that particular desire. It must have hit me at a hundred miles-an-hour, like a hammer hitting drywall. And it wasn't just the wind, because it brought cold rain and hail. The anatomy particular to the male body doesn't like cold rain or hail, and I tried to keep mine protected. However, that wasn't the only place getting hit, and I couldn't cover every part of my body. I was completely exposed. I had no help at all here.

All the white was gone by then. Imagine a storm that takes out the electricity, and all you have is the driving rain and wind battering your windows. You look outside and try to see just what's going on. All you can see in the glimpses of lightning flashes are shimmering lakes of water, with every surface of every object wet and reflecting the brilliance of the storm back at you. In other words, you can't see jack.

I didn't have anything except my arms and legs to reflect back at me, and I still couldn't see jack. The sky was black, the rain whipped in sheets around me, and when the lightning flashed, if I was looking down, I could see my hands over my personal area, and my legs below that, and then the light was gone, and it was dark once again.

I never really considered if anyone could die from shivering, but that was beginning to become a real possibility to me. Death from shivering. I could see the obit in the newspaper. "Local Science Teacher Comes to Pieces in Thunderstorm." The copy would read, "The dismembered body was found in the aftermath of the most violent storm in half a century. Doctors speculate that he shivered so violently that his ligaments were literally torn from the bone, and his body disarticulated into the segmented remains discovered by a local student. More on the news under *Weird Science Facts*. Also featured on *Too Strange to Be True*."

That sounds funny in retrospect, and at the time, it gave me a perverse sense of satisfaction; but I really wondered if it might be more on the money than not. I didn't get a chance to find out, because about the time I thought I would die, a burst of lightning hit the stone under my feet, cracking it. I jumped, but not far, because I wasn't sure how high up I was, and to die falling would leave me just as dead as dying from lightning strike. The rain and hail stopped, but what came next wasn't better. The air around me began to swirl, pulling upward in a rotating vortex, going faster and faster. It grew hot, too. Horrifically hot. And the air glowed orangey-red, like the night sky over a volcano.

"Why are you doing this?" I drew myself erect, held my back ramrod straight, and yelled the words. "What do you want? You show me my dad, and now you try to kill me. What do you want from me?"

That did something. Not something good, but something. Yeah, I can hear you thinking, Doesn't this guy know when to leave well enough alone? Of course, the answer is no. That's not part of my genetic makeup.

The mist faded just enough that I could see I wasn't alone. Laughing, grotesque faces jumped out at me, none clear, and the laughter wasn't friendly. They were all around, some close by, and others far away, but that dream thing kicked in, you know, where things happen, and the most bizarre events seem perfectly normal, like they're supposed to be that way. Suddenly, I was looking directly into my mother's face, and she had distended ears, a disfigured cranium, and she cackled at me, with spit flying from her lips. Then I saw Mary Jane. She turned sideways, and her face melted; and as a tear started down her cheek, she laughed and pulled me forward to give me a kiss. That was bad enough, but there were others worse, all the people I'd helped over the years, except they weren't being grateful. They were evil and malformed and reaching out to touch me suggestively. Naked me. Think that won't make you feel weird? And bizarrely, in the dream, it didn't seem so weird, and I just brushed their hands away as though it was okay for their nasty fingers to touch my exposed skin, except just not today, if you please, not with this many people all at once.

I knew my brain was tripping, but I'm not a naked type of guy. I wanted my corn nuts left alone. So, I brushed their hands away, as if not now, and as if them seeing me was just as natural as me taking a shower in the buff. And a lot of them were kids from my school. Think that won't make your skin crawl, recalling that, once the nightmare comes to an end?

Somewhere in there I saw Chalky's TV face, the only one that wasn't distorted. Other people were pushing him away, and I called to him, "Chalky, do something!" I reached for him, and he faded away into his television screen once again.

Then the blackness swirled around me once more, pressing in, and I felt overwhelmed with hopelessness. It ate at me, forcing itself in through my ears and mouth and nose; and when I closed my mouth and covered my ears, it seeped in under my eyelids, running like fire down my optical nerves. It was my father drinking himself to death, and my grandfather—whom I never knew—running across the world from the only life he ever knew, and my mother only coming alive, really alive, once my father was dead.

And, oh, man, it was Mary Jane being assaulted by a stepbrother night after night, and that watch I didn't have an answer to, and Chalky wanting to be my friend so badly he followed me halfway across the country, and I barely gave him the time of day.

And it was every hole in my walls that told of how much I hated my life, and all the women I'd loved and run from because of what I am. It was my own loneliness and my compulsion to help other people even when it stole my life from me.

I wanted to rip my eyes from their sockets to stop the blackness from getting inside. I pressed the heels of my hands against my face until my eyes screamed with pain, and when that didn't help, I let my voice do the screaming for them. There was no answer for being me, and to be me was to live in despair all the time, every day, every waking moment.

When the agony became too great to bear, I brazenly flung my arms wide, and I yelled again, "What do you want from me?"

The wind picked up, and it thrashed me, and the dust in the air scoured my skin, burning my flesh from my body. I expected it to lift me from the pedes-

tal and leave me broken on the ground far below.

Yet, my feet seemed fixed to the stone surface.

"What do you want from me?" I yelled it again, lifting a fist to shake it in the air. "I've given you everything, and you've taken it all. You've given me nothing back. It's my turn to have something out of life. When do I get what's coming to me?" I shook with rage. The faces and the storm and the tearing wind had eroded my patience, and I've never had that much to start with.

The truth is, it was more than the storm. It was my life. My questions were real and valid. I normally tried to cover them up with justifications and excuses, like, "Oh, well, that's just the way life is!" But it's not that way for everyone, and I deserved a break. If there were real gods out there, and judging by my nightmare, there were, then they'd beaten the stuffing out of me, and I wanted out of the cesspool.

See, I can feel sorry for myself, given the right circumstances. This was one of them. But I deserved a little self-pity, because it's true. The Big Guy up there flushed me down the toilet the day I was born, and I'm still floating in the crap, pardon my French, and some days I can wipe it off and pretend the smell's not too bad, and other days the stink makes me vomit. Holes in my walls, remember? That's the vomit in my life.

I never got an answer from the storm. Rather, I began to fight back. What other choice did I have? I drew in a deep breath, and I let the anger fill me up. It was anger at my station in life, and how I'd been boxed into too many corners, and my compulsions, and my loneliness, and all that had twisted my life into desperation. I reached out my hand, and I grabbed at something, and I twisted.

And something responded. The icepicks were back.

"No!" I cried at the top of my lungs. "You can beat me until I bleed, and I will not give in to you! Take everything I have! It doesn't matter to me anymore. I'm stronger than you. I'll always be stronger than you. Frig off, you moron. Go find someone else to manipulate, because I'm not standing still for it any longer!"

The storm raged tighter, twisting around me, grasping my arms and legs, and sucking the air from my lungs.

"No!" I screamed louder. "Give me space! This is my life, and it's the only one I have. You cannot take it from me without my permission, and I do not give you my permission. Back off and leave me alone!"

The mist withdrew. Not much, but it left a space between it and me. Something was listening, and I hoped it understood my intent. I would not be bullied any longer.

Then it hit me again, crushing me tighter than before, and the icepicks erupted in my gut. I fell to my knees, nearly giving up. I felt rage boil up in me, and I hit the stone at my feet with my fist. Surprised, I watched the stone crack. To see results from my anger gave me hope, and I lifted my fist to strike again.

Something caught my arm.

I didn't know what it was, but a feeling ran through me, as if I had been on the verge of death, and then I wasn't. I was lifted to my feet, my eyes were free of pain, and my skin no longer burned. The darkness around me released its hold on the light, and just like Oxy cleaner in a tub of stained water, the mist swirled white once again.

I was still naked, but I didn't feel exposed any longer. I felt new and cleansed, like a newborn that's happy just being alive, and clothing is an unfamiliar non-issue that's foreign to its way of thinking. Then the pedestal began to crumble under my feet, and it became powdery residue, melting beneath me, and I began to fall.

I knew that when I hit bottom, it would be all right. I was in control, and nothing could ever take that away from me. I intended to be completely in control of the rest of my life from this point forward.

—17—

THE DOCTORS DIDN'T QUITE AGREE with my version of events. You see, they think I had a heart attack. The bright light around Chalky's face and the spitting up blood? Severe stomach pains can be a precursor to stress heart attacks, and heavens knew, I'd been under enough stress. They decided a few days in the hospital were just what the doctor ordered.

That's my version of gallows humor, for those of you who didn't get that.

Once I was back in the real world, they even pointed out the bruises on my chest, where Chalky pounded on me to get my heart going again. Thanks, Chalky, but next time put a blanket over me first. I like my skin, and I like it to remain undamaged.

Of course, when I thought that, I didn't consider my hands. I'd damaged them a few times against my walls.

There were burn marks from the defibrillator, and those did surprise the docs. I remembered the vision, though. My stupid hogwash nightmare of a vision that wasn't a vision. Someone up there had tried to steal my life away, and I'd gotten jolted with lightning a few times, and I suspect it happened just when the defibrillator kicked in. Feedback. That's what I thought.

Why would something want me dead badly enough to come at me like that? What was I doing that someone didn't want done?

Still, I shouldn't have to explain all this, because you know me, but it's my teacher side. That science thing. If you can't show proof that you've reached a valid conclusion, then the conclusion is invalid. Well, this was my proof, or at least the way I'd worked it out. God No. 1 does something good, like trying to save a girl from being abused until she's dead, and God No. 2 says, Sorry. You're interfering, and I'm taking you out.

Only, I didn't get taken out. Chalky was there. So, in your face, suckers.

I said all that to point out that you guys out there know me pretty well by now. A god having a heart attack? Come on. Let's get real, now. And we know definitively that I'm one-hundred-percent full-blooded god. Or at least I have god-like powers. I think that makes me a verified god in most people's books.

I wonder if I can raise someone from the dead. That would certainly prove something. I know. More gallows humor. Sorry.

By that criteria, maybe Chalky's the god. Me? I was pretty dead, according to the docs. Chalky pulled me back from the edge. If that makes someone a god, then Chalky's got my vote. Godhood Hall of Fame. Nominated: One Chalky Hollingberry. I'm your campaign manager, man. You run for office, and I'm behind you a hundred percent.

Back to me. What it amounts to is that I'll stay here a day or two. You should have seen Chalky's face when I told the doc I was leaving, and I started to pull all the doodads off my body. I remembered my nightmare—my vision, if you will—and how only one face there was normal, and that was Chalky's. That's what made me give in. I didn't want Chalky's face to turn all gooey and melty and look evil like those others. I needed Chalky right then. Who else would I have to call 9-1-1 if this happened again?

Thanks, Chalky, for moving in with me. I really mean it.

Lying there, with Chalky hovering over that little dresser that's always filled with flowers and cards after you've been in for a couple days, I was whining about how they paint the walls in all hospital rooms the same color, and making him promise to flush my dad's picture down the toilet, when there was a knock at the door. Well, it was open. I didn't know what the hospital rules were, but I had nothing to hide. Not even any clothes on at that point, as mine had been removed in the emergency. I was covered with a sheet, and with a blanket over that, but my chest was exposed with wires attached with little pads. Cripes, but I hate stuff attached to me. They're like little antennas, drawing in all the bad juju from everyone else in the building. If you've spent any time in a hospital, you know what I mean. Hospitals are not for sick people. Sick people die in hospitals. Hospitals are for dying people. If you're sick, stay home so the dying people can expire in peace.

The knock came again, and Chalky thumbed towards the door, saying he'd check on it. Before he could move, I stopped him.

"Listen," I said, grinning. Whoever it was wasn't quiet. It was the same type of noise I got from outside my classroom door when a session was about to start, and the kids were standing around trying to catch the last few minutes of conversation, and in the process, being too loud with their friends. I picked up on one voice I recognized.

I called out, "Emilio, fries and a diet coke. I'm going off sugar for a while."

"Hey, Mr. E." Emilio leaned around the door, waved, then sauntered in with a rocking swagger, and he held up a key ring bristling with keys.

"My car, man. I got me one. There's more people outside, if you want to see 'em. Hey, you, somebody left you some bruises."

"Get over here." I held a hand up, and he clasped it and let it go. "I didn't cry. Not once. How do mine compare to the ones you used to get?"

The bruises, I meant, and I knew he'd get that. That long-ago conversation had been pivotal in our budding relationship as student and teacher. Even so, I was surprised I brought it up. I hadn't thought of it in years, but the words were just in my head, as if I had to say them.

As soon as they came out of my mouth, I knew Emilio wasn't at the hospital to see me. Like Spiderman and his spidey sense, I can pick up things through my god-thing, only without the cool suit. Something else had brought him here.

"Oh, man, you got a memory." He turned and looked out the window. "Crazy, you know. How come you not forget that?"

I heard the stunted grammar. Emilio spoke better English than that. I'd hit a nerve.

"Cause I can't forget you. Who else gives me free up-sizes?" I laughed as I said it, but when he turned, my juju antennas had started to buzz, opening Emilio's hidden hallway of doors, the whole ball-busting scenario banging open, and there Emilio was, with half his doors open, and half already closed. I tested one, and behind it was junior high, and he was in a fistfight on the front steps. I could see me looking out my window at him, shaking my head in regret. Emilio had never lived that. In a way, I felt I had a part in closing that door. Farther down I caught glimpses of bright scenes, and dark ones, too. That told me something. My bright, likeable, ex-student Emilio could still go either way. The forks in his life hadn't all been chosen, and that frightened me. Any of these doors could be his.

"So, tell me, Emilio. I guess I got my stuff together, because you survived my class. Who's butting your head, now?"

"How you read me like that?" He turned, and his eyes were red. "Man, you know me. I don't have a real conversation with you for two years, and you know what's in my *head*." He hit his temple with his fist.

I knew what he meant. I'd seen him at the drive-thru, and at a high school sports event or two, but really kept up? If he wasn't working at my favorite fry joint, he'd be out of my life. I didn't exactly hang around with seventeen-year-olds.

As soon as he said that, one of his darker doors slammed shut, and I thought, Okay, this is connected. How?

"Chip? You've got a crowd out here wanting in."

"Two minutes." I needed some time to work this out with Emilio.

"Two minutes. That's all I get?" Emilio shook his head, glancing outside with half a grin.

"It's enough." I'm used to getting everything

done in two minutes. I'm a teacher, remember? A classroom runs in two-minute increments. I heard the door click shut, and the voices from outside were silenced. "So, Emilio, do we talk about it, or let it go?"

"My friend's got a sis, the age of your kids. You know, just a kid, but not a kid anymore." He worked his mouth, forcing a smile, then it twisted off his face, and he looked away.

I thought, Mary Jane, and I cringed, but there was nothing else. Just that cringe. A cringe was annoying, but it wasn't god-information, feeding down my nerves and telling me I had work to do.

"She's got a friend, you see, and there was this thing. Now she's here. That's why we're here, me and my friends. 'Cept we can't see her, and when we heard you were here, we thought, Cool, Mr. E. We gotta stop in and check him out. Only, we got to go. School starting and all." He smiled brightly, rocking his shoulders, and throwing out his hand again, waiting for me to grasp his in return.

This time, when we grabbed hands, my juju receptors lighted up like they were wired into the national power grid. The doors around Emilio receded from him in fast forward, leaving him in a vast space that was washed out except for right around him. He was in full color, like someone standing in a fog, except the fog's every-
where except right where he is.

Then, that motion picture thing kicked in, where the director films the scene in high-speed, then runs it forward really fast, interspersed with periods of slow motion. Except this was running backwards. I watched Emilio, and we were shaking hands with lightning running down my arm, then we released hands, Bam!, but not like just releasing hands. It was with a flash of light, and our hands exploded apart. Then, still in the fog, he moved in high speed to the corridor outside my room, all in reverse, and the slow motion kicked in again, showing Emilio talking to the friends with him. I could see Conner from the drive-thru, two people I didn't know, and a girl, one probably Mary Jane's age. She looked like one of the boys, so I guessed she was his sister. They joked, bumping knuckles and kid stuff like that, although I didn't hear anything, just saw the image.

Then the image blurred, and we were at the front desk, and they were asking about someone. The receptionist shook her head as if to apologize. Conner pointed to something on her desk, and she brightened, wrote on a pad, tore a sheet off, and handed it to him. As they turned away, the image blurred again, and they were in the parking lot, getting out of a Camaro, probably Emilio's new car. Everything blurred again, not slowing for a long time, and the Camaro was sitting under a streetlight, surrounded by darkness. An arm hung out the window, the wrist exposed to the night air.

On the wrist was a black watch, with two diamonds, and two black hands.

I tried to focus on the arm, to see more inside the car, but I was yanked out of the scene, and in a spinning head-rush of dizzying proportions, the entire vision unraveled, back through the parking lot, into the glass doors, past the reception desk, into the elevator, down the corridor, and Emilio was back at my side.

I let go of his hand, and the fog disappeared. The doors, though. I couldn't get rid of those. They still huddled around my ex-student, and I didn't understand that. Just because you're a god doesn't mean it all makes sense to you. My life is proof of that.

"Are you all right, Mr. E.?" Emilio frowned, as if nothing had happened. For him it probably hadn't.

"Who came with you?" What else could I ask? What do you know about Ryan's death? What are you not telling me? Are you a lying son-of-a-gun? I didn't know that he was, not yet, anyway.

"Um, I told you." He looked vaguely guilty, though. As much as I like the boy, guilt isn't vague. It's there or it isn't. That isn't juju. That's fact.

"What have you got yourself into? I can help you, if you'll just ask." I used my god-voice from eighth grade. That was when I saw one of his doors slam closed, one of the bright and colorful ones.

"Not this time, Mr. E. I'm sorry." He squeezed his eyes tightly. "I shouldn't have come. You, you *know* stuff. Hey, man, time. School. We're outta here."

And he abandoned me, disappearing out the door without another word or a look back. None of the other kids came in. Chalky did, though.

"What was that?" He laughed, like he wanted to blow it off, but his expression said he was totally mystified. "He came out of here like he was scared of you."

"I can't stay in here, Chalky. People need my help." I turned toward the window, wondering if I could see Emilio's car if I looked in the parking lot. I didn't even know if my window faced the lot. I was tethered, though, which didn't give me many options.

"Like me, maybe?" Chalky smiled brightly at me, like he needed to convince me.

I didn't need convinced, but I did need to find that black watch, and being trapped here frustrated the heck out of me.

"Arghh!" I grabbed the wires attached to me in one hand, at first venting, thinking, How can this be happening to me? All I've done is what you've wanted me to. Give me a break! And in that moment, I yanked violently at the wires, and the pads pulled at my skin.

I shouldn't have done that.

It was that juju thing. I should ask, since I'm writing this for you as sort of a proof that I'm not crazy, not totally, anyway, if you really understand juju. You've got to think West Africa, amulets and spells. Specifically, witchcraft. Now, I know you're thinking, Queens is a long way from West Africa, but stick the pins in the map, so to speak. Put the first pin in West Africa, and put the second in South Africa. Connect them with string. Now stretch the string from South Africa to Queens. See what I mean? It's like fiber optic juju, only now it's in Houston, and I know why. Me. It's followed me here. That lady in the hospital—this hospital? This same one I'm trapped in today? She has to be the connection.

Well, I yanked those wires, and the juju kicked in, like lightning-fired, ball-busting nerve juice, and I was riding the wires in the building like a surfer on cocaine atop Waimea off the North Shore of Hawaii, and kitty whiskers if they didn't surf me right to the ICU, and Wham! There I was, in a fourteen-year-old girl's head, living her nightmares.

And chuck it all in the wastebasket, if you've been violated repeatedly by someone you trusted, then learned not to trust; and he gets out of prison and violates you again; and he winds up dead; and people tell you it's all your fault; what kind of nightmares go on in your head? Well, I got to find out, and there was nothing good about it. Not one good thing at all.

—*18*—

PLAY THAT FUNKY MUSIC!

I know some of you don't like curse words, especially those of you who adhere to Christian fundamentalist beliefs. Cut yourself and say ouch, but anything stronger and you're cursed to an eternal fiery pit of devils and pitchforks and all that nonsense.

Yeah, and some of us already live in that eternal pit of devils and other vile creatures. Like Mary Jane. I know. I spent time in there with her.

I felt the wires going in. I mean, I've been to see people in the Intensive Care Unit, and they've got more wires running to them than cables to the back of a computer. Although I hadn't seen her, M.J. had to be hooked up like a marionette waiting to be yanked to life by the puppet master in the sky. When I hit her—I didn't know it was her at first—I was split into a hundred splintered indices of high-powered electricity, and I felt each sliver of the nightmare. Heart monitors? Do you know how many circuits there are in those things? Cripes, I felt every one. And those automated IV drip machines? More circuits, for goodness sakes! You wouldn't think they could cause so much pain, but get real! What's wrong with the manual version? Twist a dial, and just control how much saline drips in. Do you have to kill the messenger? I may be a god, but I can still stupid well feel the pain of being flung through electric circuits at a billion miles an hour.

I didn't know where I was, just that I was glad to be wherever I landed, because I was no longer fractured into a million pieces. It was actually rather peaceful, all quiet and willowy, like floating in a pool in the shade, with the trees dappling the sunlight on your face. Then it got kinda funky. You know *funky*, like that old song written by Rob Parissi and sung by Wild Cherry: Play that funky music . . . and everybody gets up on the tables and starts to dance. Weird funk. That's what happened next. That dappled shade? Well, it wasn't shade at all. It was all the crud that happened to people in the real world, the stuff they couldn't deal with any longer.

I first caught on when one of the shadows started to bother my right eye. No matter how much I moved my head, it was there, pressing in, determined to make me pay attention. I should've been smart enough to realize that anything that wanted me to pay that much attention in there wasn't planning to sponge me behind the ears with warm bathwater and dab me with a soft cloth to get dry.

No, I looked, and deep in that shadowy bit of shade was something deeper. The closer I looked, the more I didn't want to see. There was M.J., blurred, an image of what she imagined herself to be, and not at all pretty like she really was. I knew that feeling. When you feel ugly, you see yourself as ugly, and when you're fourteen and you've got a big bully molesting you, and you know it will happen tomorrow night and the next and the next, there's nothing pretty in your life.

That's when I realized this was Mary Jane's world. Duh! I hadn't figured it out before. How's that for a brilliant god? I was in her head, and these little shadows were her bad experiences, all balled up and set afloat to where they didn't have to touch her anymore. She'd just wrapped them up and made them into something she could live with, each horrible night with her step-brother packaged up and sent off to float in the sky to where it looked beautiful, if you didn't look too closely.

That's the god-thing. I have to look closely. What I've got doesn't allow me to do anything else.

My M.J. was in there somewhere with all this, but I could tell that what I was looking at wasn't happening right then. Maybe it hadn't even happened this year. It was what she wanted to forget but couldn't help but remember. See, I'm a god, so I get to know some things. What happens to you, you never forget. You just box it up and put it on a shelf, and you hope the package never gets opened again. These were M.J.'s boxes, and I shouldn't be seeing what was inside.

I wasn't in control, though. Something else had pulled me in here, and I didn't know what. When I find out, there'll be some major damage to pay, I tell you that. I won't aim for any walls, either, but for whatever creature had the gall to do this to me.

Inside that little bit of shadow, M.J. held on to a stuffed rabbit. I could see it, pink, with white inside the ears, and big green eyes, the kind that have little reflectors inside, and they can wink at you in the middle of the night, like they're really alive. There was a window, and something moved in front of it, a human shape, with broad shoulders, and I knew it was Ryan in M.J.'s bedroom. He pulled his tee shirt off, and he stood in the dimness, all quiet. I didn't want to watch this. I knew, I *knew* what was about to happen, pardon my graphic references, that he was about to jump her, and M.J. would suffer for it. I also knew it wasn't the first time, and that's why she held the rabbit. It was how she survived.

He picked up his phone and began to snap pictures, first of M.J.'s face, her neck, anyplace under her clothes. Yeah, those were the pictures that had gotten him put away, the ones that were obtained without a warrant. And the lousy warrant thing? That had also gotten him released. If he'd stayed behind bars, he'd still be alive today, wouldn't he? Sometimes you get what you want, and it takes you out, in Ryan's case, with part of you already missing.

Well, I faded out of that shadow, and I was glad to be gone. You may not hear anything, but you pick up stuff in there, like M.J. squeezing on that rabbit, and wondering if she squeezed it hard enough, would it die, and if her step-brother pushed hard enough on her, would she die, and the worst part? She hoped she would, right then, just die, and she wouldn't have to live through it again.

When I got out of that shadow, I noticed the other shadows had changed. Like they were still shadows, but they'd noticed me. Like they wanted me to see what was inside, and they came at me, pleading, *Open me, open me.* Some of them were pretty insistent, and thank the powers that be, not all were of that low-life Ryan. Some were of her mother yelling in her coarse Spanish, once or twice throwing something across the room, usually at M.J., and the thing shattering, with broken bits of glass or pottery left for M.J. to clean off the floor. Her girlfriends, a few I recognized from school, pulling mean pranks, one in M.J.'s locker. That memory? I'll never see cheerleaders the same ever again.

The most heartbreaking? M.J. holding a

kitten, its head bleeding, and Ryan standing over her with a baseball bat. Now, I don't get sound in these visions, but that doesn't mean I can't read lips. And I'd seen that kitten before. I'm science, remember? We'd done a project on animals, and M.J. had sneaked that kitten to class inside her jacket. It was the most precious thing she owned. Ryan's words? "You tell again, little sis, and that cat's head is your head."

I wish it were possible to cut off dead people's nads. I so wanted a knife in my hand right then.

Something gripped me, like giant fingers, and without any warning, I was yanked out of that shadow, and I could tell the difference. The pool thing had turned jangly. Rough on the edges. Like holding a rose, and smelling of it, to realize the stem was covered with thorns, and it smelled like slime, and how the heck did I not notice this before? But that wasn't really it, either. Ozone. Like when a computer burns out, arcing, probably in a high-voltage power supply. It has that burned, acrid smell that happens after a corona discharge, ionizing the air. You know the computer's going, and you dread the moment, but you keep your programs running full tilt because you need the information on the hard drive. Well, the power supply was arcing, but I needed to find what M.J. was telling me, and I ignored the smell, and began punching at the shadows to find what they wanted to show me, hoping something would fall out, and I would know. I had to *know*. For Pete's sake, this was a fourteen-year-old girl we're talking about. How in the world could I not want to know?

So, I took my fist and started punching the shadows as fast and hard as I could. Crikey, they were tough sons-of-guns. Little tight-wads, refusing to barf out what they held inside. I was determined, though. So, I punched harder, and I started getting stuff. Broken toys, which were young memories. A broken arm, from her father. Stealing a pair of socks, hoping no one found out, because she was required to wear them in gym, and her step-father had beat her for asking.

I had to go faster, though. The smell was worse, and it had started to burn. Like taking poison through an IV, and when it hits your veins, it's like fire inside, but I guess you can picture that without me describing it. That's what it was like. I think I was being shunted out, but now I was refusing to go. I had something to find here, if I could only break open the right memory. So that's what I began doing, grabbing the shadows, and squeezing, just to see what came out. They ran black down my arm. Then I grabbed one that was different than the rest. It was heavy and dense, not filled with the neatly wrapped misery of a forgotten memory, but something that was so *now* that it couldn't be wrapped up and floated away in the pretty blue sky. It was something solid, and it burned in my hand. This was so horrible that all the other shadows were there to hide this one, because M.J. knew that if this one were ever found, everything in her life would change. Me? If I were living Mary Jane's life? I'd want it to change, every miserable moment.

Then someone screamed, and the blue in the sky and the blue in the water changed. Black roiled in, like India ink dumped into a glass of water. It filled up, black clouds punctuated with red lightning. All the dappled shadows fled, and the water whipped in a wild frenzy. I hung on for all I was worth, but there was nothing I could do. The ozone? It became a stench, and then I was in the electronics, being sucked backwards along the electrical lines, ripped through the walls, the wires scorching my nerves, and in an exhausting implosion, I shrank back into my body and collapsed, exhausted on the bed. In my hand I still held the wires that attached the monitoring equipment to my body.

My skin smoked, like when someone sits in an electric chair, and he's cooked from the inside out. Yet, I shivered, and my skin was dry ice numb. The ozone smell filled the room.

"Chip! What happened?" Chalky stood looking at me, frozen in his tracks.

My question was the same. What happened? I had been ripped apart and put back together again. Yeah. And all my monitors were screaming bloody electrical murder. Yeah, my body was screaming the same thing.

I looked at Chalky out of my tortured, freezer-burned eyeballs, and I couldn't answer. I couldn't pretend to move.

"What's that?" Chalky looked at my left hand.

I think someone noticed the machines about then, because two nurses came running in, and they ripped what little decency I had from me, leaving me sprawled naked on the bed. I noticed I had more wires, down near my groin, and they began stripping every one off. One of them pulled something out of my left hand and set it on the table where the flowers go. They covered me back up and began wheeling the bed out the door.

Whatever it was, it was still smoking, and I saw Chalky pick it up as I was wheeled by. He looked at it with a frown, catching my eye just before I disappeared out of sight. I got a glimpse as he held it up.

It was a watch, a black watch, with black hands, and a diamond on the face. I know, because it caught in the light, just as I disappeared out the door.

Now, how the crud did that happen, I wanted to know. How in the nut-crushing improbability of all that I'd just gone through did I pull a watch from someone else's memories?

And I didn't even have the strength to punch the wall. I didn't want to be a god. I wanted to be a normal, ordinary man, who did ordinary things, and that didn't include invading a girl's memories to watch her be violated by her step-brother.

Life's a crock. Have I told you that? Well, if

not, here goes. Life's a crock, and if you need any proof, here I am, the most messed-up son-of-a-gun that ever walked the face of the earth. And I'm supposed to be a god. Well, spit on being a god. That's all I have to say about that. It's not all it's worked up to be. Just look at me. Shikes, I'm a messed-up god. Chuck it all into the sewer, and I'm really through now.

Living through this makes me angry at everything in the world.

—*19*—

OKAY, I WAS WRONG.

But I know something I didn't know before. That's something, for a god.

Like, fists can go through walls. But we already knew that.
You've seen my house, so that's proof of that. Heads? Yeah,
but I'm not a head type of guy. Feet, I suppose, although who
would put their foot through a wall, unless they were a karate-
type, and that's not me, not ever. It's the body thing I'm
talking about here. Yeah, like in those shows where super-
strong guys pick up not-so-strong guys and chuck them
through walls. I mean straight through. No, that can't happen.
The body spreads out the impact too much. That's science. It's
why a ball of iron sinks in the water, but spread it out, and

give it a bit of a concave twist, and you can load that ball of iron with 4,000 people, and it'll float all the way across the ocean.

I'd always thought my god powers made me sort of invincible. I knew I didn't get money, or eternal life, at least not like extended human life, but it was a gift, right? If it was a gift, I was meant to use it, and I couldn't use it dead, now could I? So, ergo, I had to be alive. The things I can do? Yeah, they tired me out, but I always recovered. Now I've learned some visions do more than tire me out. They can bring on heart attacks. Those screaming monitors in that hospital room? The docs tell me I really did die that time.

I watched a movie once where this man saw demons and things, and he tried to kill himself once, only doing so was a mistake, and it made things worse. So, now he lived above a bowling alley, and he chased the demons out of other people. The point is, he could visit the spirit world, but only at the moment of death, perhaps in an electric chair, or with his head held under water until he about to drown. Just at the moment of crossing over, he actually did cross over, only he didn't go all the way. Something always pulled him back.

Something had pulled me back. The thing was, the only thing I can find that connected my two crossovers? Chalky. Yeah, my old friend who followed me half across the continent, and now shares my house with me.

'Cept, he now lives alone in my house, 'cause

I'm still flat out in hospital greens (with underwear, thanks to Chalky) with tubes tied to my arms. The sticky things on my groin? They said they could forego those, if I'd lie really still and not have any more heart attacks.

That's a riot. I didn't choose to have the first one. Chuckin' funny doctors. Yeah, right. If I'd not have . . . Anyway, I promised.

Oh, and that little flower shelf? It's full, now. Cards, too, and my favorite thing? It's on a piece of poster board up on the wall where I can see it from here. Miss Mulford brought it in this morning. It's from my last period class. They drew a picture of a scientist—rather mad-looking, if you ask me—standing with two blown-up test tubes. His front side is all blackened, and his eyes are really round. They all signed it, and in big letters at the bottom, it says, We love you, Mr. E.

I mean, people who don't teach wonder why some of us do. That poster says it all. Sure, eighth graders might see you as a black hole walking down the hallway, and they forget about you as soon as they move on to high school, but in the moment, they care. They really care, and unlike adults, eighth graders don't lie. If they feel it, it's on their sleeves, and it comes out. Now, what eighth graders are really good at is disguise. That's different than lying, because with an eighth grader, when you work through the disguise, the truth is always there, and it will come out. Love it or hate it, it will come out. An adult? You can know them for ten years, and the whole time they say they love your strawberry coffee, until one day they throw it at you and yell, "I never liked strawberry, anyway. Hogwash on your strawberry coffee." But that's getting personal, so I'll move on.

I heard from M.J. Not much, just that my phone rang, and it was a nurse. She said another patient wanted to talk with me if I felt like it. I said I did, and they let me talk. Funny thing? No vibes. I'd been in this girl's *head,* and not a vibe one. No juju. No tingles. No strange heart attack going on. Nothing. Just a girl from my class, sweet voice, and telling me her friend had been to see her, and that's how she knew I was in the hospital.

Well, holy hush puppies, if that doesn't shuck all.

I asked how she was doing, and she said she felt really good, and thank you for getting me through. I wasn't sure how I got her through, but there it was. She said it, I didn't know what else to say, and I said I'd do it for anybody. As soon as the words came out of my mouth, I wanted to kick myself. But you have to understand this: The god-thing doesn't make me smart. It just makes me crazy, crazy enough to chase down step-brothers who go after fourteen-year-old step-sisters.

After I hung up, I thought about things, trying to figure it out. You see, when all the bad doors are shut, and only the good doors are left open, it's like some-one cuts the cord, and that invisible connection with that person is gone. It's like I lose their cell number, or maybe they lose mine, and I don't get all the calls and texts anymore. Weird, I know, but I can only tell you how it feels. There's not a manual for this. Not even the Bible. I mean, where's the doggone verse that says I'm supposed to be able to run time backwards and see what happens when a child molester gets burned to a crisp in a garden-variety dumpster? It's not in there. It's not. I've read the entire thing, and you won't find it.

Now, the part about fire and brimstone? I can identify with that. I'd never been sucked down wires before, but I don't think fire and brimstone could be worse. That hurt like a sandy beach in Hell. Like getting fried by the daddy of all suns on a sandy beach in Hell while on shiitake mushroom *steroids*. The bullet train kind that smash into you at a hundred miles an hour.

My life is so messed up. Why does everything have to happen to me?

—20—

OH, CRAPOLA! I MUST HAVE BEEN hopping out of my mind. At what point in life do we wake up and quit doing the stupid stuff?

Chalky came to pick me up when the doctors finally decided I wasn't having a third heart attack. Yes, I had to parrot. No red meat. Easy on the caffeine. Walk more. Good heavens, I was thinking. I'm not even thirty, so what's the big deal? It sounded like Lifestyle of the Old and Retired. But, da da da da da. They asked it, I said it, and they pronounced me fit enough to brave the real world.

Then I got in my car with Chalky behind the wheel. I didn't trust his old beater to get me from the hospital to my house. There's a reason Chalky's cars are always beaters, and it's not always his lack of high-paying jobs. He can't drive worth anything. I know. Put Chalky in a parking lot, and God help anyone on two feet. They're invisible to Chalky. The same thing at crosswalks and right turns on red. Bam, and he goes, "What was that . . ." as the car bumps over their freshly dead body.

As Chalky pulled out, I was distracted by my glove box. You see, I was thinking about M.J. and what her mother said, about going off somewhere, and how I didn't get any juju vibes from the girl over the phone, and that made me think of the dumpster. Glove box . . . dumpster? Yeah, I know. No connection, right? Yet, something was telling me there was. A gut feeling had put a pin in my glove box and another in that dumpster, and stretched a length of string between the two. Now I needed to follow it.

Yeah, that dumpster wasn't over with, yet. You know which one I'm talking about. I had to know, like, was it still there, or had they come to pick it up and put a new one in its place. All that's interesting if you've climbed inside and seen a man die in there, one who's already missing his gentleman's parts, because someone cut them off just before they lit the match. Now, that's some wicked juju, and you don't have to be a god to pick up on that. It's just plain worked over, every- day shibblets. No, I acted all casual-like, just asked Chalky if he'd been back by, pointing out different things in the city as we passed, the little hospital ID tag hanging from my wrist and flopping around every time I pointed.

"There, Chalky. Take that street." It was the back way to the Education Center. I knew that, but I didn't think Chalky did.

"Hey, new way home?" He grinned brightly, one hand on the wheel, and the other rubbing at something in his ear. I told him in plenty of time, and he still nearly missed the turn, slamming on the brakes and squealing the tires. A man whipped around us, honking his horn and flipping us the finger out the window. Forget you, I wanted to call back, but I'm still a teacher, even though I haven't been there in a couple days. I didn't want word to get back to Admin that one of their finest was out badmouthing local drivers. Believe me, word like that gets around, and you can lose your job because of it.

"Yeah," I said. "Like a shortcut. Comes out by the Education Center." No big deal, like anyone with their right mind screwed in all the way would take this route. If you live in Houston, don't try it around eight in the morning or four in the afternoon. Every parent in Houston is on this road about those hours. At eight or four? Take the long way. You'll get there faster.

I could see the traffic out on W. Dallas, bright flashes of cars amid buildings decorated with vividly painted signs. Then, that's the fun in being in the Southwest. You get that cultural mix. It reminds me of parts of Queens, the part I lived in. Not all *white*, if you get my drift. I was watching that, expecting the tape to be there, and I glanced at the grounds of the Center for a moment, not looking for kids or anything, but seeing a group of students out, all in burgundy and red, and a few in white. Uniforms. I'd forgotten that, although I'm sure I've heard about them from Charisse. I only saw three Anglo kids. Like I said, I felt at home in Houston. Anyway, I was watching one of the girls kick a ball, and Chalky slammed on the brakes, throwing me against the shoulder strap.

"There," he called, pointing. "I think it's the same one."

The dumpster, he meant. It was bright green now, and with new stickers, phone numbers to call, and the company logo. Even the plastic lids were new, black and shiny. That wouldn't last long in the Houston subtropical sun. It beats plastics to death, including car seals. It was the reason I was in a house and not an apartment. I needed a garage. The holes in my walls? That came after, sort of a fringe benefit. If I'd bought a good concrete block house, my hands might be worse for the wear, but my walls would be in better shape. Maybe I should consider Ft. Myers. I understand most of the houses in Florida are built from good ole sturdy concrete block. Good for resale. Bad for my hands.

Tangents. That was one. Sorry. Can't live with 'em. (You) Can't talk without 'em. (Me) That dumpster, though. I think he was right. The burn pattern. They'd painted over the burn damage, and the finish was smooth at the bottom, where the heat hadn't scarred the paint completely off, but at the top, you could see the roughness underneath, and it exactly matched the pattern I remembered. I'd been in that dumpster. I had hands-on experience with what had occurred in there. This was definitely the same one. If I looked, my old clothes were probably off in an alley somewhere, just where I'd tossed them when I'd changed into Chalky's gym stuff.

"Pull over." I motioned with my hand.

"This is what you were doing before? Just taking a short-cut?" When he found me here before, he meant. He shook his head as he shifted into reverse and threw his arm over the back of the seat to look behind him to reverse the car. At least Chalky does that. He's never *backed* into anything that I know of. My mother? She's never had a car with a back bumper that stayed straight for more than three months, and most not that long. She doesn't even look, just guns the engine, then exclaims, "Where the heck did that come from?" Me? I'd be going, Where the holy flippin' fragdaggle did that dipstick son-of-a-gun come from, which is why my mother should probably be writing this story. More people would be less offended if she did, but I say, No, be offended, because I'm a god, and I can offend as many people as I want. 'Ceptin' you know that's not true. I can't offend anyone. Those of you out there with religious issues are probably thinking, This guy's all messed up. If I were him, I'd be saying, *Forget you* to the world, too. And I bet you feel all weepy-eyed and sorry for me, like you want to be my friend and everything.

Well, screw you. See? Now you're really my friend, because I only say that to people I really like. If I'm nice to them, they don't get it, and they walk away cursing at me, like I meant to insult them. Remember Emilio? He's my number one fan now, and Chalky? I told him to get lost, and now he's chauffeuring me around the city. That's how it works. If I told my story with nice words, would you still be reading?

I did answer Chalky. You remember, his question about the shortcut.

"Something like that." I got out when he parked the car. Now, to get this picture, you have to visit the hospital dismissal door sometime. No, don't go in, just sit in your car outside. You'll see all these people rolled out in wheel chairs, still in robes or whatever they were wearing in bed. They climb in cars dressed just like that, and that's what they wear home. Sure, I know some people wouldn't be caught dead without their Prada shoes, but when you've had two heart attacks, it's too much *work* to get dressed just to go home and recuperate for a few days. So, I had my boxers on, and over that one of those free hospital gowns they charge the insurance company $900 for. My feet? Paper booties. Chalky brought me the boxers, but he's Chalky, and let's let it go at that.

So, I climbed out of the car in my green gown, and I think my boxers might have been orange houndstooth. I like A&M almost as much as dinosaurs. That's really immaterial, but the point is, if they showed, at least my tush was covered. So, I stood at the dumpster with its fresh green paint, bright and vivid against my pale hospital gown. I hesitated to touch it. Its juju felt okay. It wasn't vibrating, or sending out major juju currents or anything. It was more like being in a great big church with one of those pipe organs, where you can't hear the sound, but you know it's there, because the floor's vibrating. That's what I felt. If you're not a church-goer, imagine the subwoofer attached to your home surround sound system. That's what I felt. It was there, but only because I knew it was supposed to be there.

"Chip?" Chalky stood outside the car. He had the door open, and one arm rested on top of the window frame, and the other on the roof. "Did you notice what you're wearing?"

"Yeah." I looked at him. "Your point?"

"There's a school right here. Um, you might want to think about that." He ducked his head, ran his fingers through his hair, and glanced at the Center.

"Yeah." I was already tuning him out again. This dumpster. Mary Jane hadn't jangled my god-nerves back at the hospital, and now, this dumpster. My nerves should be jangling away about this time. I should be standing in the middle of a pair of cymbals, and they should be crashing around my ears.

I touched it, and I yanked my hand away. It was just metal. Nothing else. Metal. Oh, the subwoofer was still there, but the tweeters stayed silent, and I couldn't hear the woofers or the bass module at all. I rested my hand on it and slid the door back, the little one on the end designed for trash bags. Then I put my other hand on it, relieved to find I was still in good ole Houston, and I didn't feel a burning sensation in my veins telling me I was about to be pulled into under time.

"Since we're here, Chip, want to toss this in? It doesn't work." Chalky put his hand on my shoulder to get my attention. "I've had it in the glove box."

I realized I'd heard him closing a car door and opening another. Mine. When he said glove box, I saw that string. I'd felt it earlier, but now it was a vivid, pyrotechnic line, zipping through the air, from my car to this dumpster.

"Toss what in?" I was focused on the line. Then I saw his hand, and I realized the line wasn't pinned to the car anymore. It was pinned to Chalky's hand, well, more precisely put, to what was in his hand. He was holding that watch. "Cowabunga holy cow, where did that come from?"

In that moment, it all came back to me. M.J. The pool. The dappled shade. And squeezing that final one, with black running down my arm, and knowing it was different. I knew now, it was what I was meant to find.

And Chalky held it in his hand.

"Just trash." Chalky laughed, and he tossed it at the opening.

Chalky can throw, but I can catch. It's reflexive for me, like blinking. My right hand was on the lip of the dumpster, and my left hand jerked into the air with my palm open, and I clamped my fingers shut. That's the crazy out-of-my-mind decision I made, to catch that watch, because that's when the stereo came on full volume, tweeters, woofers, bass modules, subwoofers, and whatever other lint-licker parts of a stereo they design to blast out the flippin' hairs in our ears. You've seen *Back to the Future*. Doc's giant speaker? Yeah, I was surrounded by those, and I was blown into the afterlife. Literally. I was there beside Chalky at one moment, and the next I was standing in fire and brimstone, with devils and ashes and pitchforks, and the whole shebang nightmare.

The funniest thing? I was standing nose to nose with Ryan Gallagher Simpson. Now, here's the interesting part. This god learned something in all this. People are naked in Hell. Holy Pokémon naked, like a baby just out of its mother's womb. Why? Heck if I know; maybe because we pass through some sort of fire gate on the way in that incinerates them. I just saw Ryan was naked, and I couldn't cut his nads off for what he'd done to poor Mary Jane. They were already gone.

Snap dangity, I don't get no fun, do I?

Now, I know this question is running in

everyone's mind, so I'll answer it and get it over with. Like I said, nearest thing I can tell, what you're wearing up top doesn't make it through to the afterlife. That applies to me, too. If you want to picture me sans briefs, go ahead. Trust me, it might be prettier than how Ryan looked, but not much. I see it every night in the shower, and I like my bathroom mirrors fogged up. That way, when I wipe a spot clear, I only see the pretty parts, and by that I mean my face.

Then Ryan grabbed my wrist, the left one holding the watch, and he thrust it in the air. From all around me, demons roared, screeched, and generally sounded like out-of-tune violins played by first-year novices. And I could have sworn they were headed my way.

I didn't know what that was about, but I was learning one thing. Walking on brimstone? It's not fun at all, and you can trust me on that.

—21—

I'VE NEVER THOUGHT OF HELL as a really bad place. You know, you go there, and maybe you don't get eighty-inch plasmas, which, by the way, have much better color than LEDs, and of course, God's in the other place, no there's none of that chapped Holy, Holy, Holy nonsense, which sounds really boring to me, anyway, unless I'm the one up there on the throne, and you know how well that's gone for me.

Still, holy demons screaming out-of-tune violins at you? What the crapola was this? No-nads Ryan? I could deal with that. Remember, I'd already seen him die a rather horrible and gruesome death, so no big deal there. I just wasn't psyched up for the rest.

So I put all that practice pounding walls to good use.

My hand. Remember what I said about hairline cracks in the bone making the fist stronger? Bam! Hit the wall, and it hurts like blazing fire, but do it again, and it gets stronger; and sure, it still feels like fire every time you do it, but you can do the same damage with less pain every time. Read that like I said it. You can do the same damage with less pain, which for the science or math teachers out there means you can do even more damage with the same amount of pain.

I have a lot of holes in my walls, and I intended to do some damage to some cheese-and-rice so-and-sos.

I saw the obvious flaw in my line of thinking, and I guess you've seen it, too, especially the perverts out there, because I'm in the buff, here, and that makes me kinda exposed. However, I've had some practice at this. I teach at junior high, remember? I've never been in the gym showers with the boys at my school, but I've been in the gym showers. The ones in Houston are just like the ones back in Queens. No walls, just a lot of nozzles. Now picture high school. It's even worse. That's a load of heavy karma to dump on a fifteen-year-old, to be unclothed in a room full of equally sans seniors. Sweet nibbits, they've got more armpit hair than the rest of us have on our entire bodies.

You learn to deal with it really fast. And watch your eyes. That'll get you beat up quicker'n cheese melts on a hot dog. That was my plug at a joke. Get it?

My solution? The same as it was in my freshman year. I went on the ramrod offensive.

First, I balled my right hand into a fist and drew it back, and I slammed it into the side of Ryan's face. He jerked away, his face twisting into a caricature of a human being, all twisty like those slow-motion face-hits you see in *Rocky*. You've seen 'em, the spit flying everywhere, and the guy's eyes looking like they might come out of their sockets. At first I thought I could see all that because I was so angry, but then it hit me, that time thing I can do? It's not exactly the same, but I can mess with time in here, too. Slow it down. The only good I saw in it was that it gave me time to think, you know, to plan out my next move. I could take time to see what muscles were being tensed by the other guy, and I could plan ahead.

Bam! I hit him again, this time in the throat. His head whipped back the other direction, but crazy sucker, he refused to let go of my wrist! I'd a kicked him in the privates, except he didn't have any, just that raw wound down there, and when I looked around, those demons were getting pretty close.

I was frantic, so I tried something desperate. I could sense what Ryan was doing in slow motion, so I considered the possibilities. How far could I push it? If I leaped and kicked him with both feet, right in the chest, maybe I could force my arm loose. It might really hurt him, though. The thought crossed my mind that he'd be pretty angry if I crushed a lung, but I decided, what the hey. I'm in Hell, already. How much worse can things really get? And somehow, I knew that as long as he held my arm, I wasn't getting out of there. So, I screamed at him to get myself psyched up, and hopefully to startle him into letting go.

"You snassa-frazzin' brat. Let go my arm!" And I jumped up, drawing my knees to my chest. Time froze there, just for a moment, and I noticed my toenails needed to be trimmed. What the heck, you may think. You're noticing your toenails, when you've got a naked hot dog between your legs, and you're fighting a man who's been castrated, and a thousand crazed demons are coming to suck out your soul? Egad, man, focus!

That's it, I *was* focused. I saw those toenails, and I saw weapons. *Jurassic Park*. Ever seen that movie? Velociraptors. My word, those monsters have toenails. So, I pointed my toes, aimed for the soft skin under the arm with my left foot and his nipple with the right. Bam, bam! I connected, and I ripped my feet sideways, just to twist the knife, so to speak, and as soon as I felt his hand release my wrist, I rotated my body and pressed harder with my legs, so as to do as much damage to that chump's body as I could.

It's stupid, but I think I tore a toenail off on the way down. I was free, though, and I lit out of there.

Here's the thing, and you won't understand this if I don't really describe what I was up against. Some people tell you Hell's just a place where you're not in Heaven, but we've already nixed that. I mean, I'm *here*. This is the real deal. I'm gonna have blisters on the bottoms of my feet to prove it. But that's not it. You know I've got demons running after me. They're in all sizes and shapes. But it's not like you think. I saw a movie once where all the demons were these skull-like creatures that slunk around across the ground, and that's pretty scary stuff, but the real thing? Hold on to your Pampers, because you'll need them.

Hell's not all red and black like you see in all the pictures. That's a campfire. This? Try for an obscene kaleidoscopic explosion. Every color out there. And see, what happens is that the demons look pretty until they move. It's how they move that's so scary. One part of them moves, and then the rest catches up, but it's like they're joined by sticky mucus. One leg moves, and an arm moves, or the head turns, and the mucus pulls the rest of the demon along after it. I looked at 'em in slo-mo, and decided really fast that I didn't want to see that again. You see, in slo-mo is when you can tell what they're really made of. People. The mucus is made of people. You can see every single one screaming through the mucus when the demon starts to move, like it hurts them when the demon runs, and mother of pearl can they run. Like little Tasmanian devils, they can run.

I wasn't sticking around to become one of their little mucus people.

It was the end of the yellow brick road that threw a hitch in my plans. I was tearing up the brimstone, holding on to that watch for creeps-all knows what I was worth, planning what I would do to get back to my dumpster and my friend, and that fast, I was at the edge of a ragged precipice. It just the heck stopped, and before me stretched nothingness. I think I found the real Hell, though. It was like I was only halfway there. Like this was the Plateau of Purgatory. The noise . . . and the stink from below? Eat a handful of habaneros and smell the toilet when it comes out. You don't forget.

Then I heard a voice scream in my ear, "Mr. E.!"

That's all it was, but I knew that voice. How could M.J. be down here in Hell? I'd just been talking to her on the phone.

"No!" I screamed it at the top of my lungs, and with my right hand, I made a fist, and I slammed it into the yellow brick road, and it hurt! And I didn't care. I wanted it to hurt. Ryan deserved Hell, and he deserved to become mucus, and to scream in agony every time one of those demons moved, but not M.J. No way did M.J., my sweet little M.J., deserve that. I pounded the road over and over, hardly noticing the cracks I was creating, and only eventually aware of the demons growing louder and closer. I stood, and I looked them in the face. I raised the watch in one hand, and I raised my other fist, and I yelled, "You want it? Come get it from me!"

I slammed my fist down onto the roadway with everything I had, and all those little cracks separated, and my little precipice began to slide toward the real Hell far below.

"Mr. E.!" The voice yelled in my ear again, from farther away, and it became harder and harder to hold on to that watch. It was like it wanted to stay on the plateau. And like if I released it, I was lost forever.

Then the voice changed, and it wasn't Mary Jane any longer, and she wasn't saying Mr. E. anymore. The voice dropped an octave, and my name turned into, "Chip!"

What the hey, I thought. My students never call me Chip.

Then it got to be too much, and I let the watch go, and I was burning up, and everything went black around me.

—22—

I SAT UP AND GROANED. I opened my eyes to find they were as bleary as Caesar's ghost, and I looked around.

"For crying out loud," I said. "Someone's punched holes all in my walls."

That used up every bit of the energy I had. Breathing hard, I tossed the covers back to see I was still wearing my orange houndstooth, which was a relief after my run through Hell in the buff. I fell back onto the bed and closed my eyes.

"Chip?" It sounded like Chalky, but like Chalky in another room, talking on an old-timey phone, in France.

"Where are you, Chalky? I can barely hear you." I refused to open my eyes. It was too much effort.

"Here." His voice was louder, like he was still in France,

but someone had turned up the volume.

Then something happened, and I thought my head exploded, and right through my ears.

"Blast it all!" I yelled this time, coming up off the bed, and slapping my hands to my ears. "Suck it all, that hurts!"

Unable to bear it, I balled up my right hand and slammed it into a wall, only to have it go right through. Then, I couldn't get it out. I stood there panting, bent over, with my hand inside the wall. I opened my eyes, and I yanked at it. It's like crocodile jaws, though. They can crush bone, but you can hold them closed with one hand. I couldn't get my arm free.

"Let me help." Chalky put his hand on my shoulder, and he reached the other one and grabbed the edge of the hole. He broke off a piece, and when I still couldn't get it out, he repeated the process, until I could pull my hand out.

"What was that about?" I sat on the bed, cradling my arm.

"You did it to yourself." Chalky dropped into a folding chair across from me. "Don't blame me if your hand hurts."

"Not this." I held up my arm, still cradled in my left hand. "My ears. What in the world happened there?" I twisted my head side to side, hoping it didn't start up again.

"Oh, these." Chalky held out two cotton balls, blackened with dried blood. "They were in your ears. You said you couldn't hear, so I took them out."

"Next time I won't tell you. Why were they in my ears, anyway?" The blood? I thought I could guess, but I didn't want to have to guess. I was still seeing demons and hearing M.J.'s voice calling out to me in Hell. I didn't want to do anything except forget that.

"You were bleeding a bit when I got you away from the dumpster, and you made me promise, so I brought you home and put you to bed."

"Oh. Thanks." I fell back on the bed, and I grabbed at my arm as I landed. "Ow! That hurts."

"Two days ago." Chalky stood and walked out of the room.

What? I called out, "Two days ago?"

"Yeah," he called back.

"I've been out for two days?" I couldn't believe it. I tried to sort the elapsed time. I hoped it wasn't Sunday, already.

He leaned back in. "That's what two days means. And tomorrow's Saturday, so you get two more days to lay in bed. I hope you're feeling better by then. Oh, and by the way, I couldn't find the toenail, so I wrapped it with a bandage."

At least I knew where the holes in my walls had come from. My hand. I'd just wrestled one out. And for me to have forgotten that? What had happened to me? I recalled the demons and M.J.'s voice, but little else; that's all I could pull out of my memory.

"Dumpster? What dumpster? And what toenail?" I yelled my questions.

Chalky had some explaining to do.

—23—

BY THE END OF THE WEEKEND, I WAS UP and moving
again. I could even work the wrist I'd jammed through the
wall. Just because I punch walls doesn't mean I walk away
unscathed. Even a god pays the price for stupid decisions and
stuff.

I called up Stefanie from the school and asked her about
my classes, explaining that I'd be on half days for a couple
weeks, although I hoped to sneak in a full day Monday, unless
someone ratted me out. It seemed my three subs had shown a
lot of movies, so I knew my lesson plans were all shot. That
meant I was starting from scratch on Monday, but on the other
hand, if I picked up where I left off, I had a couple days to get
new lesson plans put together. So, sometimes stupid people

actually help me out. How hard is it, though, to "Read pp 452-459 and list the pathogens" when it's right there in my lessons?

Of course, part of it is that they've not stared down all the Emilios, and the boys at my school? When they jockey for power, they are masters. They have to be to survive in Houston's rough environment. Their first lessons come at home, and they escalate from there. It's not surprising they're the way they are. Look where they come from.

I'd forgotten about inviting everyone over Sunday night. Chalky saved me there. It was the phone call to Stefanie that clued me in, her telling me she couldn't make Sunday, but Rod, Tamina, and Ella planned to be over about six-thirty. They were bringing dates. Ann-Kristian would be there with her husband, and was it okay if Mosi brought his girlfriend's son? She had no one to babysit. The boy was fifteen, but he was a good kid. She'd laughed at that. Some of ours we teach are fifteen, and we know fifteen. Still, I said sure, and would she pass it on? Were we still on for fajitas? Absolutely, I said. Tell everyone I'll have the grill ready.

Of course, when I told Chalky, he was all into it. He'd been to some of my parties before, but he'd never felt like he was part of them. I know, because I'd watched him. He tried. He really did, but remember Chalky's beater car? That's Chalky's entire life. Beater quality. Teachers are a pretty high-class set to measure up to.

Now, before you start thinking too much, I don't mean high class like snooty and stuff like that. No, what I'm talking about is how we can talk in complete sentences, and if someone says Nietzsche, we know who we're talking about, even if we haven't read him. And to mention Green Peace or the Peace Corps, we know the difference. Green Peace chases whalers, and the Peace Corps makes the people smart enough to chase the whalers. That type of high-level knowledge.

You know, one time I mentioned 403b investments to Chalky, and he said, I don't know if 403 would be an investment or not, because I don't know what a 403 is. See? All teachers know about those. Still, Chalky's my man. He's my house buddy, and he keeps me alive when god-crapola happens to me, and for that? I'm grateful. The party? It's like he took over. Planning. The grill. Even cleaning the bath in the garage. See? He's been in my house, and now he understands. I guess I should have trusted him more all along. Someone said to me you really know a friendship when you test it to the limit. You know it's a good one when you wake up covered with the worst life can throw at you, smelling all to high heaven, and they're still standing at your side. By that description, Chalky's the best there is. He's seen about the worst I can be, and I still haven't run him off.

The man even did the yard. Nice. Love ya, Chalky.

Everyone started showing up right on time.

That's another thing that sets teachers apart. We say six-thirty, expect us at six-twenty-five, on the mark.

"Chip!" That was Ann-Kristian, a blonde Nordic type. She's here from Finland on a teacher exchange. She has the greenest eyes you've ever seen. Of course, now that she's married Victor Ruiz, she might just stay. Victor's her polar opposite, with milk-chocolate skin and burnt-cookie eyes. He's a wiry, boxer type, middleweight. On the circuit, I think, although I've never seen him box. They brought peppers, as Victor's the maestro when it comes to stuffed chilies.

"Hey, Ann." I waved from across the yard. I was at the grill, pretending to cook. However, Chalky wasn't letting me do much except hold some tongs. Heart attacks, he leaned in and whispered, when I started to take the steaks out. I wasn't allowed to so much as carry the meat to the grill.

"How's your vacation been?" Ann gave me a kiss on the cheek. "More importantly, how's the ticker?" She was setting out her peppers. She even had a knife and a cutting board. That's why I like teachers. They come prepared. I should say we come prepared, except this is my home, and I'm already here. One of my jokes. So, sue me if you think it's lousy. It was free, so toss it out if you want.

"Some vacation. The heart's fine, but the deductible on my policy is killing me." I laughed, but it was a serious dig on Houston ISD's laughably poor bottom tier insurance benefits. I was out twenty percent until I met my deductible. Of course, that's my fault, but then, how many years have I taught here, and I've never used it? I think I'll come out ahead.

"Well, the kids miss you. They'll enjoy you being back tomorrow, even if it is just half-days the first two weeks."

"Chip, stealing my wife?" That was Victor. He was grinning, and he already had a beer in his hand.

"Hey, Vic. She needs a backup plan for when you get knocked out in the ring and don't come back up. We like her here and don't want to see her kicked out of the country just because you can't stay alive."

"Chip!" Ann-Kristian laughed, but she shushed me, anyway. "Stop that talk."

"Here." Victor pulled out two tickets. "For my next fight. Front row. Be prepared for blood." He slipped them in my shirt pocket and patted my chest before sauntering off to mess with Chalky. I felt sorry for Chalky.

Ella Lund and Tamina Kendrick came through the gate together, both with foil-covered bowls. Ella brings pasta salads, and Tamina? She's my best friend at every party. She's a dessert kind of girl, banana pudding at the last one, and I could only hope tonight, also. I recognized Tamina's boyfriend, Evan Crewe. He's been here before. A nice guy. A step up for Tamina. He has family money some-where, and Tamina drives the nicest car on the school lot. Ella's plus one was unfamiliar to me, later introduced as Michel Baudin, said with a very French pronunciation. Overdressed for a backyard barbecue, but heck, first time, so no one said anything. Anyway, his fancy dress suits Ella. She's a looker, and she deserves a looker. They make a swell pair.

Mosi showing up gave me insight to his girlfriend. Not bad or anything, just that she'd come with him once, and I'd been surprised to see my man, Mosi Maalouf, with this Amara Okoro. He changed with her. Normally he was bright and funny, the reason his students like him so much. Picture this man the way he usually is: black as midnight, and big eyes, and a bigger smile. And he smiles a lot. His voice? Double bass. When he speaks, it's like kicking in the subwoofers. Boomba, man!

Not so around Amara. I attributed it to love. He was being respectful around her. Then her son Bongani came in. Stefanie said fifteen? This guy could be with the Texans. There was a player several years ago called Refrigerator Perry, played for the Bears and the Eagles, even did the Super Bowl thing in '86. Helped his team win, too. This could'a been his boy. Yet, Amara, she pointed a finger at that boy, and he disappeared to the back of the lawn to a stone bench I kept there, and he pulled out a hand-held video game.

Wow, I should have so much control in my classroom. Still, it made me look at Mosi differently. Heck, man, I thought. What are you doing with a woman like that? Everyone loves you like you are. Be yourself, man, not who this woman wants you to be.

The truth of that hit me as I stood there turning another slice of meat. *Be yourself, man.* I should apply that to me. I mean, look at me, living a lie to the world. None of these people knew me. Not really. I didn't want them to know me, not the me who saw dead step-brothers with their underage step-sisters. I'd never be able to wipe that image from my head, and heaven knows, I wanted to.

The last guest for the night was Rod Pettersen. His girl-friend of the moment was Halina Miller, who's a fashion model. Catalog, but still, that tells you she's built. I dated her once, but she was so sweet, I handed her off to Rod quick as I could. Not that I didn't find myself attracted. She wasn't the type to live with the holes in my walls or anything like that. Plus, I think Rod's been working a part-time job to keep up with her expenses. Yeah, beautiful comes at a price. I suspect Rod thinks it's worth every penny.

Rod's our PE coach. More coach than PE, but he does both, our place of employment being at the junior high level. We have track, football, and a swim team. We're well rounded, even if we struggle to place in the overall district standings. We like to blame that on the size of the district. Houston ISD is right up there among the largest in the nation. The largest in Texas, for sure. We topped 200,000 students a couple years ago, and we haven't stopped growing. But that's not the point.

Rod's not the only coach on staff, just my favorite. He's a go-getter. Early to work, takes kids for special reward activities during his lunch, and plans after-school activities, even when it doesn't come under his job description. He's that kind of guy, and we're lucky to have him.

I'm glad he enjoys hanging out with me.

Once the fajitas were done and out on people's plates, and the salads and peppers were all distributed, and everyone had drinks, whether virgin or otherwise, Rod and I happened to find ourselves sitting beside each other in two of the yard chairs. We chatted a few minutes about me being off, and what the doctors had said, and the answers were about the same as with Ann-Kristian. Then we moved on to the real stuff.

"You and Halina. You two still doing okay?" I said it casually. I didn't have any vibes or jitters. Just asking, friend to friend. Easy and offhand, like it was no big deal if he answered or not. Small talk.

"Yeah. She's the best. Keeps me busy." He looked at me and grinned as he said that, all the while stuffing a wad of meat twisted up in a roll into his mouth.

"How's that?" Still small talk, just responding.

"That ring she's wearing? Five grand. She had to have it, though."

I looked, and it was catching the light. It should for five grand. "She's getting calls, though, right?" He would understand that. Her job, modeling. When I dated her, she told me how it worked. She'd work sometimes two days a month, then she'd have four jobs back to back. She'd be gone for two weeks. Shoots, she called them. It was another reason I let Rod have her. I couldn't handle the inconsistency. My dad, remember? He hadn't held down a steady job for years at the end. I needed to know where the income was and when it was hitting the account. Teaching's like that. You don't get a lot, but it comes every month.

"Not as many as she likes people to think. Hey, what do you think about Amara's boy?"

The kid was back there with his third plate of fajitas. He'd not been a bother, so much so that I kept forgetting he was around. Once he'd asked me about a bathroom, and I'd sent him to the garage. He was just a chillin' dude, and I'd tuned him out. I glanced at Rod and shrugged. He'd shifted the discussion away from Halina. I got it. About the boy? I told him I didn't have an opinion.

"He knows someone you know." Rod took a drink, waiting, as if that meant something to me.

"Hey, Rod, I know lots of people. Hundred twenty kids hit my door every day. Multiply that by how long I've been teaching? He could know a lot of people I know."

"You got tight with Emilio. Right?"

"Not exactly tight." I laughed that off. Maybe tighter than any other teacher he had while in junior high. "Why do you ask?"

"I just hear you visit the Burger King on Westheimer. You see him sometimes."

"Holy cow, Rod. I don't go in. Sometimes he works the drive-thru."

"Hey! Not saying anything." He held his hands up in a semblance of surrender. "Just talking to a good friend. You heard about that dumpster killing on Taft? You know Charisse Winston there, I think."

"I know Charisse. What's she said?" This was getting hoary. With the heart attacks and all the other weird nonsense that had taken place there, some things were a bit hazy, but I remembered Emilio at the hospital, and Chalky had told me about going by the dumpster on the way home. That watch? Yeah. He'd shown me that, too. It was all cracked, with one of the diamonds missing. But Charisse? Where did she come in?

"You've heard about the dumpster, though. Right?" He was insistent on this.

"Chalky—" and I pointed to him, just in case he didn't remember who he was, "—said something to me about it."

"Okay, then," and he leaned in to me, like this was impor-tant, and he wanted it kept just between the two of us, "Charisse said she saw that boy near that dumpster that morn-ing. That's all I'm saying."

"I don't get the connection with Emilio."

"You don't know, do you? They're half-brothers, even though they don't live together. Oh, there's Halina. She needs me. I'll talk to you later." He was up and gone.

With the word *half-brothers,* all sorts of things opened up in my mind. I remembered that day years ago when I had that run in with Emilio. *I don't want no bruises anyone can see.* That was falling into place for me, finally. Now, Amara, and her big bruiser of a son? What would a son like that do to keep a mother like his happy?

I was starting to get juju vibes, and I didn't like that at all. In fact, it was making me angry. This was my wretched dog-gone party. Can't I even have one ripping night off without having to play god? All I want to be is me.

I looked at Bongani. I felt for him. I felt for me. Fudge berries, I felt for anyone who came into contact with me. He saw me looking his direction, and he lifted a hand to wave, all polite-like, and he smiled. I waved back, and I nodded my head. Still, this wasn't right. Fifteen-year-olds shouldn't be caught up in this absolute nonsense.

Neither should fourteens, and that's what I was trying to fix. It was coming back to me, at least some of it. M.J. needed my help, and it seemed I'd only dug her hole deeper than it'd ever been before.

Have I said to you yet that being a god sucks? If not, here goes: Being a god sucks to the underside of the world and back. I've been there, and I know, and you can take my word on that.

—24—

HECK, CHALKY HAS EVERY RIGHT to tell me to buzz off. If I were me, I'd tell me to buzz off, and I *am* me. How's that for living a life that makes sense and shows the people around you they're appreciated?

It's my dad's fault. I'm convinced of that.

Bull, you say. Your dear ole dead daddy has nothing to do with your life now. I say, Wanna make a bet?

There has to be a reason my father drank himself to death. There always is. You know, people who self-medicate. I'm in pain, bro, so maybe a few pints to get me through. However, when pain soaks your brain, those few pints only numb something that hits even worse when it returns. Then, not only are you in pain, you lose your job, your family starts to suffer, you fight with your wife, and your son starts to think you're a loser.

You're recognizing this story, huh? Yeah. I've lived it. I was finding out something else. It also affects friends. Makes them not friends, if you get my drift. Oh, but Chip, you say. You tell people to go fry themselves, and they love you. It's not that simple. And, I would never, never tell someone to go fry himself, not in those precise words. I'd say it much more nicely, like, Hey, dude, I saw a place up off the Parkway for rent. You interested in me helping you move your stuff? If that didn't work, he'd come home one Saturday, and I'd have his stuff in the living room, telling him I was finally getting around to making his bedroom my office; and of course, I'd slowly reclaim the house, until he was in the garage. And since he has a bathroom out there, he could hardly complain. It's nicer than the ones inside.

I may have to white out that paragraph. I don't want Chalky to read that and suspect I'm talking about him, which of course I am.

After everyone left, I got to thinking about Mosi's step-sorta-son, him being so big, and that mother of his just ordering him around with a snap of her fingers, and I couldn't get M.J. out of my mind. Sure, the jeebies had faded from her direction, as if she was in the clear for the first time in her life, but she was still part of the pic-ture. She was wrapped up in the criminal investigation, and would be, regardless of what that thick-headed louse had done to her. Anyone with eyes on the news could figure that out, god-feelers or no. The real eye-zinging caseload of reality was this Bongani. The moment Rod said they were half-brothers, it set me off, and you know how I am. I could not put it aside.

Poor Chalky got the worst of it.

"What the bull is this?" I yelled the question and hit a can of beer off the bar and across the living room. The crowd had gone. I'm not much of a drinker, and I've never seen Chalky consume all that much, so I was certain it wasn't his. "Who the ice-cube barnacle-eater has been in this house?"

I was crazy, but something had me blinded, and I couldn't focus on it. It felt like a needle in my eye, one at the back that I couldn't get to or even see in a mirror. Banana shenanigans, it hurt, and I was reacting.

What was different this time was that Chalky was around. I figured that out later. Living alone I had to find other ways to act out my frustrations, hence the holes in my walls. I was learning another reason I couldn't afford *ever* to let a woman into my life. I wasn't suited to be a wife-abuser, and look at what was already happening. Chalky had moved in, and already I was abusing him. How would it be after ten years of marriage? For Pete's sake, we wouldn't make ten years. I'd be in prison by then. Or messed over with a bottle of booze in my hand, like my old man.

Maybe that's why Pops drank. It numbed him enough not to beat my mom. At least not often. Thinking of her made me laugh. If I learned profanity in Afrikaans, would the evil demons leave me alone? It had seemed to work pretty well for my mom.

"What's funny?" Chalky had a towel, and he was mopping up the beer. He didn't sound upset, rather like he had come upon his favorite puppy to find it had made a mess, and while he didn't appreciate the mess, he loved the puppy, and besides, if a puppy has to go, it has to go. You can't blame the puppy.

I guess Chalky's seen my walls.

I wondered if that's how he saw me, and it got my attention. Like a parent raising a kid who was loving and attentive at seven, and now he's fifteen and can't be bothered about his mom or dad. It's all about finding the next high and hoping to get laid for the fourth time this week. Even good kids who try to stay out of trouble are like that at fifteen. You know? Of course, if you've been fifteen, you *know*, because you're driven by all that hormonal crud, where nothing else matters . . . and there I go again, getting a bit on the personal side. You're not reading this to find out what a horny jerk I was my frosh year in high school. But trust me, we all were, and that's why I chose to teach at the junior high level. They're all randy jerks, too, but too young to figure out how to jump into bed together. Most of them, anyway.

But Ryan? That's different. He was old enough to know better.

All that just to say that I realized Chalky seeing me as a puppy is how I see my kids at school. They're almost fifteen, so they laugh too loudly at inappropriate times, try to wrangle their way out of homework, and sometimes sleep with each other and get pregnant. You try to prevent it, but you know it will happen sometimes, and you help them through the mess. Abortion? I don't weigh in, but for some people it's an option. Adoption? That's happened a time or two, and every now and then the student returns to school to try again. Sometimes the parents have beat them black and blue, and then Family Services steps in. Still, they're kids, and we expect them to do kid stuff. Like babies. They poo on themselves, but no one beats them for it. It's what babies do, and if fifteens fornicate, well, that's what fifteens do, and we clean up after them and move on.

Chalky was moving on. I could see that. He knew I was still fifteen, messing myself, and that was who I was. And he loved me anyway. See what I tell you? I can't make people hate me, no matter how badly I behave. They find a reason to love me in spite of it all. How would you like to live that guilt trip?

Welcome to my crummy life, where I can't

even intentionally foul things up. Cheesitz, crabcakes, crapola, and crimeny. There. That's out of my system, and I can move on.

I finally got around to answering Chalky's question.

"Domkop," I said, laughing. I picked that up from my mother. She doesn't use it much anymore except when she gets mad at me for moving to Houston and not going back to visit her that often. You can probably figure out what it means. *Idiot.*

"What?" He tossed the towel on the coffee table and fell backwards to sit, laughing.

"Ek gee nie 'n moer om nie. That's from my mother. It means, I don't give a rip. Here's another one she used all the time. Verdomp. That one's easy. It means, dang, man, dang!" I sat in the chair opposite him and leaned my head back. "My life is vol kak. Did you know that? I thought I could pretend it's okay with you here, but who I am is going to come out. Sorry." I sat and watched the ceiling for a bit. Doing that, I could pretend my house was still the pretty thing I'd bought years before, all smooth and unpunctured, like a kid's life should be if his father's not soused on Kentucky and his mother's not yelling at him in Afrikaans. It surprised me to have remembered my mother's words. I wondered what else would come to me.

"Vol kak?" Chalky kicked the table, just enough to get my attention.

"Manure, except something worse," I snorted, reaching and pulling the table out of his reach. I also tossed the towel towards the kitchen. It was wet and would warp the veneers. I froze, hearing what I'd said. I began to smile. "I didn't realize I remembered that. My mother used to call my father that. Crikey, how they must have hated one another."

"Both were from Africa?" Chalky looked interested.

"In a manner of speaking." I stood and went to the back door, and I opened the blinds. Outside was pretty. I had lights in the trees. I like pretty, in spite of the way my walls look, and that's why I keep my yard up. I don't punch holes in the trees. Just in my walls. Out there was nice, with the yard, and the grass all trimmed by Chalky. The grill, now closed and against the fence. Chairs still out. "We never had this in Queens. Sure, sidewalks, the basement game room Pops took over for his swill den, and Mom's garage. Never a real yard, though."

"You don't talk about him. I just knew your mother. Isabeau, I used to say, gimme a rum toddy. She slapped my head one day for that."

"Did she give it to you?" I was smiling. It sounded like her. If she loved you, she hit you. Not hard, but you remembered.

"The toddy? When I was twenty. You were at school that day, and I'd stopped by for something I'd left. Your mother was dancing in the game room. She was so funny. You want you toddy, Mr. Chalky? I give it to you today. And she twirled in a circle, wearing one of those bright dresses she always seemed to find." He laughed. "I never had so much fun as I did that day, not with the mother of one of my friends, anyway."

His words made me homesick. That was the mother I'd wanted to have. That day? I was sure she was dancing on my father's grave, or at least his memory. I hoped she hadn't buried him in the basement. What had Chalky seen in that silly little dance of hers? The fun. I knew the reality, and it hadn't been pretty.

"Your parents. Did they grow up in Africa?" He seemed determined to hear about this.

"South, not Africa. South Africa is a completely different place. Like Costa Rica and Texas. Both on the same continent, but not the same at all." I was still looking outside, trying to soothe the roughened memories with the orderly and ordinary back yard just out the window.

"Okay, South Africa. Tell me."

"My mother, yes. That's where Pops met her. She was a barmaid at a little place in Jo'burg. Once when he was mostly sober, he told me how beautiful she was the first time he saw her, her hair wrapped in a bandanna, teasing all the men who came in. Pops? He came to America as a kid, and he'd gone back to find his roots." I said the last three words big and broad. I was making fun, and

I hoped it came through.

"You knew your grandparents, then?"

"On my dad's side, only one. I see Mom's when I visit every year or two." It was an easy question, and on one hand this was easier to explain than my parents. On the other, I couldn't explain it at all. "I met my dad's mom the first time we were down there. She never came north, and my grandfather died before I was born." I shrugged, as if that was it, but it was the way my grandfather died that twisted the story into something beyond belief. Then, you know my story, so maybe you would believe it. So, if you want to know, here it is, and the rest of you, skip about a page or two, and I'll pick you up there.

You see, as near as I've been able to piece the story together, my grandfather came to America, but he never really left his homeland. And no, Queens was not his homeland. He ran from South Africa, ran like a bat away from something that had tormented him since he was a teen. As I tell this, remember, I wasn't there. This is all pieced together from oddball bits that I can only make sense of because I've lived it for nearly thirty years. Some of the information came from my mother; other bits I eavesdropped when Mom and Pops didn't know I could overhear their verbal fisticuffs. I even picked up some from my Grandmother Engelbrecht on one of my South African tours. Not much, but some. You'll understand better when I tell you about meeting her for the first time.

Gramps (my own word, not what anyone called him) was a crazy old dump truck. I don't know all of it, but he was some sort of mystic soothsayer in Africa. Made some money at it for a time. Good money. He could see inside people, knew what made 'em tick. Not the good stuff, not everything, just the freaky undercurrents. This sounding like anyone you know? Not to point any fingers, but if I were, a lot of 'em would be aiming my direction. He tried to do positive things, I guess, but as my grandmother said in her half-whispered way, he tried to do it for himself, making money out of it. And some people didn't like the good he tried to do. The "bad people" (her words, not mine) tried to shut up the man who "did good for himself out of other people's problems." She understood that, and I think I do now, but when she said it, I thought, What the heck?

Before he came north, Gramps spent some time in cuffs, and not the real kind, like in prison. I think he was beaten a few times, once dragged behind a car, and generally made to want to shut up. He wound up mumbling to himself wherever he went, and in the end, no one believed in him any longer. Sound like anyone else we know? Except for the booze, that was Pops. See why I'm so careful? I keep it all to my walls, where it's hidden, and I can live a normal life on the outside. Like my yard, just the other side of the glass. Pretty. Trimmed. Ordinary as anything, and I want to keep it that way.

Gramps? He thought he could leave behind the craziness that had tried to take away his life by jumping aboard a boat. Maybe, just maybe he'd seen some of the craziness already coming out in my dad, and he threw enough things for two into an old suitcase, fled my grandmother, and wound up in Queens. South Africa followed him, though. Gramps didn't go out slow like Pops did. No, he showered the bathroom sink with his brains and left a hole in the basement wall. It was still there the last time I looked. My dad had already dropped out of school, and somehow Pops kept the place. That means that Gramps died there, Pops died there, and you now understand why I'm in Houston.

Grandmother Engelbrecht? Meeting her was a life-changer of an experience. That old woman? The first time we met, I saw my father in everything about her. His rancid complexion, the large pores on his nose, and his jowls, the way they sagged under his jaw. I'm glad I take after Mom. I didn't have the presence of mind to think that, then. No, it was the shock of seeing my father standing there, even if he was a woman. She grabbed my face on either side with her hands, and she pulled my eyes wide and stood looking for about three minutes. Then, she tossed her hands aside, turned, and spat on the dirt, saying, "Hy is 'n duiwel."

Cripes! I was fourteen. My father'd died the year before. Smoking cripes, I didn't speak

Afrikaans, and I knew what that meant. It was a lightning connection between my father's sour death covered with puke and booze, and the strange jeebies I was already getting from other people, weird stuff, like the high school thing with the drugs. How's a kid supposed to navigate that, with no one to help him through? It's like a gay kid, not knowing he's gay, and that first realization he wants to spend all his time with the boys, and thinking all the guys want to wrestle or joke with one another or something, and then he gets the stuffing beat out of him in the locker room for looking at the wrong crotch, and he doesn't know why. He thinks all guys feel the same way. Besides, it feels stupid good to him, right in his pleasure sausage, and there's no way in tarnation he won't want that to continue. It's only when he's being pounded in the kidneys and being told to keep his wandering eyes on his own man tool that he realizes these dudes aren't attracted to him. He's different, and it's not a good thing.

Just in case you're wondering, I pulled that from *Psychology Today*. No connection to me on this one. The story fits, though. I was fourteen, and I thought everyone could sense all this juju stuff, like, how can you not *know* your mom's cheating on your dad? That one was my friend Chadsen. He never could understand why his mother was always gone when he got home from school, until once we got an early dismissal, and that happened to be the day she'd decided to do an in-house gig, and on the living room sofa, to make it worse. I'm not sure Chaddie ever got over that one. I thought everyone could see that type of misaligned karma coming. Then, I get to South Africa, and an old woman I've never met before calls me a devil and spits on the dirt.

I was, suddenly, in my eyes, my dad, and I wanted to throw up. That's the one farging person in the whole wretched world I didn't want to be. Yet, there I was, with my mother at my side, on a godforsaken-hot Jo'burg street, being told I was a fourteen-year-old devil.

Makes you wonder how I can walk and talk like a normal, well-adjusted American, doesn't it?

Like I said, if I were me, I'd tell me to shove off, and I *am* me. I should be glad I had enough sense to come home from South Africa, get high for a year, and bed as many willing participants as I could convince to let me inside their clothes. Too bad I don't remember much of it, but it kept me sane. After all, how many devils—and I mean true, Hell-walking devils—will copulate their eyeballs out, crying all the time, just wanting to be normal, and not knowing how else it's done?

Hope to heaven I never made any little Chippers that girl-filled year. I never heard of any, but if I did, they'd be about the age of those I teach. Wouldn't that be a crock of nonsense to have someone walk into my class, and to find myself looking back at me?

Yeah, Chalky, one grandparent. The one that came to Queens. My dad's other one? She's still alive, but she's not a grandparent to me. I've seen her a couple times since, but she hasn't changed her opinion. She cried the second time, and since then, she laughs and calls me her duiwel-child. It's not exactly a grandparent-grandchild connection, and I don't see her that way. I make the expected contact with my father's parent, and then I seek out my mother's side of the family. They're great people, although more casual friends than grandparents. That bar my mother worked in? Her parents wound up buying it, and when we get together, we hang out there, laugh until the small hours of the morning, and then I sleep late and catch a noon flight to Cape Town where I attempt to surf the rest of the week before flying home, glad to head back to the Lone Star State.

The lights in the trees clicked off, and I knew it was midnight. I dropped the blinds and turned to apologize to Chalky only to realize the room was empty. Had I really stood there for nearly three hours? The room was even straightened, with the towel gone, and the beer can missing. I saw a sheet of paper on the counter, and I picked it up. There in Chalky's blocky printing was an explanation: *The can was on the patio and opened, and I was on my way inside. I thought I'd pour it out in the sink, and I was distracted. I'm sorry, Chip. You're the best friend I've ever had, and I'll do better next time.*

I crumpled the paper. I'm an idiot. I blow up at him, and he apologizes to me. To *me*. I think I'm the only real friend he's ever had, and I make a cesspool of his day, and after he put all this together for me. Hey, Pops, I thought. Got any Kentucky you want to share? I'm feeling the need for a shot.

I straightened the paper, flattening it as best I could against the corner of the countertop. I pulled a pen out of a drawer, and I wrote on the back: *You're a funny domkop. Thanks for being my friend. Chip.*

I wrote my name with a flourish. I would have said something nicer, but that'd backfire on me. This was safer. I got in a thanks, but I had it tempered with Afrikaans. Maybe the karma would even itself out, and Chalky would know I really did care about him.

Yeah, read that again. Make fun of me if you want. I'm realizing I care the world about Chalky. I've never let anyone get next to me, really next to me, but if it has to be someone, I think I can trust Chalky. He might be a beater friend, but he's been my beater friend since we were boys, and that says something. And he lives with me, so I the heck better care just a little bit. Otherwise, we're going to hell in a handbasket. Been there. Done that. Don't want to do it again.

I flipped the light off, and I headed for bed. It wasn't until the next morning that I realized I didn't think of M.J. at all for a whole three hours.

How about that? Life's turning around, just like a Ferris wheel. I'm bound to have a great week coming my way.

—*25*—

ALL THE PEOPLE I TEACH WITH, how lucky can I be?

People who do this job don't realize exactly what they've got, that it's something you can't get in almost any other profession in the world. Sure, the kids are kids, and that means there are days they're total turds, and the parents are always turds, and the hours? Forget that, because this is not an eight-to-four job, no matter what the people down at the assembly plant say. We just clock eight to four, and we get all the rest of our teaching done on our off hours. Like the M.J. stuff, and days spent in the hospital, and two heart attacks. You seeing it? Teachers see *that*, and they forget the good stuff. The warm stuff. The welcoming stuff.

Mrs. Chen? Always peering at me over the top of her

glasses? She pulled me into the nurse's office and handed me a giant handmade cinnamon roll wrapped in foil. Patted me on the side of the face and told me to refrigerate it and only eat a little bit every day. Take care of the heart—and she patted my chest, too—but enjoy the roll. She smiled and held up two fingers pinched together, with about an inch between them, whispering, A small amount at a time, and she shooed me out the door.

Like I said, teachers don't realize how special this is. M.J.'s mom? She ran off and left her. See? Life outside school can be hard. Just ask our kids, the ones who are turds. They're turds because they have turd lives.

When I saw Mrs. Lamar, strong and very-much-in-control Mrs. Lamar, I made a point to tell her I'd spoken to M.J. in the hospital. She was in, also, and she rang up my room. Was there any news? I didn't tell her I'd been given unofficial custody of the girl. I didn't want to go there—tell or take—but I hoped she would give me something, at least. Poor M.J. had been left in the wings so often, it was time for her to take the stage and sing. I wanted to help with that, but it wasn't my stage she needed to be on.

"Thank you for asking, Mr. Engelbrecht. You'll be hearing this later, and since Mary Jane was in your classes, now's as good a time as any. Don't discuss this with the students, but it seems there's a residency issue.

Mary Jane has been withdrawn by her father and

is on her way out of the country."

"Withdrawn? When?" I had spoken with her only a few days before.

"This morning. I received a call last night from Admin, and I met with Mary Jane's father earlier." She smiled as if she hadn't enjoyed either the early arrival or the circumstances of the withdrawal. "It's all to be handled very quietly. Factually, but very quietly."

"Thank you, Mrs. Lamar." I got it, though. It was a diplomatic issue. Girl, accosted in the most intimate way. Brother, dead. Family, illegal. With the border issues all along the Southwest, and the national controversy about immigration, this wasn't being allowed to surface. I got it fine.

"Oh, and Chip, welcome back. Your students will be glad to see you. Very glad to see you. The staff had a moment of silence for you at our meeting last week."

I smiled. That was Mrs. Lamar. I caught the name change. Mr. Engelbrecht, then Chip. My professional name for the tough stuff, and my first name for the personal. It worked, too. I recognized what she was doing, and I felt engaged. Like she cared, which I really think she does. If not, that's stupid good technique. I usually catch stuff like that, and I only ever catch control from Mrs. Lamar.

When I saw lights on, I knocked on people's doors and spoke to them, more to let them see me alive and kicking than anything else. First thing in the morning is preparation time for most teachers. Especially Mondays. Get the head in gear. Pump up. Sort out the runoffs from Friday. Fire up the projectors, all that nonsense. Thank God for science. I had lab on Mondays. I was good to go, because Kim Whitfield taught the lab course. I only had to supervise the students.

So, there I was, heading down the hallway to my classroom, my door key in my hand. The corridor lights were on, and it was quiet, just the occasional laughter coming from an occupied classroom, either someone on the phone, or teachers already in collaboration who had found something amusing. Down by the cafeteria, which was around the corner, I caught two kids wearing student council colors putting a sign on the wall. It was too early for anyone else to be inside. Students without special passes had to wait for the fifteen-minute bell. Then it'd be a stampede of mid-weight rhinos, and the halls wouldn't be safe until the final tardy bell.

Then, out popped a face I knew, right out of Celeste Boenker's advanced lit class, and she was headed the other way.

"Mary Jane?" I ran a few steps to catch up to her.

"Hi, Mr. Engelbrecht. I'm sorry. I can't talk." She smiled, that bright and charming smile she gives everyone. Pushing her hair behind one ear, she held something to her chest wrapped in a light jacket. She turned to walk away.

"No, no." I touched her arm. She was one of my few students who always said my entire last name. Most kids call me Mr. E. "Mrs. Lamar said you were gone, yet you're still here. Your mom? She, um, left me hanging. Now, you, checked out. I've been gone, and I want to know what's happening before you disappear forever."

"I have to go. Raylene let me in, but my father's waiting." Raylene was one of the student council members working on the sign.

"Did you forget something?" I pointed to what she held, and tears began to roll down her face. "What?"

"It's not mine." She unwrapped it enough for me to see it was her advanced lit book. Rather, it was the school's advanced lit book. She was holding it in the arm with the cast. "Please don't tell."

I got it. Mexico. A father who only came for his daughter because she was now twisted up in State Department shenanigans. She wasn't leaving for a life of privilege. By her standards, life in her apartment, with a brother that took advantage of her repeatedly, probably *was* a life of privilege, although one where you were always trading off something you could never get back to have something that you needed to live. M.J. was bright. Advanced lit told that. This would probably be the only book she owned in Mexico.

I squeezed my eyes shut for a quick moment, just to gain control, and I smiled, giving her a gentle knuckle bump on the shoulder. "Tell what? All I see is your jacket. You have a good life, M.J., and I'll miss seeing you around here."

"Kay, Mr. E. Bye." She smiled, and she walked quickly towards the outside door by the cafeteria.

I didn't see her leave the building, and I had no idea what her father was driving. Or if they were in an Immigration SUV, State Department black with deep-tinted windows. It didn't matter. I had no control over it. It's what teachers do. We keep our dumplings wrapped safely in our hands while we have them, and when they walk away, we open our hands and let them go. I'd noticed the names, though. I had called her M.J.—unintentionally, by the way—and she called me Mr. E. I like to think that in that moment, we stepped aside from the student-teacher formality that we all had to dance around, and the connection became stronger. Maybe it was being in the hospital at the same time, my connection to the dumpster, or simply the fact that I had tried to help her when no one else would. Somewhere I felt a connection had been made, and hopefully it would help her out in whatever happened to be her life from this day forward.

I headed straight for my room after that. No knocks, no mini-conversations. Just my room. When I flipped on the lights, it was about as I expected. The floors were clean, of course, as the custodian would have taken care of that, but the rest of the place was a jumble. Supplies were out and opened on the counter by the sink. A chart was down, showing the periodic tables. Some smart aleck with a board marker had made a suggestive drawing on top of the colored blocks. You know, an outsized sausage attached to two oranges. Eighth grade stuff, but fixable. I took out a spray bottle and an eraser and wiped it clean. There was other stuff scattered, but what irritated me more was supplies haphazardly returned to the shelves. Crooked, like they didn't care. With my house like it is, I need my classroom to be orderly. Not a jumbled mess.

I made a point to set Mrs. Chen's cinnamon roll in the small fridge I keep at the back of the room. My desk was—and I was grateful—less jumbled. I pushed things aside, pulled my lesson planner from the drawer, and opened it to last week. This morning at lab would be my time to sort out what the rest of the week would be, but most likely I would bump everything forward, as long as it didn't conflict with anything on the campus schedule. Before I could open it, I got a knock at the door. It was unlocked, and I saw it open a bit.

"Chip? Are you back?" It was Stefanie from next door. Her light had been off when I'd gotten to my room, or I would have said something, no matter how much of a hurry I was in.

"Entrer, Stef." I gave her about half the French I know, other than bon appetite. I slid the lesson planner to the side, inadvertently knocking a metal ball off the desk. It had a magnetic clapper inside, one that only rang when it was jarred. It rang, and I jumped.

"I didn't mean to startle you." She laughed, and she pointed to the far side of the room. "I see you cleaned your chart. Did you look underneath?"

"More profanity?" I shook my head, and I picked up the spray bottle.

"Gillian and Tony drew you a picture. Your last class all signed it. I know you've got to catch up, and I won't keep you, but we're really glad to have you back. Oh, the party yesterday. How'd it go?"

"You missed the best fajitas this side of the Mexican border." I chuckled. She had, but if I knew Stef, she hadn't lacked for a good time.

"I won't miss the next one. Anyway, I've got my projector warming up. I'll see you at lunch." She waved and was gone.

Under the chart? I found a mad scientist in a white lab coat, with red eyes and wild hair. There was a black explosion going on, with smoke everywhere. Why do my students see me as a mad scientist, always blowing things up? Or maybe they want me to blow things up. Still, all around the drawing they'd written little notes, signing their names with flourishes, or circles over their letters. One said, Be bad, Mr. E., and it was signed by Gippy. I've never had a Gippy, so that one con-fused me. Others, though, said, Don't ever be gone again, or Too many movies!, or such stuff. It was heartwarming, and I decided to leave it for the day.

When I returned to my desk, it hit me. I'd talked to M.J. in the hall, and not once had I felt a twinge of juju juice oozing from her. She was a clean slate, like one-way glass. Shining on the outside, pretty and new, and only she could see through. My side had become a mirror. I couldn't see inside any longer.

That was usually a good thing. For M.J.? I certainly hoped so. Then the bell rang, telling me I had fifteen minutes. The kids would start to show in about two, though, and I had better be ready.

Heck, I'm always ready. I'm a god, and gods are never surprised. Right?

Let me say that again. Gods are never surprised. Right? Tell me I'm right. C'mon, dude, just say it, once, for me.

Even you aren't helping out today, so I'll have to do it myself.

Gods are never surprised, and who cares if you don't agree. Got that? Who cares, doofus. I will make it through this day, and I bet, I really bet, that everyone here loves me by the time the day is over.

It'd be easier, though, if I loved myself. Thanks, Pops, Gramps. You're the champs, for making me what I am today.

The door opened, and it was little Jimmy Carver. I've nicknamed him Cricket, from Jiminy Cricket. I called out, "Are you having a good morning, Cricket?"

He grinned, leaping into the room. He does that, leaps. "Great, Mr. E. I'm glad to see you back."

His voice was like his walk. He spoke in vocal leaps. See? I make fun of the kid, and he loves every moment. However, just for a bit, I felt like a real god. A skinny little kid with a silly nickname who couldn't walk or talk normally was glad I was back at work, because he would be spending part of his day with me.

Heck, that makes anyone into a god. And toss you, because sometimes I get that, and this morning? I'm not willing to share. So, feel free to turn the page or not. You get to play god with my story, but I get to live it. Lucky me.

Thanks, Cricket. Like I said, lucky me.

—26—

RYAN GALLAGHER SIMPSON has come back to dump on me again. How messed up is that? He's dead, the crazy idiot. Why can't he stay dead?

I see you rolling your eyes. Yeah, the guy's dead. Ashes to ashes, and all that crud. You can't put ashes back together again and expect them to take up their bed and walk, well, not unless you're the almighty God in Heaven. Note: I understand the difference between me, god, and him, God. He gets to be God, and I'm forced to play god. Forced. I mean forced, because I don't want to do it.

You see, I was at work, and I had the kids in Kim's lab. They were heating water over Bunsen burners and making balloons expand, and as I watched, there were all these different colors—red, green, purple, and a few yellows—and I saw the kids working. It hit me, this was just like my life. Those balloons, all exactly the same, and yet, every one as different as daylight from night. You wouldn't mistake one for another, would you? Table A has a red balloon, and when it slips and gets away, the kids shriek and leap out of their chairs, so, of course, three other kids have the same thing happen, but they don't rescue the wrong balloons. Each group ends up with exactly the same balloon they started with. They're fundamentally the same but individually as different as can be.

I saw all that, and I watched the kids, each one as different and as individual as anything on this earth, yet three of them wore the same brand of jeans, four sported the latest style of Nike high tops, and at least two had hair that seen from behind was identical. To top that, they were all fourteen, or there-abouts, had all the right body parts—the ones I could see—and listened to the same music when I had my Fun Friday activities at the end of each reporting period.

The same, yet different. Ashes to ashes, and dust to dust. To the casual observer, ashes and dust look very similar. Yet, they're different, with different properties, chemical makeups, and uses. You can use ashes as an upholstery cleaner and preservative, heck, even an insect repellant, but dust? Well, dust is dust. I kept seeing that arm with the watch, and stuff started becoming clearer to me. Stuff I'd forgotten. Chalky had told me some of it, but there was more, so much more I'd been remembering, and some of it was beginning to fit together. Not well, yet, and certainly not all of it, but any piece that would fall into place, I'd take.

Later that day, after school, I drove by the old dumpster. It'd been nearly a week. For Pete's sake, you'd think after a week and all that's gone on, the juju would have faded. M.J. was gone, Ryan was gone, and even the tape from around the dumpster was gone. Flames alive, I hadn't even felt drawn there. More like I was checking off old boxes, making sure the balloons were really red and not blue or yellow, or maybe I was making sure they were all really balloons, and not something else, like kids or dust or ashes.

Holy frijoles, I hardly know what I mean.

The real reason, though? I don't talk about this much, because it's sort of creepy, but when I've had an experience like at the dumpster, it doesn't all simply go away, clean and pretty-like. You can't treat it like a love affair with the porcelain queen, where you can wipe the rim, and everything inside flushes away, leaving life sparkly and clean smelling. No, what I go through leaves an odor like walking into a really clean bathroom, and you know it's clean, except there's that hint of a smell that suggests someone has been in recently, and they really took care of their business while in there.

Yeah, it was about as I expected. The dumpster reeked.

It wasn't a smell, either. It was a feel, a sense, a glow, if you will. I drove by, and more than once, just scoping it out, eventually stopping on the street with my engine running and the window down, just looking at it. Hoping I would get some peace out of it. Hoping, hoping, hoping, like, Mary Jane, be at peace. I wanted that connection there. I refused to drive by her apartment. You thinking Ryan was creepy? A teacher doing drive-bys on a student's apartment? That's only a step up from the Ryan thing, and I wasn't going there, not even to salve my tortured conscience.

The dumpster's mass of metal hunkered there, like a pit bull. I knew it wanted me. From the stink, I knew it was loaded up. Not being fenced off, it could be used by anyone, and probably had been. To top it off, the pit bull had bad breath.

"Crap and double-crap," I growled, and I pulled up and cut the engine. I wasn't irritated. I had gone past that. Climbing out and slamming my door, I ignored that I was outside, it was daylight, and I was still dressed for work in my second-best clothes. I went up on one foot, and I kicked the side of that dumpster with the heel of the other, and as it clanged with that hollow sound metal containers have, I yelled at it, "Leave me alone!" I did that three or four times, until I had my hands on my knees and was panting for breath.

Man, I'm so stupid. Just out of the hospital, on an easy, slow regimen, and I'm doing side kicks into an inanimate metal dumpster. I limped back to my car, forced the door open, and fell into the seat. I glanced at the dumpster where I'd kicked it, and I snorted. Then, looking closer, I saw some of the new paint had scraped away. Turning my foot, sure enough, there was some of that new paint, wedged into the pattern of the rubber. I slipped the shoe off to flick the paint out the door, when a darker spot caught my eye. Rust. A nodule of rust attached to the original paint. Slobs. Can't they at least scrape it down before painting it? How'd they think it would hold up? It'd begin to flake again within months in Houston's constant humidity.

Turns out that wasn't a piece of rust. It was evidence. How's that, you say? Remember those balloons? They didn't have to look the same to be the same. And all those kids, completely different, every one of them. Yet, they weren't different at all, not if you looked at them in the right way. If you looked at their shoes, their shirts, and the music they listened to, they were all exactly the same.

How's a piece of rust look the same as evidence? Carbon, that's what. Plain ole carbon. Everything in this world, and I mean every idiot thing is made of carbon. They're all the same. All we have to do is erase the colors, and they're all the same.

I went to flick off that bit of rust, and it was

stuck. I scraped at it, only to see a flash of color leap out at me. Holy moly, I thought. What was that? If you're into science at all (and I am) you know that compressing carbon a million times will give you something very valuable. Sometimes. Well, always, but if it happens in nature, it's worth millions, and in the lab, about fifty bucks. Remember that busted watch Chalky tried to throw in there, and it sent me into a crazy, murderous headspin? I think it was calling home, because right there in my hand, my idiot hand, when I scraped away its rust coating, was a little diamond stuck to my sole, barely more than a chip, but nevertheless an honest-to-god real son-of-a-gun diamond.

I'd bet my soul, if God's given me one, that it fit in that busted-up watch back at the house exactly. Thank you, guys, for not scraping down that dumpster. Now, to find the arm that watch went to. That would be a really big deal. I slammed the door and started up my car; and shifting into gear, I pulled onto the street. Immediately, my car coughed and died.

"What the heck!" I put it in park and turned the engine, only to get zero results. I take that back. It turned over smoothly, just refused to start. Before I had time to get really angry, my phone rang.

"Chip? It's Chalky. I'm glad I caught you." He sounded out of breath.

"Yeah?" Duh. He didn't think I could tell he was Chalky? He was the only one who sounded like Chalky. I was glad he'd called, though. Chalky doesn't carry a cell, and I needed to know where he was—because I might need him to come give me a ride.

"Um, you might want to go by the gas station before you go too far. I, um," and I could see him scratching his head, "ran around all weekend in your car, and I forgot to fill it."

I glanced at the dash to see the gauge on the bottom and found that, thank you, Chalky, he'd set the little LCD digital screen to show the speed limit rather than the range until the fuel was exhausted. I tapped the dash by the fuel tank, and the light for Low Fuel flashed once, then blinked before burning steadily.

"Chip, you're not saying anything."

"Yeah." I said it with exasperation, just blowing the word out of my mouth with a gust of breath. I didn't know what to say. A knock on my rear fender got my attention. "Hang on, Chalky."

"Chip, is that you?" It was Charisse from the Center across the street. She laughed, very brightly and pleased-sounding, and walked forward. "That *is* you. I heard you were in the hospital last week. What was it about?"

She was up to my window by then, and very pretty. She's about my age, bumping around thirty, and I consider her my friend; but working at different schools, our con-nection's decidedly platonic. By my choice. Not willingly, but for my sanity and her well-being.

She's very pretty, though, and today, especially, in a black wrap and pumps—and in the light of where I was and who had gotten me there—a breath of fresh air.

"Just a minute." I held the phone to show her, and I told Chalky I'd call him back, all the while with my eyes on Charisse. I tossed the phone aside. "You're dressed up, today. What's going on? By the way, you look very pretty." I smiled and meant it. I was responding, something that should need no explanation.

"Thank you! I had a parent conference this morning, and I didn't have time to change. I saw you over here. This was so sad, wasn't it?" She peered at the dumpster before pointing to my car. "Are you having trouble getting it started?"

"Gas." I glanced in my mirror to see a small Nissan. Charisse's. I turned to her and shrugged. "A friend borrowed it this weekend, and he didn't tell me I was out."

"Your low-fuel light isn't working?" She smiled at that, and I tapped it so she could see it blink off, then back on with another tap. "I can give you a ride to get some, if you think your car'll be okay here."

"You are a champ, Charisse. The car's not going anywhere until I get gas, so my guess? Yeah, it'll be fine. Let me lock up."

I did, placing the shoe in the glove box. I didn't suppose Charisse would think it too odd I was wearing only one shoe. To pull the diamond loose? I couldn't afford to lose it, and I didn't think I could lose the whole shoe, now could I?

"So, one shoe? That's odd." She looked at my exposed sock as I fell into her front seat.

"I injured my ankle. Stupid accident, but I can't wear my shoe for a day." Cripes. I remembered that about her. She always notices everything.

"A day?" She laughed at that. "I've had first year nurse's training. I know better than that. Besides, there's no cast, and no brace, either." She had her car moving by then, and Elvis crooned from the rear speakers, something about his blue suede shoes.

"You're an Elvis fan?" I thumbed toward the speakers behind us, immediately realizing how that sounded. Ruder'n raspberries. I sank into my seat.

"I love Elvis. I didn't think you'd know any of his songs." She tapped a button on her steering wheel, and Elvis grew in stature. "So, what was the hospital visit for? Your foot?" She grabbed my leg, my good one, right on the thigh, and she squeezed it before patting it and resting her hand on my pants leg. She smiled as she did so.

"Dizzy spells, and I wanted to have it checked out. I think we'll put this elsewhere." I moved her hand and placed it on the console. Her fingers that close to my, ahem, personal area, was giving my personal area a workout, if I can, uh-hem, get my point across.

I'm sure you can use your imagination. Like I said, Charisse looked really cute in what she had on. Really cute.

It turned out Charisse had an empty plastic jug in her trunk, and it had a lid. It wasn't much, but it would get my car on the road. And talking, we decided to meet up at a foodie joint for a burger, only to find we were really enjoying each other's company. It was nice, rather like being a normal person, and I began to wonder why Charisse and I'd never spent more time together. We, after all, had taught in the same district for years, seeing each other at workshops and once working on a summer project together for two weeks. We'd almost become a number that time, but you know me. Girl gets close, and I remember my mom and Pops, and I'm not doing that to anyone.

Well, I would have overlooked that with Charisse, at least for that summer, because I was getting really worked up over her, except every night I lay in bed—without Charisse—and remembered the pictures of my parents when they were first married. They seemed so happy. Oh, sure, Pops always had this haunted look around the edges of his eyes, but he smiled in all those pics, and my mom, well, I never saw her that happy when I was a kid. Never. I knew what it was. It was Pops. He'd driven her to become the slightly crazy, Afrikaans-slinging demon that I'd come to know as my mother.

Crum. What a memory to have when you

want to start a relationship with a beautiful woman. That summer I pictured Charisse turning from the beautiful woman I spent those two weeks with, to yelling at me in Afrikaans, and me stroking a bottle of Kentucky like a giant man rod, just hoping she would go away and leave me alone. That can turn you off women pretty quickly. At least any woman who's really beautiful, and especially one that I like.

I'm not sure Charisse understood why the end of that project was the last time she saw me that summer. It seems like I told her I had to be in Queens, the "mom" prop. Yeah, I ran away. From a beautiful woman, I ran away, like a scared little boy with his tail between his legs. Tonight? I think the M.J. thing had gotten to me, and after a week in the hospital, and knowing Chalky was at the house, you know, I suppose my iron grip on not involving someone else in my life slipped.

That was the reason I awoke at midnight, and I was in Charisse's bed, and she was lying beside me. There was light from a stained glass window just over the headboard. I discovered she rents the top floor of this funky old house, and there's a street light on the corner. I could see the glow on the ceiling. I knew before I picked up the sheet that I was sans boxers. I looked over at Charisse, and she was turned my direction, with her hair swirled across the pillow. Beautiful. God-awful beautiful. How could I ever have chosen to live without her?

But then, I know how my life goes. I'm

cursed, so why didn't I close my eyes and try to get some sleep? Seeing Charisse had to have been the trigger—remember her hand on my leg in the car—because I felt something going on down there, and that was right when my vision began to narrow, and I knew some weird stuff was about to happen. I didn't want it to happen. I wanted to be here with this woman, enjoy her company, and just lead a normal American life.

Then I was swept up in it, but it wasn't me. I was feeling it, but it was that shadow memory of Ryan going down on M.J. It was making me sick, just thinking about it, a fourteen-year-old, and I was involved, even if I tried to tell myself it wasn't really me.

I'm an idiot. Oh, I'm stupid. I fought it, but it was too late. I felt myself let go, and in that blinding rush of sensation, I fell into a cesspool of swirling nightmares that made me want to choke.

Only I couldn't. To my dismay, I discovered I was dead.

—27—

CLEARLY I'M STILL ALIVE. You're reading this, for heaven's sake. If you want to read the story of a dead guy, try *Ryan's Tale of Aborted Immortality*, because he obviously didn't make it past twenty. Or pull out the Bible. All the guys in there are certifiably dead. Me? I just wish I were sometimes.

You know how I can push back time. Sort of reach into the past and watch things unfold, a little voyeuristic joyride into moments already lived. Except it's ridiculously unpleasant when I come out, and I only do it when my god-thing forces me into it.

That night I didn't get a choice. I was sucked under time and shot off to another part of the continent. Oh, you don't know about the "across the continent" thing, yet. See? Stuff happens, and not even I can keep up, much less keep you in the know.

Under time. Let me try to explain it to you. It's like slipping your hand under a blanket to play with a cat on top. It chases, and it pounces, but you can never really touch one another. Yet, if the cat pounces too hard, it can tear your skin. I was the hand, poking around under the blanket of time, and I suppose if I tried, really tried, I could reach through the blanket and hurt the cat, too, maybe find a hole in the fabric, or create one.

I want to be clear on this. The blanket thing I just described? That's nothing like the weird-wu-wu stuff I see when I'm back time. Under time, whatever. It's to give you some sort of understanding how it works. This time was plain off the charts. I wasn't tingling, I was on fire, all over my body. You know how I've told you I start to sense things back time? Not that night. It was a slap in the face, right there, with week-old lasagna, and smelling about as bad.

Let me try to describe it to you, and maybe you'll understand. It's like using an energy transporter from the 29th century, one that disassembles you an atom at a time, and then reassembles you, except it's not set correctly, and it reassembles all the nerve endings wrong side out. And then it drags you over a million jagged rocks. Yeah, *that* energy transporter, the evil one. Then there I was, surrounded by cactus, creosote, and rocks. Great big wretched rocks. Heck, what does that mean? Mexico? Remember, back time means I don't have a perfectly clear vision of everything. What I look directly at I can see pretty well, but it's tunnel vision, and the deeper I am, the more tunnel the vision. Like fog, the kind you can't see through.

This was bright as daylight, so I suspected this wasn't back time. Back time is dark. This was like when I turn up the brightness on my electronics, and everything is, well, not washed out, but hidden behind the brightness. You've seen it, where the bright light comes forward around the object, and you can still see thick objects, but the really thin ones, like faraway telephone poles, become next to invisible. That's what I was getting.

I felt like this must be the big one. I was really dead this time. The overriding question hit me: Had I done the god-thing well enough? Had I cracked enough nuts on enough bad juju to get out of this crazy messed-up life I live? Like, do I get my wings?

Then it hit me. I don't have a god-thing. I have a god *curse*. You don't get *rewarded* when you're cursed. This was a cactus nightmare, with creosote bushes and rocks thrown in for good measure, and I was here for a reason. So, I waded through white molasses to find what had drawn me to my very own cactus purgatory.

That was when I heard Ryan's voice. For

what it's worth, I never even met Ryan, not in the real world. There had been M.J., and yeah, I was pulled into all that court stuff, but to sit and talk with him? I would've kicked the bro's backside to the other side of the room before I had a decent word to say to him. So, I had to ask myself, how the shama-lama did I know it was Ryan's voice? Yet, just like I know when my mom's calling me even before I answer the phone, I knew it was dead Ryan. The thing was, I'm the one responsible for taking the sorry jerk out of circulation. So, then, why did he sound so fundamentally *nice?*

"Hey, there, Mr. E. That's what M.J. calls you, isn't it? Mr. E.? Is that okay by you, for me to call you that?"

I turned, and there, stepping around a cactus, was Ryan Gallagher Simpson, all in one piece, and glowing with an aura that even I would have to describe as heavenly. His clothes? SoCal beach, and carrying a surfboard, to boot. Doesn't that take all? He looked stupid good. More sixteen than six feet under.

"Ryan?" His name just came out of my mouth, a simple question, but I was thinking, Man, why be so polite to the sucker? I shook my head, knowing the answer. It goes with the teacher in me, and maybe, being a god, it comes out. I wish I could be mean sometimes. I sure wanted to now.

"Hey, I'm headed down to catch a few waves. Ever surfed before?" He ran a hand through his hair, and I realized it was sun bleached. Thick and sun bleached. And his eyes, that deep blue that sucker punches all those impressionable fourteen-year-olds out there. Or at least it sucker punched one. His step-sister, M.J. He shifted position, and I realized he was carrying two surfboards.

"I'm not—" I started to say, I'm in bed, and I'm *involved*, you know, like, my gentlemen's parts, and I remembered who I'd been with just before all the weird undertime stuff took over. I glanced down and realized I was also in board shorts, with beach shoes on. And just past the next cactus, a roaring surf was tearing into the sand.

"I love Baja in summer." Ryan smiled, his white teeth flashing, and he handed me the second board.

It hit me, the looking-sixteen part. He wasn't the nineteen I remembered from the trial. I wouldn't have known M.J. then. What was up with that? I grabbed his arm, asking, "How old are you?"

"Old enough to drive. Just got my license. Gonna move in with my mom and my little step now that I've got my freedom. How's that, homie?" He did a hand thing in the air, I guess to show his approval, but it went way over my head.

"So, you're not living with them?" I hadn't known that. See how messed up this god business is? I get half the information, and I have to figure it out from there. That's why I screw up so much stuff. After I asked the question, my next thought was, Ryan and M.J. didn't grow up in the same house. Somehow I thought maybe that's what this funky juju was all about.

"Been at my dad's, Mr. E. He said I had to have a car before I could move." We were standing in the waves by then, about knee high when they were out; but they were hitting us on our shorts as they rolled by, getting us wet. The water was cold. I looked at him, and his face went red. "Sorry, man. I shouldn't keep on calling you that without your permission. M.J. tells me how much she thinks of you. She's my girl, and I'd do anything for her. I see a whoppin' set about to roll in. Follow me." He leaped forward, stepping high, his board held over his head with both hands.

My thought? Like, what would you do for her? Wax your board on her? Ride her like you do one of these waves? Then walk away with about the same concern you'd have for a wave that was great but's no longer useful to you? And I was puzzled, too. If Ryan was sixteen, how could M.J. tell him anything about me? She hadn't met me, yet. Man, this was a screwed-up version of under time, or whatever version of time I'd been sucked into.

I snorted and brushed that aside. I didn't have much sympathy for Ryan Gallagher Simpson. I wished I had my knife with me. He still had all his mojo attached, and this was my chance to cut it off. Yet, there he was, whooping it up on his board, and honest to God, I didn't think he'd bedded her yet. I think the boy's wick was clean. By all accounts, maybe he'd never been with a girl at all. There are kids at sixteen who haven't. And he seemed likeable enough. What the devil had gone wrong?

He rolled up on the end of a breaker, laughing, his skin glistening, and he waved to me, calling out, "Did you see that takeoff? I was effin stoked! Sorry, man!" He laughed, brushing water from his face, and he ran up to me. "Sorry about nearly cussing. I'll watch myself."

I thought of the camera, and I cringed. Yeah, Ryan, you'll watch yourself. I realized I'd seen more of what he had inside his shorts than he knew. He threw an arm across my shoulders, and he jerked me towards the water. Then he slapped me hard on the back, yelling at me that I was a chicken turd if I let him take all the best waves.

Man, I thought. How often do I get to Baja? The sun was bright, the sand was hot, and the water was ripping. Even if I wasn't. I yelled back that I was out to get his backside, and I high-stepped after him. I know how this looks, that I was out surfing with a known child molester, and I was having the time of my life. But, by all accounts, he wasn't a child molester, yet. He was a kid with a brand-new license, and all he wanted to do was rip some waves. And I found I actually liked the little wanker. Sometimes I wonder if that's how Jesus felt. He knew all the people around him would rip him to shreds and hang him up to die, but he acted like he liked them. But, you know, it's like me and Ryan. They hadn't *done* anything, yet. They were still innocent, and as we know, Jesus *was* God, so he had to know ahead of time he was going up big time. Yet, he still ate lunch with them, laughed with them, and he forgave them when they nailed him up. So, before we worked through the day, somehow I'd forgiven Ryan. I mean, this Ryan, not the nutcake that got roasted in that dumpster. That loser deserved his hellish death, however cruel it was. This one? He was a good kid. I did wonder what made him turn, but that wasn't anything I'd ever know, not unless it just jumped out and bit me on the tush.

We crashed on the beach afterward. Funny, the sun was still straight overhead. I didn't catch it at the time, but we'd surfed for hours, and there we were, high noon, digging our toes in the sand, and watching the best waves on the Pacific coast roll in one after another. He threw some sand at me and laughed.

"You're a good dude on the water. Where'd you learn to do all this?" He motioned to the waves stretched out before us.

"Never thought about it." Cape Town, maybe? Except, even there, I'm never all that good. I threw some sand back at him. "And you can keep your sand."

"Yeah." He fell back, his face to the sun, and his eyes closed. "Always wanted to live with my mom. My step-dad never wanted me. Now I get the chance. You ever had something you wanted so bad, and then you got the chance? It's the best feeling in the world." He was grinning like it really meant something.

I glanced at him, and I looked away. I didn't want to look at him. I felt confused. I liked this guy. Really liked him. I have kids in my class like that, the ones that engage you, and in spite of yourself, you look forward to seeing them each day. It's like the day's better with them than without them, even when those are the screw-ups that spend a quarter of the year in detention. I was wishing I'd known this kid before all the bad juju started up. Then, wrapped up in that, my mouth turned itself on, saying something I'd never ask a kid in the real world.

"You're sixteen. You ever been with a girl?" Yeah, that was tame, but that type of question is not part of my job description, the teaching one or the god one. I dropped back and closed my eyes, soaking in the sun. I felt just as uncomfortable with waiting on the answer as any normal human would be.

He just laughed. After he quit, he tossed some sand at me and said, "I'm sixteen. Whaddya think?"

His laugh didn't ring true to me. Maybe I should have dropped it, because the answer was immensely personal, but this mattered, and a lot. And when else would I have the chance to talk to the younger version of a real dead guy? I might just learn something here. And, he was already dead. What would he do, rat on me to the police? Forget that! I sat up on my elbows and looked at him this time.

"Yeah, you're only sixteen. Have you slept with a girl? The real thing, not just in your imagination." Asking such a direct question? That curled the hairs on my tongue.

"You've got a way with words, Mr. E." He glanced at me and laughed again, but this time it seemed forced. "I hope you don't talk like that around my little sister."

He didn't answer my question, though. I also thought about how old M.J. was if Ryan was just now turning sixteen. Ten? Eleven? She was still a little girl to him. Not old enough to attract his attention. I hoped.

"So, answer my question. Yes or no will do. Have you been with a girl? It's that simple."

"Why do old guys like you do this to kids?" He sat up and crossed his legs, and he looked out to sea. Then he pounded his fist into the sand. "That's why I need a car."

"Because you've done it, or because you want the opportunity?" I wasn't letting this ride. My visit under time was feeling sticky, like it was about as far as I could push it, and if that was so, I was about to lose this opportunity at any moment. When he didn't answer, I grabbed the wrist that still pounded the sand, stopping him. "Who have you been with, Ryan?"

"No one, and forget you!" He yanked his arm away, and when he turned to glare at me, his eyes were red. "I've never been with a girl, and I want to every day. There. Now you know the worst thing about me."

I knew a lot worse than that about him. I knew he'd pounded his little sister more than once, and he'd spent time in prison for it. I watched him throw both his hands to his face, then push them into his hair. He laughed.

I asked, "So, that's funny?"

"No, you are. Look at what you got out of me. I should punch you, but I can't. It feels good to admit it. I've never had the nerve, not once, case closed." He had his knees up, and he was punching the sand between his feet again. He took a deep breath, looked at me, and threw another handful of sand my way. "Why'd I tell you that? Nobody in the whole world knows that."

"I've got a trustworthy face, I guess."

"You've got a butt-ugly face. But you're a heck of a surfer. For an old-man grownup, you're pretty okay. I like you. What do you think about that?"

Man, someone tells me they like me, and after bleeding all that crap to me . . . well, I wanted to continue this conversation. However, I suspected it was about to end. Up time was yanking pretty hard on me, and the white molasses was swirling around and getting pretty thick. I had to wrap up whatever it was I was supposed to do here, and it didn't feel like a day surfing was what this was all about. I had to press harder, and this boy saying he liked me had me regretting it. Bummer. Even I had to feel sorry for me.

"Ryan, this is important. Who are you really attracted to?" I was hanging to a rubber band by then. Barely, and it was about to snap. Own up, Ryan. Your little step-sister, by any chance?

"There's a girl on the pep squad I really like—"

The fog was swirling, and I was out of time. I laid it out cold. "Mary Jane? You ever wanted to be with her?" Would you do that, sixteen-year-old Ryan? Slip one to sweet sis?

"Hell, no!" He leaped to his feet and backed way. "Who do you think you are? She's my sister. You're crazy, old man." He jabbed a finger at me and turned and walked down the beach.

Then it all snapped, and the whole day began unraveling, faster and faster, our discussion on the beach, riding all the waves in reverse, Ryan taking the surfboard back, until it was a blur. See, I know it sounds easy, but there's undertime friction to deal with, and it burns like Long Island frostbite to do this. Remember that "across the continent" thing? It does this, every time. It hurts like a knock to the nads, except all over your body. You guys get that. For you women who are still reading, I'm guessing you can compare it to a urinary tract infection, and then you realize you've consumed four glasses of beer, and you really have to go. Yeah, you're getting it, now. It feels dadgum awful, and colder'n a load of freeze-dried fish.

When I came out, I was back in Charisse's bed, but it sure wasn't like waking up from a dream. It was like being crushed back into my body, and it stupid well hurt. My undertime me hit my real-time body, and I was screaming like a banshee. My back arched until I thought it would break, and I guess the only things touching the bed were my feet and my shoulders. I scared Charisse, because she leaped up screaming, too, except she was on the bed, jumping up and down. I rolled over and fell to the floor, panting, and I remembered my heart. Holy cow, I was killing myself. I'd be stupid dead, if I didn't quit taking these repeated night trips to under time and back.

I was convinced of one thing. Ryan forcing himself on M.J.? That kid on the beach with me, and his reaction to my suggestion? He was repulsed at the very idea. Heck, no, not his baby sister.

Yeah, even I picked up on that.

And crazy as it seems, my phone starts to ring about then. Here I am in Charisse's floor, buck naked, and I scramble for my pants on the back of a chair. In the dark. Well, under the light of a stained glass window, but that might as well be in the dark, when I'm digging blind in my pants pockets. I pull my phone out and turn it on just before it stops ringing. What do I hear? Afrikaans! It's my mother calling me in the middle of the night!

"Chris, jou mot!" Not bad, as she'd only

called me an idiot. "Where you be, you fool! I come to see you, and you no home." Mom does that sometimes, falls into this fake patois when she wants to tweak someone's feelings. When I hear the "Chris," I know she's trying to get to me.

"I've been to Hell, Mom. Thanks for asking. What do you mean you came to see me?" I looked at Charisse to see her glaring at me, and I thought, *been to Hell?* That was a stupid turn of words. It might be true, but it was also easily misunderstood.

"I spend time with your friend. He no understand you, either. I am embarrassed he have to see your house."

"Yeah, Mom. Remember Pops? I'm his son."

"And I am your mother. I want to see you when the sun comes up. Goodbye." And the line went dead.

"Hell?" That was Charisse, from the bed.

"Not you. Not Hell. Sorry."

Then, she held out her arms, we kissed and made up, and, well, we were awake already, and I'll leave it at that. If you want to read the pornographic version, try the Internet. They've got all the nasty stuff you could possibly want. Charisse and me? Let's just say, it was a long time before the sun came up, and we made good use of it all.

—28—

"BE STRAIGHT WITH ME, CHALKY. What's Mom doing here?" We were outside the house in the drive, and her big Buick from when Pops still had money took up half the space. It was a monster car that spoke more of her unwillingness to give up on some old dream she'd once had than it did a desire to drive an old Buick. Mom could've traded up. She chose not to.

The garage door was up, and I could see the door to the house was open. It has a screen, and sometimes I let natural air circulation cool the house. Chalky's car was in front of mine, so this side of the drive was crowded.

"She's crazy. No offense meant toward your mom, but I've got bruises up and down my arm." He pulled up his sleeve, and sure enough, good ole Mom had been smacking him like the crazy woman I sometimes suspected Pops had turned her into.

"If she hits you, she loves you. Get past it. Why's she in my house?"

"Something about time."

"Time?" That perked up my ears. I remembered a watch, and the diamond still on the bottom of my shoe in my glove box. Now, most of you out there would think, pull up your training pants. It's a watch. Lots of people have watches, and if your mom's here about the time, it could be any watch.

Just for your juices, my mom's never "just about something." That Afrikaans she sprinkles around? It's infused with juju. When I was a kid, sometimes I thought she was cursing Pops. Then I slowly realized Pops was cursed when he was born. Mom just made it worse.

"She said your life is broken, and it's time for you to fix it. What's that about?"

"Leapin' lizards, Chalky! I should know? I haven't even talked to her yet. I just want some kind of warning what I'm walking into." I turned and leaned against the car, my arms on the roof, and I put my head down, face to the side, staring down the street. Charisse's bed was looking pretty good to me. Did Chalky want to take over payments on a house? I'd gladly give it up, my mom thrown in for free. The place has a really good bathroom in the garage.

"Why're you wearing one shoe?" Chalky bumped me on the leg with one knee. "Were you in a fight?"

"With the devil." I lifted my head. I guessed Mom was up. There was a lot of noise coming from inside the house. "I suppose I should tell Mom hello."

"You think? She was really upset when you weren't here last night." He grinned at me, as if that made everything all right.

No. Everything'll never be all right with me. But I could give my mother a little bit of my time. Now, before I tell you how it went, let me describe my mother. I've painted her as a demon from Hell, and that may be the case, but to look at her, you'd never know. She was young, still, when I was born, so she's only in her early fifties. She looks ten years younger, and downright girlish when she feels like teasing around. Her hair is creamy chocolate, and naturally curly, the kind actresses pay salons big money to get artificially, and my mom gets it for free. Except, she hates it, saying it takes too long to dry, and when it's humid, "Wat de duiwel," she'll moan, threatening to cut it all off. She never does, though. It's like Pops. She could have cut him loose and gotten back to a reasonable life. She didn't, though. Her hair? Maybe it reminds her of being a girl back in South Africa. Who knows? When she moans about it too much, I start to hate it, too. But it's beautiful, and sometimes I tell her that.

"Christopher?" Mom's voice called, and I knew she was unhappy. She never uses my complete name.

"Hey, Mom! It's good to have you here for a visit." I called it loudly, glaring at Chalky. He grinned back. "I'll be right there. I've got to get my shoe out of the car."

"Let me come help you." The screen door screeched open, and then it slammed.

"Mom, you don't have to do that." She was already out the door, though, and I held out my arms to give her a hug. She looked stunning, already in full makeup. Her dress was a sunburst yellow, with a red belt that matched her lipstick.

"My baby!" She took my arms and gave me an almost kiss on the cheek. She knows I don't like lipstick marks, even when she claims it's smudge proof. Then she stepped back and slapped me hard on the arm. "Ek sal jou donner!"

"Ow! You already did!" What was the point in threatening to smack me after the fact?

"Is what I wished to say to you last night. Now, I get my chance. We should go inside. Is food ready for you." She pointed to Chalky. "And you. You come in, too."

"Thank you, Mrs. E." Chalky had a big flippin' grin on his face.

"You, I see it in your eyes." My mother grabbed my arm. "You been with a girl. Do you marry her?"

"Mom!" I jerked my arm free, glancing at Chalky to see him laughing. I remembered the visit with Ryan, and it colored my more intimate memories of Charisse. It also reminded me of what I'd grown up with and how it'd destroyed my mom and Pops. Marry Charisse? How could Mom ask that?

"I see. It is like South Africa. The boys, they take it for free, and the pretty girls, eh, so much for them. Come. I have something for you later." She took my arm again and smiled at me. My mom is really pretty when she smiles. She should do it more often.

"Who was it?" Chalky grabbed my shoulder and whispered the question in my ear. His face looked like a kid outside a candy shop. I elbowed him, telling him to back off.

Inside, I was relieved the place didn't look totally different. I've told you I'm not a pig, in spite of the holes in the walls. One doesn't make the other. What could my mom do in one night other than rearrange the furniture? She might have tried, though. God help us, Chalky would have been in there helping her out, most likely.

It was what was on the bar that caught my attention. Steaming eggs. Sausages. Two glasses of orange juice. Freshly squeezed, if my mom had the time. I'd forgotten this. Maybe if she'd done this more for Pops, he wouldn't have been so cruel to her. Then, maybe he didn't have any choice. Anyone seen the

- 245 -

gaping holes in my walls? They don't help me like Pops any more, but they do help me understand him.

"Now you sit down to eat, baby, and I'm bringing you a plate. You, too, boy." Mom pointed to Chalky.

I noticed she'd cleaned up her grammar. She can, when she wants. It's how I read her sometimes. She uses the patois like a crutch, like sliding back to South Africa to pull some sort of magic juju nonsense out of her past to help her over a rough spot in the present. Now? With the proper grammar? She was getting what she wanted, and that meant I was about to get hit with her craziness, some gobbledygook weird nonsense, because that's how my mom operates. She can't just show up and be a mom, fix me breakfast and wash my socks. No, it's a game of tease this, suggest that, and manipulate the world into just what she thinks it ought to be. She's done it to me enough times. Too bad I didn't know she was planning this one. I'd have hung garlic over the doors.

"This is pretty cool." Chalky was digging into a plate of eggs. "She wasn't like this when you were gone."

"Enjoy it while it lasts." I had biscuits and gravy. The gravy was filled with little chunks of sausage. It was greasy. She'd probably made it with the sausage drippings, just like I like it. Egad, I bet this would be bad, if she was building me up like this.

"What's that mean?" Chalky licked his fingers. "She's here. You're here. You've got an extra room. Maybe she should stick around for a while. You think she'll mind if I borrow her car when she's not using it?" He grinned.

We turned at a noise from the other side of the room to see my mother dragging in a big trunk. The black kind that you see in old movies. It looked heavy.

"Mom, what's that?" I set my fork down and turned my chair sideways. A black trunk? No way in heck was that good.

"You!" She stood, still fresh in her yellow dress, and she pushed her hair back from her face. "You should be more a man. Take your stuff when I ask you to take your stuff." The word "stuff" came out of her mouth like she was saying dirty diaper poo; and it tasted too bad for her to get her tongue around.

"That's not mine. I've never seen that before." I looked to Chalky to see him still shoveling in eggs. He'd covered them with catsup. That turned my stomach, but then greasy sausage gravy? Whatever fits down the gullet, I guess.

"Is your grandfather's." Like that should mean something to me.

"Grandfather was dead before I came along." I turned back to my plate, and I folded a biscuit in two and pushed it into my mouth. The flavor was gone, though. I was thinking of that trunk. As a kid, I'd been a nosey little weenie, getting into things I wasn't supposed to find. There was this door in our house that was always locked. You know the kind, the dark closet under the stairs where no one ever goes. It had a keyhole in it, and one day I figured out to shine a penlight in it, and maybe I'd be able to see what was inside. I hadn't really *really* seen anything before Pops grabbed me by the arm and yanked me to the other side of the next week, except that whatever it was had been black, just the color of that trunk my mom was being so kind as to dump at my house.

What the fragdaggle was she getting me into now?

"I don't want that old trunk, either," I called to her, focused on finishing off the final bite of my biscuit. I licked my fork while waiting for an answer.

"Um, she's not in here, Chip. Those eggs were the best. Ask your mom if she can fix them with jalapenos tomorrow."

"Not here?" I turned to see that, indeed, she was not in the room. "Like, where'd she go?"

"The garage." He'd already moved back to the bar, and he was scraping little sausages onto his plate. About then we heard her car start up.

"No, you're not, Mom." I swung out of my chair, and I leaped for the door, flinging back the screen and running through the garage. Crazy woman! I had to catch her before she drove off. She'd come here for no other reason than to dump that trunk on me, and I didn't want it. Not if it was my grandfather's. You think my father was crazy! You don't know the stories about my grandfather.

I chased her halfway down the street, yelling at the top of my lungs, but Pops didn't skimp when he bought cars. That Boston whaler she drove had a monster big engine, and Mom kept it tuned till it purred like a kitten. I caught the smell of her exhaust and not much else.

So, people out there? The next time you complain about your mother, stop and give her a hug. How many of you have one that will drive halfway across the continent just to dump an old trunk off at your house, and then not even say goodbye before she hauls her backside back to Queens?

For crying out loud, I come from a messed-up family.

"Chip?" Chalky was outside the garage, and he was holding something up. "She left this, too."

"What is it?" My chest was hurting, and I wondered if I'd messed that up by running after her. Crazy woman, she has me; she and Pops screw up my life; then she tries to kill me the week after I have a heart attack. I didn't care what she'd left, but not to ask? I take that back. I wanted to know so I could call her up and scream at her about it. I love my mother, but sometimes I don't like her very much, even if she does have beautiful hair.

"Here." He held it out to me as I got to the house. It was a manila envelope. Not the flat kind, but one of those lined with the bubble stuff. The ones where you can't tell what's inside until you open it.

"Not now." No, absolutely not now. I threw myself past him, ignoring the envelope. I was thoroughly irritated, not at Chalky, but well, he was here, and Mom wasn't. Crum, she even screws up my friendships, then runs the shiitake mushrooms away.

I know why my father hated her, even if it takes this to admit it; but then, I did move halfway across the continent to get away from her.

"She said it was important," he called after me, letting the screen door slam after him.

"Finish your sausage." I was stopped by the trunk. Oh, man, it was black. Not real black. Not shiny, not flat, just black. Empty black. Crazy empty black, like light hit it, and nothing got away. Like it ate light for a snack and wanted me for the main course. Picture being in a cage with a lion that hasn't eaten in a week. I wanted out of there.

"What's wrong with the lights?" Chalky was standing next to me, and his shoulder bumped mine. "Brownout, you think?"

His question made me shiver. I looked around. Through the door and into the back yard, things looked fine. The lights in the room, however, were dim, like they were grayed out. So, that meant I wasn't crazy. The weird black trunk was doing exactly what I thought. It was eating the light, every bit of it. Then, one of the overhead lightbulbs popped, sizzled for a second, and the glass exploded. Electricity shot from the socket directly to the trunk, and for the first time I could see the surface, really see it. And it wasn't black. Not by a danged long shot.

The lousy trunk was alive, and it was reaching out for me.

"Power! Kill the circuit breakers!" I yelled it at Chalky, although I didn't realize I was yelling, and when he didn't move, just stood mesmerized by the brilliant charge of pure power streaming down from my ceiling, I yelled again, "Chalky!"

No, I thought. I realized he was leaning forward, and that the magic box was probably trying to eat him, too. No wonder Pops yanked me back from that keyhole so quickly. Light must wake this thing up.

No, no, no, no. Chalky was about to go in. I was about to lose the best long-term friend I had. I had to do something.

I didn't make the best choice, like run to the garage and hit the main box to shut everything down. No. Like hogwash, I couldn't do that. I had to be heroic, to physically move the box that wanted to eat me for an entrée.

This stinks, I decided. What can an electric shaman-box do to a god? And if it was really bad, maybe I didn't have to play the god part any longer, and I could be free, even if that meant being dead. I didn't even think about Mary Jane. In that moment, all I could see was freedom. I wanted it more than anything in the world. I screamed at the box to let Chalky go, because I was the one it wanted, and I wasn't the heck letting it take anyone else.

And I leaped, with everything I had, to get that trunk as far from Chalky as I could; and when I slammed into it, my thoughts became a series of exclamation points rattling my teeth out of my head. All I could put together was a series of ten words.

"For the love of Mike! What have I done now?"

I AM A GUY. NOT TO BE TOO GRAPHIC, but I have all the appropriate man parts. I've used them a few times, too, and quite effectively. Sometimes alone—it's a guy thing—but with the opposite sex occasionally; and I've found the experience isn't too shabby.

You gotta protect all the equipment, though. For the women out there who are still following this, skip the next three paragraphs. If you don't, I'll embarrass the crud out of you.

See, you squeeze a guy's testes, and you can take him down. Literally. Somehow, due to a messed-up God, the testes are connected to the mammary glands; and if you can imagine running a hot, threaded needle up inside a man's scrotum, through his testicles, then follow his groin past his stomach and across his chest cavity and out his nipples; and then yank the line as hard as you can to try to pull his testicles out of his nipples, you've about got the first surge of pain that comes from a good, strong impact to the nads.

Yeah, it feels exactly like that, except maybe a thousand times worse.

Now imagine you're covered with testicles, and each one has a flaming string linked to your spinal cord (as if the nipples weren't bad enough), and some crazy god is yanking the hey out of that cord, and you're sure all five thousand testes are about to come up through your spine, into your head, and explode your brain all over the room.

Yeah, I think you're getting the picture. That's exactly how much it hurt, and dadgummit, why'd Chalky have to be there in the first place; why did I ever move to Houston; and *why* the *Sam Hill* was I born, anyway?

Then I was through. Whatever it was, it tried to pull a million testes through my skin and up my spinal cord, and when it wasn't successful, it relented and let me pass.

I was really irritated. When it couldn't kill me, it let me through. Only then! Willickers, that irritated me, and I wanted to punch someone in the face. I just had to find them, first.

Sorry, ladies! I went over three paragraphs.

Now I'll have the women's rights people on my case. Shikes! It's turning out to be one of *those* days. Get over it, ladies! I just had my testicles pierced with flaming needles. I'm in pain. I deserve a little slack!

Now, I intend to paint this next picture as clearly as I can, because I want you with me, and the picture is important to what happened later. After I got my testes pierced by that branding iron, I thought my vision was gone. I had my hands on that trunk, and everything around me was ghostly dim. There was Chalky, with a look of surprise on his face, and the box was still black, and my living room furniture was in the same place, even the eggs on the counter.

There was more, though. When I saw Mom still in the kitchen frying up the morning's sausage, I thought, "What in the world?" It wasn't really her, though. I mean, it was, but it wasn't, not the here and now her, because *that* her had driven away before I could call her the lowlife she really is. This was the breakfast maniac, the one who was buttering me up so she could royally screw up my life once again. Then I looked and there was Chalky, moving his things in, like he was intending to live here, no matter whether I said yes or no. And more. I saw the walls undamaged, and there was another family living in my house, with two kids: a daughter, and a younger brother. The younger brother, I knew I should know him. He was maybe four, running and yelling, and throwing a ball into a lamp. The lamp shattered, and someone was beating on the boy. It didn't stop there, and I'm not talking about the beating. I was catching glimpses, things layered on each other, and all there at the same time. Yet, I could pick and choose. After a moment I realized I could stand and walk around, in and through the action, as if it were happening around me. I looked back to see if Chalky was still there, and that's when the freakiness of all this slammed into my brain.

I was still holding on to that chest. I was having a wretched out-of-body experience.

"Freaky weird, huh?"

I turned and felt my nads tighten. "Ryan?"

"Like I said, freaky weird." He grinned. When he did, I could see his teeth were blackened, as if he'd eaten carbon, like from a fire in a dumpster.

"How are you here? This is my house. You can't be in my house. Dead people can't be anyplace they didn't live in the real world." Remember the dumpster? Heck, I remember the dumpster, and that's the only place I should be seeing this sucker.

"That's how I can be here. Watch." He reached out his hand and twisted it at the wrist. The scene changed, and the kid was throwing the ball again. It leaped out, and just before it hit the lamp, Ryan clamped his fist shut, and the action froze.

Are you still with me? I'm still setting you up, because you have to understand this. I barely do, and if I don't describe it, you never will.

When I say the action froze, the kid froze, the ball froze, and everything that had to do with the kid froze. My mom was still cooking sausage, Chalky was standing beside the black trunk, and a second Chalky was moving his bed into his new bedroom. There were several me's in there, too, doing all the "me" things I'd done over the years, including a couple punching holes in the walls. I suspected if I looked closely enough, I've see all the me's that had ever walked through the room, and that'd be a lot.

None of them were frozen.

"Feeling the freaky, yet?" Ryan punched me on the arm, like I was his friend, and we were joking about sharing a joint together.

"I . . . you stopped the action. You can control time here?"

"You can, too, when you learn to come and go. It takes practice. For now, look at the kid's face. Really look." He moved his fingers, and the scene sharpened up. It wasn't quite solid enough to be real, and the others moving in the background didn't go away. It was like layers of images on a computer editing program where you can crank up any one to override the others, but you can't really hide any of them.

Ryan had cranked the boy to full strength. I walked around him and reached to touch him, unsure if I could.

"Try it," Ryan said. "You can't interact with him. He's dead."

"Dead?" I glanced at my mom. That panicked

me. I love my mom, even if I don't like her. I don't want her dead, just in New York where she belongs. "That's my mother over there. You're telling me she's dead? I just saw her driving away."

"The kid's dead, not all these other crazy idiots. Get with it, Bozo. You're gonna burn here if we don't get busy."

"Burn?" I'd done that when I grabbed the trunk, and I didn't want it to happen again.

"Psychic burn. Flesh isn't built for long-term crossover. Figured out the kid, yet?"

"Don't know." I wasn't thinking, and I reached to him again, like I would any kid, you know, to touch him on the shoulder and get his attention. I wanted to look him in the face, like Ryan said. Except, when I touched him, it felt like I really touched him. The little boy shimmered, and he turned to me and mouthed, "Make it stop."

I stumbled and broke the touch, but I felt the terror in those words. I'd seen the kid's whole life in that touch, and I knew every bruise and scar he carried. More, I knew the ones he would carry as he grew up, and I knew every time he would climb in bed with his step-sister in revenge for watching his father kill his mother and sister, all because he was too afraid of his father to tell the police.

I wanted to throw up.

I looked at Ryan to see the same expression on his face, and his lips mouthing the same words as the little boy. He *was* that little boy, living here in my house, and I'd never known. I watched him gasp and pull himself back under control.

"How'd you do that?" He was wide-eyed with fear.

"Do what?" Heck, I was certain *I* was wide-eyed with fear. I had no idea what was going on.

"Bridge with the dead. Man, they're not *real*." He released his hand, and the boy threw the ball. His father began beating him all over again. Ryan looked as if he was about to crap his phantasmal pants. "They're *ghosts,* living their lives over and over, trying to make the pain go away."

I sensed maybe Ryan was having a freaky sort of day, himself. I pushed him. "That boy's you."

"Just before we moved. My mom and sister will be killed next week." He sounded stronger, even if he did still look pale. At least, paler than the other ghosts walking around the room.

"And your dad married Mary Jane's mother." I watched him nod. "She never was your mother. You weren't related to Mary Jane at all."

"You shouldn't have gotten that. I wanted her to be, so I always said she was. Did you see the rest?"

Believe it or not, he looked like a wounded little boy. I was actually beginning to feel sorry for the kid. How messed up was that?

"I know why you did it, now." My gut still

turned at the thought, but at least I understood. Ryan had been through a hell of his own. Hell begets hell. I was living proof of that. My grandfather, my dad, and now me. It's karma. You can't escape it.

Then it hit me. I knew what happened in that dumpster.

"You got Emilio to help, didn't you?" My Emilio, my success story, the kid I'd butted heads with and learned to love. Ryan had pulled him into his mess of a life, and now someone else was screwed to the gills. I wanted to grab him by the throat and shake him until he was a rag doll. Then he could never hurt anyone ever again. I gripped my hands into fists and spat, "You have no idea what I want to do to you."

"I couldn't—" He choked, and tears ran down his face. "I couldn't hurt her again, and I couldn't stop. You saw the truth when you touched my shoulder. Take my hand. If you could read what happened then, I want you to know the rest of the story."

I looked at his hand reaching toward me, and the very thought of touching him revolted me. I shook my head and backed away. To my side the kid was about to throw the ball again, and I knew what would happen after that. This was a living hell whose attendees got to reenact their worst nightmares over and over again.

I wanted out.

"Take my hand, you stupid moron!" Ryan's face twisted in anger, and he leaped at me, tackling me to the floor. Where his flesh touched my flesh was like a live cable feed, and every part of his life became mine, in full living color, with every strike of the belts his father used, and the fear that swallowed him when he watched his mother and sister die before his eyes, and the nightly terror of his father threatening to kill him if he ever told.

I got to live his hell on Earth, and it was a burning sword thrust down my throat. It was being soaked in living fire, and I couldn't even scream with the pain.

I tried. Oh, I tried, but that stupid sword was in the way the entire time.

—30—

I SLAMMED MY HEAD INTO THE WALL, and I could feel the blood running into my eyes. I saw red, literally. I didn't care. I wanted to die. I wanted it to stop.

Oh, the pain!

I knew it wasn't me, not slamming my head into the wall, not the blood, not the hurting. But it was, too. I was living it, and I wanted it to stop as much as Ryan did.

"So, you like little girls. How's it feel?" The voice growled in my ear. The man—a picture of him popped into my head—was about six-nine and maybe three-twenty; and his skin was carved with more hand-scored tattoos than a carney's bum. He was sweaty, pressed into me, and lifting me up every time he pushed me forward. "Is this how your sister felt when you rode her? Moan for me, little man. Act like you enjoy it."

Except it was Ryan being forced into the wall. I was living his prison experience. This was the teenager I'd been surfing with, and now he was in with the rough crowd. He was theirs. Closer to the point, I was theirs, as long as he held me down on my living room floor.

The head bashing, that was Ryan trying to kill himself. Kill me. Kill the both of us. Concrete wall, flesh. It had to work. And the tall guy was trying to rip me apart . . . *rip Ryan apart*. I was having trouble keeping the two separated. Just to get away from what this man was doing to me/us, I was all for helping Ryan finish the job. The next time he slammed his head into the wall, I put all I had into it, hoping maybe he would die, and I'd be out of this.

Then the oversized tattooed man finished with a shudder and backed away, handing me off to another guy like a limp ragdoll. This one didn't hold me against the wall. Nah, he tossed me onto a bunk and began undoing his belt. Along with Ryan, I turned my head, not wanting to look.

Light flashed, and I was in darkness. It smelled differently. Not prison, that was for sure. A fan kicked on, and I recognized it as the furnace in my house. Ryan's house. *Ryan* recognized it as the furnace in his house. I tried to differentiate between him and me. He was living this. I was just riding along.

It felt realer than life, though. If this was riding along, how had it felt for Ryan to live through it? I might be cursed with god powers, but if this was what God allowed to happen to people, then I wanted no connection to the Big Guy upstairs. Being a god ought to give you some *control,* at least of having to endure moments like this.

A door closed in the darkness, one from the next room. Mary Jane's room. I rolled over, remembering her whimpers from the night before; my brain flashed white, and I was there, nuzzling her neck, my flesh hot against hers. It was a memory, I told myself. I didn't want to be part of it. I wanted away. In the memory, I pushed against her, and I nearly threw up. It was Ryan; Ryan pushed against her. I tried to clear my thoughts, but all I could think of was the intensity he remembered. And he wanted it to happen again. The thought consumed him, taking over, leaving no room for anything else.

I'd forgotten how all-enveloping arousal felt at that age. Being a kid is messed up, even when you're messing up someone else.

"What about Emilio?" I raged at him, as he stood and moved to the door. I wanted to do anything to stop this. I didn't want to live him being with M.J., not with me inside his head. "Where does Emilio come into all this?"

"Emilio." He stopped at the door, already breathing hard with anticipation.

Yeah, I thought. It's working. I remembered

the scene from my living room, and the little boy. I'd touched him, and he'd responded to me. I hadn't been a bystander. And now, by heck, I'm changing something here.

"Don't do it, Ryan! Leave your sister alone!" I screamed it as loudly as I could. I/we were breathing hard, and I had to stop this now. Sorry, readers, for the graphic part. I was him, remember, and I could feel him—me?—fighting and losing control. He might be a legal adult, but he was barely more than a kid. At that age, when your magic fun stick takes over, there's nothing else going on in your head. You're divining for a deep well, and for Ryan, he knew the water was in the next room, and he planned to dig to China.

Sorry, again. That's about as gently as I can say it. The grimy part? I was getting caught up in it, too. No, not the sister part, but the need part. I was having to fight it off like a bear in a molasses factory. How does the molasses-mad bear not lick every wall in the place? He does, because he can't help himself, even as the hunters track him and ready for the kill.

I was afraid for Ryan to go into that other room. You find the factory door unlocked, and all the guns on Earth aren't keeping you from licking those walls. Me? I was inside the bear, and what he felt was tripping all the synapses in my brain, too. I wondered where that concrete wall was. I wanted to slam Ryan's head into it again, make it hurt this time.

"I don't want to, M.J.," Ryan moaned into the darkness, as he stood at the door.

"Then don't, creep!" I yelled it. "Take yourself out, instead, you sick excuse for a brother. Go out and blow your head off." I wouldn't have talked like that to a live person, but since this one was already dead, I didn't see that it could hurt. I wanted to distract him more than anything. This once, maybe M.J.'d have a night left in peace. Maybe he'd be dead before he bothered her again. I really let that thought carry over. I wanted him to feel what she must experience when he was with her.

Crikey, before I go on, I knew I was living a dead man's memories, but when you're in there, it doesn't feel like a dead man's memories, especially when you're caught up in how he's feeling. The anguish, the need overriding his good sense. He was crazy with it. If I didn't get out soon . . . well, I didn't want that to be part of any memory I might carry around with me for the rest of my life.

Then he groaned, our thoughts went white, and loud music began to blast my eardrums into tiny, tiny, irretrievable shreds.

—*31*—

"LONG TIME, NO SEE." It was Emilio, and he yelled the words at me. He grinned an odd, half-friend grin, the sort that says it's not been long enough, either.

Why was Emilio meeting me at what seemed to be a party bar? I'd just been . . . and I remembered what I'd just been doing, and I forced that from my mind. I looked at my hand to see Ryan's hand. I was determined not to picture that hand doing what it had just been doing the last time I remembered it doing anything at all. Even for the guy riding along, that's hard. Those memories tend to hang around for a while, and for me/us, it'd been about a minute ago.

"Yeah, been away." That was me, in Ryan's voice. Not a bad voice, not when heard from inside Ryan's head. "You gotta help me, Emo." Emo. I wanted to laugh. What a nick-name. I guess the two knew each other. I wasn't aware of that.

Emilio leaned forward, picking up one of those cardboard drink pads with advertising on it—Gia's. I didn't recognize the name, perhaps in a part of town I didn't frequent—and tapped it on the table as he spoke. "I can't, you know, get you no drugs. I don't do that no more."

This was the gang Emilio, playing a part. The fellow never talked like that with me. He was too bright.

"Here." Ryan slid something across the table. When he lifted his hand, I saw the watch. The Watch. The same one I have at home with one missing diamond.

"Man, no. Where'd you get this? You been with a rich chick?" Emilio laughed as he picked it up and turned it in the light. "This her pimp's watch?"

"Doesn't matter." Ryan took the watch back, and he pushed a button on the side. A small display appeared on the face, black within the black. "It's got a calendar and an alarm, already set. I need you to do something simple."

"Simple's bull for illegal. Man, I'm going somewhere. I don't need your stolen watch." Emilio pushed his chair back and stood. Even with the music and the yelling, I could hear it scrape on the floor. He looked at the watch and snorted in disgust. "It *is* stolen, right?"

"Wait!" I grabbed his arm. Sorry, Ryan grabbed his arm. "You know Mary Jane."

"You in her pants again?" Emilio shook my hand off and sneered. His expression looked like the one he'd carried into my classroom all those years ago. It wasn't pretty. "They put you down already for that. Or did you forget?"

"You like her, right?" I/we pleaded for him not to go.

"Yeah? And if I do?" Emilio had his nose in the air. He was about to walk away.

"I'm not touching her again. Ever. Promise. Just do this one thing for me. For M.J. Hey, for her, you will, won't you?"

Emilio sat. "What is it?" He refused to pick up the watch.

"Just a dumpster. Pour in some gasoline and light it up. Then toss this in. That's all. Then run away." He produced a glass container. It was what I'd thought. Carbon disulfide. No wonder the fire had burned so hot.

"That's all? What dumpster?" Emilio touched the watch and turned it his direction. He was thinking about this. I could tell.

I listened to myself describe the one by the school, and Emilio said he didn't own a gas can. His half-brother might have to bring the fuel. Could he get him to help, and what would be in the dumpster?

We worked out the details, agreeing that Bongani would help, and that Emilio would be helping destroy M.J.'s worst nightmare. I watched my hand lay out ten hundreds, and Emilio covered them with his arm and pulled them his direction. Seeing that, I knew, I *knew.* That's how Emilio bought that car. That was his down payment money. It was blood money, and he didn't know. How sick was this?

As Emilio pocketed the watch and money, slipped the glass container in a pocket, and walked away, I watched him with Ryan's eyes. I'd been scared Emilio wouldn't come through. I was even more scared now that he would.

Ryan knew he'd just signed his own death warrant. He reasoned, if I'm going to burn in Hell, what does it matter if it starts in that dumpster, or after I'm dead? I won't enjoy it either way.

The music grew really loud. It was so bad, my eyes began to tear up, and I'd swear the notes began to swim around before my eyes, crashing into the walls, and exploding randomly. The colors ramped up next, in kaleidoscopic arrays, growing brighter and brighter, becoming acid eating away my skin until I screamed in holy mother torment, wondering if I was dying along with Ryan the evil monster.

Just when I thought I couldn't take it anymore, my skin was ripped from my body, and I lay gasping in total darkness.

"Chip?"

"Chalky, is that you?" I realized there was a little light, only it was coming in through the back door. Inside was dark.

"Did you forget the electric bill?"

"The electric bill?" I was on the floor, and I remembered Ryan tackling me. I must have stumbled over the trunk. Curse you, Mom, for bringing that thing here. I climbed up until I was on my knees, and that exhausted me. I must be zonked from my trip through Hell with Ryan.

"The house went dark, and I think you've got a broken bulb or two. Should I check for extras?" He had his arm out, feeling his way, and tentatively moving toward the kitchen.

"Sure. Over the fridge." I stood, looking at the trunk. In the dim light, it looked like an ordinary black trunk. I wanted it hidden away before the lights came back on.

"Maybe your switch is broken." Chalky flipped the kitchen toggle up and down repeatedly.

"Might be the breakers. Help me get this trunk into the storage closet, and then we'll get the lights on."

"What if the whole city's out?"

"The trunk, please?" I didn't care about the city. I wanted this trunk out of my sight.

We dragged it in the dark into the garage, me telling Chalky the storage area out there was the only place I had enough room. The reality? I didn't want it in my house. We moved some tools out of the corner, put it there, covered it with a blanket, and piled the tools back on top. Chalky wanted to know what was in it, and I told him it was my granddad, and that I didn't need to open it. Ever. Then, for the first time since I moved in, I locked the storeroom and put the key inside a book at the top of my closet.

The neighbors still had electricity, so I sent

Chalky to look at the breaker box. Sure enough, the lights came on while he was gone. He relayed that the main breaker had tripped, and when he pushed it back into place, everything began working again.

After living with my god-thing as long as I have, living Ryan's hell for a few hours didn't bother me too much. Notice I qualified that with too much. Of course it bothers me like the devil, but I expect it from time to time.

Here's what I couldn't get out of my mind. I affected the little boy Ryan. He was dead, and he responded to me. I had suggested the adult Ryan would be better off dead. Had I played a part in killing him? Like, I know he was a douche bag, and Mary Jane's better off without him around and stuff, but would he have contacted Emilio to burn the devil out of that dumpster, if I hadn't stepped in?

This is a new one to me. You think a god would never be surprised, but this one's worrying the bejeesus out of me. I'm supposed to save people. If I've switched over to killing them, what does that make me? The devil? Crud, I don't know what I think about that.

Oh, and a second thing. I think I'll have a mother lode of an electric bill this month. Thanks, Mom. Thanks for nothing at all.

—32—

DID I EVER MENTION I'M A GOD?

Now, before you split a gut, that's a rhetorical question. Remember, I'm a teacher. I can say things like "rhetorical question" and expect you to understand. So, what's rhetorical? It's a question that doesn't have to be answered, because the answer is already obvious.

So, let me ask again. Did I ever mention I'm a god?

I watched a Keanu Reeves movie once where he played the part of a dead guy. Well, not really dead, but he'd committed suicide and got to come back to life. The Reeves character killed himself, because, like, he saw demons and stuff, and he couldn't quite cope. My opinion? God should have taken him to Heaven for all the abuse he'd already endured, but no, that's not God's way.

Heck, I know how that feels. I've been telling you about it all along. Welcome to my life, and a messed-up life it is, too.

Anyway, Reeves tries to earn his way back into Heaven by trashing all the demons on Earth he can find. He becomes the demons' worst nightmare.

Here's the point in this story. Reeves in the movie tried to do good. Real, honest-to-helping-people good, making people's lives better, Mother Teresa style. The cruel part? Gabriel spits on the Reeves character (metaphorically), telling him there's nothing he can do that will get him back in God's good graces.

Man, all I've done is help people. I've never tried to commit suicide. I'm a teacher, for heaven's sake! What can be nobler than that? We sure don't do it for the money or recognition. So, why's my life still so twisted up?

Remember that envelope? Holy cow, but I'm an idiot. I actually opened it. Thanks again, Mom. Guess what? I'm booked on a flight to South Africa. One way. Compliments of my mother.

The ticket isn't the problem. I've been to South Africa. Parts of it are pretty cool. Maybe not the parts where my family lives, but I've spent time on the coast. Nice. I can leave Houston for a week or two, blame my time away on the heart attack, and people will probably congratulate me, saying it's about time I got away.

So, what's the problem, idiot, you might ask. Remember my mom? I love her, but she's a messed-up crazy woman. Just the fact the envelope came from her was bad enough. My dad? Even more fouled up. Then there's my gramps. Poor guy, ran halfway across the world, and still his worst nightmares drove him crazy in the end.

Then there's the old lady that saw the devil inside me, my grandmother. Remember when I went to visit as a teen? South Africa messes with your head.

So, what's the problem? Inside that envelope, along with the airline ticket, was another envelope, one old, yellowed, and folded in half, then in half again. I flattened it, and in a script I recognized as my grandfather's, it said in a heavy, inked print, Old Sterkrivier Farm. Underneath was scrawled Potgietersrus with two heavy slashes underneath. The end had been torn away, and before I could catch it, an old iron key clattered to the floor.

This is where the god-thing would have come in handy. Sterkrivier? Potgietersrus? What the devil did that mean? If I'd had any sense at all, I would have never tried to find out. Then, that wouldn't be me, would it?

Cripes! Every day of my life is just another disaster in the making. I should learn to expect it by now.

—*33*—

SOUTH AFRICAN HISTORY is a messed-up story of greed, murder, and overhanded prejudice, leading to attempted and sometimes fulfilled genocide. By all that's good and right, this makes M.J.'s story seem almost mundane.

As if that's possible.

I googled Sterkrivier. It used to be outside Potgietersrus, but it's not anymore. Now, before you think all those trips down time have fried my brain, that doesn't mean Sterkrivier's moved.

It means Potgietersrus isn't there anymore.

I know, I know. How's a place get zapped off the map? Here's where the history lesson kicks in, so if you're not into that sort of nonsense, turn the page, and start reading in about six paragraphs, 'cause I'm about to bore the crud out of you.

The city of Potgietersrus is now the city of Mokopane. Mokopane is near the city of Polokwane, which used to be the city of Pietersburg, until Pietersburg was renamed. They've even tried to rename Pretoria, the capital, to Tshwane. At least the city center's retained its original name. Whew! If I get lost there, I can at least find my way home again.

Confused, yet? All the renaming stuff's because of the genocide thing.

Now, as interesting as the genocide thing is (think Nazi Germany), hold on, because I'm about to get to the *really* interesting part. The Dutch surged north to the area where Sterkrivier is today nearly two centuries ago, killed off the locals, and took their land. This guy Piet Potgieter got himself knocked off, and the village of Vredenburg was renamed after him. Hence, we have Potgietersrus.

That's only mildly interesting, I know, but hang in there.

A hundred fifty years later, the world learns the rest of the story. Old king Mgombane Kekana, the ruling monarch, was brutally murdered by Potgieter's bunch of Dutch Voortrekkers. This being South Africa, I'm pretty sure it couldn't have happened any other way. Okay, now here's the interesting part. Grandmother Engelbrecht, remember, the crazy kook who stayed in South Africa? Well, what the holy banshees if she wasn't a Potgieter before she married.

Are you getting it, yet?

If I have any fourteen-year-olds out there whose parents are twisted enough to let you read this under your covers at night, let me string it together for you. (That's what teachers do.) Gramps was crazy, but my grandmother was crazier. Her family murdered an African king. Then my father went crazy, and you know my story. What's to bet there's a connection running directly from 1840 to today, and on that string we'll find old Piet, King Kekana, my grandfather, my father, and now me.

That old trunk locked safely in my garage probably plays a wicked hand in there somewhere. Or it would if I dared pull it out again.

See what I mean? This is interesting stuff, and I'll be kicked in the behind if I'm not right in the middle of the dirt pile as I speak.

You know what this boils down to. I'm going to Africa!

—34—

I WAS THROWING MY THINGS in a suitcase. Hard. Chalky was at the door, and he was like a gorilla on my back.

Dang it! All he wants to do is be my friend, but how the heck do I make this all about him? It's all about me and Grandmother Engelbrecht. I don't even have any good places to punch more holes in my walls. I wouldn't do that with Chalky watching, anyway, so I was throwing my things in my suitcase.

It's not quite the same. A suitcase doesn't break the bones in your hand.

I watched a documentary once on Thai fighters. Those guys actually pound trees and brick walls to break the bones in their hands. As the micro-breaks heal, they become the strongest parts of the fighters' physiques. They can actually punch their opponents harder because they've broken their bones so many times.

My walls have done that for me, and it has nothing to do with my hands. It's made me stronger emotionally. God-knowledge wise. When I go under time, I don't vomit quite so hard when I come back out. I knew Sterkrivier was going to hurt. Maybe not my hands, but everything else in me.

"Hey, Chip. Won't you even look at me?"

I looked. Chalky had his hands in his pockets, and he worked his lips between his teeth like he was trying really hard to control his emotions.

"I'm looking, and no, this is something I gotta do." I threw another shirt at my suitcase, but not quite so hard this time.

"Can we get the doctor's opinion?"

"It won't change things." I didn't intend to look at him again, because he was right. I knew that. I was claiming medical leave from my teaching position, and that meant bedrest and all that other nonsense. But there was bigger stuff hitting the fan, and I was getting splattered. How did I tell the guy that I might be dead of a heart attack if I went, but I was dead with crazy if I stayed? I had the proof in my genes, too. Just ask Gramps. Ask Pops. If being dead gets in the way, ask Mom. She's bona fide proof of the crazy part. If that's too much trouble, look at my walls. That's all the proof anyone needs.

"Then I'm going." He stepped to the bed.

I wadded up the boxers in my hand and ground my teeth, wanting to say, "Like a load of shiitake mushrooms you are." Instead, I shook them out and methodically began to fold them. It was the control I fought to show, to keep from crushing him too badly. I needed to go alone. Maybe I wasn't coming back. Maybe what I'd find there wouldn't let me come back. Heck, I didn't even know what I'd find, but it wouldn't be anything positive.

"Are we good with that?"

"So, you're rich, now." That was my angle. Deflect.

"Rich? Why do you ask that?"

"You know how much it costs to fly to South Africa?"

"Um," and he forced one hand into his hair. It was the look that said I'd topped his reservoir of worldly acumen, and he had no clue. "A lot?"

"Two grand. You got that under your mattress?" I put the boxers in the suitcase, carefully this time, and I took a deep breath. I looked at Chalky. He was blinking, fast. I grabbed his shoulders, and I shook them. "Chalky? You with me?"

"Yeah." He sniffled.

"Two grand's a lot. I don't have two grand. My mother paid for this. That's how I'm going."

"You told me." He tried to smile, but it wasn't a good one.

"Now, while I'm gone, I've got a job for

you." I slapped him on the chest twice, and I backed away, calling as I stepped into the bathroom, "Can you do a job for me?"

"Think so. What're you needing?"

"The house." I was back with my bathroom bag. I dropped it in the case. "Have you noticed? It needs a little work."

"Yeah. The rat damage." He chuckled, and his color improved. He balled up his fist and worked it in and back out of a hole beside the door. "Buggers about the size of your fist."

"Thought you might have seen that. I've got a delivery coming in this weekend. I need you to open the garage for them, then see if you can work on this." I grabbed the spot he'd worked his fist into and pulled a chunk of sheetrock loose. I dropped it into the cavity in the wall.

"I can do that." He had a full-blown grin on his face by then. "And if I need more stuff, I can use your car, right?"

"I didn't say that." I threw an arm over his shoulder. "But, if there's an emergency, okay. It's just every now and then, not all the time."

"Not all the time." He was still grinning wide as could be. "This is great, Chip, you setting this up for me. I didn't know you trusted me this much."

"You're my friend, Chalky. Friends do that for each other. Now, get your butt in there and fry us up some eggs. I bought bread, so that's toast. I'm hungry."

"Got it. Eggs coming up."

Screamin' tear-jerkers! Now I had to call the home improvement store. I had supplies to order.

My car? Double dang. It was that smile on Chalky's face. After almost seeing tears, how could I say no to that?

Like I've said more than once before, dang, dang, and dang again.

—35—

THAT PLANE WAS AN ERASER wiping all the events of the past months from my thoughts.

At least that's how I thought of it on the drive to Bush Intercontinental. No funny tingles. No juju hovering just outside the car windows. Not one single premonition that anything bad was about to happen.

Holy frijoles, at the passenger drop-off, I even gave Chalky a hug before handing him the keys to my car.

My first stop was to check in my big bag. I had two layovers, Charlotte and London, so I knew I wouldn't see the bag for a while, probably never, if my luck played out like it usually does. I've got enough sense that I only put replaceable items in it, like underwear and extra shoes. What the hey, in

South Africa, it was likely to all be stolen, anyway. It should be part of South Africa's travel motto: Come See Our Country, But Leave Your Good Stuff at Home.

My most important items I had in my carry on. That key. Yeah, it's what this trip was all about. I had no idea what it meant, but it was at the core of everything. Some of you may be asking, "For crying out loud, Chip, call your mother and just ask the woman what she's trying to mess you up with now." Let me send you back about six or seven chapters to reread the crazy part. Then, once we're on the same page, we can move on. I'm better off just going to Africa and figuring this out for myself.

I also packed the watch from Hell. Literally from Hell. I put it in an old watch case, and I stuffed the diamond in with it. I didn't know the part it played in all this, but it was the only thing I'd ever brought back from a downtime journey, so it had to be really important.

I also bought the cheapest Triband phone and a SIM card compatible with South Africa's mobile networks. It's one of those things they always tell you: Don't Leave Home Without It. Of course, they say to always wear clean underwear, too, but if my airplane goes down, I don't expect to survive, and my underwear won't matter. For what it's worth, though, maybe I'll come out alive in spite of the evil juju, protected by my god curse, wearing those dirty underwear, just to be embarrassed by my scrambled sense of self-importance.

What I couldn't take with me on that flight was the normalcy of ignorance.

You heard me. Ignorance. The normalcy everyone else in the entire world gets to enjoy. Yeah, that's the state of the human race. I'm not complaining about the people around me, either. I'm the abnormal one. I like ignorance. I just don't get to enjoy it. You know the difference between ignorance and stupidity? You can teach the ignorance out of someone. Stupidity is permanent. Well, my condition has been pretty permanent all my life, so you see which category I fall into.

I wanted to be part of the ignorant crowd, smiling, greeting the flight attendants, sleeping without a care in the world, having small conversations, like the businessmen chatting about deals done well (or badly, as the case may be), couples whispering hand-in-hand, and even one set of cheerleaders in identical apparel who looked as though they were returning from a competition, calling out across the aisles to each other. I figured out the thing about the competition because they all wore blue ribbons pinned to their shirts, and they were irritatingly bright and bubbly.

That's what I wanted, a normal, average life back, as if I ever had it in the first place. Normal for me is slightly crazed for everyone else. Remember, I'm a god, and it's not all it's cut out to be, not from the god viewpoint, anyway.

As the airplane readied to lift out of George Bush, it seemed as if I might get to experience normal for a while. The ignorant kind, the normal version, rather than my variety of an early taste of eye-watering afterlife. I was already seated, and a businessman I guessed to be in his forties came down the aisle. You know the look: briefcase in hand, overcoat draped over one arm, carrying a hat. Yeah, a fedora. I thought no one wore those anymore outside of old movies and freshly minted entertainment wannabes. He saw my empty seat, and he nodded with his head, catching my eye.

"Do you mind?" He gave a bit of a smile, just being friendly.

"Sure." I smiled back, and I picked up the magazine I'd been flipping through, sliding it into the seatback ahead of me. I sat as unobtrusively as possible, keeping out of his way, impressed with his efficiency. He checked his briefcase locks, slipped it in the overhead, rolled his overcoat, and laid it on top of the briefcase as if he'd done this a hundred times in the past year. Truth was, he probably had. He slipped his suit coat off, pulled out a slim paperback from the inside pocket, tucked it into the seatback in front of his seat, put the coat in the overhead with his other things, then slid into the seat next to me.

"Tanner Hood." He held out his hand.

"Chip Engelbrecht." I gripped his hand, then released it. No juju. Funny, that was my only real thought. No juju. Not that his grip was firm, or that he smelled good. I might not be interested in men, but my nose works fine. Some colognes are invasive, designed to cover. Tanner smelled *good*, although I couldn't have told you what the fragrance was. It didn't really occur to me until after the flight was over.

"Headed home?"

Home? Sterkrivier, with an iron key under my seat, and a black watch from under time? Heavens above, I hoped not. Even so, it was an innocent question, very politely asked, and offered with a warm smile. Polished, as if Tanner might be in public relations. A normal question in a normal conversation, and I liked that. It made me feel, well, normal. I chose to answer without sarcasm.

"I live here in Houston. I'm off to South Africa, courtesy of my mother." That was true, although it shaded the facts somewhat, leaving out all the juicy parts, but then, that's not what he'd asked. He'd asked if I was headed home, and that was the information I shared. It felt good, like being ignorant. That was a positive thing. For a moment, I was almost glad my mother gave me this trip, whatever the reason.

"I'm not a movie watcher, so I came prepared. I happened on this in the airport bookstore. It's about the African Dutch."

He pulled his book from the seatback and held it out to me.

"African Dutch," I murmured as I looked at

it. It was titled, *The Great Karoo*. The tagline at the bottom read, "The Dutch East India Company's landing at the Cape of Good Hope was only the beginning. Then came enslavement, brutality, and eventual genocide." I flipped to the back and read, "The Great Trek took the Voortrekkers into the darkest parts of an Africa they could only dream of in their nightmares, populated by savages, ripe with disease, and overrun with wild animals. Conflicts were often violent, native tribal boundaries were ignored, and only the lure of gold and diamonds gave these intrepid adventurers a common goal."

"I recognized your name, from the book. With your blue eyes, I thought maybe you had some Dutch ancestry—" He took the book from me and flipped through several pages, then pointed out a passage to me. "Here it says, Herman Engelbrecht . . ."

He kept talking, even as the flight attendants began their departure speech, telling me about Herman and his adventures in the African bush. I was scanning the page, though. I had caught something else that leaped out at me.

Sterkrivier.

Yeah, you read that right. Now I was looking for Potgieter. How did I not think about this, that there must be books written about this stuff?

"You can have the book when I finish, if you're interested, since you're headed that direction. Maybe you've got some family history in here."

"Seriously?" I thought not. Better, I hoped not.

"You never know. Anyway, I'm on the last chapter." He laughed. "I had a long layover today."

"Sure. Thanks." I watched Tanner open the book towards the end and settle into his seat, then I turned to the window. We were well into the air by then, with clouds pulling at the plane, tugging us back to the ground, as if gently whispering to the wings that heading towards Africa wasn't a good idea. I could see glimpses of ground. Charlotte would come in about two hours. Then Heathrow in London. What did the clouds know that I didn't? How did they know where I was headed? What else was Mother Africa telling them to whisper into my ears along the way?

I've never thought of myself as African, and especially not as Dutch, even though I do have Dutch-blue eyes. I'm a New Yorker. Even then, New York is Dutch. It was originally named New Amsterdam. Not everyone knows that. My family came from Africa, so the connection with Europe's never been there for me. However, Voortrekker. Pioneer. People at the forefront of the expansion. Brutality. Slavery. Death. Genocide. Piet Potgieter and Mgombane Kekana.

One black watch, and one iron key.

Grandma, Grandma, what sort of funky juju have you woven into my life? What African curse have you brought down on my head? I thought of a passage I'd had one of last year's classes memorize from a book titled *The Collapsing House*. It seemed prophetic, now.

Perhaps the slaver ships all those years ago had brought more than hard-working field hands to provide free labor for the Southern plantation owners. Perhaps they had brought a piece of African Mother Earth with them, and as they had tilled the dirt, something besides the sweat of their skin had remained. Perhaps when growing children walked the soil of South Carolina, the language of Earth rose out of the soil and entrenched itself somewhere deep down in their souls.

Gramps came to Queens on a slaver ship. Nah, not in iron manacles, but he was bound as surely as any slave ever shipped to America back in the day. He'd brought a bit of African Mother Earth with him, and it had bled into my soul, becoming my hell on Earth. From the walls of our house, through the floors, and deep within the screwed-up lives of my parents, it had been there, soaking into me all the years I lived in Queens, and now it was entrenched deeply in my soul.

Sitting there on that airplane, I watched those clouds, and my eyes blurred with the purity of their voices calling to me. Turn around, Chip. Or, maybe they were teasing me along, offering me a chance for redemption, a "washing away of my terrors" so that I could become one of the ignorant crowd that never had to see what I've experienced in my life.

Fudge berries, if I didn't miss Chalky at that point. The man might be ghosting between the ears, but gosh darn it, he believed in me, even if I didn't. I was going to Africa alone. What had I been thinking?

Charlotte seemed a long way away. A stupid long way away.

—36—

I DECIDED I CAUGHT THE FLU somewhere over the North Atlantic.

Jitters. That's what you feel first, that inability to sit still, because your legs hurt, and your elbows are sore. Then there's that feeling in the back of your throat, the one where you think it might be because you haven't had enough to drink, and maybe you're dehydrated. I couldn't focus, and I made a trip to the toilet, but I still felt like death warmed over when I got to my seat.

I had pulled out Tanner's book. He'd headed off to Miami. He was meeting his wife, and they were flying down together. Exiting the plane, I thought he'd decided to keep the book. Heading down the corridor to the terminal, he felt in his jacket.

"Hey, I offered this to you." He chuckled, pulling out the book. He hefted it once, shaking his head. "Quite a story. You want to learn some of the history behind your name? This is your source."

"You sure?" To give it to me, I meant. The farther east we flew, the more ill-at-ease I'd begun to feel. Not sick, yet, I hoped, and I kept putting off thinking about it, because it might be nothing. And this was just Charlotte. What would Africa be like?

"You might be correct. It's pretty graphic." He held out the book with a visible shudder. "You're lucky your branch of the family came to America. I wouldn't have wanted to live through what those poor souls survived."

"That bad, huh?" I pictured Gramps and Pops.

"Only if you believe in that mumbo-jumbo stuff from all those Tarzan movies. You never know. They say the guy who opened Tut's tomb died of a curse. Who knows, maybe there's something to this, also."

We'd made it into the terminal, and a woman's voice called out Tanner's name. He clapped me on the shoulder, said it was his wife, and wished me a good trip, finishing up with, "If they start to chant, get your butt out of there. Take care, man." He laughed and was gone.

I stood for a moment, watching his wife throw her arms around him. She planted a kiss on his cheek, asked him something, then looked my direction and waved before walking off with him arm-in-arm. I hefted the small volume and wondered if she enjoyed dark reading material, or if it was something he indulged in alone, like would he have thrown the book away if he hadn't been able to find someone to give it to? That was when it crossed my mind that his cologne had been for her.

Now, what made me think of that?

Maybe it was bigger, the two of us happening to sit beside each other. Fate. That's what they call it. I'd researched Sterkrivier just before leaving on this trip, then Tanner happened to be reading a book about the exact same topic. That couldn't be chance. No way.

London was a long leg, and I watched a movie for the first two hours. I started to feel better once we were in the air. We were heading *away* from South Africa, but I didn't consider that. The tingle in my throat faded the longer we were over the water. I was fine, and then I got bored, pulled that book out, and opened to the first page. I began to read:

The Dutch East India Company was founded in 1602 to make its owners rich. Within 200 years, it would be corrupt and seriously in debt. It was dissolved in 1799 by the Dutch government, but the corrosive disease of European territorialism had already infected the Cape of

Good Hope and its surrounding lands. In 1652, Jan Van Riebeeck built a fort and a supply station that would one day become Cape Town.

In that singular moment of Dutch intrusion, the Bushmen and Hottentot tribes of southern Africa were already doomed . . .

"Sir, soda or water?"

I glanced up to see an attendant in the aisle. Setting the book aside, I pointed to a bottle of water, and he handed it to me with a cup of ice and a paper napkin before moving on. I closed my eyes for a minute. The tingle was back. However, that was what made me notice something. When I released the book, the tingle faded. When I touched it, it returned with a vengeance.

Dread, I thought. That's all it was. I was on this massively idiotic trip because of my effin crazy mother, and I was making something of nothing, all because of Grandmother Engelbrecht, that stupid iron key, and this book. No matter what anyone might say, the words between the covers were just a story that happened centuries ago. There was no way any relationship between this book and how I felt was anything other than something in my head.

Now, I know what you're thinking on the other side of this page. That was your clue, Sherlock. Toss the stupid book away. Take Tanner's advice. If you hear chanting, get your butt out of there. Well, that book might have been chanting to me, but if it was, I had no clue what it was saying.

What good's a god who can't read the signs in the heavens, you say. Leave me alone, I say. Let's let you be me and try to pick up on all the juju floating around in the ether.

I downed that drink, still thinking thirst was the problem with my head, and I picked the book back up. I opened to the second page.

During that first winter, extremely harsh weather whittled Van Riebeeck's small troupe by nineteen men. This should have been a warning. Instead, before the decade was out, Van Riebeeck was sending out search parties to ensure his foothold in the lands that had traditionally belonged to the native Khoikhoi people. No known records of the names of the first settlers survive, but it is now thought that among them were the Potgieter, Naidoo, Kruger, and Engelbrecht lines that dominate the country's roll books even to this day.

Of these, the most celebrated is the Engelbrecht name, a family founded in Holland, elevated into nobility, and with old family seats at Arnhem, Yzendoorn, and Middleburg. For a younger son of the noble Engelbrecht clan to not be with Van Riebeeck on this historic mission

About then was when the flu symptoms hit in earnest. I tried to read on, but my hand was shaking, and I had sweat on my forehead. I pressed my paper napkin against it, trying not to be obvious. Who wants to be trapped aboard a sardine can with a sick man, when the nearest exit is in the next country on the distant side of a very deep sea? I closed my eyes and laid the book on the empty seat next to me. My stomach began to settle, and I breathed deeply, convinced it was helping. I felt for the cup and put a cube of ice under my tongue. It was advice from Mrs. Chen. It worked with my students, so I figured, what the heck?

After a few moments, I had distinctly begun to feel better, so I decided Mrs. Chen was the best thing since sliced bread. No wonder she'd kept her job at the school so many years. I also tried to find other reasons to explain my sudden illness and its equally quick remission. Altitude sickness might do it, but we were fully pressurized. Nerves, maybe, but I didn't feel especially anxious. Lack of food; my heart; being a god. Any one of those could be the culprit, but I wasn't ready to admit to any of them.

As the airplane began its descent over London, I assembled my things to pack them away. I felt a twinge as I wrapped that book in my magazine, but as soon as I stuffed it into my bag, my stomach settled, and my headache cleared.

That's the flu, though. It comes and goes until it takes you out for two weeks. What a great time to come down with a bug like this. I wondered if the airport sold flu medication. At least if I tanked up, maybe I could get through this trip. If not, then what the heck. Once I got to Sterkrivier, I might not have to worry. A god's gotta go home sometime. Jesus was taken out on a cross. Maybe I'd have it easier. Perhaps my exit strategy was as simple as an old iron key.

Yeah, right. That's about the stupidest thing I've ever thought in my life.

—37—

READY FOR THE THIRD LEG of the flight? I thought I was. I was dreading a raging flu that would be enough to ruin anyone's aerial journey across the vast African continent. As it turned out, that was the least of my worries.

I did learn one thing that every transcontinental airline passenger needs to know. You can't punch a hole in an airplane toilet's wall. I injured two fingers finding that out. But then, you know me, crazy stupid, even when I don't need to be. Still, how the devil do you prepare for a twenty-four hour flight to the other side of the world? Leaving London meant we were only halfway there. Heathrow to Tambo International in Johannesburg was still another fourteen boring hours.

I was packed up on flu meds, though. See? Occasionally I

try to do the right thing. It's *not* doing the right thing that knocks me flat every time. It's my god-thing, and once we hit airspace over the continent, it slammed me like a fist in the face.

"Sir, we have tiramisu, steamed shrimp, or roasted chicken. What would you like to order?" A flight attendant stood at my side. I jumped at the sound of the woman's voice. I had Tanner's book out, and the stories were making my eyes burn. I was considering the meds, but I needed something to drink first. She had a drink cart with her, and I smiled.

"Shrimp, please, with tea. Oh, and water, if you don't mind."

"Certainly. Perrier or Evian?"

"Nice choices." I was impressed. Premier brands. I remembered that the first was sparkling, and I didn't want that. "Evian. Lower carbonation."

"Ah, a connoisseur. Enjoy." She offered me a bottle, rather on the small side, but it did say Evian on the side. She immediately moved to the next row and began the same question.

I set my book aside and unscrewed the lid. I took a sip and noticed my head felt better. I shrugged and decided to let the meds ride awhile.

That was when it hit, only I didn't know it at the time. Get it? I didn't know it at the time. Sorry, it's the downtime thing. It sends me loopy sometimes. I felt the plane vibrate, and I looked around, blinking my eyes. They'd gone blurry for a minute, and I reconsidered the meds, but then my vision cleared. I wondered that no one else seemed to feel the vibration, but it had stopped by then, so I guessed it had been me. Like old Scrooge said, a bit of undigested beef or something like that.

Then I frowned, focusing on the aisle seat three rows ahead. I knew that head of hair. I saw it every time I drove through Burger King. How could I have missed seeing Emilio when I walked on the plane?

The attendant had moved past me toward the rear of the cabin, and I unhooked my belt and stood, excusing myself when I accidentally brushed a man's shoulder, although he didn't seem to notice and ignored my apology. Some people. It's politeness that makes the world go round. I try to teach my students better manners than that, and usually they show it, at least when I'm around.

"Emilio?" I leaned around tentatively, just in case I was mistaken. I smiled when I saw it was really him.

"Mr. E., I was wondering how long you'd take to notice me here. You want fries with that burger?" He put his arm on the back of the seat, turning half to face me, and his eyes twinkled.

"You got your stuff together?" I grinned, and I popped him gently on the back of the head, just like I'd done that first day he was in my class back in eighth grade. He ducked his head and laughed. "I've never had a better student than you, Emilio. Have I ever told you that?"

"More than a few times. Thanks, Mr. E."

"Where are you headed, if you don't mind me asking?" I'd knelt down on one leg by then, and I punched his knee with my balled fist. He was hard as a rock. Knowing Emilio, he probably had to be to survive in his world. He sidestepped my question. He'd learned well in my class, and I was impressed.

"I'd be a gangbanger if it weren't for you, Mr. E." He looked away for a moment.

"And I wasn't real sure I could back you down." I'd been pretty sure, but I'd also been prepared to hit the emergency call button on my walkie if I needed it.

"Nah, don't tease me." He smiled, and he seemed pleased.

I followed his eyes and noticed that the plane must have changed directions. The sun had been on my side when we took off, and now it was streaming in on Emilio's side. I thought I'd have noticed that, but for all I remembered, I might even have dozed, missing lots of stuff. Flu does that to you, and I hadn't taken any of my meds, yet. I must be sicker than I thought.

He glanced at me, holding my eyes with his. "When you turned that walkie-talkie off, I knew I was dead."

"I turned it on. I wanted the office to hear."
Well, on, but the volume was down, so it wasn't

transmitting. I never wanted to embarrass a kid, not without his knowledge.

"That's funny." He dropped his head and laughed, but he whispered his next words. "Every day that year I pretended you were my dad, and I was going home with you." He glanced up, and his eyes were red.

"Sometimes things turn out all right." What else could I say to that? I put my hand on his shoulder and squeezed, holding it for a moment.

"Not always, Mr. E." He'd begun to twist his hands together.

"What's bothering you?" I was watching those hands, and I was thinking that I didn't recall seeing Emilio at the check-in counter, or anywhere in the airport. Surely he would have said something then, if he'd seen me.

The next thing that hit me made me remove my hand from his shoulder. I remembered how Emilio had filled out during his year in my class. At the King, he'd turned into a good-looking young man. You know kids that age, late teens, and no longer fresh-faced boys. They've lost that eighth-grade, baby-faced smoothness to their cheeks.

The eighth-grade Emilio was the one sitting on this plane with me.

I got the chills, remembering that vibration earlier. This didn't feel like under time, however. Under time always visited the past. I was still on my flight to Jo'burg. Nothing had changed that I could tell. Time was moving forward at a normal pace.

"You don't know why I'm here, do you?" He asked the question as if I should.

"Maybe you could explain. I saw you last at Burger King, and you yelled out you loved me. Remember that?" I needed to see if this eighth-grade Emilio remembered something that had happened to seventeen-year-old Emilio.

He leaned his head back and laughed. "I wish I'd said it that year I was in your class. Maybe things would have turned out differently. Maybe no one would have died." He paused, as if getting control, before saying, "I didn't know what was in the dumpster. You have to believe that." He shook his head and glanced at me. "You met my half-brother at your party."

"Bongani?"

"I saw you when we made that deal."

"What deal?" Now I had sweat running down my back. I knew exactly what deal he was talking about.

"That watch is bogus. Sabe? Bogus. It's why the plane's going down. They want it back."

"Emilio, you're scaring me." And I was about to soil my underwear, but I didn't say that.

"All you need's the key, Mr. E. Put it in your pocket. Keep it safe. That book you're reading will help you understand, but it's the key that's important." He looked at me for a moment, then he glanced back towards my seat. He smiled, but it was more an apology than a real smile. "You'll be safest in the toilet."

"How do you know—" The book? I didn't even have it until Tanner gave it to me. And the key? Only Chalky knew about that. How could Emilio know? I followed his look, glancing back at my seat to see myself there, my head back, my eyes closed, just in time to observe the attendant tucking a pillow under my neck.

"Five minutes and it happens. You've been asleep a long time, Mr. E., and I'm real sorry about this, but you really need to be in the toilet. Be sure to keep that key with you."

"And you? What will protect you?" My breathing had ramped up. I thought of my heart. I was worried that maybe Chalky had been right about me needing recuperation. I wouldn't get it if the plane was about to crash, and worse, if it did, I wouldn't be able to apologize to Chalky and tell him he'd been right all along.

I should have been worried about getting to the toilet.

"I'm not here, Mr. E., but you already know that. I'm sorry about not helping M.J. sooner. Don't blame Bongani. He's a really good kid. I needed his help, and he had no idea what was in that dumpster, either."

The airplane vibrated, violently this time, and I glanced back at myself. I was still snoozing. I turned back to Emilio to find an empty seat. The airplane vibrated again, and I jerked awake. My seatbelt was still attached, and the sun was back on my side of the cabin. I pulled the pillow from behind my neck and unlatched my seatbelt in one smooth motion.

Could I do this? Five minutes. I dug in my bag until I found that key, and I slid it into my pants pocket. I looked at that book, remembering the headaches, and making the connection. Before I stood, I pulled out my new phone, breaking out the SIMM card, and inserting it into the case. My hands were shaking. Snapping it closed, I fought to find the charger and the adapter the salesman had guaranteed would fit all South African plugs and finally dumped my bag into the empty seat, digging violently until I located it.

I glanced around for the time. Stupid! How long had it been? I should have checked the time first thing, and I didn't think. Double stupid. I never think, and that's the problem. However, dumping things out was a good thing, because I saw my wallet and my paperwork with my passport. I grabbed it along with Tanner's book and slipped it in the waistband of my pants. As I adjusted the book to make sure it was secure, the realization of my situation punched me in the stomach: This was really happening, and I nearly ran for the toilet.

I was sick to my stomach, and all I could do was hope everyone survived. I couldn't even warn them. Who would believe me? I would become Chicken Little, crying, "The sky is falling, the sky is falling." Well, I'd be saying, "The plane is falling," except it wasn't, yet. You get to deal with stuff like this when you're a god. It sucks, huh? Welcome to my world.

Once I got there, and I closed the door, I leaned my forehead against the wall and pounded it hard with my fist. My cold medicine was *out there!* Pain shot through my hand, telling me my bones would soon be stronger in two fingers— once they healed.

My brain finally came to, and I started stuffing everything I had in my pockets, as far inside as possible. The paperwork? It went inside my pants. If they found me dead, I wanted them to at least know who I was.

I backed into the corner as far from the door as possible, and I wrapped my arms around myself. I closed my eyes and prayed for everyone on board. My last thought was of that hated watch. What had Emilio said? *That watch is bogus. They want it back.* Five hundred people might die, and all because I'd brought that useless watch with me in my carry-on.

Then the airplane shuttered violently, and all hell broke loose.

—*38*—

YOU DON'T EVER, EVER WANT TO BE in an airplane
that's going down. Trust me. It's unmitigated terror, from the
first sound of rushing air to the final violent cacophony of
shearing metal.

At precisely five minutes—give or take a few, since I
don't wear a watch—the floor of the toilet dropped out from
under me. It was there, and then it wasn't, and my shoulder
slammed into the wall. For a moment, I thought we hit something, stopping the aircraft dead. Then the air around us began
to scream. I could hear it through the walls, with the engines
whining in an ever-increasing wail of terror. The toilet began
to shake, and I looked for separation cracks in the corners,
wondering how long it would take things to come apart while

we were thirty-thousand feet over the ground.

You think of things like that when you're not sure how much longer you have to live.

Something crashed into the toilet door. It shivered, then was still, as if someone had walked by and fallen against it. I realized I could hear screaming over the sounds of the engines and rushing air. God, I prayed, there are some frightened people out there. I closed my eyes, thinking, And I'm one of them. I wanted to step outside, to help people, because that's what I do. It's my god curse, even if I don't like it. If I'm there, people do get helped, or at least some of them, the ones I somehow make contact with.

Yet Emilio's words echoed in my head. *It's the key that's important. You need to be in the toilet.* And I could tell the pilot was trying to recover the airplane. He just wasn't succeeding. You know how an airplane rises sharply in the nose when taking off, and aims down when approaching the runway? We were doing that, although in a very wobbly, frantic fashion. We were also skewing side to side, and I was being tossed about like a Mexican jumping bean in a very giant tin can. Five hundred beans in a shiny aluminum tin can, all being shaken to bits, just hoping that the tin can didn't come apart on the way down.

Here's something you can compare. Go to Coney. Pick the biggest roller coaster. Get on it, but don't hook up any safeties. Then stand up in the seat, ride it holding on with one hand, and you get pretty close to how it felt on that airplane by the end of the ride. I braced for impact, thinking, clean underwear wouldn't have mattered in the first place. Nobody's underwear was staying clean in this hell-bent maelstrom of maleficent terror.

Then my vision flashed white, someone rammed a fist into my solar plexus, I was shaken like a rag doll, and I was sprawled out on the ceiling of the toilet like Linda Blair in *The Exorcist*. Somewhere at the edge of my hearing, the high-pitched screech of ripping aluminum sheets wove a background symphony of cacophonous subharmonics, like the jet was screaming out in pain as it gave up its final, tenuous hold on life.

Fly the friendly skies. Just watch out for the landing. It's not a bit friendly, not one wretched bit.

I grew really cold, and everything around me went black.

—39—

I LEARNED TWO THINGS my first week in South Africa. Everyone in this country gets free health care, and free health care in South Africa is really crummy.

When they learned I was American, and that I had recently undergone heart surgery, all that changed. Like, the second time I was conscious, I found myself in a private room, with curtains on the windows, soft music playing, and a big flat screen on the wall across from the bed.

My second thing to learn? Private health care in South Africa is really sweet.

"Good morning, Mr. Engelbrecht. How are you today?" A very pretty arm grabbed the curtains and flung them to the side. The track at the top whistled with the rollers, and I pictured the engines on the airplane as they began to scream with the air being forced down their throats. It wasn't the same, but that's what I heard.

"Fine, I think." I steadied myself, closing my eyes against the glare of the sun. "Where am I?"

"In hospital, but you can see that." She laughed, and it was bright and friendly. "You're quite a survivor. You made the headlines."

"Headlines?" I was still coming to grips with the sun. "What country is this?'

"South Africa, very near your destination." She was folding a blanket, and she laid it across the foot of my bed. "Later, there are some reporters that wish to speak with you."

"Reporters?" I felt like an echo, doing nothing more than repeating what she said.

"This will explain." She picked up a folded newspaper from a table in between two chairs, and she offered it to me.

"Is there a table? One of those rolling kinds for meals?" I raised a hand to take the newspaper to find an IV in my arm. That couldn't be good.

She laughed and pulled one up, positioning it and locking the wheels. It had been off to the side out of my vision, and I hadn't seen it. That was when I realized I couldn't turn my head.

"Don't try to look sideways. There's been a slight fracture of one vertebrae in your neck, and we have it braced until we can get it pinned. You're fine moving your head up and down, so no worries there." She adjusted my pillow and opened the paper for me.

Pretoria News took up the top of the sheet, with a red band just underneath. I glanced at the date, shocked to find nearly two weeks had passed. Then the headline hit me. "Unexplained airline crash. Hundreds dead." A huge photo showed a mangled aircraft spread over nearly ten acres. One wing was folded around a tree, or what was left of the wing was folded around the tree. Luggage had burst open, and the traveling effects of the dead were strewn everywhere. It didn't look as if anyone could have survived. A helicopter was small in one corner, and there were numerous people about in brightly colored First Responder gear. In smaller type, at the bottom, it read, "Three survivors live to tell tale." There were photos of me, the attendant who'd taken my meal order, and a tight-haired boy of about ten.

"I didn't get your name." I rested my arm on the paper, leaning my head back to let the information soak in.

"Nurse Sheckley." Still bright and effusive. "You can feel perfectly free to call me Moriah."

"How do you know my name, Moriah? I wasn't in my seat when we went down." I hadn't told them, and my destination.

How did she know that? Then it hit me, the hospital had access to the airplane's flight plan.

"Oh, you were very easy to identify." She

opened a drawer beside the bed. "You had all your identity papers on you."

I could just see inside without turning my head. My passport was on top, with other paperwork underneath. I recognized the edge of Tanner's book. The key was out and unwrapped. My phone. I'd never used it. They set it up at the store, then I never had the chance to make a call. Maybe my first should be to Emilio, to thank him. He saved my life, although even I have to admit, it isn't much of a life. I'm not even thirty, and I'm pretty beat up, first my heart, and now my neck. Gramps took himself out fast. Pops went the slow way. I wondered if someday I'd wish I hadn't seen Emilio sitting in front of me. That would have resolved a lot of issues in a very decisive way.

"Where did we come down?" I brushed the paper, unable to focus on any of the details. It was too much at the moment.

"Just outside a little place called Sterkrivier, near Mokopane. That's where you spent your first week." She shivered visibly. "You were lucky the pilot held his plane together until you crossed out of Botswana. Botswana is perfectly safe, but to navigate the border for medical care?" She shrugged, then brightened. "When the paperwork got sorted, we airlifted you here."

"Sterkrivier." The word was a black cloud, filled with Gramps, Grandmother Engelbrecht, Chalky, Emilio, even Tanner. What was the cologne he wore? I could still smell it. And he left me that ridiculous book. Was there a connection? I touched the name emblazoned across the top of the paper. "We're in Pretoria, not Johannesburg?"

"You'll love it here. Don't mind me, but I need to check your connections." She picked up my forearm with the IV inserted, checked the area around the port, and patted the skin in the crook of my arm. She studied a blinking box while she talked. "Do you have family around here?"

"Why's that?" She was very friendly, and with her holding my arm, I felt especially relaxed. "Can't a man just come to South Africa without a plan?"

"Your name, Engelbrecht. You're bound to be related to someone." She put my arm down, pressed a button on the box that made it beep, and crossed her arms. "The press will ask these same questions."

"My grandfather was from here. I've been back several times to see friends, but I spend most of my time at the coast. Cape Town." I didn't mention Grandmother Engelbrecht.

"Your grandfather was someone important, perhaps?"

"Hardly." I laughed sourly and looked out the window, remembering the stories of him being pulled behind a car. He'd been a rough, hardcore case, even before he made it to Queens with my father in tow. Then his life had gone downhill from there.

"What did he do while he was here?" Moriah

had moved to my IV rack, and she exchanged a bag of a clear fluid, swapping out some plugs, with her eyes busy on them and not me.

"A mystic, perhaps? What's someone like that called here?"

"Shaman works, or sometimes a sangoma." She laughed lightly. "I have a friend whose grandmother practices as a sangoma. She heals people with goat blood and medications made from plants and animals. Be glad she didn't get to practice on you."

"My grandfather could have been a witch doctor, according to the stories I've heard." I decided to laugh it off. Moriah was, and I didn't want to get into all the craziness that made up my life.

"Oh, don't call him that." She stopped what she was doing and looked at me, very seriously. "We don't say witch doctor, not in public, anyway. Your grandfather was a sorcerer. It runs in families. How about you? Do you practice?"

Practice? How about them Yankees? Think they'll win the Series this year? I pulled an Emilio on her and asked, "Those reporters, how long have they been waiting?"

"Since you checked in. You can see them as soon as you feel up to it. Doctor's orders, approved and in your files." She picked up a tablet device hanging from the end of my bed, and brought up a screen to show me. I didn't bother reading it, waving it away. "Are you ready now?"

"I'm front page news. I might as well be."

"That's a trooper. I'll give you about five minutes, then I'll give them ten. We don't want you tired out before you head back to America. It wouldn't make for very good public relations, would it?"

She laughed, and I laughed. As she exited, however, my thoughts were more jagged. How's this for public relations? Arriving in South Africa via a plane crash, spending two weeks in hospital, only to find my plane had crashed in the same location that an ancient iron key had drawn me to, an iron key given to me by my crazy mother in an envelope covered with my grandfather's handwriting, and he was an African sorcerer.

Yeah, being tired out wouldn't make for very good public relations. Surviving would make for better ones. How's that sound? Just get me back to America in one piece, and that'll be a pretty good trick.

Just don't ask the other 497 people on board my flight from Heathrow. They weren't standing up for South African public relations promos. They were already dead.

—40—

"MR. ENGELBRECHT, WE UNDERSTAND you were traveling to South Africa to reforge connections with long-lost family members." The reporter held out a small microphone on a very thin shaft. He was young, with black eyes and mocha skin. He smiled a lot. A whole lot. That was suspicious in itself. "Now that South Africa knows your identity, has anyone reached out to you?"

"Well, um, I don't have any text messages on my phone, if that's what you mean." I hadn't even turned it on. It was a stupid question. I'd only been awake half an hour.

"When you realized the plane was going down, who's the first person you thought of?" That was from a woman, and she was more rumpled, like she'd been outside waiting for a lengthy amount of time. When she smiled, it looked as if she really cared, and I liked that.

"My fellow passengers. I said a prayer for them." All the reporters responded to that, whispering into their mikes, or scribbling on small note pads. They looked as though they approved of my answer.

"Did you know Angela Limpkin, the flight attendant, one of your fellow survivors?" A third reporter stood and leaned forward.

I began to see how this was going. They wanted a human interest story. This interview had nothing to do with finding out the facts. They had those. They wanted something to sell papers, and maybe, just maybe, put a positive spin on what I imagined could well become a debacle beyond all public relations debacles for the country of South Africa.

I remembered Angela, although I hadn't caught her name. I decided to help them out. Angela's family would appreciate it, if she had one.

"Angela took my dinner order." The group of interviewers fell silent, and all eyes were on me. I laughed to lighten the mood, inviting them to picture a very good memory. "She offered me Perrier or Evian. When I chose Evian, she told me I was a connoisseur. She was incredibly sweet, a perfect hostess, and I'll miss her very much."

There. That's more sugar than I usually belted out in a month of Sundays. Still, it was the same as in parent conferences at my school. You said what people expected, then it became the truth. However, what I said about Angela *was* true, so in this case, I guess it was all right.

"The boy. Did you get to meet the boy?"

I didn't see who called out that query, but I wondered why, after two weeks, they were asking me these entry-level questions. Surely they had interviews with the other two survivors. The newspapers should be soaked with sob stories by now. Pretoria and all of South Africa must be sick of the plane crash.

"I saw his picture in the paper." I held it up, and I pointed to it, trying not to growl when the IV line snagged on the side of the bed. I worked it loose before asking, "How's he doing?"

"You don't know, then." It was the rumpled woman.

"What should I know?" The reporters were silent again.

"He never came out of his coma. We lost him this morning."

"Rachel, don't tell him that." It was the smiling man. His face was serious, now.

"He deserves to know."

"How about Angela?" Crikey, I thought. Don't tell me she's dead, too. You said survivors, creeps. Make it true.

"The doctors aren't making any promises." I missed who said that, probably the man from the back.

"She's here in the hospital?"

"Pietersburg Hospital, Polokwane?" Said like

a question, as if they weren't certain, and it didn't really matter. It meant she wasn't in this hospital.

"Why not here?" I remembered Moriah's remarks about me being transferred when they learned I was American. What nationality was Angela? Shouldn't she have been transferred, too?

"You have private insurance. You're from the U.S.A. You get only the best of care."

I wanted to throw up at that. Who the devil did these people think they were? I was hardly injured, and the doctors couldn't offer Angela any promises. I wondered why the kid died. Did he not have private insurance, either? Was that all it took, and it was your day to kick the bucket in Pretoria?

They had more questions, but I didn't have the stomach for it. I tried to answer one or two, and thankfully Nurse Sheckley called time and ran them all out.

"I apologize about the boy." Moriah pulled the folded blanket off the foot of the bed and shook it out. "I should have told you. That paper's not the most recent, and the updated ones tell more about the boy and the flight attendant."

"Did the boy have a name?" I squeezed the bedding at my side, wadding it in my fists, trying to be polite.

"It wasn't in the paper I showed you, because of his age," and she smiled, "but I have a more current one. I think it tells." She knelt and rifled through some papers I couldn't see, and she stood with one in her hand. She opened it and scanned the words before folding it back and laying it on the rolling table. It was an obit section, and she pointed. *Kobe Potgieter.* His photo, the one from the previous paper, was there, also.

Potgieter. Of course. I should have known. What else? I remembered the name from Tanner's book, and I asked Moriah to hand it to me. I was double-stupid, asking for the book. A messed-up, double-stupid idiot. The connection between that book, my flu symptoms, and meeting Emilio on that airplane was obvious. They were all tied together. As soon as I touched that book, it kicked me in the face like a billy goat on speed, and I knew I was going under.

Under time. Get it? Going under?

As I lay there, my fingers just grasping one side of the book, everything grew glassy and still, the room not quite in focus, as if something was in the way. That wasn't what I was used to, and it took me by surprise. You've seen underwater images shot under melting sea ice where the fresh water sits on top of the salt. It creates a barrier like glass, only you can swim through it. When you do, it shimmers, liquid glass that flows with the touch of your hand. That's what the hospital room did all around me. I looked at that book, still in Moriah's hand, and in my hand at the same time. She wore a smile, and I realized what was happening. She wouldn't sense anything unusual. Down time was like that. It affected me and no one else.

Well, almost no one else. That hadn't held true on several of my most recent trips.

Then the scene shifted, like a movie speeded up a hundred times just for a second. Everything changed, jumped fast forward, jerky, and Moriah was at the door, frozen behind shimmering saltwater glass, waving, with one hand on the door, already pulling it open. Everything jerked again, the door was closed, and I was alone. I looked at my hand. I still held the book. It was my connection. Something in this book wanted to tell me something, or more likely, wanted me to learn something. That's what down time was always about. You go under, meaning *I* go under, and I move outside of reality, until I discover whatever I'm supposed to learn. Putting the book down might break the connection, but I was getting psychic burn no matter what, and if I didn't give in and go through this now, it was coming back for me. I'd learned long ago that it was best to deal with it and move forward.

I unplugged the IV and checked to see if I was attached anywhere else, only then realizing I wore a hospital gown and nothing else underneath all these bedclothes. As if being sucked out of my reality wasn't enough, I had to do it with a cold, naked backside. How's that for being a god? I held on to that book and walked to the window, reaching to touch the air around me as I moved past, watching it swirl in a kaleidoscope of colors. LSD. I've been told stuff like this happens when a person is tripping. If that's so, it's not for me. My life is weird enough without it.

At that point, I was actually thinking that this wasn't too bad. Yeah, I'd survived worse. Maybe this would be an easy trip, I could find out what I was supposed to know, and I'd wake up back in that hospital bed, with Moriah coming in and adjusting my IVs while we had a pleasant conversation. I could stand for some of that.

Will I ever learn?

The windows were saltwater glass, too. I pressed on them, and I floated on through. It was wonderful for a time. The sun sparkled, the traffic on the street below gave off comforting city sounds, and I was about to decide South Africa was a pretty nice place to be, especially floating in the sky above it all. The sun grew hot, and it began sparkling off the buildings and cars. Then the sparkles started hurting my eyes. I put my hand up, only to realize I was saltwater glass, also, shimmering in the sunlight, my hand melting away before my eyes. When I stopped moving, I coalesced again, becoming solid once more.

I was about to dampen my shorts, except I didn't have any on.

That's when I heard the chanting. It might have been in Afrikaans, or maybe I was hearing through saltwater ears, but it grew louder and louder. The voices were coming from the light. Each glaring sparkle of brilliance took on a face. They were alternately beautiful and horrible, smiling sweetly at me, then shifting to crude caricatures of angry emotions that I couldn't begin to guess. I closed my eyes and tried to focus on the repeated sounds, "Koning, help ons asseblief. Koning, help ons asseblief. Koning, help ons asseblief."

Hands grabbed my arms, and I jerked. That shouldn't happen. Downtime things can't affect me. I'm not really there. And yet, someone had my arms. My eyes flew open to see a wizened old man dressed in African finery, with elaborately beaded clothing, and designs worked into his skin. He wore a cheetah cape, with more cheetah skin worked into a sort of crown. My arms flowed around his hands, my saltwater skin shimmering and becoming invisible as it coated his. I was disappearing into him, becoming him. Oh, crikey, I thought, and before I could think anything else, I was looking through his eyes.

The city was gone. Instead, the pristine African landscape stretched to the horizon. The sun cast harsh shadows, and in the distance was a primitive city. Then, the scene jerked, and we were in that city. Then it jerked again, and a battle raged, white men against dark, guns and knives, manacles and locks, male European victors mounting female African conquests in a horrific rape of the surviving population.

It was devastation and genocide come to a land that had boasted a strong and vibrant culture for centuries before the white man stepped in to screw it up.

Then I reached into myself—rather the old man reached into himself—and I pulled out something brilliant and pure, a shining golden light, and I held it up as if in offering. Its brilliance turned everything else into shadows and whispers. I stood in a worshipful pose for some minutes, my body lighted by the golden aura and filled by its warmth, when out of the shadows, a sword flashed, and pain lanced through me. I fell to one knee, feeling my lifeblood spilling onto the ground. I heard myself whisper, "Koning, help ons asseblief," finally understanding. *King, help us, please.*

I jerked, and I awakened in my hospital bed, with the curtains open, the sun shining in, and the monitor at my side wailing its alarms. The door flew open, and Moriah charged in with two other nurses. She looked at the machine, put her hand to my neck, and yelled for the defibrillator.

"We're losing him," she called out.

Losing who, I wondered. I felt just fine. I was surprised to see that my skin didn't melt into saltwater glass when they cut the front of my gown away, and it felt cold when they put the paddles to my chest. Funny, I could see the scar from my heart surgery. It embarrassed me to have it out there and exposed for all three of them to see. What would they think, me all scarred up?

About then I heard Moriah call, "Charged."

Oh, fishsticks, I thought. The psychic burn's going to be bad this time. Then, whump, my body jerked, lifting my naked butt off the bed, and everything around me flared into incandescent fireworks of unimaginable beauty.

—41—

I WAS DEAD THIS TIME. REALLY, TRULY DEAD.

At least I should have been. As far as I knew at the time, I was.

Oh, yeah, you say. Turn the wheel one more time. We've been there, done that, what else is new? How many times are you planning to die in this story?

Trust me, sucker, try dying. It feels fresh and new every time.

How did I know I was dead? By all that's great and glorious, how do you know you're alive? You reach out and touch things, your manwich hurts because you get it caught in your zipper, and you feel as if you're about to dirty yourself on account of you ate a plate of onions the night before. Heck, put your finger in a light socket and flip the switch. You'll stupid well know if you're alive or not.

My finger was stuck in the light socket. The light socket from Hell. An African Hell, if they call it that.

"Welkom om my huis." The words came to me out of the blackness, in a musical voice that carried laughter woven into every word. They made perfect sense to me, even though I didn't understand them. *Welcome to my house.*

I heard chanting similar to that from earlier, only different. Musical instruments, yeah, but these were instruments that rattled, clattered, and banged in odd, cacophonous rhythms, and yet, somehow, it was beautiful. I was warm, and I felt welcomed, really felt it, like someone had been waiting on me for a long time, and I'd finally come home.

"Is jy gereed om wakker?" Laughter followed. The words were clear this time, as if I'd heard through raging wind before, and now the air had stilled. *Are you ready to wake?*

I opened my eyes. A man was beside me sitting on an enormous seat carved from a tree trunk. One glance and I knew he was important. He was huge, wearing a more elaborate version of the outfit I'd seen on the old man in my vision outside the hospital window.

"You must know me." He waved a hand to indicate everything around him, and I could see a bonfire, with dark-skinned dancers bound up in grass skirts and tall headdresses bobbing fitfully as they twirled and ducked around the flames. In the distance, less visible, there were musicians with vibrantly festooned instruments of all shapes and sizes.

"Have I met you before?" I pictured the old man, but this one was sturdily built and virile in every way.

"This is my land. This is my people. Everything you can see, it is all mine."

"I can understand you. I couldn't before." The words tumbled out, but they expressed my amazement. When they hit my ears, they sounded like, *Ek kan verstaan.*

"Of course, you can. How can you not? You are of my own blood." He laughed, and the deep-throated sound rumbled across the landscape, shaking fireflies from the bonfire. The sparks rose into the air, forming a roaring lion that exploded in a shower of shooting stars. "Come, my woman will join us."

And she was suddenly there. No one had been at his side before. Yet, I knew she'd been there all along, just not within my ability to see her. The king stood—I knew he was a king, just as I realized the elderly man from earlier had also been a king—and he offered his hand to his mate. She stood, wrapped in brightly colored cloth, with a towering headdress of fabric and feathers twisted around a mane of glorious tresses. She could shame a fashionista with her magnificence, and she knew it.

"She is truly a woman, is she not?" The king

laughed. "She is mine alone, but she has a sister. Her, you would not want to know."

He laughed again, and she looked at me and smiled. Then she turned away, and we began to move toward the fire. As we drew closer, the heavy beats in the music increased in tempo.

I didn't know how those dancers managed to hover so close to the heat. That fire was hot. I was sweating buckets by the time we got near enough for me to realize it was a dome of flames, and the inside was empty. Okay, not empty, but there was no wood inside. It was a cocoon of flames, like a giant pizza oven, ready to slip the prepared crust directly inside.

"Is this a feast?" *Is dit 'n fees?* I couldn't picture anything else the fire was useful for. Not heat. This was Africa, and it was wretched hot, already. An oven was the only reasonable explanation.

"Nee, man." *No, man.* "You will see."

As he spoke, something began to coalesce within the core of the fire. It was no more than a vague twisting of the flames at first, then it grew arms and legs. I realized it was a person, and I was horrified that I was watching a sacrifice. How had I not seen someone inside before? I picked up wailing, and in a shower of brilliant sparks, the person inside the bonfire solidified and burst through the edge, trailing embers, and running screaming into the night.

"Oh, my God," I said. "Poor woman."

"Geen." *No.* "Is her time to die. She is welcome to my house. You, you must return." He motioned to the flames.

I caught his woman looking at me. Her eyes were dark and incredibly beautiful. They carried magic persuasion in every glance, and I wanted to step into the flames. She nodded towards the fire, and the scene shifted, as if I were looking at them from a slightly different angle.

I caught myself, and I glanced down. I'd taken a step that way without realizing it. Then I noticed my feet. They were dark chocolate, creamy around the ankles, and lighter at the edges of my feet. I held out a hand, and it matched my lower extremities.

"What's going on?" I narrowed my eyes, as if that'd make them explain.

"It is not yet time for this to become your home." The woman closed her eyes slowly and opened them again, as she partially bowed her head.

As soon as she spoke, I knew who she was. Mother Earth, Queen of the Underworld. Her nod wasn't a gesture of respect toward me. It was a command, one that I knew I was unable to resist. She was the one who regularly invited me to step out of my world and visit down time, to engage with past events, and to connect with the people who needed me in their lives. She was the old woman from the hospital, showing me my father. She knew the way into my soul, and I existed at her largesse.

Her nod was my dismissal, and my exit from her presence was through that bonfire.

Crapola. This meant I really *was* dead. And in Hell. Wait until I tell everyone about this. What if Christianity's had it wrong all along, and the devil's really a woman? Wouldn't the Catholic Church love that? They'd have to change the pictures in every one of their Bibles.

Mother Earth stepped to me and gently took me by the shoulders. My heart settled, and a wave of peace flooded through me. She was no devil. She was kindness, compassion, and love. I felt all that flowing from her. As soon as her hand touched my skin, I wanted to step through those flames. I had to. It was as if there was nothing else in life except those flames, and walking through them was what I'd been created to do. She leaned in and gently brushed her lips against my forehead before pressing her cheek against mine.

"I welcomed your grandfather, and I welcomed your father. They were not strong enough to complete the task. They are here, and they are at peace. It is up to you to undo the wrongs that have been done. I wish for you, my son, to find your way to who you are."

She stepped back, and I fell into those flames with my arms flailing. It was every bit as hot as I'd imagined, and a thousand times as painful.

I began to scream with everything I had for the burning to stop.

It seemed as if it never would.

—42—

I DIDN'T SO MUCH WAKE UP as get rudely vibrated back to life.

I opened my eyes to the sound of a drill. All I could see was the floor. Crum, but I hurt all over. I wondered if I was in burn therapy. The flames were still real to me. Someone touched the side of my face, then pulled my eyelid up. Get away, I wanted to say. I've already got my eyes open. I couldn't speak, though.

"He's awake."

Stupid right, I am, I tried to get out, but there was nothing. I heard electronic beeps, which I figured were medical monitoring equipment. What were they doing to me?

"Lie still, Mr. Engelbrecht. We have you on a local, and

we're pinning your cracked vertebrae. We suspect a pinched nerve caused your adverse reaction earlier. We were lucky to pull you back, and we want this taken care of so there's no further complication."

The voice was bright and cheerful. I thought it might be Moriah by the effusive tone, but I wasn't sure she was a surgical nurse. I knew, however, they hadn't brought me back. I'd been sent back. I was confused, though. Finish the task? Undo the wrongs? What did that nonsense mean? I was just Chip, confused godlet, bumping into trees in the dark, and totally clueless about where my life was headed.

That fire pit transporter, however, between this world and the underworld, if that's where I'd been? That was cool, refrigerated crabcakes cool. It felt like the inside of an oven, too, but I liked it. The concept, anyway.

"We're putting in the final screw. Mr. Engelbrecht, blink once if you understand what I'm telling you." A mirror appeared below my face.

I blinked. I just caught a woman's eyes looking back at me before the mirror was pulled away.

"Good. I'll be putting in three stitches, and then I'll apply your bandage. We'll flip you over, so be ready for that. You should regain the ability to speak in about twenty minutes or so. Until then, we'll try to ask you yes or no questions, and you can reply with one blink or two. Do you understand what we're about to do?"

I saw the mirror again and blinked. The mirror disappeared.

"Good man. Are you comfortable?"

I was face down, watching the floor, and seeing the shoes of whatever doctor was toying with my neck. He, or she, had a black mark on one shoe, and it was driving me nuts. The mirror was there, in the way of the shoe for a moment. I blinked twice, and then I was looking at the shoe again.

"Oh, you are such a kidder, Mr. Engelbrecht. The last stitch is going in. Tighten, tighten, the knot is tied and clipped. Now for the bandage. Good. You didn't feel that at all, did you? Ready to flip. One, two, three, flip."

Apparently the anesthetic was very local. I felt hands on my legs, my torso, and one on either side of my head. I was lifted, the scene in front of my eyes rotated, and I was staring at the most beautiful, exotic face I think I've ever seen.

I blinked. Yes, I tried to say. You can stand right there for as long as you want, my vision of loveliness.

"Good afternoon, Mr. Engelbrecht. I am Dr. Akeelah Ihejirika. You gave us a bit of a scare, but you're all sorted out now. We'd hoped to wait a day or two for the bone repair, but—" and she shrugged, flashing a big smile, "—we thought it time to move ahead. You should be able to move about freely once you feel like getting up. I should think a good meal will be your first step, but as you've not eaten real food in over two weeks, we'll start with small portions. For now, we'll hook your IV back up. How does a strawberry daiquiri sound? I think you're about ready to come back to life."

Light-dancing angels, yeah, I thought, and I blinked once.

"Good. When the anesthetic wears off, your neck may be a bit sore, but being a young man and in reasonable health, I expect that won't bother you too much. I'll leave you with Moriah."

She stepped away, and I saw my nurse move into the picture.

"We'll wheel you to recovery for a time, just until the numbness fades." She was unfolding a sheet as she spoke, and she began to pull it up over me. "Are you warm enough?"

I blinked twice.

"I thought you'd say that. I came prepared." She reached under the bed and pulled out a blanket, and she spread it over me. "We're moving now. You may feel a little drowsy. We thought you might like a rest, and there's a bit of sedative in your IV bag."

The woman must have access to an entire storage locker under my bed. I wondered if she could pull out a turkey and cheese sandwich. That'd taste good about now. Instead, she walked beside me, maneuvering a wheeled device with my IV bag suspended from it, probably with my turkey sandwich inside. I figured there were other people manhandling the bed. The lazy good-for-nothings. Turkey, I wanted to scream. Get me some wretched turkey, so I can quit feeling hungry.

The ceiling continued to slip past, light fixture, light fixture, light fixture, just like that. I could see my feet, and occasionally I glimpsed someone's arm, but lifting my chin to see behind me was impossible. I simply had no control over my head. Before we got to my room, I saw the ceiling going dark at the edges, and I left the hospital staff to their duties long before we got there.

—43—

DOCTORS IN SOUTH AFRICA must be incredibly opti-
mistic. The numbness faded in about three days.

What I mean is that the numbness didn't so much fade. I
lost three days. Out. Cataleptic. Insensible. I lost three
wretched days. I remember fading in and out on occasion, and
perhaps there was a meal or two in there, a blurred moment of
nonreality that spoke more of enforced wakefulness than real
awareness. Then I'd be gone again. Poof. Into a black world
of nothingness.

At least the drugs didn't make me dream. Think what it'd
be like if I'd spent those three days with African Mother
Earth. The doorway to her cozy residence didn't make visits
there exactly a fun day at your grandma's house.

Then, you've met my grandma. Maybe it was about the same.

Still, didn't these people know that I had a job waiting back in Houston? Didn't they consider that I might want my three days back?

One thing, however, and for this I'm grateful: I could walk when I woke up. Really, truly walk. That was good, because I suspect I may have used up my insurance benefits, and they were about to boot me out the door. Oh, Moriah was her usual cheerful self, and I got a last meal of Salisbury steak in a brown sauce, with carrots and peas, and a tiny plastic bowl of applesauce to finish it off. But the door was open, and the boot was on the kicking foot. When I realized that, I thought, what the hey. I'm ready to get this adventure back on the road.

"Mr. Engelbrecht, let's get you dressed." Moriah smiled brightly, and she set a stack of neatly laundered items on my bed.

"My clothes?" I hadn't thought about those. Spending weeks in the critical care unit makes normal things like socks and underwear seem nonexistent. More to the point, in critical care, underwear *is* nonexistent. I was hoping I'd find at least one pair in there.

"We can't let you walk the streets in your gown, now, can we?" She laughed and placed a hand on one of the drapery panels. "Would you like these closed for privacy?"

"Open. I've got nothing to show that people haven't seen already."

I caught what I was saying. No, that's not quite it. I caught *how* I was saying it. I flexed my fist and realized I hadn't hit anything in weeks. It dawned on me the last wall I punched was in the airplane. Then the craft had exploded around me.

"How's your hand feeling?" Moriah took my fist and straightened the fingers, massaging them.

Oh, wow, but her touch felt good. Not the massaging, either. Yeah, the massaging, sure, but crimeny, the texture of her skin against mine. I'm a guy. You know what I mean. I tried to pull my hand away.

"No, don't do that. Just relax." She laid my hand on my stomach, and she moved the stack of clothes to my waist, placing my hand on it. "You, sir, need to get these on. We've got another paying patient waiting on this bed, and we can't get her in here until you're out the door."

She winked, and her words were light-hearted, but I didn't doubt that she meant it.

"My personal things?" The book and that key were a pit in my stomach, a growing rock of unease. Even so, that was why I was here. That book was a connection, if an unwelcome one, and the key I hoped would answer all the questions I'd attempted to find answers to over the past thirty years. The other, more mundane things I was less concerned about, more like glad I'd had warning to gather them so I wouldn't spend weeks at the United States Embassy in an attempt to get my passport replaced and all my credit cards up and functioning again.

"In the bedside table. We've provided a small bag," and she opened up a wardrobe door next to the television, taking out a dark gray backpack, "for the things the emergency responders located of yours. All travelers should pack like you." She placed the bag on the foot of the bed and began to unzip the different pouches. Inside the largest she pulled out a zippered case of pencils, erasers, and markers. She set them to the side, remarking, "It's a school bag. Sorry. You won't want these. Usually the school supplies are donated to the children's ward."

"I'm not taking anything they need, am I?" I still had the bedding pulled up to my waist. She shook her head no and waved off my question with one hand and a smile. "What do you mean, pack like me?"

"I understand you had all your vital information on your person. What traveler does that? Fannypack?" She smiled, clearly teasing, and she began zipping the different parts of the bag.

"Hardly." I laughed it off. I wouldn't admit to it if I did. My mind raced for a good explanation. "Worry nerd. I'm not much of an international traveler, and I'm paranoid about losing my passport. I never leave my seat without it."

"Or your phone with all its accessories, or your iron key." She looked toward the door as if expecting to be interrupted, and she licked her lips before glancing back at me. "What's that about?"

"E.T., call home? Isn't that what phones are for? I didn't expect I'd find all the appropriate doodads for charging it in the African bush, so I grabbed everything." I totally missed her question. I could tell when she pursed her lips and gave me a hard look.

"No, Mr. Engelbrecht, the key. Tell me about the key." She looked to the door again, and that didn't bother me, but where had my pleasant and charming Nurse Sheckley gone?

"Have I said something?" I balled my fist again and re-laxed it, crumpling the clothes. I was actually growing to like Moriah, and a sense of rising frustration flooded me. I might never see her again, but the possibility that I could had been warm honey on my oh-so-male gonads, and I needed that about now. I was ready to head into the African bush to un-lock what could very possibly be the door to the underworld. I'd been doing fine in this hospital, and I'd stay awhile longer if they didn't have to give my bed to another person. No night-mares. What the heck was wrong with that? It was a pretty good tradeoff, in my estimation.

"The key, Mr. Engelbrecht. Now." Moriah grabbed my wrist, and it hurt. She put pressure on it, squeezing. "Where did you get the key?

What's it for? Why have you brought it back to this country? I must know."

"Criminy, woman. I was starting to like you, and now you're turning abusive? What does my key matter to you?" I jerked my hand, watching her fingers turn white with the pressure she was applying, but I couldn't wrest it free. "And one question at a time. Holy frijoles, nurse, just tell me what's going on."

"I have no more time." Her voice growled the words. I looked into her face, and my eyes widened.

"Gadzooks, Moriah. What long teeth you have." How had I not noticed that before? Her skin had taken a darker tone, and her eyes? Where had those dark rings come from? Good gravy, were those red contacts? "Sheesh, let go of me."

"We have the watch, and you cannot continue to run. It is only a matter of time until you are ours." The words were hissed, and tendrils of ghostly steam began to emanate from Moriah's body.

I knew this wouldn't turn out well. What was Nurse Sheckley? She stupid well wasn't the sweet nurse that had so gently coaxed me back to health. It dawned on me that it was unusual for a patient in hospital, any hospital, to not have multiple nurses throughout his stay. I'd seen Sheckley on a daily basis, at least the days when I'd been cognizant of my surroundings. Where had the other nurses been?

Had there been any other nurses? Why couldn't I remember? Had the crash fried my memory banks?

I fought to get free and wound up on the floor, sending the bed against the wall, and the tray of supplies on the bedside table scattering around me. The monitoring devices off to the side took a tumble, crashing, and the sound was loud in the confines of the room.

"Help!" I felt desperation building. Each time I scrambled away, Nurse Sheckley grew bonier, her arms became longer, and her face more emaciated. Her hair was now a tangled nest of paper, sticks, and feces. I knew this really, really wouldn't turn out well, and my only hope was to get out of this room. "Anyone, help," I yelled, struggling toward the door.

Nurse Sheckley had begun to steam quite profusely by then, and I fully expected her to explode, showering me with maggots, blood, and excrement. I'd seen *Constantine*. I knew how the exploding demon thing went, and I didn't want to be anywhere near when she went off. I was kicking, she was dragging, and she was making better progress. She was able to reach the bedside table, and she pulled on the drawer, yanking it free of the cabinet, and scattering the contents around us. The key landed just out of my reach.

"Take it. Pick up the key."

"No, you can have it." I was still trying to get away.

"Take it." The words slithered from her lips,

this time causing me to glance around to see if there were any actual snakes in the room. I could barely understand her next statement. "It is not for me to touch."

Her eyes were full red, and I locked on them, certain I saw desperation in there somewhere. She'd become translucent, and the steam was heavier. She wailed until it turned into a shriek, and she exploded in a violent twist of light, leaving a falling shower of glowing dust to settle to the floor. The sudden release of her hand caused me to slam backwards into the wardrobe, and the door thudded with a booming sound. My head slammed into it, and stars swam in my eyes for a moment. Why wasn't anyone coming to check on the commotion? When my vision cleared, I saw my bare legs askew in front of me. The bed was rumpled, with bedding spilling to the floor. There were my passport, the book, my unused phone, and the key, tossed willy-nilly. The clothes were equally disarrayed, in a tumble of plaid and denim. I looked toward the door, back to the clothes, and I crawled forward until I could pick them up. I stuffed the boxers into the pants; and pulling myself erect using the bedframe as ballast, I shook out the pants and slipped my feet inside, pulling them up under the gown and snapping them at the waist. I stepped to the door and opened it, looking for assistance. The corridor was oddly blank and empty. Not only of people, but of anything. Chairs, decoration, anything. I let the door shut and tossed off the gown. I retrieved the phone and checked it for signal. It was fine, and I slipped it into a back pocket. My passport went into my other back pocket. I pulled the drawer from under the bed and found the rest of my paperwork in there. I folded everything together and slipped it into my front pocket. Then I looked at the book and the key. I didn't want to touch either one.

Tanner, I thought, I'm blaming this on you.

I walked to the window, and that's when I began to get nervous. The Nurse Sheckley thing had been bizarre enough, and the hallway had surprised me, but remember my life. This was mild compared to what I'd seen down time. Flames alive, if that was down time, I'm go under more often, just for the thrill of it. Out that window, where did the world go? I mean it. This was Pretoria, one of the busiest cities in the country. You couldn't cross the street in Pretoria without bumping into a hundred crazed idiots.

There was no one there. The city was blank and, I realized, silent. I had thought it was the room and the sound insulation, but I'd heard cars and other city sounds before. Now? It was dead. Even the sun looked flat, with no clouds in the sky, and no birds, no airplanes.

I wasn't in under time. But this wasn't my world, either. Upwelling rage at my continued inability to exercise any control over my life overcame me, and my fist slammed into the window ledge. Being granite, the only damage was to my hand, and I stepped back, panting with pain, holding my hand at my chest. With tears running down my face, I turned and rested my back against the glass. This place was a half-world, real in one sense, but not quite complete in another, as if someone had started a painting but only bothered to color in the details that were right next to me. I was in some sort of limbo between under time and wherever I was supposed to be, and that rock in my stomach from earlier? It was about boulder size by then.

I made my way back to the bed, and I sat on the edge, rubbing my hand and looking at the book and the key. The book had already been a catalyst sending me to under time. I was hesitant about touching it again. The key? It looked odd lying there. I remembered it in the drawer, and now I realized why it had seemed odd even then. It had been wrapped when I was on that airplane. The envelope had Gramps' writing on it, telling me just where to go. In my mind, I could see the paper still wrapping the iron. Why hadn't Nurse Sheckey known what was on the envelope?

And she had asked, very strongly, too, in unequivocal terms. She'd tried to pull off my arm to get at the answer. On the floor, the key was the same, odd, as if what I was looking at wasn't what I was supposed to be seeing.

"No," I said, hitting myself in the head. "No, this is all *wrong!* I've been seeing it, and I haven't been *seeing* it. How messed up am I? I'm *up time.* Stupid, stupid, stupid, stupid, stupid. No wonder nothing's pulling me back. I'm on the other end of the spring."

I kept looking at that key, and I knew it was the key. Yeah, key and key. I'm a teacher, of eighth graders. I think like that. No apologies. Still, the point is, it had to be the link. My word, this was going to hurt. It was going to hurt bad.

I knelt down, with that book on one side, and the key on the other. I wanted them both. I felt I *needed* them both. The key, it was the link to all this going on around me. I was convinced of that. The book? It was a hot time on the old town tonight, and I suspected I'd regret leaving it behind. I reached past them, pulled the shirt from under the crumpled bedding, and slipped it over my head. Then, with both palms flat, I slammed them down on the book and the key at the same time.

Did it hurt? Dadgum! I hadn't imagined the half of it. I felt like someone reached down my throat, shot an anchor rod into that giant rock in my stomach, and began to yank it out with a Humvee revved up on steroids, pulling willy-nilly, forcing me to vomit it up. Then just as I thought my face would explode, the room began to vibrate harder and harder. Air was rushing by in a screaming torrent. I heard other people wailing around me, and the lights went out.

What now? I thought. Then, the building's coming down. Earthquake, terrorist attack, I didn't know which.

Or if. Then a whine assaulted my ears, and I recognized when I'd last heard that particular noise. Aluminum screamed as it was ripped from around me, the sound of the shearing metal threatening to burst my eardrums. Five hundred voices called to me, five hundred pairs of hands ripped at my psyche, and five hundred souls knew they were about to die.

"I'm sorry, Angela," I screamed, but I couldn't hear my voice. "I'm sorry, Kobe."

That was all I had time to get out, and this time, the airplane crashed for real.

—44—

FLAMES COVERED THE AFRICAN BUSH, dotted here and there; and a steady beat of drums accompanied their flickering dance. And it smelled *rank,* like diesel fuel mixed with blood. I rolled to my side, barely able to focus on the devastation. My stomach churned, and in a violent burst of incandescence, my gut emptied itself into the grass at my side.

A voice moaned, and I looked to see the flight attendant who'd taken my meal order, with her arms around the remains of a torn leather seat. Angela. I couldn't remember her last name. Her hair was matted in the back, and one leg was twisted under her. She was alive, if crumpled and tortured could be called that. At least that part of my nightmare rang true. I wondered if the boy had survived, and if so, if he'd die anyway like the newspapers said.

And I thought the nightmare was over weeks ago. Instead, it was just beginning.

The drumming grew louder. I turned, and behind me, dirty smoke boiled from a mass of torn and decimated metal. It lay across the ground, a blackened fog of death. A large tree burned. Luggage was broken open and spread across the landscape like color sprinkles on a birthday cake, all festive and gay. Instead, it was mocking laughter, thumbing its nose at the last few weeks, saying, In your ear, Chip. You thought you were home free, and now look where you are. Ha, you ramen-head. Are you done in or what?

Hope grabbed me when I saw movement in the smoke, the swirling morass telling of what looked like hundreds of people. "Kobe," I called, searching for the boy, as I coughed, a searing pain slashing my chest. "Angela, there are other survivors, after all."

I tried to stand, to make it to Angela. I wanted her with me to join in the life that I could see just on the other side of that wall of deathly fog. I wanted to cheer her up, for her to be well. I remembered the news from my dream, that she didn't make it to the "good" hospital. I didn't want her to relive that experience. I wanted her well, rejoicing, and as she had been just minutes ago. I wanted Angela to get up from that cushion and be whole again.

I worked one foot under me, keeping my

hand on the ground, and I tried to stand. Honest to God, I did. My head spun, and my stomach roiled again. A knife slashed my chest, just where the incision from my heart surgery had left a long scar. I dropped, my face to the ground. The drumming stopped, and silence surrounded me. Angela moaned at my side, and I looked up to see ebony feet with feathered and beaded anklets just in front of me.

"Jy wakker is nou." It was a man's voice.

I understood the words immediately. *You are awake now.* Awake now? What the heck did that mean? Had I been taking a nap, and I'd decided to get up? Was I a little boy who wanted to sleep in on Saturday morning? I tried to bark at him, to growl my response, but when I went to speak, I began to cough, blood splattered, and I thought it would rip my chest from my spinal cord.

And to top it off, the dude was speaking in Afrikaans. My grandmother used it all the time. I didn't speak Afrikaans. How the devil could I understand what he was saying?

"Jy is wie jy is." *You are who you are.* "Welkom tuis, my seun." *Welcome home, my son.*

I raised my head, and oh, my heavens, I almost did my business in my pants. It was the ruler of the underworld, larger than ever, with Mother Earth at his side. Mind-numbing African Mother Earth. I remembered how warm and secure she'd made me feel. I dreaded what she'd ask me to do this time. The flame elevator?

Mother Hubbard, yeah. Sticking my arm into dead people? Malkovich, yes. Cutting out my own heart to give it to her? Stupid right, I would, just to feel that warmth and peace again.

Totally screwed and run over by a train was where I'd found myself, and I couldn't even get up and stand.

"He struggles to believe." The words floated over me in her voice. Mother Earth. Her speech was the gentleness of a spring shower and the freshness of moss crushed underfoot. Oh, man, why did she have to speak to me?

"Angela's dying." I wiped blood from my mouth, and tears flooded my face with those words. The emotions came unbidden as a surge of empathy overwhelmed me. "And I can't find Kobe."

"See, Mother. He cares for others when he himself is in pain. He is, too, my son."

"As are all men." The freshest leaves of spring whispered her response, and a cool breeze carried them to my ears.

"Ah, we will see. Ek is vervul met geloof." *I am filled with faith.*

"As ever you are."

The drumming started up again, and I looked behind the king to see a massive army of midnight warriors in African regalia wearing weapons of music, their long-fingered hands working the surface of their drums. The smoke swirled, and as they turned to disappear into the black fog, they began to dance, the soles of their feet stirring the dust of the dissected soil, raising a great cloud that mixed with the oily fog and bore them away. The drumming faded, and the king held out his hand.

"My son, the time has come."

That hand drew me, a magnet of energy and desire broaching the air between his flesh and mine, filling me with all the possibilities that ever were and ever would be. The feeling was tangible, as if a bridge had spread from his hand to mine, and we were one. I felt his desires, his disappointments, and his anguish at something that had been lost many years ago. I felt connected to the planet, as if it was more than soil and sky and water. I knew the heartbeat of a world that had come to life a billion years before, each heartbeat taking a thousand years, and each breath bringing life to the unyielding rock that formed her, becoming the air that all creatures breathed, and the sustenance that allowed life to continue.

This was no ordinary king, no matter how vast his domain. I had met God, and everything else was swept away. I was no longer Chip; Houston was a distant dream; and Angela and Kobe were people I'd never known.

I had met God, and he held out his hand to me.

I had met God, and . . . I could think of nothing else, except that I had met God.

—45—

I TOUCHED GOD'S HAND, the air shimmered, and we were someplace else.

"Zonkers! That was weird." Equally weird was that I said that. What happened to the awe and majesty that had overwhelmed me minutes before? God's response was to laugh. "Well, it was," I said, almost petulantly. For some reason, I felt like a little boy, not the little boy who'd survived the stories of my gramps' suicide, not the little boy who'd lived through my dad's destructive drinking, and not the one who'd tried to drive away my teenage demons by sleeping with every girl I could get my hands on.

"You have known many unusual things in your life. How was that so very different?"

"I don't know." I thought about it, however, and I realized what it was. I didn't control it here. It wasn't me. I wasn't the one stepping down time or up time. Someone else was in charge. It wasn't my responsibility, and that was sweet. I'd never *not* been the one responsible for all the mumbo-jumbo that happened in my life.

"You must have questions of me."

"What do I call you?" Dang! What an asinine question. Why didn't I say something smart, like, how did you manage to cause an entire plane to crash, and did you have to kill five hundred people just to bring me here?

"I am known by many names." And yet, I heard more. I heard regret. It was as if I could read God's mind. Sort of.

"Are you a shaman?" That made me wonder where Tanner's book was. It had been on me, and now it wasn't. My passport, either, or my cell phone.

"Among other things. Look around you. What do you see?" He held a hand up and indicated what was behind him. All I could see was a swirling mist.

"Nothing. Hey, where's Mother Earth?" She'd just been here, and now we were alone.

"Think of her." He moved his hand, and I realized we were sitting, he on his massive tree-trunk throne, and me on a smaller tree trunk beside his.

I closed my eyes and pictured Mother Earth. When I heard her voice call to me, "Boy, I am here," I breathed in and smiled. Her words recharged me.

"Open your eyes, my son."

I did, and there she stood, at the edge of the mist. She held a hand to me, and her compassion for me softened the edges of every fractured memory I'd ever lived. Then she faded, returning to the mist. No, becoming the mist, as if she hadn't been there in the first place.

Double weird, but I didn't say that out loud, not with God sitting next to me.

"Am I really here?" I remembered the hospital. That'd felt pretty real, too.

"You are wherever you are. What else do you wish to know?"

"Kobe, the boy. When I was up time, he died. He's alive now. Can he be saved?"

"Up time, your word for reaching forward. You are correct. He is alive. Look into the mist. See him there."

I closed my eyes, only to hear God laugh. I looked at him, wanting to glare, but I didn't dare.

"Imagine. You don't need to close your eyes. See?" He waved his hand, and the mist coalesced into a savannah, with trees grouped in small clusters, and green grass surrounding us. Off to the side, a pride of lions rested, with two cubs chasing each other and tumbling over their mother. At one point, she swatted at one of the cubs, and it hissed at her before running after its sibling. A stork spread its wings, coming to land on a marshy delta. In the far distance, a waterfall tumbled from a high plateau, sending mist rising into the air. The sun's light created a halo of color around the waterfall.

It was beautiful, and it took my breath away.

"You, too, can do this. I felt the mist would make it simpler for you to understand. Perhaps this way is easier for you. Now, imagine the boy." He reached and touched my hand, and power surged through me.

"Kobe," I whispered, as I pictured the image from the newspaper. The air in the distance shimmered, like heat distortion on a summer's day, and out walked a brown boy wearing cloth shoes, neat khaki slacks, and a dark blue pullover shirt. He raised his hand to wave, and a bright smile burst across his face. "Kobe," I called.

"Patience, my son. This is a dream for him. He still lies among the wreckage."

"He can hear me, though?"

"Of course, as in a dream. My woman has visited with you in this way many times. Often I have joined her."

My head recoiled with understanding. The dream of my graduation door slamming shut, me running down the hallway, desperate and afraid, and finding the door where we were burying my dad, only to learn the next morning that he'd cut his wrists with the broken lens from his glasses.

"Yes, my son. You were here with me then. And others." God sighed. "It's not always a help, but it's what I can do, to help you find your way when you would become lost otherwise."

My mind was still reeling, seeing the stone pit and the mist, with M.J. melting away in front of me; every dream I'd ever had of people who'd needed my help; remembering the ones I'd followed through on, and the ones that I hadn't; and I knew the regret I'd heard in God's voice.

It was the regret for all the good he hadn't been able to accomplish, and I felt tears flowing down my face.

"My son, there is only so much one man can do. If we regret every lost opportunity, then we can never find new ones. How can we help your boy?"

I wiped my eyes, certain now, if I'd ever doubted before, that I truly sat in the presence of a powerful being that knew who I was from my inner core to my outer skin. Every thought I had was his to peruse, and he found compassion for each and every one.

"I want him to live." Too many people had died. Just one little boy, that's all I wanted.

"And if he doesn't wish to live?" God had his hands out, as if I wasn't seeing things as they were, but rather as I wanted them to be.

"How can you say that?" Anger boiled in me. This might be God, but to say this kid wanted to die? He was there, right *there*, alive, and of course he wanted to live, to be fifteen, and twenty, and have a family, and have his grandchildren sit on his knee and listen to the story of his life. I thrust myself from my tree chair, and I threw my anger at God. "It's stupid to even say that. He's a kid. Don't you have any compassion?"

"See what I see." God moved his hand, and we were among the burning wreckage of the plane. Helicopters were hovering, one with a news logo on the side, and more with medical insignias telling of priority access. Sirens wailed, and First Responders dotted the scene. Kobe still stood off to the side, except now he looked around, confused.

"What? What am I supposed to see? A boy's dying. Help him."

"Look closer, my son." God moved his hand, and we were vaulted forward, to see paramedics carrying a form on a stretcher. I looked, and beneath the blood and torn skin, I recognized the boy from the picture. One shoe was gone, his khakis were stained with red, and his blue shirt was shredded. One paramedic held a darkening cloth on his chest while trying to press his scalp against his skull.

"Oh, my word," I murmured. I had no idea. Truly no idea. Surely he'd not make it to the hospital. How could he? Not alive.

"And if he doesn't wish to live?"

"He's been shredded. How can he survive

that?" I fell back onto my tree-trunk chair, the fires still raging around us, as my energy drained from me. "You can make it all go back, can't you? Undo the crash, save everyone?"

I was clinging to an impossible hope. I'd been down time. I knew what it was like there, how it tried to spit you out, and it could never be changed. But this was God, right? He could do anything.

"My son, the truth is already in your thoughts. What is done is done. Only the future remains for us to shape as we wish."

"He can still be saved, then." Kobe, but I didn't need to call his name. The boy stood to the side, watching himself being loaded into a waiting helicopter. "He's dreaming this, isn't he?"

"We invited him in, and he dreams what he sees. The boy can be saved. I offer you caution, however. To truly understand, it is important for you to know the life he will live."

God shifted three fingers, making little more than a motion, as if he didn't want to do this. I knew he did it for me, and I needed to pay attention. I suspected I'd wish I hadn't asked. Isn't that me, though, hard-headed stupid, even sitting next to the God who controlled everything.

That's me, total jerk. I can't do anything right, can I?

—46—

A TORNADO OF POSSIBILITIES swirled around us, and in an instant, they stabilized, shifting until they became completely solid. We were in a hospital room. Kobe lay in a bed, tied to machines. A nurse was pulling bandages from his legs, and each time she drew the cloth back, he screamed.

"She's hurting him." I jerked forward as if to stop her.

"He's burned. She's helping him." God touched my shoulder, and I couldn't move. "We can't interact with them. These things are showing what might be if the boy lives. None of this has happened, yet."

"How long does he have to endure this?" It may not have happened, but I remembered that hospital visit. It never happened, and I could still feel the pain of dying on that bed and having my neck screwed back together.

"Many months, with many surgeries. He lives, however, as you requested."

"I had no idea."

"This will pass. Let's move ahead." The tornado swirled again, sucking up the bed, the nurse, and Kobe, with everything coming to rest again, shifting slightly and becoming a school hallway. Students, brightly dressed and laughing, made their way around us. There were signs on the walls telling of an upcoming dance.

"High school." I smiled. "Kobe must love this, having a car and girlfriends. I don't see him." A tangle of students were laughing around a locker, drawing my attention.

"Search, my son, for he is here."

The knot of bodies separated, and I found him. One arm was so damaged as to be useless. His face sagged on one side. He stood at a locker, and tears flowed down his cheeks.

"He's crying."

"Look inside the locker. He sees this every day." God nudged me forward.

Inside, everything had been trashed. Food was smeared over his books. A sign was stuck to the back, scribbled in wide-tipped marker. *Freak.* I turned away, unable to endure his pain.

"Again."

The tornado swirled, and we were in a darkened room. Kobe sat in a chair, and in the dim light, I could see needles gleaming on a small table at his side. In another room, someone yelled, and I heard glass breaking. Kobe lifted one of the syringes, jabbed it into his damaged arm, and pressed the plunger. "At least you're good for something, effin useless arm." He leaned his head back and closed his eyes as his face relaxed into an expression of bliss.

"Someone could have helped him." I quivered with desperation. I'd been there. I'd pulled through it, fighting my demons until I had them under control, but this boy was sinking into oblivion. He was about to go under.

"He doesn't want help. He wants to die."

"No, not Kobe." I pictured the little boy in the dark blue pullover and khakis. He was so sweet and full of life. Not this, not like this. No one should have to become this.

"He wishes every day he'd died in that crash. He envies those who did. He lives that day over and over, his parents and his sister, the people he loved who died while he lived, and he curses the God that saved him and let them die."

"He curses me." Remorse flooded my brain and my heart and my soul. I had wished for him to have the chance to live this life, and look where it had taken him. I'd condemned him to a life of torment and misery, and all to relieve my own personal suffering and misgivings. "Let's go back."

"See the end." God nodded his head ever so slightly, stirring the tornado, and when it settled, we were in the same room. The light was different, and the walls dirtier, so I knew time had passed. Forensic people filled the space.

"How long?" A pretty woman, probably in her thirties, choked before regaining control.

"The neighbors smelled it several days ago but just called it in." The man offered her a paper mask. He already wore one.

"They know who he was?"

That was when I realized what I was looking at. The walls, they weren't dirtier. I was looking at the remains of a person. Whoever it was sat in Kobe's chair, or at least his body did. Half of his head was gone.

"God—" I started. He shook his head, and I listened.

"Kobe Potgieter. The prints match, at least on the one hand that has them. Thank God. We'd never pull dental records from this mess." The man was flipping through a chart, and he stopped on one page. "Here, airplane crash thirty-seven years ago. He's been a drug addict for over thirty. No wonder he did this. He was horribly disfigured." He flipped out a picture showing Kobe after the accident. Most of his face was scar tissue.

"He probably wishes he'd died back then." The woman took the picture, looked at it, and handed it back. "I would have. I'm surprised he was able to live with himself this long. Poor guy. Some people don't catch any of the breaks."

I closed my eyes and wanted the green veld back, with trees, lions, and the waterfall in the distance. I wanted Kobe's life not to have happened, for him to remember none of it, and to be a boy once again. I wanted to undo my life, my father's life, and my grandfather's life. I wanted to undo it all, to erase all the pain of all the people I'd known all the years I'd been on this earth.

"And Mary Jane? Do you wish her to endure her hell?"

"Her hell? What's that got to do with all this?" I opened my eyes, and blurred through my tears, the waterfall appeared in the distance, and I wanted to sob with relief.

"You saved her. Do you wish her to live her life without you there?"

I wiped my arm across my face, and I sniffled. I couldn't look at God. I'd just seen the inside of Kobe's head, and his brains spattered across the wall. I wanted life undone. All of it. Especially mine.

"Life can't be undone, especially yours. You must use your gift while you still hold it. This is the way life must be."

"What does that mean? Don't forget, this *gift* killed my father and grandfather." I laughed sourly. "You should see the holes in my walls at home. Stuff happens, and I punch holes just to cope."

"My son, I see you still do not understand. Your expressions of anger and frustration are what cause events to react around you. This is a portion of your gift, part of who you are."

"That's the stupidest thing I've ever heard," but as I said that, the realization of the truth washed over me. On the airplane, I'd punched the wall in the toilet, and minutes later, the craft had come apart around me. Then, in the hospital, I'd punched the window ledge, and look where I was now. The falling dominoes of holes punched in my walls and events that had taken place just afterwards made me stagger. How had I never made the connection?

"You see, you are my son, and you can be no other way. Your father and your grandfather refused to accept the gift. Your grandfather, for a time, tried to control it, but he used it for himself. You use your gift to help those in need. This is the favor I find in you."

"You killed five hundred people to tell me that?" I couldn't let that go. I didn't want any part of a god who'd kill people for his convenience.

"The plane's destiny was already written. I simply reached in and saved you."

I remembered Emilio. Thank God I'd made a friend of that kid all those years ago.

"It is time for you to return. You will find your answers here." God opened his hand, and inside lay the key. He took my hand and placed the key against my palm, wrapping my fingers around it. "This is the most precious thing you carry. My protection will be yours, my son, as long as this key is with you. Do not let it get away."

He released my hand, and lightning struck that key with concussive force. My vision went blank, I felt my insides swell up and rupture, and the explosion of sound in my ears made me want to scream. I opened my eyes to find myself in that airplane toilet, the engines were screaming, and we were going down. No, not again! I grabbed the door, flung it open, and threw myself into the cabin. I yelled, "Kobe!" I looked to the front and the back, to see people hugging, screaming, and wrestling with items falling from the overhead bins, some doing all three at once. How could I not find one kid? Then I saw him, and he was looking at me. He knew me! The kid knew me! I fought over people in the aisle to get to him. I took the arm of the frightened woman I thought was his mother, and I yelled over the din, "I can save your son. Please."

She didn't get the chance to answer. The fuselage cracked just over our heads, and the window at her side evaporated into the sky. Kobe flipped his seat restraints off, and he leaped for me, grabbing me around the waist. Together we fought for the toilet. I pushed him inside before me and forced the door closed.

It was the least I could do, and curse you, God, this boy's not dying, not today, not when I've got a chance to save him.

What's a god for, anyway, if everyone has to die? Can't he save just one, every now and then, just to prove he's still a god?

Holy macaroni, if no more did I think that, and Kobe and I hit the ceiling, and I was living my rerun of *The Exorcist* once more.

Oh, no, I thought. Here we go again.

—47—

UP TIME IS UP TIME, just what it sounds like. In back time, I travel *back* through what's already happened. It's thick, like refrigerated honey, because it's in the process of gelling. You've seen those little insects in amber. The amber's hard as a rock, but not when they first get trapped. Initially, it's still soft and gooey. They're stuck already, so they're dead, so to speak, because they're already trapped, but they feel like they're alive, because they still have volition. They can swim in the stuff, try to get free, even if it's too late for that.

In up time, none of the events are stuck, yet. No honey. No superglue. No hardened sap that can be polished to a gem-like shine. It's more like dropping a noodle in a pan of water. It'll fall in and remain in one spot, but give it a stir, and it'll swirl around pretty as you please. Then, heat the water, and you've got a heck of a dance going on. A jig, like dancers from the Golden Age of movies leaping and tapping to a hip-hop beat. Fred Astaire getting down. That sort of exciting stuff. That noodle can't stay still, because the water's too stupid hot.

I think grabbing Kobe turned up the fire a bit.

Once the *crash! bam!* happened (and I think we must have skipped along the ground a bit), I lay in the dark awhile, my arms wrapped around the boy, both of us breathing hard and hoping nothing was broken, punctured, or missing. It didn't feel like it. The pains I felt were more akin to getting slammed around in a fight, not that I'd had many of those in several years. I figured I'd be screaming if one of the other things happened. The boy, too.

I could still hear stuff falling, and the sound of cracking wood. Tree branches, I thought, overloaded with debris, and giving way under the strain. Sketchy grass was under my arm, and I smelled damp earth. And what might be lion scat. God's uptime cats had been out here somewhere, and maybe they'd relieved themselves right where we were.

"Kobe?" I whispered the word as I cupped my hand around the back of his head. "Are you okay?"

"I think so," he whispered back. "My mom and my dad, and Anashe, are they okay?"

"I don't know." I was hearing sirens in the distance. I tried to focus on that. "We've got help coming. Think they'll find us?"

"We can climb out." He shifted in my arms, pushing on what covered us, and it wouldn't budge. He stiffened at one point, whispering, "My leg's caught."

We worked on our situation for about fifteen minutes. The first sirens had died away, but I could hear more growing closer. The sound of a helicopter's rotors, too. I remembered the scene from God's point of view. It wasn't good, and it wasn't getting better anytime soon.

I heard voices, and I began pounding on anything I could reach, telling Kobe to yell as loudly as he could. You do desperate things in the dark, especially when you've just fallen out of the sky in an airplane, and we yelled everything we could think of to say.

"I'm American!" "We're on the ground!" "I smell diesel fuel!" "Where are you fish mongers?"

I regretted the last one, but as I said, desperation takes over when you're buried in the dark, and you don't know if you'll ever get out. Crikey, I wasn't sure this was even real. What if I was wandering up time again, and all this was just effluent for hitting the fan? I was tired of airplanes that couldn't stay in the air. Son-of-a-squeegee, I was tired of Africa. I hoped I never saw this milk-curdling place again.

We heard metal shifting, and glimpses of daylight began to filter in. An engine roared, like a machine was hooked up to something, and it was giving it all the stuffing it had. It sounded like something snapped, and I heard someone curse, like something had gone wrong.

I yelled, "We're in here! Get us out!"

The sounds stopped for a minute, and I heard someone scrambling just over us. Then a voice yelled, "Hook it up again. We've got a live one under here."

"Don't squash us," I yelled, but his voice sounded great to me. It was us they were talking about, me and Kobe, the two dudes from the toilet. We'd spent the trip down on the ceiling, and I was about ready to get out of here, wherever exactly we were.

"Cover your faces—" The words from up top, out there in the real world of sunshine and freedom, were eaten by the renewed grinding of masticated metal, with the high-pitched shearing of aluminum panels shrieking their complaint directly into my ears.

Heavens! Irresponsible suckers, all! I grabbed Kobe around the shoulders and covered his ears. This was stupid, and I thought the ride down in the toilet was bad!

"Are we going to die?"

I looked at the kid to see his big eyes looking up at me, the centers dark, all rimmed with white, in a beautiful, sunbaked mahogany face. I remembered the boy who'd grown up with another face, and he'd chosen a violent exit to this world rather than deal with the dumpload of ridiculous nonsense that God had tossed on his poor, inadequate shoulders. No, Kobe. No one else is going to die. I should have said it, but that face, so innocent, and yet I knew he remembered being up time. I did. I always remembered, even when I wanted to forget.

"Are we?" His eyes glistened.

"No. Everyone lives from this point on. I promise."

"Thank you for coming for me. Who was that man?"

"A First Responder. They're the good guys, always out to rescue people who need help." I remembered a little about New York back at the turn of the century, and the World Trade Center. First Responders had died in there. I didn't remember the number, but it'd been a lot. Over our heads, the machine continued to roar, but I think they were being more careful, now that they knew we were under here. At least I hoped they were. I didn't want to live that crash all over again.

"No, that other man." Kobe shifted, trying to sit up, and he sucked in a sharp breath. Tears began to run down his face.

"What is it?" The hole above us was widening, and I was about to climb out, enough room or not. I looked at his leg. A metal rod entered one side, and it came out on the other. No, I thought. I'm falling down on the job. "Hold still, Kobe. Don't try to move. Let me see if I can get these guys' attention."

I yelled until I saw a face peering down at me.

"We're almost to you. Can you hold on?" The

machine roared, and he turned to wave at someone, silencing the worst of it. "We have to winch part of a wing off. It's keeping us from moving this big section of fuselage." He slapped something I couldn't see, and it resonated hollowly around me.

"A boy's down here, and his leg is impaled on something. Be careful what you pull on."

"A child?" He disappeared, and I could hear him yelling that a *pikinini,* a child, was impaled, and this took priority, and heck, yeah, get the stupid ambulance to this spot ASAP.

"Were we in Heaven?" Kobe wiped tears from his face.

"Before the crash?" I closed my eyes and replayed those moments. "You dreamed of me, didn't you?" I felt him nod his head.

"I grew up, and you were there."

"It was a very bad dream. Let it go." I squeezed his shoulder for a second and released it.

"God was in my dream, and he talked with you." Kobe rested his head against my chest, and as his tears soaked my shirt, he whispered his words. "He said he couldn't help me, and you saved me. I think you're more powerful than God."

"No one is more powerful than God." I didn't want to talk about God, not then, maybe not ever. I'd lived a life doing his work, when I should have been a normal guy doing normal things and having normal problems. Not this nonsense.

"I think God wanted you to save me because he couldn't. I wish you could have saved my family." His comment was very matter-of-fact, like someone who plays the lottery and tosses away a losing ticket.

"So do I, Kobe. So do I."

The engine from outside roared, from farther away, it sounded like, and the mass of metal over our heads groaned and shifted. Kobe screamed out, light poured in, and strong arms reached in with hands wrapped in thick gloves. Rods, girders, and wiring tumbled from around us.

"Close your eyes. Don't want insulation in them. Rani," our rescuer called to someone out of sight, "I need the Jaws. I've got an inch rod to cut, then I've got a child, maybe ten years old, to transport. Stat."

I realized I'd been hearing an ambulance for some time, very loud, meaning very close. Maybe these men weren't losers after all. Maybe I'd be glad to have them around. By all accounts, I *was* glad to have them around. They were my rescuers, come to save me and the boy I'd helped pull to safety.

I lay as out of the way as possible while they got Kobe out. The boy held my hand as long as possible, looking at me with tears in his eyes as he was pulled away. One of the men, may God forever smile on him, untangled our fingers, peeling the boy's back, and telling him that everything would be okay now. I'd be coming out next. Some men have hearts of gold. I guess that's what draws people to be First Responders, the desire to help others, even when they risk their own lives to do so.

Me? I tried to sit up once the boy was gone, and I felt my head spin. I grew cold, and the man above me yelled to his compatriots, "Come on, we're losing this one. Get me some equipment down here now."

Where'd the refrigerator come from, I wondered. Ice was forming on my arms, and I considered how many toes I would lose from frostbite. I tried to keep them from closing the door and locking me inside, but I didn't have the strength. Did they know how much I hated the dark? Was that what this was all about, making me prove I wouldn't go crazy? Sorry, guys, I'm already crazy. Just ask my mom. Ask Chalky. Jumpin' Jehoshaphat, ask Kobe. He was in crazyland with me, and look at him now, being pulled out of a toilet with a steel rod rammed through his leg.

Just before the last of the daylight disappeared, I had the presence to think one last thought.

Crap. Third time to crash, and my back's *still* broken.

Crap.

ALL MY LIFE I'VE BEEN MESSED UP and angry. My walls are proof of that. Then there's the girls I went through like toilet paper when I was a teen, and the relationships I sabotage because of my out-of-this-world "god-i-ness" that keeps me buried in down time almost as much as I get to spend in real time.

Now? I'm tired. Feeling worn through and exhausted. I won't bore you with the hospital scene again, except this time Moriah wasn't there. I had normal nurses who could barely remember my name without checking my chart first, and toss all, if I never made it to the private hospital. The private hospital was much, much better, I can assure you of that. I was admitted as indigent, and that meant any care I got, while designed to keep me alive, was only scraps off the table, because there were too many dogs sitting around begging for any meat that got tossed to the floor.

I also had flowers from people I knew. I'd visited South Africa a few times, you remember, Jo'burg and Cape Town. I guess some of my old friends saw me in the paper and took the time to look up where I was interred. By the time I was in shape to be dismissed, some of the more fragile blooms were starting to fade. I stood there my final morning, wearing the plaid shirt and denims from before—that hadn't changed—with my new backpack on the bed, and I fingered the blooms, taking in a final whiff of their pleasing scents. I flipped through the cards, wondering if I should contact any of the people who'd been so considerate to search me out. Unsure what I intended, I slipped them in a pocket to look at later. I redistributed the flowers that were still fresh enough to enjoy to other rooms, just trying to liven the place up. Remember, this was the freebie hospital. It needed livening up.

I stopped by to see Kobe before I left. He was in a cast. That rod had shattered his femur, and he'd be in bed for several weeks, then on crutches for a while after that. I asked him what he would do, since, well, his family were gone in the crash, and he shrugged, telling me, "I'm your boetie." Then he laughed, his smile wide and white in his beautiful face. "You be my china. Everything's okay just now."

I laughed, having no idea what that meant, and I shook his hand. As I walked away, the nurse, a large, jolly woman with April on her nametag and wearing her hair in a knot on top of her head, pulled me aside. "I see your face. You be confused. He say he now your brother, and you be his mate."

"Whoa, April," I said, stopping, with the intention of going right back in there and setting him straight. "He's got family, maybe? Surely? People he can go to?"

"Everything be okay soon."

"That's not what he said. He said it's okay now."

"You misunderstand." She laughed, and it was rich and deep. "Just now not mean just now. It mean soon. He hope you be back, be his china; so soon, everything be okay."

She chuckled as she walked away and disappeared into another room. I looked back at the door where I'd left Kobe, wondering what all that meant. I couldn't figure it out. I'd saved the kid, for sure, but he wasn't mine. After a few moments of indecision, I shrugged it off as a friendly greeting and nothing else, and I headed off to get in touch with Houston. I had people who needed to be kept apprised of what had happened to me. I was a little jittery about making the call to the school, as I was on medical leave and *in South Africa,* but at some point, I would have to. I wasn't heading back to the States until I had this wrapped up, and I thought they'd miss me when there was no one standing in front of my class for a week or two.

Yeah, Admin tends to pay attention to things like that.

I sat on a bench in the front lobby and unzipped the school bag I'd been given. I suspected my new bag and the clothes I had on my back came from one of the staff, some kind soul feeling sorry for the poor American getting toughened up in the South African health care system. Still, nothing had been stolen. All the stuff I'd had stuffed in my pants was in there. Not too surprisingly, the key was back in its envelope. I was careful not to touch either it or the book. The phone was all I cared about just now. I was grateful the staff had charged it for me. I dialed my home number and listened to it ring.

"Yeah?" Chalky, sounding out of breath and panting.

"Hey, chommie." I was trying out one of my new South African words. I smiled at the sound of his voice.

"Chip?" His voice leaped an octave. "It's been two weeks. Were you on that plane that crashed? Did you hear about it? I've been so worried, and nobody knows what's up, you rushing off like that—"

"Whoa, Chalky!" I cut him off, laughing. "How's the house coming along?"

"Okay, I guess." He sounded a bit hurt, but then he brightened. Vintage Chalky. "You won't believe how good it looks. The hallway's done, painted and everything. I didn't know I could plaster, but I watched a how-to on the computer, and it's easy. When are you coming home?"

"A week or two. I had a little ripple in my plans, and I haven't been to Sterkrivier, yet. I'm hoping to get out there in a day or two. I'm proud of you, bro." He sounded very self-confident, and indeed, that did make me proud of him.

"For what?" He breathed audibly into the phone, calmer than before, but still out of breath.

"What's going on? You sound winded."

"Some of your friends are over—"

"Chalky, what did I tell you?" Now I was irritated. No one was allowed in the house.

"I didn't invite 'em in, just out back. They planned a party for you, but you didn't show up. So, they're here, anyway. I like your friends, Chip. Thanks for letting me stay in your house."

"Our friends. Hey, you keep them outside, and I'll look forward to seeing what you've done. Later, china." I grinned and hung up, He'd never get that one. Then I thought, stupid me! I didn't ask about school. Were there messages for me, anything like, maybe, Chip, you are scheduled this Monday at 8:00 for instruction in Science 101?

I began to dial Stefanie's number. She'd have all the answers. I hoped they were ones I wanted to hear.

"Stefanie, here." The television was going in the background. It sounded like The Late Late Show.

"Stefanie, this is Chip. I didn't think. What time is it there?"

"Nearly eleven, but I'm up. We've missed you, Chip, everyone. How's the party?"

"Party?"

"Don't be silly. Yours. Charisse is there." I could hear the wink in her voice. "Are you two a number, now? Like, do I hear wedding bells?" She laughed and said something to someone in the room with her.

I diverted her question with, "I won't keep you. I need to find out how my class has been." Wedding bells? Yowie, I'd better be careful, if that's getting around.

"Mrs. Palty hopes you're out another three weeks. She loves it." This time I could hear her say to someone else, "Remember when Craig Ferguson was on? He was funnier."

"Miss you, Stef. I'll let you go." I'd gotten what I wanted to know. The school wasn't searching for me, so I wasn't going on the missing person's list just yet.

"Enjoy the party. Bye, Chip." The phone clicked twice before hanging up, and she was already laughing at a televised joke before the connection broke.

I dropped the phone in my new school bag, zipped the pouch, and stood. I wasn't about to call Mom, and I didn't have anyone else to call, not if it was nearing midnight in Texas. It was the middle of the afternoon here, though. I considered that key. I was in the right part of the country, Limpopo, just south of Botswana and Zimbabwe, so theoretically, I wasn't that far from my goal. South Africa's big, though. Heck, Limpopo Province is a fifth the size of Texas. I wondered how far it was to Sterkrivier. It could be hours away. I dug in one of the compartments and pulled out my wallet. April had told me at one point they'd cut my clothes off, but they were *verdelg* already, she'd joked. At my puzzled look, she'd chuckled and patted my arm, popping her palms together and making an explosion noise. I got that pretty well. I'd seen Kobe's blue pullover the first time he'd come out of the wreckage. I guess mine were about the same. Still, I had everything except my clothes. Thanks, again, God, I breathed, for sending Emilio along at just the right time. My medical insurance card was in there, too, and that's why I'd breezed out of the hospital so easily. At least I supposed they'd accessed it. They hadn't asked me for any money, although I could still get hit with a really big bill when I got home.

I stepped to the door, looking out into the brightly colored world outside. South Africa. People with skins of all shades. The intensity of it all, and the robust sounds bleeding through the glass. In a better hospital, I could probably get a concierge to book transportation straight to my destination, but this wasn't a better hospital. I was on my own. I slipped my wallet into my front pocket, because I knew all the stories about South Africa; I hiked the pack onto my shoulder; and I headed out the door. I had an appointment to keep, and I had the key to let me in the door.

Behind that door, what would I find? Probably another life-sucking nightmare. That, however, was exactly why I'd flown halfway around the world in the first place. I love adventure, and I love living-in-the-dark nightmares.

And you haven't paid a bit of attention, if you believe that.

I just wanted to get this over with, go home to Charisse, and hold her. All the other god-nonsense? I was really, really tired of it, every wretched bit. You ever tell me I'm lucky, and I'll punch you right in the kisser. I won't apologize, either, not even if you tell me how much you enjoyed my fist meeting your face.

That'd probably backfire on me, though. I couldn't get God's words out of my head. I don't hit the walls because funky juju happens. Funky juju happens because I hit the walls. I was keeping my hands to myself, at least for the time being. No more funkiness needs to happen to good ole Chip. I'm done with funky juju.

And that key was against my side, two layers of fabric from my skin, telling the lie to everything I was thinking. I could feel it, like it was warm, imbued with some sort of power, and ready to unleash it all over me.

Bang my head against a wall, am I a glutton for punishment or what?

I pushed the door wide and stepped into the afternoon sun. The city was loud and boisterous, with occasional pieces of trash littering the curb, but the people I saw, while not luxuriously dressed, were clean and focused. It didn't feel dangerous, not like Jo'burg at all. Even so, I kept my pack strap firmly gripped in my hand, and I headed to find someone to point me to Sterkrivier.

I had places to go and things to do, and I had Charisse waiting at home for me. Were we a thing, now? Stefanie had gotten me to thinking. Right then I was thinking, Dear God, I hope so. I absolutely, to the depths of my immortal being, hope so.

—49—

SOME PEOPLE SAY AFRICA'S the cradle of life, that we came from here, and that this continent has been inhabited longer than any other place on the planet. I see it differently. It's Eden in my book, and these lucky people never left the garden. As far as me? I was ready to soak in some African flavor. Maybe it's the wildness of it. Head to a wild animal park in the States, and you get electric gates to let you in and out, air conditioned restrooms, and a well-appointed gift shop and restaurant at the end of the day. Here, get away from the city, and you're really in the wilderness. It's like being in bear country, except these bears hunt at night and like to climb trees to eat your skinny backside.

I was ready to get out there and discover it all, but first I had to get me some transportation.

I stopped in at this little place called the Hungry Lion. I ordered the Mash Pack Plus and headed to a table, chilling, just sitting there with my chicken and biscuit, and wondering what to do next. I was watching people through the glass, not sure I wanted the mashed potatoes, but the cold drink was hitting the spot right where it needed to go. A man walked in, about my age, with his long, kinky blond hair in a torrent of braids gathered and protruding from a garishly patterned bandana wrapped around his head. His jeans were more faded than blue, with tears across the knees and the hems rolled up several times. They bunched at the bottom and covered more of his canvas shoes than they left exposed. His jacket had more pockets than my pack, and he pulled these giant sunglasses from his face and hung them on the collar of a tee shirt that had seen better days a decade before.

Still, the man sauntered to the counter, held up a hand, and did a three-step handshake with the employee, a man who'd been efficiently polite in good English to me. These two? I only caught half their words. I shook my head and looked back out the window, taking a bite of my chicken, and washing it down with Coke.

"Hey, my bru, howzit? Mind?" The blond-headed man nodded to the seat across from me, and he held his meal in his hand.

"Nah." I motioned. Once he was seated, I

held out my hand. "Chip."

"From the crash. I know. Ritchie Holmes." He shook, then began laying out his napkin and organizing his food in a very fastidious manner. Before eating any of it, he closed his eyes for a moment, then looked at me and smiled as he pulled a sanitary wipe from one of his jacket pockets, tearing open the foil pouch and pulling out the moist cloth. "Sorry. No offense. OCDC. The moment of silence is for my grandmother. She used to thrash my knuckles with a switch if I ate without showing respect to the man upstairs."

"Hey, I got my own issues. Obsessive-compulsive doesn't bother me." *Own issues.* I'd spent time in the underworld and carried on a conversation with God—while in under time, by the way. I was geez-Louise crazy. *Issues* was skirting the reality of who I was, but I didn't know this guy, and heck, probably never would, so I didn't mention any of that.

Then it hit me what he'd said. From the crash? Ouch. I hadn't even considered I might get any face-recognition time. I'd seen the newspaper from my first visit up time, but I hadn't asked for one on my last hospital stay. It was a public facility, anyway, so I hadn't been sure they provided the news to their indigent, freeloading foreign patients, and I hadn't bothered to ask. By Jove, I was lucky to get my spine screwed back together and still be walking, and I wasn't complaining about that, not one bit.

My companion folded his towelette into a

neat square and put it to the side, squared up with the edge of the table, before lifting a chicken leg and biting into it, leaving juice running down his chin. He laughed and grabbed a napkin to wipe it clean.

"Holmes. That doesn't sound very South African." I watched his eyes, crystal blue with gold specks. He had a pretty face, except for his hair and clothes. I wondered if that was the point, dress grunge to offset the other. His clothes might give off a homeless vibe, but he smelled clean—even good—and the clothes were faded, but they weren't dirty. It didn't matter. I taught kids who were weirder. Hey, I was weirder.

"Tallahassee. I came one Spring Break to surf and never made it home. Later I wandered north for the scenery and a Peace Corps volunteer working over the border, then decided to hang around a while. Now I'm sharing a table with one of the two survivors of the worst plane crash in South African history."

"Three." I corrected him. "The boy's on crutches, but he'll recover eventually and go on to live a happy life. At least that's my plan."

"But," and Ritchie frowned, pulling a folded piece of paper from inside the massive jacket. "Look."

I wiped my hands on my spare napkin and unfolded the paper. It was a news article clipping, the same one showing me, Angela, and Kobe.

Another article fell to the table when I unfolded the last section. The second paper said, "Airline attendant succumbs." I looked at my new friend hard.

"This can't be. Angela survived." I glanced between the first and second articles, the one I was familiar with, and the second that had Angela's name instead of Kobe's. This sucks, I thought. It's not fair. I saved one, and God took the other. It's stupid. It's not supposed to work that way.

"She did, for two days. She never pulled out of the coma. Sorry, bru. You knew her?" He wiped at his mouth and pointed to my potatoes. "You eating that?"

I motioned, and he pulled it his direction, wiping his hands with his towelette before taking his spoon and digging in. I suspected his OCDC was selective if he didn't mind eating out of my potato cup, even though I hadn't touched it.

"I only met her on the plane." I folded the clippings and set them on the table between us. "She was nice, though."

"Sorry, again. Life sucks like that." He was scraping the bottom for the final bits of potato, licking the spoon each time. "You lived, though. How about that?"

"Yeah, how about that?" I felt the oppression fall over me, the one that said I wasn't in control, no matter how I tried. I endeavored to make little stabs at changing the world for the better, and all I got was screwed. I hadn't wanted to save one person *instead* of the other. I had wanted to save Kobe *in addition to* Angela. It was so stupid. It wasn't fair!

And before I realized what I was doing, I balled my fist, and I slammed it into the wall at my side. Have I told you I'm nutcracker stupid? Why did I ever do that? was my immediate thought. I take that back. My first thought was, Flames alive, that hurt! Then the table began to vibrate, and I saw that Ritchie was holding to it with both hands, and his eyes were wide.

I remembered God's words. The juju happens because I hit the walls. My stomach churned, and my chicken tried to come back up. What had I done, because it wasn't just the tabletop vibrating. The whole building was shaking.

Ritchie managed to get out, "This is bigger than the '13 quake. This is really cool."

I knew it wasn't a quake, though, not the natural sort. It was me, being stupid.

Then the window beside us cracked, and I vaulted forward and grabbed Ritchie's head, forcing it to the table and leaning over him for protection. I got him almost all the way down when the glass shattered into a million pieces, spraying over the both of us.

One normal day, I wanted to scream. Why can't I have just one normal day?

Then, I don't suppose a god ever has a normal day.

Then the table collapsed, and an explosion sent a fireball tearing over our heads.

Crap, literally! I think I dirtied my underwear on that one.

—*50*—

AT LEAST I DIDN'T GO UNDER TIME. Some mysterious god didn't yank me into Hell—or Heaven, although in my experience, they're one and the same. Once the screaming stopped, and the restaurant got its gas pipes shut off, Ritchie and I were able to get outside and see exactly what had happened.

"Wow," Ritchie said. There was a crack in the ground running right up to the window, just where we'd been sitting. "Would you look at that?"

"My fault." I flexed my hand. It still hurt. I knew where that crack had come from.

"Yeah, cool." Ritchie ducked his head and shoulders in a this-is-so-fine manner, and he grinned. "You surviving that crash, now this. We could'a been sucked into the ground." His face glowed.

"Where to now, Ritchie?" I was sick to my stomach. I'd caused this. Me. Idiot me, getting angry, and somehow doing this. It's so stupid, not at all fair. I'm forced to play the role of a god, and now I can't even vent my anger about it. I reached to scratch my head and realized I still had glass in my hair. It tripped me out, and I dropped my pack and began shaking my head and beating at my hair, desperate to have the glass gone.

"Whoa, bru. I see it." Ritchie grabbed my neck, and he worked my hair for a moment before proclaiming me glass free. "Where you need to go? I might can help you out."

"You know a place called Sterkrivier? I need to get there." Up and down the street, people were gathering to see the damage from the quake. Funny. I didn't see any other damage. It was all centered here, on the Hungry Lion. I knew why. I'd been the epicenter. It was too surreal to be believable, and I wanted to be away. I felt for the envelope holding the key that had brought me here, and I showed him the name written across its face. All it had been through since receiving it from my mom hadn't helped much, but it was legible.

"What's special 'bout Sterkrivier?" His eyes sparkled with interest as he read it, as if he knew the answer, already.

"I've got this key, and it's taking me there." I tapped the faded words written in my grand-father's hand.

"North." His face brightened, with his eyes wide, and a smile spreading across his face. "Not much there. Farming country." He actually laughed, like he was enjoying this. "I do tours, if you're interested."

"*You* do tours?" I slipped the envelope away, and his eyes were glued to it as it disappeared. I didn't put anything to it, except he was memorizing the location.

"Among other things. I got a car, so you put gas in it, and I'll do you a tour."

"Now?" I hadn't expected to get there today, but it was good for me.

"Nah. It's a couple hours away, and we don't want to be out after dark. You can crash at my place for the night. Deal?" He held his hand up in a fist, and I bumped it with mine.

"Deal." I hefted my pack to my shoulder. "How far to your place?"

"Come with me. I gotcha covered."

As it turned out, we weren't headed back to Ritchie's to crash. Or I should clarify, not only to crash. He liked to party. It was two locked compound gates to get to his apartment, then three keyed locks on his personal security gate, and a thumbprint lock on his actual door.

"You live in a bank vault?" I watched as he held his thumb for several seconds, then entered a code too fast for me to see.

"Nah, bru. I live in Pretoria." He grinned

when he said it, then he pushed the door open and keyed a security system off. "Wait while I check the place out."

That was when I noticed his knife. He held one in his hand, poised as if in defense. He disappeared into the apartment. I heard a television turn on, and Ritchie returned after a moment, folding the knife and slipping it into a pocket inside his jacket.

"Welcome to my pad." He pulled me to the sofa, patted it, and said, "Your bed. Now, though, we take a little night life. You got any different clothes?" He looked me up and down critically.

"You're seeing 'em." I shrugged, tossing my pack on the sofa.

"That's right." He snapped his fingers, chuckling. "Airplane crash. You'll get us mugged in that. I got plenty, though. You hit the shower, and I'll grab you something more appropriate."

"Sounds good. This way?" A hall led off one side of the room, and I nodded that direction. Across the space, the TV was telling about an earthquake that had damaged a restaurant in Pretoria just hours before, and activists were blaming it on continued mining activities from the Premier Mine, Cullinan, with protesters once again demanding new restrictions on underground mining near populated areas.

"On the left." He looked at me, jerked his head sideways, and laughed in a punctuated *ha-*

ah. "Man, we're going to have such a *good* time tonight. Ole Ritchie out with the *extreme.*" He pointed to the TV. "Like we were *there.*"

I headed down the hallway. Yeah, we were there. It had nothing to do with Premier Mine, however. It had to do with me. The quake was there because I was there. The crash happened because I was on the scene. I wondered if Ritchie would be glad he'd invited me to "crash" by the time we returned from Sterkrivier. It seemed I wasn't good for people's safety. I was an accident waiting to happen.

Maybe I did want to party after all, and with lots of booze. Holy guacamole, at that point, anything to soften the edges. I didn't wonder but for a moment what Ritchie's idea of party gear might be. Perhaps I should have. Instead, I closed the bath door, flipped on the shower, and stripped my clothes off.

Getting clean would feel pretty good, and at that moment, I couldn't think of anything better.

51

OKAY, SO I EXPECTED SOMETHING a little classier than ripped jeans and a ragged Gatsby driver cap. Ritchie had tossed his jacket for a tight white tank, retaining his rolled up and faded jeans. I learned why when I put mine on. He had zippered pockets built inside.

"For your valuables," he said, clapping me on the shoulder. "Keeps what's yours, yours." He tucked his hand into his pants and pulled out a wallet, and he grinned.

My shirt was looser, a ribbed knit, with a vee-neck and a tie printed on the front. Yeah, classy, what I'd choose to wear for a night out on the town. This was Ritchie's turf, however, and who was I to complain? I didn't know Pretoria, hardly knew South Africa, and the man was my tour guide for the next few days. Holy kachow, I was wigging out on fortunate circumstance, and I didn't want to foul that up. So, I made a fateful decision: Fake ties were great by me, especially if they got me to Old Sterkrivier Farm the next day.

Ritchie's choice of venue was a big place called Bonzo's, with one wall open to the street. Lights were flashing, and the noise was deafening from half a block away. I understood the reason for my clothes as soon as I saw the first people heading into the club. Ritchie and I were tame compared to some of the others.

A woman in pink stockings, a white miniskirt, and the biggest hair I've ever seen waved at us, calling, "Ritchie, dear! You brought him. Good for you!" She ran up to my companion, gave him a kiss while standing on one foot, then grabbed me on both sides of my neck and pressed her cheek to mine, saying, "Ritchie's so lucky to have found you."

"Oh?" I was a bit stunned by her greeting. I heard Ritchie smart back, "It wasn't luck, Tamara."

"Oh, poo," she said, laughing, and putting a finger on Ritchie's nose. "We make our own luck. Now come inside. Everybody's here."

Inside the door, Ritchie leaned in to tell me something, but the music had ramped up, and I shook my head at him. Above us, colored spots were swinging around, resting on various tables for a time before moving on. At one table, a couple were kissing very heavily when a red light landed on them. They ignored the intrusion, even as one of them waved the light off. Several people around them cheered, clapping their hands and laughing. On the dance floor, half a dozen twosomes gyrated up and down, their skin glistening under a glittering disco ball and throbbing colored spots. We reached the bar, a gleaming stainless sheet backed by racks of booze in front of a lighted wall. The bottles had silver nipples attached. The light shimmered through the liquor, creating a cacophony of colors ranging from light yellows to ambers and greens. One of the bartenders pulled a bottle down, turned it expertly upside down to fill a glass, and had the bottle back on the shelf as smoothly as could be.

"Ritchie," I yelled into his ear. "Where are we sitting?"

"There." He pointed across the room, past two half-dressed women on trapeze swings, to a raised area with just enough light to see a crowd of people gathered with drinks in hand. He waved, and the crowd lifted their drinks. I could hear their cheers even through the din.

"Okay. What are we drinking?" I wanted it to be strong. This seemed to be a wild crowd. I wasn't sure I'd survive sober.

"Trust me." He leaned toward one of the bartenders and yelled, "Two Springbokkies, and two whiskeys straight. We'll be there." He pointed, and the crowd on the other side of the room cheered again, although only about half this time. The rest were hunched over something on one of the tables, and they were preoccupied.

We made our way past the dance floor on the way to Ritchie's friends. He stopped once to give another man, older and heavyset with dark skin, a hug. The man looked at me as I followed Ritchie, and I shrugged and moved on by. Ritchie waved to the DJ, who lowered the music, announcing into his microphone, "Hey, and Ritchie's here tonight, so let's keep the tempo up. If you have a special request, I'll honor all those I can. Now let's see if we can keep the 'J' in jam with a little Shakira for a retro mood."

"They seem to know you." I leaned into Ritchie's ear, having to yell to make myself heard.

"They should. It's my club." He laughed and pulled me along, rubbing shoulders through the most crowded spots, and finally making the raised dais to his friends. He began the circle, introducing me to them. "Cirque, Memo, and that's Cherish, there. Oh, and Seraph, everyone's angel. You'll love Seraph."

There were more, too many for me to remember all the names, but Seraph, yeah, I caught something from Seraph. She had jet-black hair pulled severely back, *Matrix* style, with dark-ringed eyes and brilliant-red lipstick. I grasped her hand to shake, and it seemed as if the music faded to nothing, the strobes quit strobing, and everyone melted into the background. It was a charge of ecstasy, although not in a sexual sense, but it was the same, too, that heightened feeling of intensity, where nothing else in the world matters, only the feeling coursing through you and lighting you up from the inside. Seraph went wide-eyed, and I knew she felt it, too. Then Ritchie moved on, I released Seraph's hand, and the music returned, full volume, and the voices around me ramped up louder than ever.

That thing with Seraph. Yeah, it had nothing to do with romance, in spite of that super-flash charge of ecstasy. It was way deeper, even sinister, although I hadn't been able to decipher it. I let it go. It was probably nothing, thankfully from someone I'd never meet again.

Before Ritchie finished the introductions, the music fell silent, the lights dropped, and a voice announced, "Time to top up drinks; half price for five minutes." The music stayed muted, and Ritchie and I found empty seats and could finally talk. It was as well, as our drinks had arrived. The two small whiskeys I recognized, with their amber liquid in clear glass, but the other? Light-brown foam on top with green liqueur filling the bottom? I picked it up, looked at it, and laughed.

"Never had a Springbokkie?" A redheaded, dark-skinned chick introduced as Felicity giggled. She had a bag of candies in her hand, and she popped one in and chewed rapturously. "You'll love Springbokkies. You'll really love Spring-bokkies." She slid down in her seat, and her eyes rolled up in her head as she went limp.

"Is Felicity all right?" I was eyeing the

Springbokkie. If it was high on Felicity's list, then I wasn't sure I wanted to partake.

"Yeah, she's all right. I think Seraph wants to dance. The music's about to come back up. Go with her. First, though." He held out the green drink to me in one hand, the whiskey in the other. "Wash it down with this."

I laughed, lifted the Springbokkie, and took it completely down, coughing as I set the glass to the side. Then I chased it with the whiskey. Ritchie grinned at me, held up a paper napkin, and motioned to my mouth. I tasted my lips, then wiped brown foam free.

Seraph touched my shoulder, and the world slowed down again. I was filled with the ecstasy of simply being *alive*. I turned to take in those dark eyes. Seeing her standing, I could tell she wasn't the lissome runway type. Rather, she carried a solid woman's body, filled out in all the right places. She took my hand and pulled me to my feet, and we drifted toward the dance floor, arriving just as the lights began to throb and the music began to pound the gathering dancers. Seraph had one arm over my shoulder and the other around my waist. She pulled me tight and whispered in my ear, "You've come home. We've waited for a very long time."

Heck, what did that mean? I was so lost in the continuing state of rapture from simply touching her that I couldn't focus on anything else, not even to wonder how I could hear her whisper with the pounding of the music. I didn't know how long we danced, ten minutes, an hour, or two or three. I didn't know and didn't care. We moved, lurched, and thumped with the beat, until I was soaked with sweat. I don't know how long I would have continued if I hadn't slowly come to realize someone had a hand inside my pants, feeling around for something. It was like a switch flipped, and I jerked away from Seraph, the music throbbing louder than ever, and finding perspiration running into my eyes. I latched on to the arm down my pants, pulling the thief off balance, and knocking another dancer off the floor and onto a table. The table fell over, spilling drinks, and causing a separate commotion of its own. Me, though, when I got that arm out of my pants, its hand had my wallet in it, and the man didn't want to let it go. I balled my hand up and began to punch him in the head, over and over. Who the dragonflies did he think he was, and how the didgeridoo did he know my wallet would be inside my pants? And was Seraph part of this? I grew angrier the more times I hit him, and still he refused to let go.

"Turn loose, you sucker!" I screamed at him over the music. The thought flashed through my mind in a white-hot arc that maybe I shouldn't have let Ritchie dress me in my fake tie. Then I wouldn't be here just now. We were sprawled on the dance floor by then. Couples who hadn't realized there was a fight in progress were still stepping around us, their feet inches from my face, but I'd been in a few fights, both with people and with my walls. That hospital stay might have sapped some of my latent power, but I knew how to dodge feet and land a wallop at the same time, and I wasn't taking no for an answer.

He was giving me a run for my money, however, and he had an arm around my neck pounding my head to the floor. My eyes were seeing stars, one blinking away something red, and I no longer knew self-control from self-fulfillment. I aimed for his temple, yelling, "I – *wham!* – survived – *wham!* – a plane – *wham!* – crash – *wham!* – three times – *wham!*" I paused for a moment, looking him hard in the face. His eyes glowed. In that moment I understood what he'd hoped to find. The key. We both held that wallet, and I knew I had to do him in, or he would find me again, over and over, until he had what he wanted. No way! He squeezed my neck in a massive hand, and I felt things going dark. It was now or never. "For- get you – *wham!* – Let – *wham!* – go – *wham!* – of my – *wham!* – wallet – *wham!*"

He finally went limp. I pulled my wallet from his greedy hand and tried to stand. Surprisingly, the music still blared, and the dancers were going full tilt. I looked around for Seraph, finding nothing more than gyrating bodies and flash- ing lights. I looked down to see the limp arm of my attacker trailing off in a streak of red, carried away by some gothic goons with black mascara forming raccoon eyes underneath black, spiked hair. The table had been righted, and a couple of new people were already moving in, not Goths, but equally bizarre, brightly dressed in a butterfly sort of way.

Marauding matchsticks, where was Ritchie?

No more did I ask myself that than the lights changed, going from reds and yellows to greens and blues. The music followed, the beat driving harder. The dancers had changed, too, now sporting leathers and spikes, with Seraph's Goth looks and garishly bright slashes of isolated color. It was Ritchie that got my attention from the sound booth, however.

"Hey, all you okes, drinking up all my mampoer." He paused, and laughter rippled over the club. "Got me a bru tonight, there on the floor, so keep him happy. We're heading to Sterkrivier tomorrow. Chip, raise your arm. This is Chip. Give him a welcome."

I lifted my arm. Ritchie threw his hand in the air and cheered, and the better part of those in the club cheered, also. I had arms around my shoulders. Glasses half emptied pressed against my chest, were put to lips, and against my chest again. It felt intimately welcoming, and odd at the same time. I didn't know these people, and had just met Ritchie. What the heck was going on? As they pulled me from the dance floor, I looked back and thought I saw someone wiping away blood with a wet towel. I glanced into the sound booth to find my host gone.

"Where's Ritchie?" I had a man about forty

sporting muscled biceps and gold teeth with his arm over my shoulders. He was part of the crowd, and we were moving toward the balcony. His glass clinked each time he took a drink. He was looking at me about two seconds out of ten, and I hoped he'd point me the right direction.

"Wherever he wants to be." He rumbled the words, and as he shifted his arm, pushing a drunken sot out of the way, I saw the glint of metal just where his pants met his shirt. Black metal, the heavy-duty, kill-you-now, ask-questions-later sort.

That made me think. Just who was Ritchie, anyway? I was getting sweaty under my armpits, and I never liked being sweaty under my armpits. As we made our way onto the balcony, a door in a darkened area at the back was closing. It disappeared to become part of the wall, and Ritchie materialized out of the shadows. He did his shoulder and arm thing, bringing laughter from the crowd, before making his way to me.

"I want to know, Ritchie—" I had my arm over his shoulder, speaking just to him, "—what you've gotten me into." That was nicer than what I really wanted to say. What was on the tip of my tongue was, I didn't come to your crazy country to be robbed blind on a darkened dance floor. That's what I was thinking, but the memory of Seraph held me back. She was a connection with something I wasn't certain I wanted to connect to, ever again. It hadn't been under time. We hadn't gone there, but we'd sure as heck gone somewhere, and I hadn't been in control of it. I'd been drowning in it. Except for that slimy hand down my pants, I'd be underwater gasping for breath about now, so, yeah, firecrackers, Ritchie, what the cheese is going on here?

"These are my *people,* Chip. It's all cool. I've taken care of everything." He motioned with his hand around the club; and the lights were flashing, people were dancing, and it looked like a normal club night. Even the butterfly people were at their table, laughing as if they'd been there all along.

He squeezed my neck before pulling away from me to fall onto a red leather Victorian sofa, putting his arm around a chick in black tights and blonde hair held aloft with silver wire; and as he released me, my neck twinged, shooting a sharp pain down my back. Yeah, that wasn't taken care of, Ritchie. I could have been killed, so toss you, Ritchie. Toss this whole stupid country, for all I stupid care.

Maybe being a god back at home wasn't as bad as I'd made out. At least in Houston, people weren't trying to kill me every time I went out at night. Under time might be torture, but I always made it back to work the next morning. Well, mostly, when I didn't have heart attacks on the way back out.

"What will you have?" A pretty waitress leaned forward, whispering into my ear, although with the sound of the partying, I was fairly sure she was yelling. She had a low top on, and there was a pretty clear line of sight down her cleavage. I was certain I saw several wadded bills inside.

"What's cheapest?" I'm not a skinflint, but I

did have to watch my expenses. Hospital; South Africa; I wanted to get back home. Soon. That type of stuff.

"Everything's on Ritchie's tab. Whisky sour?" She smiled with pouting red lips, like that would make me order something stronger. Heck, maybe it would.

"Straight, a double, and if Ritchie's paying, have another ready, just like it. I need to step out of my life for a night."

"You're my type of man. On its way." She gave me an air kiss with those pouty lips, winking before turning away. No electrical charges, no trip to under time, just a little rise in the man cave. I shifted position to relieve the pressure, thinking of Charisse. Charisse, beautiful, sweet Charisse. What happened on that dance floor was your fault, Chip. Why'd you even step out with Seraph? What did she have that Charisse doesn't?

I didn't get an answer to that, or time to begin figuring it out. Ritchie had disappeared, so he wasn't answering my questions. Anyway, after that next whiskey made it down my throat, the rest of the night was history. Somewhere in there I think I taught the crowd a new move on the dance floor, but what the hey, maybe that was only a dream.

The lipstick on my face the next morning wasn't. And my underwear? I had them on inside out. How the cheeseburgers did that happen? Crimey, if there's another little Chippie running around South Africa in about nine months, my life's twisted beyond repair.

As you've seen, I'm my own worst enemy, and there's nothing I've ever been able to do about that.

52

"HEY, BRU, GET YOUR BACKSIDE UP!"

Those were the first words I heard the next morning, then someone leaped on my bed. Okay, okay, on Ritchie's sofa. I was face down, and Ritchie crashed into me, pummeling me on the back.

"What the shish kabob?" I covered my face with my pillow. I said a few other things, hoping most of them were smothered by the feathers. When he didn't stop, I twisted my torso and pushed, forcing him off. "You a gay freakin' trucker?"

"Oh, yeah." He laughed and hooted, falling backwards and off the sofa, and catching himself before he went to the floor. "And you're a pimento loaf, still in bed, and that's worse. Get up, creampuff!"

He yanked at the blanket, pulling it to the floor, leaving me open to the air, and that's when I found my shorts were wrong side out.

"Oh, no." I rolled off the sofa, stood, and turned down the waistband. Dismayed, I moaned, "I wore them this way all night?"

"You're asking me?" He laughed. "Only part of the night. The last part. Come, we need to make a plan." He motioned with one arm and walked toward the kitchen. It was then I saw he was in his shorts, too, and the waistband shouted Calvin Klein. I was beginning to suspect my new friend Ritchie was better heeled than I'd suspected at first. Well, it was about time I had one friend who was, and him being in South Africa, right here, right when I needed him? That wasn't too bad, was it?

"What's this?" I paused in the dining room, to see newspaper clippings all over the table. Newspaper clippings were never good. Angela and Kobe. I'd wanted them both to survive. It hadn't happened that way, had it? Newspaper clippings meant people were about to die, and I was tired of people dying. I grabbed one that caught my eye. It was yellowed, but the name Engelbrecht jumped out at me.

"Engelbrecht Not a Hoax." There was a picture of a youngish man, looking roughly like my grandfather, but with innocence dancing around his eyes. He was beside a fire, holding what looked to be two long lances, with feathery things tied on the end. I wasn't sure, but he could have been dancing.

"You know him?" Ritchie's voice came over my shoulder, right in my ear, a whisper that rang like a bell in my head. His question was less a question than a suggestion, and I knew exactly what he was saying. He hadn't found me by accident. Nope. No, siree.

"Gramps." I scanned the yellowed paper, the words telling a tale of twin girls found locked in a cellar. It seemed Gramps knew where they were, squirreled away, and being pimped out to the highest bidders. They were thirteen.

"He already had a name for himself by then. Look at this one." Ritchie moved several aside, and I saw they were layered two and three deep. He shook one to get it free. "Look in that picture and see what you find."

An image of a circus placard painted on the side of an old wagon dominated the photograph, with the name H. H. Bell larger than life. A woman in a skimpy outfit twirled a baton on one side, a lion tamer stood over a roaring lion on the other, with several smaller venues around them. One was labeled, "The Magnificent Engelbrecht," and it revealed a man with a top hat and a crystal ball. Gramps? Maybe. It showed a very young man, one who only somewhat resembled the grandfather I recalled.

"Now look at this one. I'm pretty sure these

are connected, although the names are different." He moved several layers of the papers aside, pulling out one in a plastic sleeve. It was yellowed to brittleness, and part of the text was faded. "I have it memorized, if you have trouble reading it."

"This is old." I recognized some of the words, but others were totally unfamiliar to me. The date was perfectly clear, however. 1854. The title read *something* ". . . Makapan's Grot."

"It's Dutch, mostly, but some of the words are similar in English, so you could probably get the gist of it." He pointed to words as he interpreted. "*Siege* at Makapan's *Cave*. Here you read the old king's name, Mgombane Kekana. He died there, killed by this man, according to sources." He pointed to another name, Pieter Johannes Potgieter.

Kobe Potgieter. The name hit me like a brick. Then it hit harder. Remember, Grams had been a Potgieter. Still, for there to be a connection? That was a stretch. Old Piet had been Dutch, a Voortrekker, not African. Besides, Potgieter was one of the most frequent surnames in the country. Even I knew that, and I'd never lived here.

"Coincidence," I murmured.

"Coincidence, like a monkey's rump," Ritchie spat. "Don't delude yourself. I've been collecting this for years. That's why I knew you when your flight went south. This—" he pointed to Kekana and Potgieter, "—connects to this—" he picked up the article with the circus wagon, "—and directly to you." This time he pulled his jacket from the day before off the back of a chair, dug in a pocket, and retrieved the newspaper clipping with my picture in it. He laid the three on top of the table in a row, oldest to most recent, and tapped them in order. "King, grandfather, you." He poked me hard on the chest with two fingers.

"Coincidence," I said again, sifting through the yellowed articles on the table. A newer one caught my eye, and I lifted it free. *Houston Chronicle.* "Step-brother Imprisoned on Rape Charges." I looked hard at Ritchie. I knew this story. It was mine.

"Look at it this way, Chip. You only met me yesterday, but I've known you for years. Well, not really known you, but of your family. And here you are." He grinned and slapped me on the shoulder with the back of his hand. "In the flesh. This is great, you think?"

"You made this connection how?" I scanned the article for my name, because I didn't remember it being in there. Yeah, I knew this article. I had a copy of it myself back in Houston. I'd refused to let my name be included, and being a teacher, the newspaper had worked with me and the police. Sometimes having the police on your side helps with things like that. It only said "a Houston ISD school employee." If you're interested, that could be any one of ten-thousand different people. Houston ISD is big.

"Google. Everything's there."

"This wasn't supposed to be connected to me. My name's not in this article." I let it fall back to the conglomeration covering the table. I was scanning other titles. "Local Man Proclaimed Witch Doctor," "Limpopo Province Invaded by Ghost of African King," and the most infuriating one, "Engelbrecht Dragged Behind Wagon." I picked up that last one, thinking, So, the old story's really true.

"That's the saddest of the lot. Man, I can't believe anyone would do that." Ritchie slipped it from my fingers, and he carried it to the sofa, pushed my bedding aside, sat down, and read from it aloud. "Engelbrecht was lacerated from head to foot by his ordeal. His supporters, of which there are many, were highly agitated at the news of the faith healer's attempted execution. They claim he's being run out of the country by white factions that trace their heritage back to Piet Potgieter. Engelbrecht claims to also be a descendant of the original Potgieter of Voortrekker fame, but that's vehemently labeled as absurd by his detractors. Doctors have stated that Engelbrecht should recover fully, given time and adequate medical care."

Ritchie tossed the article on the coffee table, and he leaned back on the sofa. "Your gramps was the best. Like, rad. He said, Up yours, and he left 'em all behind. I knew you'd come back eventually. I counted on it." He shot me a hand sign, with two fingers curled to his palm, and the rest extended. He leaped up, punched me on the shoulder, and headed out of the room, calling back, "Want some clothes on. We're on the way to Sterkrivier. Wah-hoo!" He yelled the last word as he headed down the hallway, and he turned and disappeared into his bedroom.

This morning I wasn't so sure about Sterkrivier. Emilio, what have you gotten me into? I liked my life in Houston, well, parts of it. The Chalky part, Charisse, and teaching my students. Oh, I liked that, seeing them grow past their wasted home lives to become normal, productive human beings.

I didn't like that stupid key that had brought me here. I took the article about Gramps from the coffee table, and I looked it over, taking a deep breath and letting it out. I remembered Nurse Sheckley's words. *It is only a matter of time until you are ours.* I suspected it was that key she wanted, and I would be no more than collateral damage. And, yeah, reading that story, I was pretty certain that back then, I might have fought on the Voortrekker's side. I knew the dark side of Gramp's story. I lived it. I'd want to drive it out of my country, too.

Perhaps I understood him a bit better, though. He'd dealt with his "gift," even making a life for himself, and he'd been worked over by the people he'd tried to help. Here I was across the globe from home, and the same thing was happening to me. I was getting dumped on every single day, and all because some almighty someone somewhere up there thought it was funny to give me god powers, ones I didn't want, couldn't use in any manageable way, ones that always backfired on me. And I'd been rude as sin to Ritchie, and just like Chalky, he was treating me like a god.

Then, that's what I am, so what should I expect?

Toss it all. Toss being a god. I just wanted to go home. As if that would make life any better. Just ask Ryan. I messed him around pretty good, even if he was having it on a regular basis with his baby sister.

I placed the paper back on the table in line with the others, thinking, I guess life screws with everyone. Then we get on with living. Isn't that the way it's supposed to be?

My last thoughts as I walked away: What does a dead African king have to do with my dead grandfather? And Gramps was a Potgieter somewhere in there, also? What did that mean, that my grandparents were cousins? Distant, I hoped, if it was true. It was too much to get my head around, and I come from a mixed-up family.

But who doesn't?

—*53*—

RITCHIE AND I APPARENTLY WEREN'T the only ones headed to Sterkrivier.

He didn't tell me in so many words, just that we were catching breakfast at a favorite place of his with some friends. Some friends. I'd seen Ritchie's friends. I'd survived, but just. What would we be having for breakfast, pickled porcupine with the quills still attached? That beefy enforcer with the gold teeth could eat one of those as a snack and never know what had gone down. Heck, he'd been big. Me? I'd be happy with a muffin and some butter.

"Hey, bru, come see my bonsella." Ritchie jangled a wad of keys in the air as I walked from the bathroom. He had a bulky backpack at his feet. Other than that, he was wearing the same as the day before, the ragged jeans, the oversized jacket, and the hair thing going on. I wondered where he kept the knife, because I was sure it was in there somewhere. The bandana was different, a bright lemon-yellow infused with some pattern I couldn't quite make out.

"About the gas thing . . ." I fished for my wallet. He'd promised to be my guide only if I anted up.

"Nah, my boet! I was teasing. I got gas money. Plenty of gas money." He laughed, hiking his pack on one shoulder, and throwing his arm across my neck. "I got to secure the place, then we head out. Jislaaik, I'm excited! The *extreme!*"

He punched my shoulder, which I was getting tired of, by the way, but he was my ride, and never diss a ride, especially one that's free. He accessed the security panel again, and it began blinking in a steady on, on, off pattern. He nodded at me, and out the door we went, lock, lock, lock, and across the outside compound to a steel door set in the side of a concrete block wall. It also had three locks and a thumbprint ID. When it released, I was certain I heard a mechanism cycle bolts from around the perimeter. Ritchie swung it back, revealing holes punched in the framework.

"Crazy, man, like this is Fort Knox." I touched one, realizing the holes were in quarter-inch steel.

"Insurance. Keeps my car where I parked it."

He pulled me forward into lights that clicked on overhead, glowing dimly at first, then brightening to full strength. "My bakkie. You like?"

Crazy Annie, did I like? It was a massive, armored people carrier, and it gleamed like a new penny. Heck, yeah, I liked it. I moved forward to brush my hand along the fender. Ritchie stopped me by grabbing my shoulder. I turned to him.

"What? It's precious?"

"Armed." He pulled out a key fob and pushed a series of buttons. The vehicle shifted position, the lights came on, and it gurgled to life. "Now it won't bite back."

"This is a . . . bakkie? That must be a South African manufacturer." I used the front wheel and a side mirror to pull myself up to peer in the front window. "Snails' tails, it's huge."

"Marauder, civilian version. Cost me a few rand, but worth every one." Ritchie leapt to stand on the front bumper, dropping his pack with a thud on the hood.

"What's a bakkie, then?"

"Truck. Sorry. I've picked up a few words from around. Still, bakgak! That means awesome, for us Americans." He slammed a fist on the hood, giving off a dull thunk, and hooted. "Fully armored. I love this car. Now, breakfast is waiting, and I'm hungrier by the minute."

I shook my head. In spite of the previous night, I really liked this guy. Inside, the "bakkie" was no slouch. Leather seats, carpeting, and navigation. My new friend hit a switch, and something thudded dully. I looked in the mirror at my side to see a massive door rolling upward. Overhead, the drive system for the door told me it was as heavily armored as the bakkie. Not too bad for a Tallahassee boy making a home for himself on the African continent.

Ritchie's favorite breakfast spot turned out to be Felicity's flat, a third-story walk-up in a neighborhood I wouldn't have felt comfortable driving though, except for that armored vehicle we left parked at the curb. Ritchie walked away with a shrug, tapping his fob, ignoring the massive beast settling on its haunches to await our return. I hoped it would be there when we got back. We'd passed one burned-out car, still smoking, a homeless person I wasn't sure was alive, and a crowd of teenagers, one of whom I was certain had an assault rifle over one shoulder. The odd thing was, in Houston, I would have seen several patrol cars in the distance we drove. Here? It was like the cops had wiped their hands of the place, and were content to let it slide all the way into Hell.

Perhaps they thought it was already there.

Felicity was in a ragged tie-dyed tee that clashed with her red hair, in a kitchen that was an afterthought, with dishes stacked on the counter. They were clean, just that there were no cabinets, only a counter with a single sink. It had a patterned red cloth gathered underneath, hiding what, I didn't know. Stuff, I supposed. Sitting around an old Formica table was the crowd from the previous night. I shook hands with Memo and Cherish;

endured a hug from Tamara, still in her white miniskirt; waved at Felicity, who was cooking at a countertop hotplate; and paused as Cirque took my hands, stood, and kissed me on both cheeks. Her fingernails were brilliantly green and long, matching her eyes in color, and her eyelashes in length. She had an elfin face, with lush features that would have seemed out of place on another woman. She was perfect, though.

"Ritchie's so smart, finding you. He be our boet; we come to love him as family. What wonders we will find today."

"Brother." Ritchie's hand was on my shoulder, and he tapped me on the chest, explaining. "Boet means brother. Sorry, Cirque. I have to interpret sometimes."

"Ah, my Ritchie, I think our friend understands more than you think. Come. May I call you Chip?"

She took my arm and led me to a sofa that could only have been pulled out of a dumpster. Its redeeming quality was the clean blanket draped over it.

"Cirque, be nice." Ritchie chuckled and moved to Felicity, who handed him a spoon, pointed to a pan of eggs on the hotplate, and began slicing a loaf of French bread.

"Did you enjoy our little tête-à-tête, Chip?" Cirque still had her arm wrapped in mine; and she drew her legs under her and leaned against me.

"Tête-à-tête?" I hadn't spoken with her last night, except in greeting.

"You are so literal." She laughed, running a

hand down my arm. "I love literal."

"Where's Seraph?" I offered the name as a distraction. I realized she was the only one I hadn't seen, except for the bruiser with the gold teeth, and I was certain he'd show up at some point. Seraph? Heavens, I hoped not. However, I wasn't sure I wanted a tête-à-tête with Cirque, either. The thing with Seraph had turned me off women for a while, at least until I got back to the States and Charisse.

"Oh," and she pulled away. "Seraph. Such a mampara, so silly, an idiot, really. She found some boy to go home with. I think breakfast is ready. Come." She stood, pulling me up.

I could smell it. The eggs, and butter, lots of it, with something spicy. Curry? That was when I realized I was hungry. The others had plates in hand. Felicity waved me over.

"Come, Chip. This one's yours." She held a plate to me. It had a large slice of bread hollowed out on one side, filled with the curry I'd smelled earlier. Eggs were tucked in at the side. Cans of beer appeared out of a chest and soon made their way around the room.

"This is good." I dipped my finger into the curry and licked it clean, before taking a fork and shoving egg inside after the curry. "Wow!"

"Bunny chow. Felicity makes the best." That was from Memo.

It was the first time I'd heard the man speak, and he had a rich, honeyed voice. His face looked familiar, with dark lashes, smooth chocolate skin, and rubies in both ears. His hair was in a kinky pageboy, shoulder-length, but his voice was what caused me to remember. I'd seen him on a CD cover belonging to one of my students. Man, but was Ritchie ever egalitarian. Poor girl, rich boy, he picked his friends because he liked them, not for who they were. I actually was impressed by that. I watched the man who was my guide for the day, and I saw him in a new light: Ritchie, collector, friend to all. He was a magnet, drawing people together who otherwise wouldn't give each other the time of day. He'd certainly drawn me in, and I hadn't even known what was happening.

I was back to the sofa by then, and Ritchie threw himself to my side, with a plate of bunny chow of his own. He took bacon from his plate and slipped two slices alongside my eggs.

"When do we head out?" The bacon smelled good, and I broke off a piece and chewed it.

"We're waiting on Kwame." He picked up his bunny chow, rolled it slightly, and took a bite, laughing when it ran down his chin.

"Kwame?"

"Gold teeth. Now, you got that key with you?" He sat up, licking his fingers, before cramming a slice of bacon after the bunny chow, watching me as he chewed. He was waiting on my answer. He slipped a foil-wrapped towelette from a pocket, tore it open, wiped his hands, and made it disappear without glancing down. Then he patted the front of my shirt with the back of his hand until he felt the key, and he grinned. "Yeah, this is a good day."

I was beginning to think so. You know, I was with a bunch of Ritchie's crazy-wild friends, and somehow that seemed pretty all right with me. Maybe that was why this seemed to be a fairly good day. They were so messed up, that I actually felt quite normal around them. Crud, what did that say about me? Back at home, I had tough standards to live up to, what with Mrs. Lamar, so in control of the school, and Mrs. Chen, always looking over the top of her glasses at everyone. Then, Chalky, normal as anyone, even if he is messed up in a totally different way. And what about Rod, Tamina, and Ella, all leading normal lives, as if the world was their oyster, and all they needed to do was slurp the gravy? Maybe Africa was where I belonged, all voodoo and scrambled religions, with its crazy, non-understandable English, and massive armored cars that could run my American heap under their wheels and not know anything was there.

I wondered if M.J. would have been happier living in Africa. Would she have been safer, perhaps? Maybe not. I'd seen the assault rifle, and there was a reason Ritchie bundled up in that bomb-proof tank he called a truck. Africa wasn't safe at all, especially not South Africa.

Then there was that key in my pocket. Remember, my grandfather had run from Africa. He'd run long and hard, and he still hadn't been able to escape whatever had haunted him. Those news articles back on Ritchie's table; that meant something. What was the man looking for? How was my key connected? Dang, until I got it from my mother, I hadn't known there *was* a key. Richie, though, had accepted it like it was a given, like, Of course, Chip. Of course you have a key to Hell (or Heaven, or wherever). Just let me come along, because I want to see inside. I didn't want to see inside. I knew what Hell was like, and trust me, this world is better.

Oh, right, you have to point out my family's heritage. Gramps and Pops didn't think so. Cripes.

I leaned my head back and closed my eyes. The curry didn't seem so appealing any longer. I pressed my hand against the key, feeling its distinctive shape through the packaging. It was warm, even through my shirt. The voices in the room curled around me like smoke from a campfire, and I suppose it was the key, even that half-contact through my shirt, but the essence of each person's soul became a rich aroma telling of who they were, where they'd come from, and the dreams they'd once had, perhaps even given up, or traded in for more practical things like companionship, a roof over their heads, and a chance at seeing the sun rise on each new day. I reached out and brushed Tamara, her essence silky and smooth, turning into chocolaty wisps at a touch, and hiding three abortions she'd never told a previous boyfriend about, afraid he'd leave her; and he'd gone off without her, anyway. Cirque, beautiful, a fashion model, I realized, her personal integrity compromised by sleeping her way to success, and no longer caring about the recognition that had seemed so important to her once.

Memo surprised me. He'd lived on the streets as a child, and he was now haunted that his successful music career could one day crumble if discovery of him as an underage teenage escort should come to light. It had been survival for him, but it had also led to his discovery as a talented musician.

Cherish? She was a hazy blank, unknown to me in my smoke-wreathed haze.

Felicity was interesting. Privilege coated everything in her life. Money was there, still, in the background, waiting on her. Yet, she chose this, living on the edge, whipping up bunny chow for a rag-tag group of friends. Where did Ritchie fit into my fog-filled fantasy? Need. I saw need in him, the drive to put the pieces together. That's what the man did, put people together, deals together, turned things into what they should have been in the beginning.

Maybe that's what this group of friends was to him, people who needed to be put back together. Maybe that's what drove Ritchie. Maybe that's why all those newspaper clippings were strewn across his dining table. The man had found something fractured, and he was being driven to complete something that had been left undone for too many years.

Like me.

God knew, but I was undone. I came from an undone family, and I'd been undone all my life. Only Chalky had been there for me, constant as a headache, yet there for me every single day. Sometimes too much there, but there, nonetheless.

Could Ritchie do that for me, complete something that had left a gash in the way things were supposed to be? Would that heal my life?

I was startled back into the real world by a slamming door. Kwame dropped two black cases, huge suckers, on the floor. The others were instantly tuned his direction. He caught my eye and nodded as if he wasn't sure I'd be there, but he was satisfied that I was.

What would I have gotten from Kwami, all burley and business? I remembered his eyes, searching, looking at everything. I also remembered the gleam of his gun in the waist of his pants. Suddenly, I was glad I hadn't seen inside who he was. I was certain I'd find death there, lots of it, and I didn't want any part of it connected with me.

Yet, when we moved to the Marauder, I was in the second row, and guess who was at my side? I had plenty of time to wonder what was in those black cases. I'd seen *The Matrix*. Black cases usually held very big guns.

Crud, I thought. And it had started out to be such a good day.

—*54*—

YOU DON'T KNOW NOW FROM THEN until you've spent time in Africa.

South Africa, to be precise. Sure, parts of the continent are beautiful, stark in their simplicity, and vibrant with life. Even lush, in spots. Well, whole countries, to tell the truth, but Africa is so big that the lush spots get swallowed up in our minds.

Not so South Africa. While it has its arid sections—many countries do—and they have a visceral beauty of their own, mostly South Africa is a stunning feast for the eyes.

The drive to Sterkrivier across the platteland was no exception.

I hope you don't think I mean the Alps, or Indonesian rain

forests. It's not postcard Austria. Picture coastal Australia. I've not been there, but Evan Crewe (Remember Tamina?) once lived there. The Twelve Apostles, of which there are fewer now that some have fallen into the sea. The Gold Coast. Actual rain forests on the northern coast. Desert across the interior.

Yet even Australia's desert is filled with life, unlike the Sahara, with sand dunes that eat you alive when the haboob winds decide to peel back the world to see what's underneath. Sand, deep sand, that's what's underneath the Sahara.

Underneath northern South Africa is life, stunningly lush life. Miles of verdant farmland. I loved it, driving out, even packed in the SUV. While the vehicle was huge, we had all eight people from breakfast shoehorned inside. In the front, Ritchie was behind the wheel, having an animated conversation with Felicity. She'd pulled on a white, string-poncho type thing that gave her a furry, teddy bear appearance. Anyway, she looked pretty in it. When Ritchie said something funny, she'd lean over the massive console and grab his arm with both hands, hooting with laughter. I think the point was to make physical contact. Ritchie ate it up.

There were three of us with our backs to Ritchie and Felicity. Well, two in actual seats, the big comfortable leather ones, but there was a jump seat in the console that folded out, and that meant Kwame wasn't exactly *next* to me. The console was still there, but Cherish was on the jump seat, sort of offset in our little line of ducks, giving me a clear view of Kwame's huge arms and dancing eyes.

Cirque, Tamara, and Memo were at the back, facing us. Memo took the jumper, leaving the ladies in the big seats, and that meant he was knee to knee with Cherish. I had no idea if there was anything in that. I felt like I should. I wasn't getting much, however. Like I said earlier, I'd drawn a fuzzy blank from Cherish. She seemed to be normal enough. To most people *I* seem normal enough. We know how that goes. Anyway, about Cherish, she was very elegant, if understated, with amazing bone structure. Beautiful, in a statuesque sort of way. She was also focused on Memo, the way skillful diplomats make every person they're around feel as though they're the only person in the world that matters. She was good. Very good. Memo was eating it up, his honey and oil voice coming across as undertones in the conversations among the occupants, never clear enough to catch every word, but more a subwoofer that keeps everything else grounded to the real world.

I watched the landscape outside passing me by in reverse as words swirled around me.

"... in his arm. He nearly died ..."

"... so amusing! There were these lighted streamers ..."

"... decided to abort the baby. Thank God she had the sense ..."

"... said she felt like she'd lived it before.

Déjà vu! The medium said . . ."

That last one caught my attention. It was Cherish, facing away from me, remember, so I couldn't see her expression. Memo was leaning forward with his arms on his knees, his pageboy caressing his cheeks with each movement of the SUV, and his eyes glued to Cherish's face. I missed the end of what she said, jerked into the conversation by the words "déjà vu," and remembered my three airplane crashes. Each one was sharp and clear in my head, even if I knew the last one was the only one that really counted. Déjà vu! To have been there and remembered, even when you knew it wasn't part of your real life.

Still, there it was. Déjà vu. Someone knew my life. Somewhere. Somewhen.

I watched Memo's face. His eyes sparkled when he smiled, part of his stage persona, the part that earned him teen-age girls' attention, I suppose, but it was there and looked very real. He took Cherish's hand in one of his and covered it with the other, laughing softly.

"You mustn't look away from the truth. Even you, surely you have seen something that you know is real, because you've lived it before."

Yeah, I thought, watching the conversation. Every day of my life. Cherish was having none of it, however.

"You cannot tell me you believe in true déjà vu." Cherish put her free hand on Memo's. Yeah, there was something going on there. I was dense, and even I could see that. "Look at yourself. You've made your success, and you've done it all on talent, one day at a time. You've told me so yourself. The next thing, you'll be telling me you believe in reincarnation."

"True." He chuckled and looked outside the window for a moment, before glancing back at his hands, then releasing hers to wipe his palms on his pants. "Sometimes, a song comes to me as if I already know it, out of a dream. Those times, then I remember a time before. That's all." He shrugged.

Felicity called over the thickly bolstered front seat, "Sing to us, Memo. One no one knows."

"Voetsek!" *Buzz off!* He said it with a laugh, taking the edge off, and he waved a hand dismissively in the air.

"You must. For our new friend. Make him, Ritchie. Please?" Cirque's elfin features lighted up, all charm and persuasion.

"Leave it, Cirque." Tamara ran long fingers through her voluptuous hair, yawning. "He's a big boy and can say no if he wants. "

"Memo?" Cherish's hand was on his knee. I knew her question. For me, please, Memo?

Ritchie called out, "It's up to you, bru. We're just your wing men."

"And women." The words resonated, like a subwoofer. It was the first thing Kwame had said since we'd gotten on the road. I looked at him appreciatively. I'd not have thought him one for women's rights. It raised him a notch in my estimation.

"And women." Memo laughed. "Strusbob."

As true as Bob. The gospel truth. I got that, although I didn't know how. Maybe some of South Africa was bleeding through. Since leaving the hospital, I'd been mostly normal, making it through normal minutes, then normal hours, and almost a normal day, with only a minor slip-up or two. I'd been letting myself relax. Maybe this was my reminder not to.

Memo began to tap his legs with his flattened palms in a catchy beat, several times on one leg, then a quick interruption on the other, with a back-and-forth jump that pulled me in. He used his mouth to fill in with additional beats, the sounds mimicking different musical instruments. He closed his eyes, his head began to sway and dip, and I felt his song wafting through me and changing who I was.

"Na na na na na . . . feel the dark, it come for you . . ."

It was there, the memories, and I closed my eyes, sensing the tingle of touching something that might pull me under, that feeling in the back of my skull. I was afraid to look around. I might see the dark, that translucent quality that told me the real world was about to disappear.

"Jesus love you . . . ahh-um-ahh . . . take you home . . ." Memo was humming in between his lyrical phrases, you know, with those musical mouth noises, and his hands carrying on their erratic dance on his legs, reminding me of the drums from Mother Earth's underworld choir. It was as if I were there.

"No cry, my love, I there for you . . . she-sho-she-sho-um-po-pu-do . . ."

Who was there for me, had ever been there for me? My parents? Good gravy, no. I was alone in my godforsaken, god-woven life. I didn't like it, and I couldn't break out of it, and bullfrogs knew, I'd tried. I was so wrapped up in Memo's song that I didn't feel the tears running down my cheeks.

"I be the one to pull you through." He followed with a series of crackling, humming, and bopping sounds, occasionally popping his tongue, and making amazing noises. He whispered with broken emotion, "Che-shu . . . che-shu—" The mood was shattered when Ritchie slammed on the brakes.

"Whoa, look at that! Crazy-cool elephant!"

"Where?" Felicity. She cheered, clapping her hands excitedly. "I see it. There, beside the road."

I glanced at the elephant. It was exciting, sure, to see a real-life gargantuan creature wandering alongside the road and pulling branches off trees, but what I really noticed was the haunted look in Memo's eyes.

Man, I thought. Memo's been under time. I've seen that look in my own mirror. It's been there in the eyes that I dread, that haunted look staring back at me. I wiped my face, glad everyone's attention was on the elephant. The others didn't seem affected by Memo's song, not like I had been . . . not like Memo had been.

Yeah, you don't know now from then until you've spent time in Africa. That's God's truth for sure.

—*55*—

ABOUT AN HOUR INTO THE DRIVE—halfway, I figured, from what Ritchie had said—Felicity saw a little roadside collection of buildings. A sign showed an arrow, pointing.

"Ritchie, let's stop."

"Here?" He glanced at the massive navigation screen built into the dashboard. It showed the route continuing on for a good distance. He did take his foot off the gas, and the big machine began to slow.

"Now. You'll miss it."

"Sure, if you want." He called to the rest of us, "Break time."

I climbed out first, offering a hand to Cherish, who used my help and Memo's to exit. Kwame got Cirque and Tamara on the other side.

"My God, it's beautiful here." Ritchie stood in the sun, shading his eyes and looking over the landscape.

I had to agree with him, one hundred percent. This view, rolling countryside as far as we could see, was God's gift of farmland to the whole of South Africa. Beautiful fields, lush grasses, and stands of trees. In the distance, magnificent buttes gave a stark beauty to the horizon, allowing the sky to undulate against the land in a slow-motion dance of tender affection.

This was the Africa people dreamed of, the one few people got to experience. Even I saw that. I wondered why I was being drawn here. I didn't get to ponder that long, because Tamara screeched and called out, "Fresh fruit! This is to die for!"

Memo and Cherish joined her, making a studied selection. Kwame and his muscles seemed to be on patrol, his eyes everywhere, even if he had smiled at Tamara's reaction. Ritchie called out that he'd found a little eatery in the back, and we should all come see.

The eatery was little more than a shed roof with half a dozen tables and an open-air cooking area. A young girl looking to be about nine wore a sundress with a white apron. An elderly woman standing at a large pot, her dark skin heavily lined, and her gray hair fighting to get out of a headtie, called to us.

"Come! Plenty potjiekos!" She smiled and lifted a spoon filled with meat and vegetables, before dropping it into the steaming cast-iron cauldron.

"Will you be eating with us?" The girl welcomed us in. "My tannie expected guests today. She felt it in the winds and has prepared a special meal."

"Do you hear that?" Ritchie twirled to face us, threw his arms out, and laughed. "This is just for us. Everyone pull up a chair."

The chairs were in a stack off to the side, as if there wasn't usually a crowd at the little shop. I noticed that, but it didn't really register. It was just another fact that I filed away, like so many others since I'd met up with Ritchie. Kwame pulled a stack to the tables and began setting them out, and Memo was quick to help. They were almost done by the time I got into motion, spending more time adjusting their position than anything else.

We didn't really *order*, as there wasn't a menu. Potjiekos, I learned, meant little-pot food, although the pot looked massive to me. The girl brought us glasses of ice, along with cans of cold drinks. Spoons and cloth napkins appeared, then bread and bowls of steaming stew filled the tables.

"You enjoy?" The old woman wandered among the tables as we noisily consumed our meal. We were so busy eating that we didn't reply much. Ritchie nodded enthusiastically, dipping his bread into the stew and holding it high in the air before stuffing it into his mouth in one bite. Our cook laughed, touching him on the arm, and saying something in Afrikaans I couldn't catch. I found the interchange very enjoyable, and was beginning to wonder why this country had such a bad reputation for violence. Sure, back in the city, but here? All I saw was warmth and charming manners.

As the woman continued to make her way around, chatting and visiting, our group grew louder and louder, with laughter and ribald jokes called to one another. Eventually, she reached my table, where I was sitting with Memo, Tamara, and Tamara's bag of fresh fruit. Cherish was at Ritchie's table, her arms in motion, regaling him with some sort of tale. They'd seen a statue of an African fertility god in a courtyard, and they pointed to it repeatedly.

"You be the rooinek." Our hostess smiled at me indulgently. "You enjoy?"

"Very much." It *was* good. I smiled, asking Memo out of the side of my mouth, "Rooinek?"

"Red neck. Sunburn neck, because you're not from here."

"Ah, you no rooinek? I think otherwise." Our hostess laughed, her eyes hidden in the folds of her lined cheeks. "This tell the truth." She reached gently toward my collar.

Here's where my morning began to collapse around me. Her remark had been so simple. Red neck. I got it. The sun was intense here, and if you weren't used to it, you'd have some crazy sunburn. I knew I wasn't prepared. I barely had the clothes on my back, and they were borrowed. How could I be expected to have sunscreen, too? It wasn't my fault if I stood out like a lion in a lamb's paddock. She didn't have to touch me! Maybe if she'd known, she wouldn't have.

Anyway, she placed a hand gently on my neck, no big deal, except it became a big deal. When she touched me, I felt a jolt, and my eyes went wide. I knew because her hand was like a cattle prod, only it didn't hurt. Rather like I came more than alive, just fishsticks frozen, stiff, and in shock all at the same time.

Even odder, everyone around me stopped eating. Not quit eating, stopped, hands partway to their mouths, Ritchie leaning back in his chair with his drink can held high to drain the last drop, Tamara laughing as a bit of beef fell from her spoon into her bowl.

The drop from the can was frozen in the air, hovering, and the beef had yet to hit the bowl. Across the covered area, Kwame was half standing, a pose no one could hold for any length of time, yet he wasn't moving.

At my table, my male companion was looking my direction, Memo's hand to his mouth, as if covering laughter; and Tamara's eyes peered into the old woman's face, as if seeing something there besides an old woman asking about how her guests liked her cooking.

Me? I stood, even as I knew I was still seated, with an ancient African woman's hand resting on my neck. I could still feel it there, warm, the skin soft, the gentle pressure of an innocuous touch by someone who truly wanted her visitors to enjoy their time in her establishment, if only for an hour of their day.

The world was frozen, the whole dang world. What was I supposed to do now?

That's when I heard the laughter. Oh, no, I thought, as I turned around. I recognized that laugh, and I had no doubt exactly who it was.

—*56*—

THE SHOP, THE COURTYARD WITH the fertility statue, all the buildings in the little compound faded into a mist. I knew exactly what was going on. It irritated me, too. After all, this was my *life*. I'd escaped this for *one day*, and it had felt so good. I suppose I thought maybe I could have it forever.

Dang it all to the center of the world. I balled my hand, and I wanted to strike out, but there was only the mist. He couldn't even give me anything to vent my frustration!

"Hey," I called. "What the heck is this? I'm tired, you control freak, you. I want my life to myself. Can't you give me even one day?"

"My son, you still have no understanding." A voice was all there was. No person, no one to strike out at. Just that voice reverberating through the fog.

"Understand what, jerkwater? I'm tired, don't you get that?"

"And yet you do not give up."

"And yet you don't give me any help." I yelled the words into the mist, only to get laughter in return. "What? What have I said that's funny now?"

"You still do not understand. Soon, my son. It is not time to be with me. You must return. Your companions await."

I readied another outburst, when I felt a hand at my face, the touch one I recognized, that of Mother Earth. A breeze caressed my cheek, and it whispered in my ear, "Be at peace, for your questions will be answered soon."

The world wrenched, and the old woman snatched her hand from my neck, hissing, "Pasop! Pasop, each of you!" She put her hand to her mouth, her dark eyes landing on each one of our group, and, trembling, she walked away, pausing at one empty table to rest her hand on it as if she had to regain her strength before moving on. She disappeared around one of the buildings.

Tamara burst into giggles, and she fanned herself. "What was that about?"

I was in a daze. Mother Earth had touched me, and I could barely think.

Memo placed a hand on my arm, murmuring, "You been there. I see it in your eyes. The dark, it come for you. Now, you must trust in Jesus to bring you home." He began speaking softly in a language I didn't understand, as if praying underneath his breath.

Everyone was talking, until Ritchie stood and called, "Hey, my bru, are you all right?"

In the confusion, the girl who'd seated us appeared with a small basket of doughnut-size bread rolls, deep fried to a crispy brown. She handed it to Ritchie, dipping her head respectfully, saying, "Tannie says you must go. Please take these to make your journey a good one."

She was gone before anyone could ask her what it was all about.

I wanted to know what pasop meant. I made my way to Ritchie just as he dropped a large bill on the table. I bumped him on the chest with my knuckles.

"Pasop. What the heck does that mean?"

Before he could answer, Memo realized what was in the basket, calling, "Vetkoek! My day is complete!"

"Ritchie?" I prodded him.

"Pasop means," and he threw his arm across my shoulder, leaning into my ear, "beware, to watch out. Vetkoek is fat cake, and you want one of these." He pushed me off, and he held up the basket, calling, "Get 'em while they're hot. First come, first served!"

They must have been good, because hands came out of everywhere. Me? I'd just been halfway to Hell. I wasn't hungry at all.

And dang it, they did smell good. Always, always, the rotten luck for me.

GRAMPS, GRAMPS, WHAT DID YOU DO to bring me here?

I stood beside Ritchie's massive Marauder, waiting as the others disembarked. As soon as my feet had hit the ground, the place seemed *aware,* the feeling seeping into my soles and running up my legs. A bird chattered off in the brush, irritated, I was certain, by actual humans interloping into its private territory. Not many had, not anytime recently, I was convinced. No wonder, if everyone felt this when they first set foot here. Anyway, a lesser vehicle wouldn't have made it down the trail, and it was a trail. The machine had mowed down small trees, forded a shallow river, and traversed a swampy area I thought we weren't getting past.

The farm? I'm sure it had been quite a place at one time, but everything had collapsed in on itself. The grand manor house, with its stone windows done in a Gothic cathedral style, arched high against the horizon. Peaked gables of timbered masonry showed the one-time grandeur that must have set someone back a pretty penny. The roof that connected everything? It was gone, and sunlight streamed from the inside of the ruin to the outside, though the remains of leaded glass that sparkled in the midday light.

Low stone walls stretched long fingers into the distance, dividing the property. Lines of trees formed the borders of additional fields, although smaller trees were established in the midst of the large, leveled areas, taking over once again. Yeah, I remembered Mother Earth. This was her land. Rising to the escarpment at the edge of the horizon, I could still make out the grid that would have divided coffee from cotton from grain crops when this was a functional farm. Actually, with the size, plantation might have been a better description.

"Old Sterkrivier Farm." Ritchie stepped beside me. "I've heard about this place. Never thought to actually see it. It has quite a reputation for hauntings and other mystic phenomena. There, the old chapel. That's where the really bad stuff took place."

He indicated a partially collapsed building to the right in a copse of small trees. A round stone tower about sixty feet high had a pointed tile roof partially collapsed, with grassy material growing around the remainder of the guttering. Arched openings bordered by Romanesque columns revealed an old bell still hanging inside. The nave of the structure had fallen in, leaving an overgrown foundation outlined by partially standing stone archways and a lone rose window with a few panels of stained glass still sparkling in the sun.

A dusky doorway in the stonework at the bottom of the tower revealed the treads of a staircase leading upward. If I hadn't known better, the key in my pocket seemed to lurch at the sight of the shadows inside. Something was there, something in the darkness, something pulling me, perhaps something my grandfather had disturbed many years before. I knew without asking that this was where I'd been drawn. The house? That was history. This chapel? It would take me into the pits of under time and beyond. I was certain of that.

"Good lighting." Cirque held her hands in front of her, framing the old manor house with her fingers. "What a location for a fashion shoot. I think I'll explore." She kissed Ritchie on the cheek, wrapped one arm in Memo's, and off they went, tromping through the golden-headed grasses and weedy tufts of knotted plants.

"Watch for snakes—" Ritchie called.

"And lions and tigers and bears. I've lived here all my life." She called her dismissal of his warning with a laugh and a hand over her shoulder, wriggling her fingers, before wrapping her body around Memo's arm, and continuing on.

"How dangerous is it?" I remembered the elephant. I was glad they weren't heading to the chapel. I didn't know what we'd find there, but it didn't feel good.

"Not very. Rotten floorboards will probably kill them if anything does." He turned to the rest of the group: Felicity and Tamara pulling on rubber boots; and Cherish helping Kwame remove the black cases from the SUV. "Let's go see if old Kekana's ready to come home."

Kekana. The king from Tanner's book on the plane. I started to ask Ritchie if that's who he meant, but I didn't get the chance.

"Equipment's ready." Kwame gripped one case in each hand, lifting them as easily as I would pick up a sack of potatoes. I'd seen Cherish struggling to get one out of the vehicle. Whatever was inside was heavy.

"Can I take pictures?" Tamara had a cell phone out. She touched the glass face, and it dinged. She looked up, smiling.

"No flash." That was Kwame.

Ritchie looked at him for a moment, then made a decision, nodding his head, repeating, "No flash, Tamara. We want this to work."

"Yebo." She touched the phone again, it dinged, and she looked up, smiling, giving Ritchie a thumbs-up. "Got it."

"Sometimes I think I should leave her home, except Felice can't live without her, and Felice makes the best breakfast south of the Botswana border. You have any idea what we're doing here?" Ritchie looked me in the eyes, raising his eyebrows in question, before slamming the door to his SUV and shifting his jacket to fit more comfortably on his shoulders.

"It's through that door, whatever it is."

"I knew you were the man." Ritchie grinned. "You, me, that key. We're making history today." He held up his hand in a fist, and I did the same, giving him a bump.

Okay, I thought. Let's go make some history, however we were supposed to do that.

—*58*—

FELICITY AND TAMARA DISAPPEARED, laughing, into the shadowed doorway. Their feet vanished up the stone steps. I could hear echoes of their voices from the openings around the top. Kwame and Chasity were probing the ground with telescoping rods they'd pulled from one of the cases, searching for hidden chambers, I supposed. Ritchie pulled me around to the backside of the ruin, offering me words of warning as we stepped around fallen stones and small trees.

Being this close to the structure had me itching like summer camp after a romp through poison oak. I pushed it aside as nerves.

"Hole, badger, probably. Give it a wide berth." Ritchie laughed, pointing with one of the rods. "Honey badgers. What a name. If my honey were in as bad a mood as these little devils, she'd be out the door. What do you know about what we're hoping to find?" He paused, looking at me inquisitively.

I shrugged. "You tell me. I'm from Houston, Texas, North America."

"Nah, bru, you know more than that. You've got the *key*." He had one hand resting on the wall, his fingers wrapped around a protruding stone, and he tested the soil with one foot. Above us, we heard something ding. We looked up to see Felicity overhead, leaning out of the tower, her cell phone in hand. She waved.

"Got you," she laughed.

"Turn the shutter noise off," Ritchie called back.

"I have the sound down." She looked at it petulantly, as if the camera should know what to do already.

"It's not the same. I'll check it when we get ready to start." He looked at me and shrugged. "Like I said. Anyway, Old Kekana was reported to have powers over his subjects. Magic powers."

I noticed how he said that. *Magic powers.* As if he were laughing it off. If he *were* laughing it off, why were we here?

"You keep saying Kekana. King Kekana, from two centuries ago?"

"Mgombane, yeah. You saw the article, killed at Makapan's Cave. That's about thirty miles overland, that way." He pointed west. "Here's

- 453 -

what I brought you to see."

He dug at the base of the tower, pulling a vine away, then kicking back dirt with his foot. One of the stones at the very bottom was different, carved instead of roughly hewn, and it contained a weathered inscription I couldn't read. Part of it was missing, as if it had been chiseled off.

"I thought you'd never been here." I was kneeling to see the design and rubbing it with my finger. It felt . . . malleable . . . permeable . . . maybe even alive. It was odd, but at the same time, it felt exactly as it should, a connection to *something*. I traced the carving, feeling a chill run up and down my spine.

"Haven't." He brushed at one side of the stone to reveal a four-leaf clover, barely visible. I'd not have seen it if he hadn't run his fingers inside, making a noise with his tongue, as if to say, Check this out. He also pulled a package of hand wipes from a pocket, tore it open, and began to wipe his palms.

"So?" I rested my arms on my knees and looked at him. His eyes were laughing at me.

"This place is famous." He swept his arm to take in the fallen manor and the overgrown grounds. "No one lives here because it's *haunted*." He chuckled.

"So, it's famous. You've never been here, and yet you know exactly where this stone is."

"Okay, I give." He let out a sharp breath,

laughing as he did so. "You've heard of *Hauntings Revealed,* the TV show?"

"American?"

"Bru, come on, you're forcing me to start from the beginning." He shook his head and settled on a stone block that seemed to be growing out of the grass. He had a smile on his face, so I knew he wasn't upset. "They did an episode on Old Sterkrivier Farm back in the 80s. They made a big deal out of this stone. The clover is supposed to represent the four points of the cross. The name is supposedly King Kekana's, written in Ndebele, which some sources say was his native language. It's been mutilated, so no one's sure any longer. It's supposed to trap his spirit here forever, keeping his curse off the Voortrekkers who killed him."

"Voortrekkers." This was straight from Tanner's book. "As in Pieter Johannes Potgieter, Voortrekker, I presume."

"Whoa, the man catches on quick!" Ritchie laughed, leaning forward and slapping me on the shoulder.

"The boy who survived the plane crash with me is a Potgieter."

"Um-huh," was all Ritchie said, grinning all the time.

"I haven't told you this." My heart was pounding. "I have a grandmother here, maybe still alive." I laughed. "Holy hummus, yeah, still alive. She's too crazy to die. She's a Potgieter, or she was before she and my gramps married."

"Kwame, hear that?" He yelled the question. He grinned when he got his answer.

"Mike's up and running. Getting everything. Yelling does not help." The words were muffled, sounding a bit peeved, and coming from around the old ruin. I saw a red light at Ritchie's waist. I wondered where the actual mike was. It didn't matter. Still, it told me they were serious about all this.

"What was on that envelope?" Ritchie stood, grinning, his hands on his hips, clearly knowing the answer he expected from me.

"You saw it. This place."

"Crazy right, this place. And you're the *extreme,* the one here to right the wrongs done by an old fart who didn't know enough to leave well enough alone. Your grandfather, I expect. I bet that key you're carrying fits the empty crypt in the basement, you think?"

Crypt? I thought of Edgar Allen Poe and *The Cask of Amontillado*, and the horror of being buried alive in the walls of the catacombs. I looked at Ritchie, all happy with himself and excited over me. I couldn't be happy. His words reminded me of what Mother Earth had said. *It is up to you to undo the wrongs that have been done.* What wrongs? Love a duck, I didn't even know what I was doing here, except that I'd had to come, and I couldn't be anywhere else. I had no idea what I was supposed to undo.

Hey, God, I could use some help about now. Sabe? If there was an answer, I couldn't tell.

HOW CAN PEOPLE BE SO CRAZY STUPID? By people, I mean me, Chip, absolute idiot, chump that can't put two and two together and get four.

Shiatsu, I'm stupid!

You can already see where this part of the story's going. Yeah, I should have run when Ritchie said "crypt." Like, crypts are all about *dead people,* Chip. Bones, spirits that won't move on, that sort of crazy, downtime stuff.

I didn't get it, yet. Was I fooled by *Hauntings Revealed?* Perhaps. I had watched some of those back home, the American version, and I always wondered who the fools were that believed such nonsense. Me, the god-guy, the jerkwater who travels under time and speaks with dead people . . . are you seeing the stupid part?

Making our way around the remains of the tower, Ritchie was talking about the episode on Sterkrivier Farm, filling me in on more than I wanted to know, how they'd tried to read the spirits with all sorts of technical devices, but being the 80s, of course, their technology was primitive, and they'd gotten nothing except lots of video of old stone walls and a few rats scrambling in the darkness.

That was enough for me. I'm not much of a rat fan. I prefer to make my own holes in my walls.

So I guess that was part of it, me feeling the dread of those nasty little critters, but more, I'd been fooled by my time with Ritchie. That had to've been it. I even laughed with him about the people I worked with always tuning in to catch the 21st century American version of *Hauntings Revealed*.

"It's all camera angles and bad lighting." I chuckled as I brushed at my arms. Ritchie had donned heavy gloves, pulled from a hidden pocket, and he was stripping vines from the rock wall. Clearing up, he said, to make the energy flow better. The falling debris was getting on everything, meaning all over me.

"I suppose. This, though, is different." He yanked at a thick vine that reached into one of the tower openings, and as it released its hold and began to slither through the stone window frame, one of the women inside screeched. He yelled, "It's just me. Kekana hasn't returned from the grave." He looked at me and grinned, saying more softly, "Yet."

He ducked as it tumbled our direction, and I jumped back just in time to miss being hit on the head.

"Ritchie, are we ready?" Felicity leaned out, holding the cell phone. It made its dingy-ding sound, and she waved. "Thanks. For Tamara. The last one was blurry. You should see the view from up here. I think there are bats in the belfry." She waved again and giggled before disappearing.

Something rustled in the brush behind us. I didn't see anything until Ritchie pointed into a tree.

"Black mamba." He pressed on my chin to aim my eyes the right direction. "Long and thin, right there."

"Ouch, don't those kill you with one bite?" It was the skinniest snake, and easily ten feet long. It was twisted on one branch, and draped across another about five feet away. "Why's it not black?"

"Not everything in Africa is fortunate enough to be like me." A deep-throated chuckle accompanied the words as Kwame appeared, stepping around the old tower.

"Kwame, we're set up?"

"Now-now. Cherish taking care of it. The mamba, you see the black just before she bite. Then you die." Kwame shrugged, then he laughed, showing off his gold teeth. "But the tannie no like to bite us. We too big for her to eat."

"Tannie? You said it was a mamba, right?" I was shivering. I had heard of mambas. Deadly mothers.

"Auntie. Old woman. For all we know, she could be a boy. There's no way to tell unless you see little mambas around." Ritchie grinned. The snake continued to watch us.

"Babies?" I cleared my throat. "You think there are babies inside there?" The tower, but Ritchie and Kwame would know what I meant.

"Struesbob, you no African." Kwame chuckled. "If she be a tannie, she no bother with her children. She lay the eggs and go away."

"We're making sure." Ritchie dismissed the snake and continued around the stone structure, kicking at the foundation and pulling away any attached undergrowth. "They generally run from people, and we're giving them time to make their escape."

"Should we warn Felicity and Tamara?" I glanced up, just catching the phone held at arms' length, and once again hearing the sound of the shutter.

"Nah." Kwame's deep rumble. "The mamba, she like to go down. We be clearing the crypt. If she there, that's where we find her."

"Don't worry, Chip. That one?" Ritchie nodded his head the mamba's direction. "That's probably why we're seeing her. We disturbed her, and she's being wary. When we're gone, she'll head back into the building, ready to lay her clutch and let the next generation spread through the veld."

"So she's what haunts this old place." I said the words lightly to counter my racing pulse. Mamba, old ruins, crypt. You can see why I was jittery. Not scared, not leery, just jittery. Justifiably jittery.

"In America, snakes might be the only things haunting old Indian grounds the Europeans violated. Here, the spirits run back thousands of years. Hauntings go a lot deeper than simple snakes."

About then, Kwame barked out, "Got me one!" He leaped to a low shrub, and with a quick motion, he pulled out a light brown snake about a yard long, his hand firmly pressing at the base of the animal's head.

"Holy cow, is that one of those?" I looked back to the mamba tree to find it empty, the snake gone.

"The big one, she a tannie." Kwame squeezed the head to reveal a black mouth, with short, spiked fangs. "Here her baby. Look inside. You see why she called a black mamba."

"That wasn't wise, Kwame." Ritchie was uncharacteristically somber. He stopped and glared at the man. "I need you, and we're a long way from medical care."

"No worry. He a bit deurmekaar. The shade, it make him sleepy. Watch out." He tossed the snake into the brush.

"That's enough mamba for me." Ritchie

reached to his mass of hair and pushed it behind his shoulder. "Kwame, are Memo and Cirque joining us?"

The big, black bruiser spoke into a tiny microphone I just noticed he was wearing, reaching about an inch from an earphone in his right ear, and running along his jawline, asking, "Are they back?" After a moment, he looked at Ritchie and nodded.

So, you see, I'd been distracted. Egad, I *was* distracted, otherwise I'd never have entered that building. I wasn't putting things together. Two plus two always equals four. How simple is that?

Ritchie called loudly, "Cherish, we're on the way."

"She heard you." Kwame shook his head.

"I heard you," came from the other side, just before we rounded the building, stepping toward the collapsed nave.

I was caught up short to see Cherish in a weird priestess getup. She wore a metal headdress fitted with black stones, a flowing robe also covered with similar stones, and wide arm bands that matched the headdress in construction and style.

"Ritchie? What's this about?" I turned to him to see Kwame helping him into a similar getup. Surely they weren't planning a ritual sacrifice, because I suspected if so, he was Abraham, and I was intended to play the part of Isaac. I had my eyes out for sharp knives, the throat-slitting kind.

"Protection from negative energies." Cirque

appeared out of my peripheral, also wearing a robe, but with only one large black stone on an expansive gold chain hanging around her neck. She grasped the necklace and glanced at it. "The stone's obsidian, and as I'm only an observer, one's all I need. I'll probably be safe from the feedback, as long as Ritchie and Cherish do their jobs properly."

She gave them a stern look, and Ritchie laughed.

"We all have them, except you, of course." Ritchie had his "protection" on, his hair tall and flamboyant in the headpiece. He looked like a white African shaman. He smiled broadly, as if this were the most normal thing in the world. "The gems transmute negative energy to positive energy, so we're not harmed. This protects the thought process," he touched the headpiece, "and the rest protect whatever they cover. You're our link to the power. You have to be able to absorb whatever energy we find in order to make this work. You'll see Felicity and Tamara wearing a single stone each just over their hearts. We only have two full sets, which is why not everyone can participate."

"And Memo?" His song told me he could go under time. Where was he? Had he acquired the good sense to run away from this nightmare before the fireworks started?

"Memo's your guide into the spirit world." Cherish spoke. "He's our resident psychic. He's inside preparing now. You think we look weird, he'll blow your mind."

"What about him?" I pointed. Kwame was to the side, unadorned, wearing no robe and no gems.

"Me? This land run in my veins. All spirits be of me and part of me. My ancestors spilt their blood in this soil, and I be connected to everyone who ever died in this place."

"Eish!" Ritchie shook his head. "He's immune. I think he's too thick-headed for the spirits to get through." The others laughed good-naturedly.

"So tell me, anybody. If this didn't work in the 80s, why now?" All this talk, well, I needed to talk, to get answers, specifically. They seemed to know exactly what was happening. I didn't want to get thrown in the looney bin tied up in a white jacket. I wanted some verification that *these* people weren't the crazy ones.

"Chommie, it works because you've got a connection." Ritchie put his arm across my shoulder.

I'd grown tired of him doing that, but I wasn't bringing it up right then. Not here, two hours from Pretoria, not when we were miles down a mud track, and on the lost side of a flowing river I'd have to ford to get back to civilization. I didn't dare think about lions, elephants, and black mambas. Cheese whiz, I'd mess my pants before I got a hundred yards.

"And that is?" I kept my eyes on Ritchie expectantly.

"You're breaking my heart, Chippie. My *heart*. Are you with us? You have the *key*." He rapped his knuckles against my chest.

"That makes a difference because . . ."

"Amateurs, amateurs. Everyone in the world of spirit intervention knows that having an *object* that is *directly related* to the deceased is how you contact the spirit world. How can you not know that?"

"So, we're having, like, a spirit reading?"

"Oh, yeah. We're contacting old Kekana right here, today, in the very crypt he was buried in. You're how we're doing it." Ritchie made a fist and jerked it downward in an expression of triumph.

I thought, No! Making contact with the dead? I've been there and done that, and it's never been fun. These guys were crazy jokers! How did I not see this coming? Am I an idiot or what?

—*60*—

OKAY, THEN, I THOUGHT. LET'S DO IT. Let's bridge to the afterlife. Let's see if the dead king is still around here, because, kind sirs, I've been there, done that, and returned home again, if sometimes worse for the wear.

"A spirit reading?" I smiled broadly, as if this was something I'd never thought of. That part was true. I threw an arm across Ritchie's shoulders, and I gave him a quick one-armed squeeze, the sort we're allowed to give students back in Houston, before stepping away and clapping my hands together to hold them in front of me. "How will you know if we actually contact any dead people?"

"Nobody's sure, not really." Cherish, in her robe of ebony stones, smiled. "Everything you see on TV is just a theory."

"Spirits, Hauntings, and Things that Go Bump in the Night has a website that explains everything." Ritchie was still smiling, as if he were a kid in a sandbox, and the new kid had come to play, bringing the only shovel in town.

"If you believe '38 Outward Manifestations of a Haunting.' One, objects may move around by themselves. Two, objects may disappear and not be found again. Three—" Kwame was pulling electronics out of one of the cases, something like a radar gun, muttering to himself, until Ritchie cut him off.

"No need to go on, Kwame." Ritchie chuckled, turning to me. "The man thinks I'm obsessed. But, note, he's here, running my equipment every time we do this."

"So you don't make a moegoe of yourself. Three, objects may appear from nowhere. Four, odd lights may be seen. Five, religious objects appear or disappear—"

"Enough, Kwame." Cherish touched his shoulder, resting her hand there for a moment. "Everyone knows you and Ritchie have a difference of opinion on this. Let's record the interactions with the spirit world and see if science can tell us what we've got."

"Ja, Tannie." Kwame grinned when he said it.

"Somebody, can you people interpret for me? I don't know Afrikaans that well." Moegoe? Ja? Tannie, I think I'd figured out from the snake lecture. Mother, aunt, or matriarch.

Once again, I didn't get my answer. Tamara

and Felicity breezed from the tower's shadowed doorway, Tamara with the little smartphone out in front of her, pausing every few steps to let the machine whir, then moving on. Felicity peered over her shoulder at each new image, clapping, as they joined us.

"Pick up anything good?" Kwame. He adjusted the legs on a tripod by touch, as if he'd done this a million times. His eyes were on the two women. He seemed to be teasing.

"She'll be a fabulous photographer someday. Don't you make fun, Kwame. Someone can do worse than take beautiful snaps from the top of an abandoned bell tower." Felicity took the phone, and she stroked its surface, stopping on one. "Here you can see Memo and Cirque just through the window. What do you think that glow is?"

She held it out to the big enforcer, and he glanced at it casually. "Poor focus?"

"You are a bully." She smiled as she retrieved the phone.

"Can I?" I held out my hand. The image showed the dilapidated manse from an aerial vantage point, the gables not able to mask the interior. Memo and Cirque were visible through the remains of the largest of the rose windows. The scene was sharp in every detail except through the stone filigree just where they stood. It sent a chill down my spine.

"Do you see it?" She tapped the screen.

"Can you make the picture larger?"

She stroked it, and the image grew in size,

still crisp and focused. A large bird sat on a decapitated wall preening its feathers; the brilliant South African sun streaked the window openings into patterned shadows; and a small tree on a staircase landing stretched brave arms to catch the light. I took the phone and moved the image around, centering on the two people I knew. As sharp as the rest of the image was, through the stonework, bits of old leaded glass, and shadows, something wasn't quite right. Hazy. Ghostly, Ritchie would probably say. Felicity touched the image, adjusting it to show just the rose window, and she indicated several areas.

"What's that look like to you?"

"It's been done before, Felicity. Don't make the man see what's not there." Kwame shook his head.

"Who did this before?" She had my attention. If you looked at the glass shards in the opening and let your eyes play with the shadows and fuzzy bits, well, it resembled a face. A dark, brooding face. It was eerie, but it could be anything. You remember that face on Mars, then they sent an orbiter up and snapped a photo from a different direction. It was just a pile of rocks. This was a window with most of the glass missing, the sun streaming in at an odd angle, and two friends who happened to be exploring the ruined remains of a bygone era. Besides, who knew what faults the tiny camera in that phone had? How good a lens could it be? I ignored the fact that the rest of the snapshot was of incredible quality. I think I was distracted by the thrumming I felt in the ground, like when standing right beside a train track, and the soil itself vibrates with the weight of the passing behemoth, jarring your teeth until you want to scream for it to stop. *Except.* Except when I looked, the dirt was perfectly still.

"Chipper, *Hauntings Revealed,* Sterkrivier Farm episode." Ritchie moved his hand in a loose circle around his ear and grinned. He took the phone and made a quick adjustment before returning it to Felicity. "They got that exact shot from the tower, minus Memo and Cirque. Memo's our trump card, and you, of course. Come, we're about ready. Felice, feel free to click away. The sound is muted."

About ready meant everyone was robed up except me, Memo, and Kwame. Ritchie and Cherish were in their stone and metal headdresses, Cirque wore her single stone over her robe, and Felicity and Tamara were attaching their obsidian necklaces over their freshly donned outfits. Except for the peaked hats, it could have been a Clan gathering from Selma back in the sixties. Cirque had a microphone out, with a small transmitter, and she clipped it on my belt, worked the cord up the back of my shirt, and slipped it over one ear. It was just like the one I'd seen on Kwame.

Perfect. When I foul myself with fright, everyone will hear how badly I screw up. Great.

Ritchie asked for the key, telling me there was a specific process for this. We had to ritually unlock the door to show we had permission to broach the spirit world, and Memo'd be the one to do that. We'd sit in a circle in the crypt; there were certain prayers Memo knew; and we'd give the spirits free rein to say hello to us. He said it like you'd say to someone, "I'm buying ten lottery tickets, and then I'm going to win and live like a rock star," when you knew it was only a pipe dream, like the last fifty times you'd bought lottery tickets, only to tear them up after the drawing, because they were no more than worthless pieces of paper. I pulled the envelope out, handing the entire thing to Ritchie, not wanting to touch the object inside. I hoped the man knew what he was doing. For all I knew, that key could suck us all under time, straight to Mother Earth and that very strange African god from my dream. I didn't think any of these people were ready to die today.

I hadn't seen Memo, yet, so I had no idea if he was ready to play his part. Or how he'd be dressed. Two thumbs up, Memo! I'm not making fun, because I like the guy, and I couldn't imagine keeping my sanity together after I'd been an underage male escort. His song in the SUV had been a hit with me, also.

Kwame was at the radar gun, erect with his arms crossed over his chest. He looked serious business. Tamara had a real-to-god, movie-quality video camera on her shoulder. Bam! Where did that come from?

"What are Felicity and Cirque doing in this?"

I was next to regally dressed Ritchie with his wild, braided hair, and I was starting to feel the African vibe. The voodoo stuff. The ancient magic. I couldn't imagine either Felicity or Cirque as the stuff of magic and wispy dreams.

"They're neutral observers. Nonbelievers. Neither one gives me a shot of picking anything up, but they've got an open mind."

"Cherish?" She'd been a blank for me from the get-go. There was something there blocking her from whatever I'd seen that morning.

"I forget you don't know." He looked at her in her flowing, stone-bedecked robe, with her obsidian amulet around her neck and resting on her chest just between her breasts, and her grand headdress. He chuckled. "I know I seem to be the center of all this, but Cherish is the one that really got me interested, especially in Sterkrivier Farm. She's true-born African, like Kwame."

"I got that. Is there something between you two?" I'd noticed how he'd stopped and looked at her. A man didn't do that unless there was something there.

"Between me and Cherish? Right! How would I get close to the likes of royalty like her?"

"Ask her out, maybe?" I was thinking of Charisse. Oh, I missed her.

"You don't know, yet." He nodded her direction. "That's the granddaughter of King Kekana, with a few greats in there, of course. She wants to bring her grandfather home. She doesn't know where his final remains are, and we're here to ask him where to look."

I froze. Granddaughter. I hadn't been able to see her through the mist. All the others at breakfast had been open books to me, and I could have perused every page of their lives. Why hadn't I been able to read Cherish? Then, there was Tanner and his book, with its tales of an African king killed by white settlers. My grandmother named Potgieter. Kobe, same name. Old Piet Potgieter, the idiot who'd killed the king. I knew my grandfather was connected, and Pops? Why else would he have offed himself?

Crikey, yeah, it was finally making sense. Sort of, in a weird, screw-you sort of way. This might be no more than a spirit reading to these jokers, but I had an inside track. I hadn't forgotten God's words.

My son, the time has come.

The time for what? That's what had the hackles up on my back. The time for what, passage through the fire, visiting the underworld, perhaps Heaven; or maybe I was to be elevated to archangel status, the next Michael or Gabriel. Should I try on Archangel Chip for size? I knew my church doctrine. The archangels didn't exactly lead a life of ease and luxury. They were always battling with the demons and spirits, sometimes for days on end.

Crikey. I'd done enough of that in my life. I just wanted peace, a quiet life with Charisse, and someone to hold in the middle of the night. Is that too much to ask? Anyone? Are you out there, anyone?

I thought not.

Memo distracted me, appearing from the back side of the SUV. To top everything else off, the singer had changed into full African regalia, with a beaded headwrap, a black and orange snakeskin necklace, a zebra-skin loincloth that was less a loincloth than a panel of zebra tassels that reached past his knees, and lots and lots of bare skin. He was barefoot with beaded anklets, and he walked through the red dirt our direction.

Jinkies, yeah, I thought. Now we've got the spitting image of King Mgombane Kekana in our midst. Sorry, Memo, you're going down. I didn't know you wanted to sacrifice yourself to become an old dead king, 'cause there's a good chance that if he returns, he's gonna want a home to return to.

You know my life. Stranger things have happened.

By then, Ritchie was headed to the bell tower, the key out and in his hand. We all fell in line, the others chatting merrily. Only Memo seemed appropriately somber.

That and Cherish. I felt her eyes on me all the way. I wasn't sure what it meant, but I was absolutely convinced, this couldn't come to a good end, not by any measure in my book.

Like I said, you know my life. If your eighth grade science teacher taught you anything at all, you know how this is going down, and it won't be pretty.

Not pretty at all.

—*61*—

NOW, I'VE NEVER PARTICIPATED in a spirit reading, so I wasn't sure what to expect, but I anticipated something with candles, a hexagram on the floor, and a table that would rise into the air. Oh, and curtains at the window that could blow in, so that a ghostly gust of air could sweep past, extinguish the candles, and leave us breathlessly nervous in the dark.

Am I a great science teacher or what? That's the most unscientific scene I can paint, but truly, I expected to walk into the basement of that ruined chapel and see all that nonsense I just described to you. The truth of it was slightly less dramatic—at the beginning.

The ending? Read on, valiant book lover. If you've gotten this far, then I've somehow managed to keep your attention, and I suppose you want to know how this turns out. Did I die? Well, I'm writing this, aren't I? So, no. However . . . I might have enjoyed that better.

Before we went inside, Memo took my key from Ritchie and pulled it from the envelope. He handed me the packaging with a shrug, and he turned the key over and looked at it. It wasn't much, just a rusty old iron behemoth, the kind you might picture a monk wearing on a rope around his waist when he wanders the monastery. He looked me in the eyes, and I shrugged back.

"It'll work, Memo." Ritchie encouraged him. "Just follow Cherish's steps. Chip and I are both miked, and Kwame's doing a full scan of the energies. Nothing's happening like last time."

"Like last time?" I felt my armpits swell with moisture. The sun was shining, it was near midday, and I was warm. I got a wicked chill, anyway. "Nobody said anything about a last time."

"Slow down, Chip. It was no big deal, and no one got injured." Ritchie was whispering.

"Seriously, you mean," Memo interjected. He held out an arm to show me a scar just down from his shoulder.

"Only a broken pane of glass." Cherish put her hand to Memo's face. "We've taken all precautions, and there's no glass here. Can we head inside, now?"

"Certainly."

Memo stepped forward, the first adventurer in our small group of four intrepid explorers. As I moved toward the shadows, I expected something big, like me dropping into another dimension. Been there, done that. When I crossed the threshold, I broke out in goosebumps, as if I'd walked underneath an air conditioning vent. I shivered and rubbed my arms. I didn't notice any ground vibration, but as I was already shaking, I wouldn't have felt that, anyway. It was musty inside. Not damp, just old, like rot had already set in and been arrested, and the floorboards and rafters were waiting for a signal so they could catch up, fall in, and bring the whole place down on top of us. On the backside of the steps leading upwards, there was a set leading down. Ritchie and Cherish each produced a flashlight from somewhere in their robes, helping me to breathe easier.

At the bottom of the steps, on the opposite wall, a thick wooden door stood ajar. The hinges were rusted, making me pretty certain it wasn't moving today, not under our muscle or anyone else's.

"What if we can't close it?" I whispered the words to Ritchie.

"We don't have to, just insert the key and make like we're unlocking it. It's all symbolism, so the dead will recognize our authority to be here."

"Ah, the dead will recognize us. I don't know if that's good or not."

"It is if we want them to talk to us, and we do, or at least Cherish does. Look, we're starting. When we get inside, you need to be between Cherish and me. We're the insulators to keep the spirit world from jumping from Memo to you and back again. It has to flow over us. The stones absorb the negative power of the afterlife, transmute it, and charge us up with spiritual energy so we can ask questions and hear the spirits answer." His voice had risen in pitch, revealing his excitement.

I was excited, too, but not in anticipation. I'd burned the pictures of Pops after he killed himself. One or two had been taken at the very end, and they weren't pretty. Gramps? I could run my hands over the pitted walls every time I used the downstairs toilet. Stuff like that tends to kill anticipation. What was I excited about? Finally getting this over with.

The words Memo chanted/sang/caressed the key with before inserting it into the lock were Afrikaans to me. No, really, they reminded me of my crazy grandmother. Real, holy pantalones Afrikaans, the kind the old Dutch Boers still speak. I didn't get a word of it. Then he inserted the massive key into a pierced iron plate in the door, pulled it out, and we made our way past it into the darkness. The flashlights were placed in opposite corners so they aimed upwards. The chamber was very small, with a stained, vaulted, and ribbed stone ceiling, reminding me of an Old World wine cellar. Everyone moved confidently to their places, for which I assumed I could thank *Hauntings Revealed*. The only people in the world who didn't know this place like their bathroom in the middle of the night were probably from America. Me. Memo placed the key in the center of the floor, and we took our positions. Directly overhead, the keystone holding the arches above us extended down to form a water-blackened, upside-down urn, eerily reminiscent of a funerary vessel for holding dead people's ashes. Creepy, if you ask me. No one did, so I shivered and followed everyone else's lead.

Ritchie, Cherish, and I sat first. The two insulators tucked their stone-decorated robes and dropped to the floor, Cherish as gracefully as if she participated in spirit readings in abandoned crypts every day, and Ritchie with enough enthusiasm for all four of us. Cherish took my wrist and pulled me down, and in trying to get my legs crossed with dignity, I caught a foot on one of the stones on Ritchie's robe, slipped, and fell partially onto Cherish's knee. Ritchie saved me from total embarrassment by yanking my arm hard his direction. We cracked heads in the process. We laughed it off, but it hurt. I wanted to joke, Was that a sign? But Memo was still standing in his African king garb with the zebra loin cloth below his bare stomach, and a look of intensity on his face that unnerved me. I figured my joke would fall flat. I didn't want my joke to fall flat. I wanted to go home, and I needed these people I hardly knew to get me there.

I still hadn't connected the chill from earlier

with anything. My bumps hadn't faded, and I continued to put it down to nerves. We three sat knee to knee. When Memo breathed out a moaning melody, I jerked, one of those uncontrollable muscle movements that takes over your whole body, bumping our kneecaps together.

"Be calm." Cherish held out her hands, one to me, one higher for Memo's. "Take my hand so we can begin."

Ritchie was doing the same. Cherish's hand was cool and dry, and Ritchie's was warm and sweaty. Polar opposites. Memo clapped his hands, looked at the three of us, and grinned.

"Okay, we can start now." He sounded too chipper in my estimation.

"I thought we'd already started."

"Nah, chommie. Everyone holds hands for the spirits to flow. Only then do we begin."

"All that chanting . . ." I looked at Ritchie, then back to Memo. "That was . . . ?"

"To set the mood." Memo grinned, and he settled to the floor, his knees making contact, and taking the hands next to him.

"Kwame?" Ritchie called loudly, startling me. "We're beginning."

"You're miked up. I'm hearing everything. I'm bringing in the reader."

"Gotcha." Ritchie released hands, pulled up a place on his robe, and spoke directly into it with a grin. "Did we bring the second mike for Chip?"

"I have it with me. I think Cirque set up one on him already. Check the power switch and see if it's on."

Ritchie pulled up the hem of my shirt, looked at me, and gave me a thumbs-up sign. "His main mike is wired and ready," he whispered into his robe, as he adjusted my earpiece before offering me his hand again.

Our official recorders and observers joined us, disappeared as much as possible into the gray shadows around the small room, and everything grew quiet. Kwame clipped a second mike to my shirt lapel, and he dropped its attached power box at my side. "To pick up sonic resonances," he muttered, looking at Ritchie as he spoke.

Ritchie grinned, and Kwame took his position behind me, joining the others at the wall.

Memo took a deep breath and intoned, "We come to speak with Mgombane Kekana. We are four, and yet we are one in intent. We request permission to enter the spirit world. Our key of passage lies between us."

My chill grew stronger, finally forcing me to pay attention. I looked at Ritchie, and he grinned and winked at me. Cherish and Memo had their eyes closed. Cherish held my hand limply as Memo continued.

"As proof of our common intent and unified spirits, we place our hands on the key which invites us into your realm."

Oh, no, I thought. I'd done my best *not* to

touch that key. Ritchie and Cherish were leaning toward it, pulling my hands after theirs. My heart pounded, I was now in a total sweat, and I was freezing. "Geez," I muttered in dread. We might get a true visit to the afterlife after all. I wondered if I'd be the only one participating, or if we'd all get to go under.

Hold on to your underwear! I closed my eyes, not wanting to do this, and I felt the cool metal of the key against my skin. It was just metal, rough, old metal like it was supposed to be. Awesome! I could play Ritchie's psychic game, enjoy a little South African culture, and catch the next ride back home. Charisse, I exulted, Baby, I'm headed your way as soon as I can board a plane.

My hot air balloon was punctured by Memo's voice. In a lowered pitch that was the singer's voice, and yet wasn't, seven words brought me crashing to the ground.

"My son, are you ready to wake?"

My skin burst into flames, and I knew exactly where I was. I was in the underworld. Or Heaven. It all depends on your point of view. Like I said, dying certainly would have been easier. Not my luck. I got to do it the fun way. That's called sarcasm, for those of you who don't know me. This wouldn't be fun. I knew that. I just didn't have any other choice.

Then, with my skin crisped from my bones, leaving me screaming with pain, I fell through to the other side.

—62—

HERE'S THE CREEPY, MESSED-UP part of all this. Oh, it's not what you think. I've been under time. It's like my second home, the one where goofy things happen that you don't dare tell the rest of the world. I hated it, but it wasn't creepy to me, not any longer.

I couldn't cross all the way over. And I tried. Like crud I did. It was like being on a lake, stepping from one boat to another, and your feet are stuck, one foot on each craft; and they're moving apart; and the water is flaming volcanic lava! This was the first time I'd been in both worlds at once, as if I didn't have a good connection, and we were constantly shifting radio frequencies between stations. Sterkrivier, under time, then Sterkrivier, under time. Bsszt, static overload, bsszt, then Sterkrivier for a moment, and bsszt, back to under time.

Holy moly! It burned like hellfire every time the channel changed, too. It was that stupid bonfire gate to the underworld, I was certain. I probably had Mother Earth to blame for that.

Through the pain I caught glimpses of God on his throne, surrounded by a writhing outgrowth of brown, interweaving branches, looping and unlooping their woody fingertips, and continually reinventing the throne's ultimate configuration. It hadn't done that before. Mother Earth stood nearby. The dancers in the background were a pointillist accompaniment to a reddened scene of undulating nightmare.

Then I was caught. Mother Nature's hand rested on my arm, and the slippery connection between worlds solidified.

"No thanks for the pudding," I spat, my stomach still trying to rip out my throat and chuck it on the ground. "What was that?"

"You have broached the doorway, and you stand in the middle. It is now both open and closed. You cannot remain in one world, but you cannot leave the other. Only by touching me can you continue to visit our side of the passage."

"Smurf it. I've done this all my life. How is this any different?" I'd fallen to my knees, and I gasped for breath. I didn't try to pull free from her arm, however. I believed every word she said.

"My woman speaks with wisdom." God had arisen, and he stood over me in his feathered and beaded paraphernalia. He made Memo look underdressed. "Are you ready, my son?"

"For what?" My anger was fading, and filling its shoes was an intense sorrow. I knew, because I felt tears running down my face. For what, I didn't know.

"Rise, my son. All your life you have carried a burden that was never yours to bear, and yet, you have done so with grace and love for your fellow man. You have called it a curse, and in that, you have been closer to the truth than you knew. It is time to learn the past. Grasp my hand."

His fingers were thick and meaty, the skin dark and glistening in the light of the fire. Drums pounded in a unified rhythm, picking up the beat, and the dancers in the background gyrated viscerally. Through the scene, I could still see a ghostly image of Ritchie, and I could feel his hand in mine. Cherish's coolness filled my other hand. Across from me, Memo, trim and youthful in comparison to God, looked regal in his beaded headwrap and flayed zebra. The hated key gifted to me by my crazy mother still pressed against my skin. Yet, those things had become a dream. Only God and Mother Earth were real. Only this fire-flecked underworld carried any semblance of *feeling,* of *truthfulness,* of *destiny.*

God was right. I lived under a curse, and I've never known what it really was or why it was mine. It had killed two of my family members, and those were just the ones I knew about. I was afraid it would do the same to me. Did I want to know the truth? Jinkies, yeah. I didn't know where God's hand was offering to take me, but I was on board a thousand percent.

What is that old saying? *Be careful what you wish for, because you may just get it.*

"Might as well eat the soup," I whispered, and I reached out, and I made contact with the awesome and inconceivable hand of the almighty God.

I HAD NO IDEA what I was getting into. Yet, why should today be any different?

And with that thought, the world twisted around me, the wind was hot on my face, and I stood on a green landscape, with a series of bare, bulbous rock outcroppings rising over my head. A battle was in progress, with occasional gunfire shattering the scene. Dying men lay all around, some moaning in pain, white-skinned in cumbersome European dress; and others, silent and black, elegant in their tribal war regalia. Underneath a rock overhang, one richly skinned man boasted more elaborate regalia than all the rest. He could only be a king. He was alive, if barely. He sat on a stone, held erect by a younger man who was little more than a youth, who pressed a hand to the king's bleeding side. The king spoke in a terse, fluid language, stopping to gather his strength from time to time, sometimes coughing in vile fits. Blood began to leak from his lips. A fresh round of gunfire echoed across the rocky outcroppings, and the king collapsed into the younger man's arms. The youth wailed with despair.

"It began here."

I had forgotten Mother Earth, and her words were an inrush, filling in the details of the mysterious scene. King Mgombane Kekana was now dead. He had cursed the Potgieter line, bringing dishonor and confusion to everything they put their hand to. Before I could question her, the world twisted again, and the manor house at Sterkrivier Farm towered above us in newly framed majesty. Broad-shouldered masons chipped at stones, preparing them as the partially finished walls grew from the red African soil.

I looked toward the copse where we'd set up our spirit reading. The chapel stood complete, the tilework on the roof brand new, with a priest in clerical robes intoning indecipherable words in Latin.

"Mgombane Kekana now rests in peace." God spoke, and I saw the wider scope surrounding this Christian blessing over a dead African king. This was bribery, a way of canceling Kekana's curse. A way of sealing the powers of his final words into a prison that would contain him forever, protecting the Voortrekker family line that had stolen his kingdom away.

"He's not there, now." I mumbled the words, remembering the empty crypt and the solitary stone that had been defaced.

"He was at peace for a time. Then, this . . ." Mother Earth waved her hand, and it was dark.

We were inside, and the chapel rose around us, the stone walls creating a barrier against the world. It was cold. Scrambling sounds came from behind the altar. In the light of a flickering oil lantern, white skin overlapped brown, and a voice hissed, "The child you bear will be coloured, no longer Kekana royalty. Your line will carry Potgieter blood in its veins. You will soon share this family's curse, witch." A female voice cried out, then was quickly muffled, as the man leaned heavily into her.

"Do something," I wailed, wanting to go to her and provide assistance. "He's violating her."

"She is your great-great-grandmother. Her son will carry the man's name."

How could I have imagined this? I knew Grandmother had been a Potgieter, but not like this. I was sick to my stomach, but before I could lose the contents, the scene changed again, although we were still in the chapel. The lighting was different, and the roof leaked sky, allowing the moon's ghostly fingers to caress the room. Two shapes in dark clothes and carrying a black trunk walked furtively down the aisle.

"Pieter, you sure we should do this?" A young man's voice, whispered and frightened. "We mebbe executed for even being here."

"Forget them. My grandfather no belong on Potgieter land. I be taking him away." The new voice, equally young, was angry and fiercely determined.

"How he be your grandfather?" The first man sounded puzzled as they navigated towards the same door I remembered walking through before our spirit reading began.

"He be my verloofde's grandfather, and mine, also. We be cousins and soon to be married, so there be no difference to me. Our family be dishonored because of the whites that took our land. It happened in this very place, over our grandfather's bones." The youths dropped the trunk, and the one named Pieter kicked at a pew violently. Dust flew, telling of the decimated condition of the old structure. It made me aware of the cobwebs and the film of dissected age covering everything.

"You brought the key to the burial chamber?"

"And a sledgehammer, if we cannot gain entrance. Grandfather Kekana be leaving this cursed building in this trunk if I must take down a wall. Let's go, Njabulo. We take the king home, then I have a date with Ntokozo. I tell her I rescued her kinsman, and she marry me tomorrow."

"That be all you think about, Pieter, sex?"

"I be a man. Of course, Njabulo."

"You be seventeen."

"As I say, a man," and Pieter laughed as they disappeared through the door.

Ntokozo. My grandmother. Pieter, Gramps. Of course, I never knew them by those names, but I knew of them by those names. Sam Hill, yeah, steal a dead body to get into a girl's shorts. Go, Gramps. I guess it worked. I had that trunk in my garage.

Trunk. *I had that trunk in my garage.* It was more, however. I had Mgombane Kekana in my garage. I got it now, the whole shebang. My grandfather stole Kekana's bones, became a psychic, and killed himself because of it. My dad inherited the trunk, and ditto. Mom sent me the trunk, and it delivered me into under time where I actually spoke with a dead person. Talk about juju to the nth level!

The boys were returning, and they crashed through the door in a run. Pieter was yelling angrily, "Somebody already stole the old man. I knew we shouldn't have waited!"

"They missed this!" The light had increased, telling me morning was on the way, and Njabulo held up a jawbone. "Lock it in the trunk, and Ntokozo will never know. You be in her bed before the night is over."

"If you ever tell!" Pieter laughed, released the catches on the trunk, and threw the lid back, stirring a swirl of dust in the gloom. "I swear I beat your face to a pulp."

"Hope to die!" Njabulo tossed the bone inside, the trunk was slammed, and the boys hoofed it outside, one on either end, leaving the final traces of moonlight to dance among the dust motes alone.

"It is in your possession." Mother Earth spoke, her words brushing my ears like feathers of dust and evensong, confirming my intuition.

"In my trunk, I know." My heart pounded inside.

"It must be returned." Not a command this time. Pleading.

"How, for heaven's sake? It's nine thousand miles away."

"Mother, he asks how. Perhaps he is not my son after all." God chuckled.

"Imagine." Mother Earth whispered the word as the mist rolled in, and the world faded to white.

I should have known it couldn't be as easy as all that. Imagine? I knew under time. It's diving through Hell, itself. I did it, though. I pictured that trunk, and as soon as I got it firmly in my mind, I heard God speak.

"Go, my son, and return with your prize."

Then I was stretched nine thousand miles in an instant, held in Africa, touching America, my mind in both places at once, a mental rubber band that wanted to snap at the earliest opportunity. My head pounded like a thousand icepicks were piercing my skull.

Did I mention I'm off work for recuperation? From heart surgery? If I can survive this, well, chumps, I guess I can endure just about anything.

—64—

I WOULD HAVE PUNCHED CHALKY'S lights out, that
was if they'd been on. I forgot about the time difference. It
might be noon in Sterkrivier, but Houston was barely pushing
four. That's AM. He was chilled on my sofa, the TV was running up my electric bill, and he wasn't awake to watch it.

Then there were the supplies from the home store, all
spread across the living room and the kitchen. Chalky, *clean
things up.*

But, yeah, the walls looked better, as seen through the
fractured vision of under time. Repairs had been started. And
at least I wasn't in *back time,* to be caught in honeyed amber,
frozen and unable to move. I was in the present, so I was
nearly unrestricted.

Except for that rubber band and the thousand icepicks.

I groped in my closet until I located the key to the storeroom, then I made my way to the garage, remembering the last time I messed with that trunk. Were God and Mother Earth still holding to me? I supposed so, otherwise I'd still be changing channels, unable to get a fix on what I was supposed to do. I had to trust them. I was here on their meal ticket. I had so little control that I really had none at all.

I pulled things from off the trunk, asking myself, We covered it with everything I own for what reason? Yeah, talking to dead people, but for *what* reason? I took a hammer to the lock, busting it off. I no longer cared about damage to the trunk. I threw the lid back, expecting to see the jawbone right there, and it wasn't. Crud, it was packed with everything Gramps could have possibly collected in his entire life. And my head. It was about to explode. I saw one problem with traveling halfway across the world. I suspected that when the rubber band snapped, I would hit Sterkrivier pretty hard. Nothing to be done about that, however, so I began tossing items from the trunk. Paperwork, old clothes, even some African tribal art. Then came items I had seen in Ritchie's old newspaper clippings from Gramps' days as a psychic. Playbills. A collapsible top hat.

All got tossed out.

I was getting desperately close to the bottom.

Finally, I turned the trunk over, dumping everything into the floor. A hard object wrapped in an old shirt tumbled out last. I grasped it in my hand. It felt the correct shape. Yes! I thought. Except, I was still in Houston. I had to get back. I was nearly blinded with the pain in my head. I closed my eyes, imagined the chapel and my friends there, and opened them to my storeroom.

"You know how this works," I muttered. "Unwrap it, Chip, before your head explodes. You know that's how this works." With trembling hands, I pulled the shirt away, exposing a portion of the bone. I recognized the same artifact I'd seen Njabulo toss inside the black trunk decades before. It was just a jawbone, yet it was something much, much more. Deaths were invested in this. My life was invested in it. Cherish wanted it back; it was her ancestor's. It hit me, that elegant woman was a cousin of mine. Shuzzbutt, but imagine that, an African princess is a cousin of mine. The other side of that hit me. Was I a prince to her princess? It seemed so. Diluted, certainly, but this had been my grandfather, also. I gritted my teeth and hissed, "King Kekana, you're going home."

I grabbed the old king's jaw with my bare skin, wrapping it tightly with as much force as I could muster, and that rubber band released with a violence I hadn't thought to imagine. And it was cold, stupid cold, as I zipped along through the under time, covering nine thousand miles in about a second. It was, like, go-ahead-

and-give-me-frostbite cold. The icepicks were so bad that I was past caring.

I made it through, in spite of the pain. I slammed into that crypt about a million miles per hour, hitting that floor and smashing on my back directly onto that iron key. I was smokin'! I was told later that I had ice crystals on my eyebrows, and that my skin was blue. I had no clue. I held up that jaw bone, and I yelled, "Got it!"

"Man," I heard Ritchie call out. "What happened to you?"

I do remember asking how long I'd been gone. Memo, wide-eyed, said in a sharp voice, "Domkop!" *Idiot!* "You didn't go anywhere. You jumped into the circle, nearly breaking my arm." He held his right one protectively.

Kwame stood over me, and he pulled the second mike and its power source off, looked at it disbelievingly, and returned to his computer. He clicked several keys, before announcing his judgment.

"Jumping into that circle, Memo, took our friend about four hours."

"Go lick a duck!" Ritchie grinned. "I knew all this was real. Didn't I say that, Cherish, that I knew all this was real? Hot dog!"

"How do you figure four hours?" That was Cirque.

"His mike has a recorder built in. It's recorded that much time since I put it on him and turned it on. It's uploading to my computer now."

All that was fine, but what impressed me most was that I was still holding that jawbone, and I was getting nothing. No channel changes, no static, nothing. Had I "completed my mission," "done what needed to be done," and "righted the wrongs that needed to be righted"? If I had to go back under, I wanted to do it now and get it over with.

But heck, you know me. If I never went back under, it was good with me for the rest of my life.

—*Epilogue*—

WE HAD A CEREMONY for the old jawbone. All eight of us. We hiked out to Makapan's Cave. I recognized it from my undertime visit. I pointed out just where the old king had breathed his last. You should have been there: Memo, recognized recording artist, provided the music, via his mouth band and his extraordinary hands on his legs; and Cherish spoke words over her grandfather. Over mine, too, because I knew now why that bone being in with Gramps' stuff had affected the men in my family so strongly. Kekana's blood was in our veins. Gramps got the whammy because he was the one who'd stolen the final part of Kekana's remains. My dad, he had royal blood from both my grandparents. The old king was crying out for us to release him, only we didn't know what he was saying. It took Mother Earth and God to finally arrange circumstances to relieve my great-grandfather's suffering, to bring him back home again. You see, as long as the bone was in Sterkrivier, Kekana felt at home. It was when Gramps toted it away, then to Queens, that the trouble started. He never knew what it was all about, either. And poor Pops. He wasn't a bad guy. He might have been a good father, too, if old Piet hadn't killed Kekana, wrecking my family's lives for a century and a half.

I'm pretty sure even Kwame had a tear in his eye as we covered the last of the old king with African soil.

I know all that sounds like a funeral, but I don't think you could exactly call it one, because we weren't supposed to do what we did; but we did, so that's that. Just don't tell the South African government, because they'll be out there digging up a UNESCO World Heritage Site trying to find what we buried. The truth was, the final piece of King Kekana needed to go home. It was the only way he'd find any rest in the afterlife.

The last night I spent in South Africa, I went with Ritchie to the club. Amid the pounding beat coming from the dance floor, he told me he might be thinking about returning to Tallahassee. His African adventure felt like it was winding down, and he needed something new to fix. His family was a pretty good option. He has a sister there, and maybe he could get to know his nieces and nephews. Maybe she'd forgive him for abandoning the family. I gave him two thumbs up and laughed, but it got me to thinking. My African adventure was also winding down. Maybe I also needed something new to fix, and if so, Mom was a pretty good option. I wondered if our relationship could be repaired.

I finally got to put my satellite phone to good use. It was after midnight, and I was on Ritchie's sofa. The lights were off, except for the green indicator inside the smoke alarm; the fan had cycled off on the air conditioner; and somewhere in the distance, a dog barked. I had my hands under my head, looking at the ceiling, seeing nothing at all. That sentence seems like no big deal to most of you, but see it from my eyes. I've spent my life seeing things no one else could. Seeing, sensing, living, and for a while when I was a teen, running from them. My "visions," my "god powers," had brought me halfway across the world, for no other reason than to give peace to a dead man who hadn't known peace during his lifetime. And all I was seeing was the ceiling. How sweet was that? The ceiling! No violated teenagers, no burned bodies in dumpsters, no undertime gods or goddesses. It was just paint and plaster and right now, without the future or the past getting in the way. The phone rang, and I jumped. I reached to the coffee table and lifted it, seeing a number I recognized, and I smiled. I answered it.

"Hey, Charisse." I whispered the words,

enjoying the feel of her name on my lips. "I've missed you."

"Give me a second, Chip." A muffled conversation came across the line, then Charisse returned. "I'm pulling through Burger King. Emilio says hello."

"Thanks, Charisse. Give him hello back. How've you been doing?" I was more interested in how Charisse felt. I'd run scared before, afraid to let any woman get too near. I'd carried something inside that no one else could be allowed to see. Only Chalky had gotten close, and he was too blinded by worship to see anything other than what he wanted to see. Charisse mattered, too much for me to put into words.

"Missing you. I went by your house yesterday. The police were there. Someone was in your garage and trashed your storeroom. They couldn't find any signs of a break in. If you're interested, I can get you the number of a good security service."

"Thanks. When I get back, maybe." I'd been the intruder, but that wouldn't make any sense to her. "How's school?"

"Our two campuses had a combined staff meeting last week. I'd hoped you'd be back." She chuckled longingly. "I sat next to Stefanie, and she says you're in Africa. Your students miss you. Are you returning soon?"

"It's my last night here. I've been staying with a friend, Ritchie. He owns a club, and we've used his car to explore a bit."

"Don't you have a grandmother there? Have

you seen her? Oh, my food's ready. Just a minute."

This time she didn't cover the phone. I heard Emilio say, "Here, Ms. Winston. I put in extra catsup. Is Mr. E. still on the phone?"

I called, pretty loudly, "Hey, Emilio!" I thought of that dumpster. He hadn't known what was inside when he torched it. Besides, who was I to cast stones, a god? Not anymore, thank heavens for that.

"Yo, Mr. E.!" Charisse must have handed him the phone, because his voice became stronger, and I could hear restaurant sounds in the background. "It's Mr. E., everyone!"

A rousing chorus of greetings erupted, including one, "We love you, Mr. E.!"

"I love you guys, too." I smiled. I was no longer privy to Emilio's doors, but I bet the only one left open was the one where he was receiving a college degree to the cheers of his family and friends. I promised myself I'd be there when it happened.

"Come on by, anytime, Mr. E., for a free coke, on the house. Here's Ms. Winston back."

"See, you've got fans here."

"You're one, I hope?" Oh, man, I missed Charisse, and I was on a different dang continent.

"Always have been, as if you didn't know. Call me later tonight?"

"It's nearly one AM here. How about in the

morning?" I enjoyed her voice so much.

"I forgot. Maybe when you get in. Who's picking you up at the airport?"

"Don't know. Chalky, I suppose, unless you have a better option."

"We could stop by my place for a bite to eat." She sounded hopeful.

"Seven, then, day after tomorrow, Bush Intercontinental. I'll text you the details. I love you, Charisse."

"I love you, too, Chip."

I heard the phone shut off, and I watched the ceiling for a time, the little green light painting a glow across the plaster. That's all it was, though, just a ceiling. I suspected that's all I'd see in the future, ceilings and walls and floors; and people, the real, outside people, and not the stories behind them. I'd helped some, or at least I hoped I had, but I was tired of being a god. It's not all it's cracked up to be, especially when you don't have a choice.

I'd rather be me, Chip Engelbrecht, ordinary guy, no superpowers needed.

Charisse asked about my grandmother. I smiled, then I began to laugh. Maybe next year. I didn't want her to spoil what looked to be a very normal first day of a brand new life. Now, Kobe, he was different. We had a connection, now. A good one, too. I'd make a point to look the boy up before I left, then send him a card every couple months to let him know I was thinking of him. Heck, he might even want to visit Houston one day. Who knows?

What I did know was that I actually looked forward to tomorrow, for the first time in a very long time. Oh, man, forget that, I looked forward to the rest of my life, as long as Charisse was with me, of course. How do they say it? God works in mysterious ways. I say good things come to those who wait, and I'd waited a long time for someone I could share my life with.

"Love you, Charisse," I whispered in the dark, feeling like the luckiest guy in the world.

About the Author . . .

Levi Kristoffer Castle was born in Finland. His family moved to Johannesburg when he was five, and he spent his youth exploring the bushveld around Sterkrivier in the Limpopo province of South Africa. After high school, he settled into NYC life as a college student. His surreptitious boyhood exploits into the Makapan's Cave region fueled his interest in Boer history and was his inspiration for this story. Now he splits his time between his Houston, Texas, home and his family's mountain cabin in western North Carolina. His wife, son, and two dogs happily join him when they can.